THE REALM OF THE DEEP
Ride: **Mariana Trench Dive** — a journey into the sea's deepest chasms
Explore: Underwater Observation Pods
Dine: The Captain's Table

THE R...
Rid...
rea...
Exp...
Din...

THE REALM OF THE CELL
Ride: **Amoeba Escape** — a thrilling battle with microscopic predators
Explore: The Molecular Mazes
Dine: The Protein Palace

THE REALM OF LIFE
Ride: **Paleozoa** — a riverboat safari through the primordial jungle
Explore: The Primeval Zoo and Aquarium
Dine: The Dragonfly Dining Terrace

OmniPark 1986

This univers

...ARS

voyage the furthest
...eyond
...al
...afe

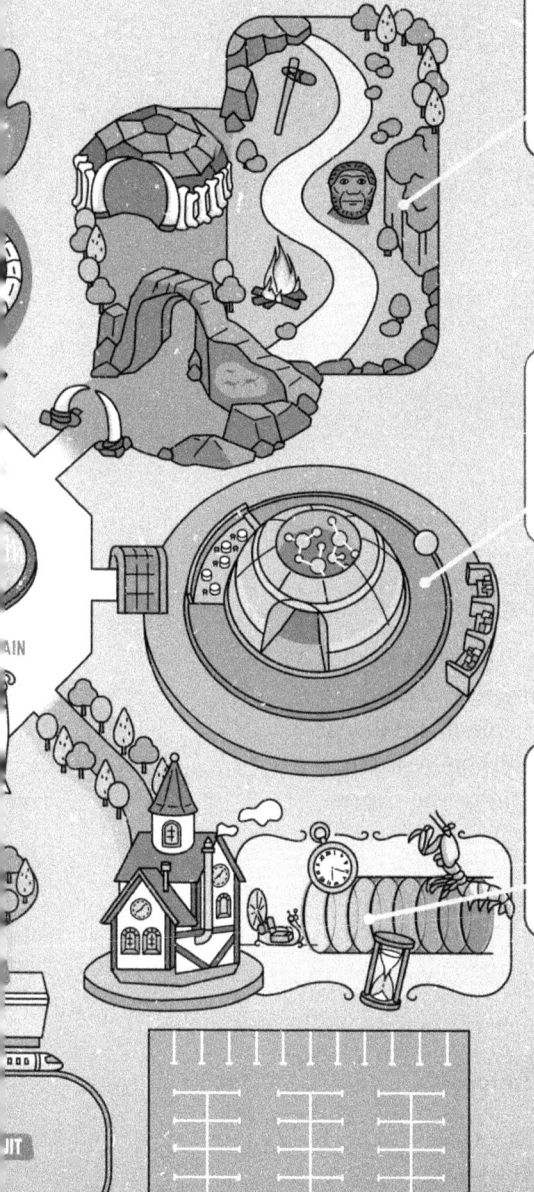

THE REALM OF MAN

Ride: **The Story of Man** — a face-to-face encounter with humanity's ancestors

Explore: The Ice Age Cavern Complex

Dine: The Feasting Cave

THE REALM OF THE PARTICLE

Ride: **Quantum Catastrophe** — a race across the microcosmos within an atom

Explore: The Electron Shells

Dine: The Outer Inn

THE REALM OF TIME

Ride: **Time Tunnel** — a marvelous journey to Earth's distant past and future

Explore: The Inventor's Mansion

Dine: The Conservatory Parlor

PARKING STRUCTURE

s yours to explore.

Copyright 2020 by Ben Thomas

This is a collected work of fiction. All events related in this book are fictitious and any resemblance to real people or events is purely coincidental. All rights reserved including the right to reproduce this book or portions thereof without the express permission of the publisher.

Introduction copyright 2020 by Ben Thomas

Interior art and design copyright 2020 by Trevor D. Richardson

Printed in the United States of America
10 9 8 7 6 5 4 3 2 1

ISBN: 978-0-578-83617-1

First Edition, First Printing: 2020

TALES FROM
OMNIPARK

18 STRANGE STORIES
OF A THEME PARK THAT MIGHT'VE BEEN

TABLE OF CONTENTS

The Dark Ride	Ben Thomas	1
Uncertainty	Gemma Files	21
All Those Lost Days	Brian Evenson	35
Quantum Summer	Jesse Bullington & Brent Winter	55
The Robot Apeman Waits For the Nightmare Blood to Stop	Orrin Grey	73
The Secret of Invention	Brad Kelly	89
Stellar Nucleosynthesis and the Infinite Power of Love	Alicia Hilton	97
Outside of Everything, There Is Nothing	T.M. Morgan	113
Here There Be Dragons	Katharine Gripp	131
The Ultimate Technosopher's Guide	Anna Maloney	143
The Bottom-Dweller	Pedro Iniguez	157
The Fisherman's Last Call	Maxwell I. Gold	165
Beyond the Confines of Man	Marshall J. Moore	177
The Selkie Who Loved Buttermilk Biscuits	Susan MacDonald	193
That Which Skulks Among the Stars	Ethan Hedman	207
Down Came the Rains	Patrick Bates	223
This Universe Is Yours to Explore	Ryan Clement	235
Cadence: A Coda	Tina Marie DeLucia	257

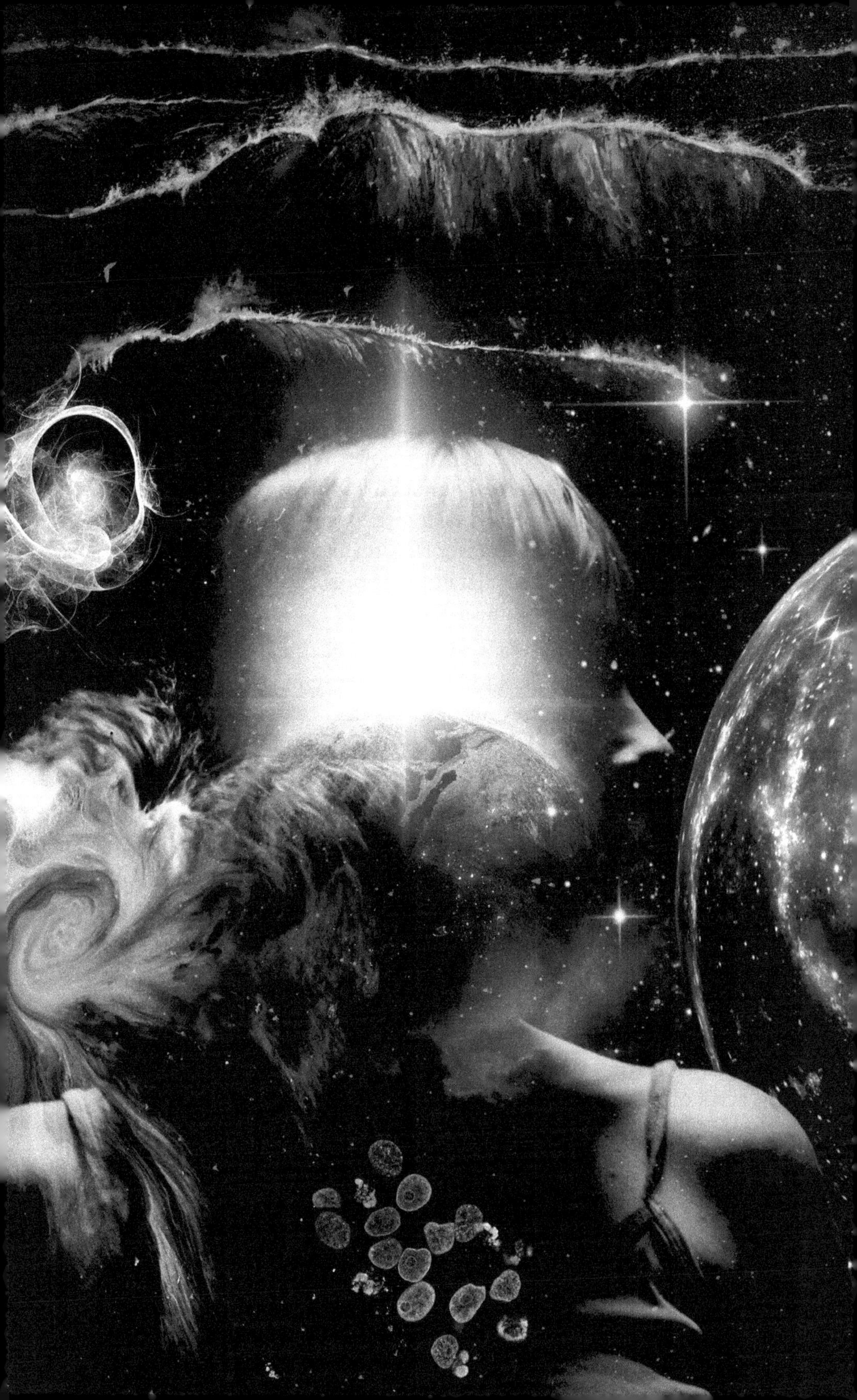

Introduction
by Ben Thomas, *Editor*

On May 19, 1977, a little-known West Texas theme park first opened its gates to guests. Founded by Odessa oil billionaire Dalton Teague, OmniPark thrilled, astonished and educated visitors of all ages. Its seven Realms transported travelers to the furthest reaches of the universe, to the distant past and future, and down to the microscopic and quantum scales.

In a 1979 interview with *Life* magazine, Teague attributed his original idea for the park to his own wide-ranging scientific interests, as well as to his realization that "California has its Disneyland and Florida has its EPCOT Center — so why shouldn't the great state of Texas have her own world-class theme park?"

Dr. Teague himself remained shrouded in mystery throughout his life. In 1967, the geo-engineering Ph.D. sold his petroleum drilling firm Omni Oil for an undisclosed sum, retiring as a multimillionaire at the age of 44. He and his wife Evelyn spent the next six years traveling to remote corners of the Arabian desert, the Amazon rainforest, the Himalayas and the Arctic Circle, for reasons they declined to discuss with the press.

Dalton and Evelyn returned to the U.S. in late 1973. The following May, they dipped into their private funds, purchased 120 acres of farmland near Odessa, and hired a team of "Technosophers" — including engineers Harry Peale and Roger Clarendon, designers Beth Bachmeier and Elijah Shattuck, science fiction writer Chuck Walcott, and storyboard artists Denise Olivetti and Yamasato Masaru — to begin work on an undisclosed project.

That project, of course, was OmniPark.

It wasn't only the park's hit attractions like Nebula Quest and Amoeba Escape that enticed tens of thousands of guests to Odessa each summer. The Teagues' self-imposed veil of secrecy proved fertile ground for a profusion of conspiracy theories — some more eccentric than others.

In backpage mailing lists (and, later, online forums), fans obsessed over rumors that the Realm of the Stars concealed a facility for extraterrestrial communication, that geneticists were breeding monstrous marine creatures beneath the Realm of the Deep, that physicists in the Realm of the Particle had created a portal to an alternate universe, that Technosophers in the Realm of Time had unlocked the secret of time travel... and those were just the more coherent speculations.

Outrageous as these theories appeared to most, they served only to enhance OmniPark's beguiling mystique. Over the years, fans' relentless pursuit of conspiracy evidence became as powerful a draw as the Realms and attractions themselves, fostering an underground subculture that continued to flourish even after the park closed its gates for good in August 2003.

Here in this anthology, we imagine an OmniPark that might've been; the park many of us secretly dreamed of — one where all the wildest rumors were even truer than we dared to imagine.

In these stories you'll meet sentient sea creatures, time-traveling siblings, creeping cosmic horrors, mad inventors — and a full cast of equally memorable characters. You'll travel to alternate universes, distant solar systems, ocean trenches, paradoxical dimensions, and dozens more realms of the fantastic.

Along the way, you'll discover for yourself why OmniPark remains vibrant in our thoughts and memories — and alive and well in our hearts.

Is any of this true?

Well. That's entirely up to you.

— Ben Thomas
Editor

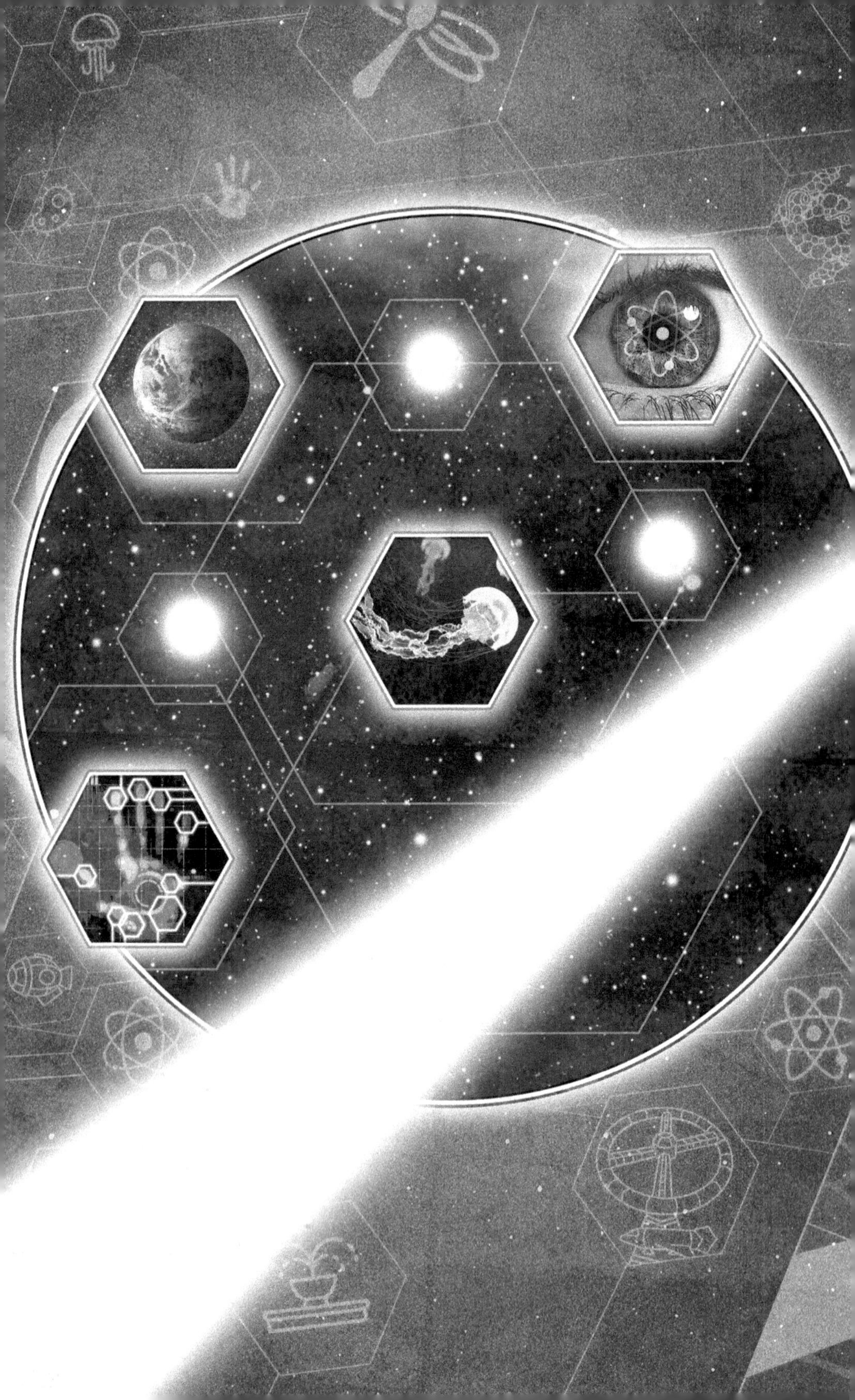

THE DARK RIDE

BEN THOMAS

1

I'll always remember OmniPark the way I first experienced it as an eight-year-old: a wonderland whose rides carried me on spellbinding voyages millennia into earth's past, light years into outer space, fathoms beneath the sea, and down to the microscopic and quantum worlds.

If you grew up in a family that revisited OmniPark several years in a row, as mine did, you may remember the shock of discovering that Park Management had revamped or replaced one of your favorite attractions — and not always for the better.

Take the classic Time Machine ride, for instance. Those of us who visited OmniPark in the '80s cherish fond memories of steampunk vehicles rocketing through subterranean caverns packed with leering animatronic Morlocks, then catapulting us billions of years into earth's future to narrowly escape the pincers of a monstrous mantis shrimp, before returning us safely to the Inventor's Victorian laboratory.

The Time Machine was an undisputed OmniPark masterpiece — until 1991, when Management (led by the park's founder and CEO, Dalton Teague) made the bizarre decision to replace it with Pterry's Time Tunnel, an incoherent flop narrated by a cartoon pterodactyl. Today, our beloved Time Machine survives only in YouTube uploads of shaky VHS recordings: tributes kept alive by sheer force of Gen-X nostalgia.

But even as monetizable cartoon franchises took over our favorite rides, we always returned — watching OmniPark evolve as we ourselves grew into adulthood. We took pride in our knowledge of hidden nooks left untouched by the garish redesigns: the old "Antarctic Expedition" ice cream parlor nestled in a back corner of the Realm of the Deep; or that little-used stretch of monorail track that ran through a cave populated by jerky robotic Martians, green tentacles twitching in ceaseless clockwork rhythm since the late '70s.

On "OmniParchaeology" message boards, passionate fans dissect rides like Nebula Quest and Amoeba Escape with all the devotion of UNESCO curators documenting Roman ruins. Sometimes a blogger even tracks down one of Teague's original Technosophers for an interview about the projection effects in Quantum Catastrophe, or the LED systems for the luminescent fish in Mariana Trench Dive.

We do all this because OmniPark was, and is, far more than just a theme park. No Universal Studios or Magic Kingdom could awaken the same sense of awestruck revelation that OmniPark's journeys did. Where most theme parks simply entertained us, OmniPark *changed* us. Its rides swept us to the strangest corners of space and time, to confront the dire beasts looming in those shadows.

Who could forget that moment in Palaeozoa where the giant dragonfly swooped down and knocked the tour guide into the primeval swamp, sending the boat careening backward down the waterfall? Or that cave scene in The Story of Man where everything went pitch-black for a solid minute while a troop of ravenous *Homo erectus* sniffed and pawed you in the dark? Those rides gave me nightmares for weeks. Maybe that fear itself was what made OmniPark so endlessly fascinating to me; made me beg Mom and Dad to keep taking me back there every summer we could afford it.

If you'd asked eight-year-old me to classify the rides at OmniPark, I wouldn't have had the slightest inkling where to begin. But I would've been eager to point out that OmniPark's rides were clearly designed to evoke more elevated sensations than mere nausea or a cheap adrenaline rush. They rarely resorted to gimmicks like abrupt plummets or tilt-a-whirl spins. Instead they cruised with ethereal smoothness, gliding along embankments and around curves, sometimes tilting back or even rotating full-circle for a panoramic view of some cosmic vista.

That's why it feels dismissive to me when people call OmniPark's attractions "dark rides"— direct descendants of the cardboard-and-plywood haunted houses at county fairs. Sure, these attractions might technically fit into the "dark ride" category — in the same way that *2001: A Space Odyssey* belongs to the same film genre as *Cat-Women of the Moon* — but that taxonomy conveys nothing of the scale and majesty of the starscapes in Nebula Quest, or the fog-shrouded menace of Palaeozoa's invertebrate predators, or the perplexing questions Quantum Catastrophe raised about the nature of reality itself.

Those automated voices as you entered each ride reminded you to remain seated, to keep your hands and feet inside the vehicle — but above all, to *behold:* to bear witness to the wonders about to unfold around you.

OmniPark seemed inconceivably vast to little-kid me. The three days my parents allotted for each visit felt like barely enough time to explore all the pavilions and re-ride all the rides. If you'd asked me how many attractions the park's Seven Realms contained in total, I would've guessed a dozen, at least.

You can imagine my surprise, then, when I downloaded a scan of the OmniPark guidemap for summer 1985, and realized the park had housed a grand total of only eight attractions.

And also — what the hell? — one of them was a ride I'd never heard of.

In all my visits to the park, I'd somehow failed to notice a small cylindrical pavilion at the dead center of the Seven Realms. The summer '85 guidemap labeled it "The Wild World of Life."

On a hunch, I downloaded the guidemap for autumn '85, just three months later. As I suspected, the ride's cylindrical pavilion had been deleted. In its place sat a gray rectangle marked "Under Renovation." And in the guidemap for spring 1986, that rectangle had been replaced by the OmniColor Fountain, which continued to perform its hourly light-and-music shows on the same spot until the park's official closing in 2003.

I clicked over to the 'Parchaeology forums, searching for any mention of the vanished ride. All I found were a few posts that included Wild World in bullet-pointed lists of summer 1985 attractions. None offered details about the ride's nature, or even a photo of the pavilion or the vehicles.

After twenty minutes of fruitless searching and scrolling, I stumbled upon a cached copy of a post from a long-defunct OmniPark message board. It was titled, "1985's Wild World of Life — Did Anyone Ever Ride It?"

Only one commenter had responded:

[Posted by Miami_Dave78 on 03/15/2001 @ 3:57 pm]

Yessir, I was one of the lucky (or unlucky) few who took a spin on "Wild World" in July '85. This weird ride only ran for a few weeks before OP shut it down.

My memories of the ride are kind of a blur (I was only six) but I remember it rushed through the evolution of life on earth, from the first cells, to invertebrates, plants, fish and reptiles, and finally to humans. I think there was a part where we went inside a giant human body (I'm not sure). It was creepy as hell, with a lot of loud noises and jump scares — super strange for an OP ride!

I don't remember how the ride ended, but I remember my dad looking really pissed when we got off, talking about how that wasn't appropriate for kids. Which it definitely was not, LOL! I'm sure that's why it got shut down after just a few weeks.

On an odd note, though — local legend around Odessa says the REAL reason "Wild World" closed was that it was making guests sick. According to the story — take it or leave it — some people got rushed to the hospital and OP management covered the whole thing up. (If a coverup sounds farfetched, remember that any time a guest vomits on park grounds, OP staff are trained to call in a "Code 27," rope off the area, and rush the guest off park property as fast as possible, to avoid legal liability. I'm just sayin…)

Anyway, '85 was a while before camcorders got popular, so I've never seen any footage of the ride. Anybody else remember riding it? If somebody's got photos of the sets or animatronics, I would love to post them on my blog (with full credit, of course).

That was all I could find: a solitary plain-text post from 2001, on a message board that'd been dead for years. If anybody besides me had even seen Miami_Dave's post (which didn't seem likely), they hadn't had anything to say in reply.

Besides, the post raised more questions than it answered. How had a ride like Wild World ever gotten built in the first place? OmniPark's rides were famous for evoking astonishment, awe — even terror, in carefully measured doses. But why would a park built to showcase the wonders of the universe greenlight a ride that portrayed life itself in the most nauseating way possible?

More to the point, who had bankrolled such a project? Most of OmniPark's attractions were sponsored by big multinationals like BP and Pfizer, who wanted their logos stamped on exciting journeys through inner and outer space. I couldn't imagine any company wanting their name on an attraction that made people sick.

A fresh-eyed Google investigation returned nothing but links I'd already clicked; forum posts regurgitating the attraction's brief life and abrupt death, and the colorful fountain built over its grave.

I was starting to think someone at OmniPark wanted Wild World to *stay* forgotten. This could be serious: "World-Famous Theme Park Builds Deadly Ride, Then Buries Evidence — Literally!" I might have some real-live investigative journalism on my hands here; a story that wins awards — or at least some new social followers.

So I circled back to ground zero: the original forum topic that Miami_Dave had responded to. That thread had been posted by someone called ShadowQueen362, who'd left no other posts on that message board.

Her profile did, however, link to her blog — which, surprisingly, wasn't about OmniPark at all. ShadowQueen posted mostly about evolutionary biology, and occasionally about the fiction and poetry she enjoyed reading. The science was definitely my taste; the literature, not so much. ShadowQueen was an avid reader of Aleister Crowley, whose short stories I found just as lurid and incoherent as his "magickal" religion; and of a French poet named Isidore Lucien Ducasse, who I hadn't heard of, but quickly learned I disliked with equal intensity.

It was ShadowQueen's love for these writers (she explained in a post from March 17, 2005) that had sparked her interest in OmniPark's lost ride. The Technosopher who'd spearheaded the Wild World project, she wrote, was an eccentric engineer named Elijah Shattuck, who'd made his name with the famous *Homo erectus* tunnel sequence in The Story of Man — that dreaded minute of crawling pitch-blackness that gave me nightmares as a kid.

When OmniPark had unveiled plans to open a new pavilion with a life science theme, Shattuck submitted storyboards for a ride called "The Tragedy of Life." ShadowQueen had somehow gotten her hands on a scan of the proposal's cover letter, in which Shattuck explained his designs were inspired by a Crowley story, "The Testament of Magdalen Blair," along with a cycle of obscene poems by Ducasse.

Somehow, Shattuck convinced OmniPark's board of directors to build the ride. Dalton green-lit "The Tragedy of Life" in February 1983.

Funding proved a hairier problem. Corporations weren't lining up to stamp their logos on an attraction with the word "tragedy" in its title. OmniPark changed the name to "Wild World," yet they couldn't land a corporate sponsor. The storyboards were too upsetting; the ride's message unpalatable.

The board was on the verge of canning the project when a mysterious investment firm threw down $230 million. Just like that, Wild World was a go. Construction proceeded at feverish speed, wrapping up just in time for the ride's ribbon-cutting ceremony in June 1985 — and its short-lived, disastrous run that summer.

ShadowQueen concluded her post by lamenting the fact that she'd never visited OmniPark herself, in 1985 or any other year. So that was another dead end.

What about the engineer, Shattuck? I wondered. His name didn't appear in any interviews on the blogs. None of the Elijah Shattucks on Google looked the right age. If the old guy was still around, he seemed to be fighting fiercely to stay under the world's radar.

I left a comment on ShadowQueen's old post, in case anyone happened to find it. Then I downloaded my meager collection of evidence, dropped it in a folder, and put the project aside with vague hopes of a "Eureka!" moment to come.

When Shattuck himself reached out to me, I just about fell off the couch.

2

The email sat in my inbox, staring back at me from the pale window of my monitor. In the darkness of my living room, I re-read its terse sentences, stunned into disbelief by the message they conveyed:

From: elshattuck@protonmail.com
Date: Feb 10, 2020 22:26:12 EST
Subject: The Tragedy of Life

Saw your question on ShadowQueen's blog. I am the Elijah Shattuck you seek. Would be delighted to discuss The Tragedy of Life — or "Wild World," as my bosses idiotically renamed it. It is indeed quite the story.

That was the whole email: just four lines.

My first instinct was that somebody had to be putting me on. Which scenario was more likely — that the real Elijah Shattuck had somehow seen my comment on ShadowQueen's blog, and had jumped at the chance to talk to an unknown journalist; or that some Parchaeology troll was catfishing me for fun?

All the same, this was the only lead I had. I typed up a quick reply saying I was very eager to hear Elijah's side of the story, and sent it off into the ether without much hope for a response. Even if I did get an answer, I figured it wouldn't be long before I outed the imposter.

Shattuck's reply arrived a mere fifteen minutes later:

> From: elshattuck@protonmail.com
> Date: Feb 10, 2020 22:47:01 EST
> Subject: Re: The Tragedy of Life
>
> *Glad to hear you are interested. I'm not much for typing these days. Perhaps we could do this by phone?*

A whole pageant of doubts unfurled in my mind. If somebody was catfishing me, they were taking things pretty damn quickly. It didn't seem likely that a random prankster would be pushing for a phone conversation with a no-name journalist.

And if Shattuck really did want to talk to me, what was I supposed to ask him? I was nowhere near prepared to fence with a cagey engineer whose ride had sent people to the emergency room. My "evidence" comprised three old OmniPark guidemaps, the cover letter for an old ride proposal, a few semi-anonymous posts, and a personal hunch. For all I knew, Shattuck might hurl me into the jaws of the park's litigators.

But my gut told me Shattuck hadn't been on OmniPark's good side in a very long time. He'd most likely spent the past thirty years moldering in cramped apartments, strategizing how and when to expose Papa Teague's heartless sabotage of his magnum opus. Perhaps the trumpet was finally sounding on that long-awaited day of judgement.

I dialed the number.

He picked up after two rings.

3

"Shattuck," said a voice like sandpaper soaked in bourbon and cigarette smoke.

I fumbled a moment. "Uh, hi. This is — we spoke over email? About ShadowQueen's blog?"

"I know who you are," he rasped.

"Good," I replied. "That's good."

"You're a chick," he said. "I wasn't expecting that."

"Um." My mouth worked soundlessly. "Yeah. I am. Is that — I mean, is this a good time?"

A long silence. "A good time for what?"

"Well," I said, "I'd like to talk to you about the ride you designed."

"What do you want to know?" Shattuck asked.

Words failed me. I'd been on this call for less than ten seconds and the interview was sliding off the rails. I scrambled, summoning a question to keep Shattuck from hanging up.

"Well, for starters," I said, cradling the phone with my shoulder as I reached for my notepad, "I was curious how you managed to get your storyboards approved."

Silence on the other end.

"Is that really what you want to ask me, honey?" Shattuck cackled. "You tracked me down through the bowels of the internet so you could ask me how OmniPark's storyboard approval process worked in '83?"

Anger flared in my chest. "It seemed like a good place to start," I told him.

"A good place to start," Shattuck sneered. "Are we here to make small talk, or are you going to ask me about my fucking ride?" He coughed, thick and hard. It sounded painful, and it kept up for a while. I heard Shattuck hawk-spit into the sink, followed by the sharp hiss of an oxygen mask.

"What was the ride about?" I asked, hoping he could hear me. "The Tragedy of Life. What was the story?"

Shattuck hummed, low and long, over the hiss of his oxygen tank. "Now that," he said, "is a good question." I heard him tap his fingers on the counter, pondering an idea. "Might be easier to show you."

For a moment, I thought I'd misheard him.

"*Show* me?" I realized my voice was trembling.

"Hmm," he said. "Yeah. Probably easier that way. You got a VR rig?" He coughed again.

"I — no," I stammered. "I mean, I don't really play games all that much."

"They make cheap ones now," he said. "Just snap your phone screen into the headset. Feels just like a personal movie theater. Cumbersome, but it does the trick. But you know —"

"What?"

He chuckled. "You really want the full experience, you better shell out for a serious kit — an Oculus or something."

I was still reeling, doing my best to keep up. "You're saying you've got a VR recording of this ride?"

Shattuck scoffed, which set off a fresh coughing fit, followed by another series of pulls from the oxygen tank.

"I designed the damn thing, remember?" he said, once he'd wrestled his breath back under control. "We were running simulations and ride-throughs for six months straight. Shot every room from every angle, *ad nauseum*. Mid-eighties recording media wasn't that great, I admit, but I've stitched it all together over the years. Fiddled with the RGB, got it looking pretty sharp."

"*Ohmygod*," I whispered, then added, "Sorry. It's just — this is a lot to process. I thought OmniPark destroyed all records of this ride."

Shattuck barked a laugh. "They did! Tried to, anyway. But I had the tapes. What are they gonna do, raid my house? They're a theme park, not the fuckin' FBI. Made me sign a nondisclosure, obviously, but who gives a shit? I'll be dead before I see the inside of a courtroom." He hacked a long, harsh chain of coughs, and I heard the hiss of his tank again.

"All right," I said. "Yeah." I smiled. "Hell yeah. I'll go buy a headset right now. You've got the files on a private server?"

"Damn right I do," Shattuck grunted.

"Okay, just hang on," I said, as if he might cough himself to death before I got back from the store. "Send me the download link and I'll call you after — you know. After I've ridden it. All right?"

Shattuck laughed softly. "Yeah, sure. Call me afterward. If you're still up for it."

I thanked him in exquisite prose, tapped "End Call," and scrambled to the closet to grab my shoes and purse.

Holy shit, was all I could think as I laced up my sneakers. *I'm about to ride the ride that sparked an honest-to-God OmniPark coverup conspiracy.*

Stuff like this didn't happen to people like me. It just didn't.

Except now it did.

I shoved my wallet in my purse and dashed out the front door, almost forgetting to lock it behind me.

4

The video faded in on a shot of the ride's boarding area. At the upper right-hand corner, a pixelated timestamp flashed *10/30/1983*, then disappeared.

I swiveled my head to the right, then to the left. The video lagged, jumped — then caught up. I raised my gaze upward and the ceiling materialized: multicolored spiral patterns hand-painted across a matte-finish dome.

Shattuck had done it, the bastard. He'd resurrected his ride.

A series of identical vehicles — ovoid cradles of slate-gray polyvinyl, seating two riders in front and two in back — traced a broad semicircle around the room. At the center, a worker in blue coveralls adjusted knobs and flipped switches at a small control panel.

"*Your vehicle doors will close automatically,*" chimed a piped-in voice as the person carrying the camera entered one of the ride vehicles. The voice's gravelly timbre tantalized me: it wasn't Attenborough or Irons, but some other Royal Shakespearean whose name lurked just beyond my memory's reach. "*Please keep your hands, arms, feet and legs inside at all times,*" it reminded riders.

Trembling with what I assumed to be eagerness, the cameraperson entered the nearest ride vehicle. A void loomed ahead, soft winds carrying the crackles and hisses of inscrutable static. We glided through emptiness, and I started wondering if this was going to be the whole ride: an immersion in hissing darkness, meant to test the rider's mettle or awaken some long-postponed confrontation with the Self.

Then the narrator spoke:

"*In the beginning, there was a Bang.*"

Thunder shook the tunnel as waves of coruscating color erupted from behind, arcing overhead. My gaze leaped frantically to scan the floods of pink and blue that rushed outward from the chamber's apex, glimmering with the protean dust of Creation.

"*From this blast, a symphony of chaos thundered forth,*" spoke the voice. "*And in that spontaneous chorus, Space and Time were born.*"

A Moog synthesizer sounded a deep foghorn note, while a white laser grid rotated across the vault above.

"*As spacetime twisted and clutched at itself,*" said the narrator, "*it tangled into particles and waves: a hologram of rare device. Energy broke fellowship with Matter. Quarks began their dance.*"

The synthesizer chirped out an arpeggiated rhythm as the grid coalesced and distorted around spinning circular shapes.

"And at long last," said the narrator, "*there was light.*"

A chorale sang rapture as laser patterns danced all around us; strings and loops vibrating, a kaleidoscope of patterns shifting from red to green to yellow to blue.

"*Across millennia,*" the narrator explained, "*this howling inferno cooled. Quarks coalesced into electrons — then into protons and neutrons, which crashed together to form atoms. Hydrogen and helium became the first of many elemental siblings.*"

Tiny glints of yellow and red danced about the tunnel, colliding and throwing off sheaves of sparks; gathering into greater masses that flickered and flared against the dark.

"*Eons passed,*" the narrator said, "*and space grew colder. Quintillions of atoms swarmed together: the first stars. And in the hearts of those stars, radiant fires forged new elements: carbon and iron.*"

A titan sun's horizon loomed before us, surface churning with plasma, alive with leaping flame. Great chains of many-colored particles looped outward from the star's mantle, coalescing into spheres that spun wildly through space as the view zoomed outward — revealing, at last, the Milky Way galaxy: a two-armed panoply of glimmering stars rotating serenely in the boundless void.

The synthesizer sounded a regal note as we emerged into a vast new chamber. Gas-giant planets waltzed and promanaded about the star-dome. Some worlds' surfaces bore swirls of reds and browns; others sumptuous blues, greens, teals and burgundies.

"*A cavalcade of planets,*" said the narrator, as our ride vehicle rotated to encompass the spectacle. "*Each an unparalleled, unauthored work of art. Splendid. Perfect. Pure.*"

An angelic choir raised a joyous chorus while elegant crystalline forms soared among the planets. Violet labyrinths of fluorite, iridescent fractals of bismuth, cerulean petals of azurite and towering prisms of white quartz shone in the heavens.

For a time outside of time we floated in that pristine space, ensconced on every side with watercolor worlds, each more lovely than the last.

But suddenly, into our paradise erupted a wail of lamentation.

Gemstones and planets spiraled away; trash circling a drain. The vault of stars lay empty and barren, devoid of sound or color.

At last a single planet loomed up before us, monstrous in its blueness. We hurtled toward the rippling surface of its world-encircling ocean.

"*Until,*" said the narrator, "*on a small blue world on the outer spiral arm of this perfect galaxy... something strange began to happen.*"

As we plunged beneath the thundering waves of that enigmatic sea, our ride vehicle neared the chamber's exit, converging on a tunnel that opened on the next room.

All around us in that boundless azure, chains of molecules clicked and inter-rotated; a chemical clockwork that grew more intricate and complex by the second, folding and twisting in on itself until it vibrated with energy that cried out for release.

"*A molecule called ribonucleic acid,*" the narrator was saying, "*developed the ability to replicate itself. And something new came into the universe. Something called... Life.*"

We emerged into the next chamber. A twitching network of pinkish helices knotted floor-to-ceiling; rig-work of tendons that rattled, cranked and shivered like a butchery line in some self-driven meat processing plant.

"*And Life,*" said the narrator, "*began to grow.*"

The synthesizer blared a baleful note. A klaxon like a radar ping echoed in that chamber, as beams of pale light swept across the pulsating web. A sea of bruised membranes undulated, and from their gelatinous surface rose wriggling strands of yellow proteins stretching out blindly with grasping hooks, clutching and crawling along one another like a hive of molecular centipedes.

"*This was not action — but reaction,*" the narrator said. "*Blind force drove these gyrations. Life gnawed upon itself, festering and multiplying in the deep.*"

Threnody swelled as we entered the next chamber, where armadas of pulsating cells swarmed, gravid with translucent mucus. The protoplasm divided; subdivided; split again, spawning legions of incoherent nuclei that fissioned in feverish heaps, crawling up the walls and piling in upon our flanks.

Pseudopodia loomed on all sides, swallowing smaller cells whose whip-like flagellae wriggled in obscenely frantic ecstasy. Euglenas and paramecia whirled and writhed in the bellies of amoebic predators, dissolving in digestive juices, unable to escape.

Now we converged upon a door where many cells gathered, linking together in labyrinthine clusters. The music rose to a piercing chord.

"*As Life's cells devoured one another,*" the narrator said, "*They swelled to colonies — then to macroorganisms, which sculpted the sea itself into their feeding trench.*"

We emerged into a gloomy chasm of the primordial ocean, where branchlike creatures clutched at the current with fleshy fingers. Feathers of skin filtered food from the cold brine. Discs of pale meat squirmed along the seafloor, arms lined tiny mouths that plucked prey creatures from the sand, forcing tiny creatures into maws of chewing muscle.

As we passed beneath the gateway to the next room, the narrator lamented, *"But even this was not enough for Life."*

Cold twilight surrounded us now. Segmented things swarmed in these depths. Chitinous predators with feathered feet and mouthparts wriggled in the naked dark, snapping up their prey and relishing each bite.

Those invertebrates, too, were snapped up in their turn — by glistening squid, by octopods and nautiloids, by lampreys and long-toothed worms, and by wide-eyed fish whose bodies grew longer, their fins extending into writhing tendrils that clutched in the mud.

"Life demanded more," said the narrator. *"Life clambered up from the seas, and battened itself upon the land."*

The seawater receded. Mud-flats and mangrove forests rose around us. Slime-streaked amphibians wriggled among the roots. Pink tongues flicked out to snatch insects and taste the air.

Soon the amphibians rose proudly upright; became reptiles that lunged at one another in that murky jungle, rending hard-scaled flesh with dagger teeth, spattering blood upon the leaf-strewn soil. Every blood-pool fed fresh colonies of worms and larvae, pale bodies fat and pulsing as they lunged onward with wide and eager jaws.

Our ride vehicle rotated to the left as we swept into the next room, where a rotating vault housed tall screens that showcased predators falling on their prey. Scaled lizards crashed clumsily together. Sharks with eyes like onyx tore at whale-flesh. Lions sank their hooked claws into flanks of antelope, gazelle and zebra.

"Behold the Great Banquet of Sodom!" intoned the narrator. *"This orgy's insatiable lords eternally eat themselves to death — pausing only to spend their seed in the creation of fresh morsels for their delectation.*

"In every sea and sky, atop each mountain-peak and in every lightless cavern, in the lushest rainforests, driest deserts and coldest glaciers, Life gnaws upon itself in ravenous abandon — bursting with excess even as it slavers and gropes for the next course."

On a central dais, a sequence of ghostly creatures reared up, roared, and died in turn: tyrannosaurs and pterodactyls, mastodons and rhinoceri, long-necked predatory birds, towering sloths and muscular apes; all falling prey to one another, or to the hordes of squirming invertebrates that teemed within their body cavities, feasting on their blood and sinew, devouring their flesh and bones even as they devoured those of others.

As we neared the outer edge of that blood-spattered chamber, a new series of creatures rose upon the central dais: upright apes whose faces grew flatter, skins more pale and hairless; eyes afire with uncanny recognition.

"*Yet among all Life's hungry prodigies,*" growled the narrator, "*none devours more gluttonously than Man.*"

Our vehicle proceeded sideways across the next room. Before us rose a great stone wall, where myriad battles erupted with unnatural speed. Stone-age hunters raided enemy tribes. Warlords clutching bronze swords slaughtered slaves in mud-brick cities. Roman legions clashed with fur-clad Gauls. Vikings and knights thundered in hails of steel. Cannons bombarded fortresses while bayonets skewered ranks of uniformed infantry. Soldiers trapped in barbed wire cried out as tanks thundered over trenches, lobbing shells that ruptured earthworks and bodies without distinction. Clouds of yellow gas engulfed flaming jungles, where children ran screaming from the mindless rattle of automatic rifles, and from the frenzied laughter of the men who loosed that iron hail.

Turning from these tableaux, our vehicle pushed slowly into the succeeding room: an enormous sphere whose screens thronged with thick-pressed masses of humanity. We teemed in our towns, in our offices, on our farms and in our suburbs; myriads of mankind rushing panicked amid the lights and wirework of a thousand urban sprawls.

"*And what Man, in his arrogance, has forgotten,*" said the narrator, a sardonic note creeping into his voice, "*is that he, too, is Life.*"

Our view zoomed in, focusing on a man standing in a city street. His gaze turned upward to behold the sky. We fell, plunging into the man's yawning mouth: a blood-webbed cavern harboring a writhing, bloated tongue-worm whose papillae clutched at us like pale anemones. Wave after wave of hot breath swept over us; the panting of an idiot behemoth.

The great throat convulsed, forcing us down the esophagus. That chasm of slime-covered flesh crushed us without mercy, pressing us toward the clenching sphincter below.

As the muscle yawned open with a sucking hiss, we tumbled through empty space — landing with a splash in the frothing, bubbling slime of the stomach. That organ's roof arched high above us, a swollen membrane honeycombed with pits and trenches; and we were tossed about like sailors on waves of belligerent acid.

At last the stomach's churning sea, too, sucked us under. For a moment all was dark, until we plunged into the deeper waters of the frigid labyrinth below. Lead-colored chyme squelched and swept us against walls of contracting muscle, whose rills of jagged boils and craters probed and clutched at us, driving us deeper into the duodenal maze.

Pinkish worms crawled those charnel vaults. Currents of ashen slime bore us closer to the whip-bodied creatures that tore at the muscled walls with hooked mouthparts. Leechlike flukes battened on veins and arteries, gulping with fierce thirst til at last they fell aside — bloated and blood-drunk even as they grasped for more.

"*Within the body of every man and woman,*" the narrator snarled, "*Life devours Life — for Life's appetite cannot be satisfied.*"

We burst through the intestinal wall, hurtling through many other regions of the body in dizzying quick-cuts. Long-tailed spiders gnawed at the stems of eyelashes, eight plump legs pumping excitedly. A slender white worm wriggled across a green iris. Mites clawed about ragged rims of sweat and oil glands, gulping up secretions, forcing out clutches of eggs.

"*We are born to serve as food,*" said the narrator. "*Life's epicures gnaw at us without ceasing, each moment of each day, until at last we perish. And even death itself is not the end.*"

The view zoomed out, framing a wall-length mirror — which reflected a person who wasn't me, of course. A lanky man in his mid-thirties, clad in an engineer's blue canvas coverall, sat in my place, balancing a bulky black camcorder over his shoulder. His sable hair hung long and stringy, and stubble covered his bony chin.

Shattuck! I realized. *It's Shattuck himself!*

A "Pepper's Ghost" projection effect, which I recognized from other OmniPark attractions, rendered Shattuck's body aswarm with translucent parasites: mites, worms, larvae of all shapes. As our vehicle traversed the passageway, the crawling host convulsed, molted and multiplied, overwhelming Shattuck's mirrored twin.

"*This, then, is the Tragedy of Life,*" the narrator lamented: "*that even death itself offers no escape. For Life will always be fiercer. Hungrier. More terrible than death.*"

Then without warning or preamble, Shattuck terminated the recording, and the video cut to black.

5

Now I understood why Wild World sent a few guests screaming to the emergency room back in '85. Even thirty-odd years later, in mere VR, the ride still inspires a sharp-edged revulsion against the raw experience of being alive — which, I realized, had been Shattuck's precise aim all along.

I also realized why Dalton Teague and the OmniPark board killed their $230-million attraction just a few weeks into its first seasonal run. Unlike the park's other rides, Wild World failed to ascend to Teague's sought-after sanctum of cosmic awe. Much as Dalton loved commissioning rides that challenged his guests' preconceptions about reality, not even he could find merit in an attraction that made riders physically ill, while teaching them very little they didn't already know.

This drama's closing act was all too easy to piece together: Teague and the board had eaten their sunk cost, shuttered and demolished Shattuck's ride, and told the engineer to seek employment elsewhere — or perhaps let him save face by "voluntarily" quitting. Either way, a disappointingly banal ending to a story almost as wild as the ride itself.

Maybe it was that ending's very banality that conjured the idea of a final twist — the possibility that the ride might've driven already *me* to madness, as it'd done to those unfortunate guests back in '85. I wondered if, even now, I was on the verge of sprinting out into the street to proclaim Shattuck's gospel of annihilation. Perhaps a small part of me — just the teensiest little part — was even hoping that might happen.

But it didn't happen, of course. Things like that don't happen to people like me.

6

I extracted my head from the VR helmet. I heard the rattling hum of my apartment's furnace; the soft hiss of my refrigerator. I saw white dust on my coffee table, and recognized it for what it was: millions of flakes of dead human skin.

I hurried to the bathroom, overpowered by the urge to cleanse myself in hot water. The instant I flipped the lightswitch, I recognized a brown smudge around the faucet as a colony of bacteria and fungi — breeding, festering there in the darkness.

That infestation reminded me of the eyelash mites. I grabbed my phone and found videos of them. Somebody'd even made a movie: *Life On Us*, all about those plump, clutching, many-armed things on Shattuck's ride, teeming and gnawing around all our follicles and pores.

As I stepped beneath the shower nozzle and felt hot purity rain down on my shoulders, I remembered the ride's scenes of humming, rubbing nucleic acids: the hot, wet meat factory that churns in every living cell, each moment of every day.

I cranked the water temperature to near-boiling, remembering the great chamber where I'd beheld our universe *before* the infestation of Life: a fountained paradise of watercolor planets and crystal works of art. I reflected what a beautiful, pristine place such a universe would be.

And to restore it, all I had to do was eject the interloper: Life.

Razorblades. Bottles of pills. Drain cleaner. Carbon monoxide: though any of these might bring my subjective suffering to an end, none would pluck out the disease at its root. Even after my own end, my body would become a banquet for fresh generations of gnawing, wriggling things. They would breed in flesh festering with gardens of bacteria, and Life would thrive on, chittering in mockery at my failure.

No, I would not — *could* not — let Life win. Now was the time for decisive and final action.

I laughed aloud when I realized how simple the solution was.

7

A jug of lighter fluid lay ready to hand beneath the kitchen sink, left over from some long-forgotten barbecue. I doused the bathroom's white tile til it dripped, then upended the bottle above my head, scenting acrid sharpness as the liquid soaked my hair, spilling in rivulets down my chest and belly. Suitably drenched, I tipped the bottle against my lips, choking down the last few mouthfuls with a coughing, gagging smile.

I dug a matchbox out of the drawer beneath the sink, next to the scented candles I'd placed there in a different life so long ago.

I drew out a match and struck it.

My fingers parted, letting the miniature torch tumble to the pool between my feet.

All roared with light and heat. How rapturous, this coruscating dance of purification. Soon the pain came too, sinking myriad needles into my flesh; digging deeper into me; lancing through me.

I smiled. Oh, how I smiled; because pain was the sound of a quintillion tiny Life-motes screaming their last agony. How they howled in their defeat! I knew myself as their scourge; their chastisement: Heaven's Flail.

At long last, Judgement's trumpet roars. And I, humble worm that I am, stand sentinel amid these roiling flames.

8

— I am become —

9

— the Shatterer —

10

Let there be night.

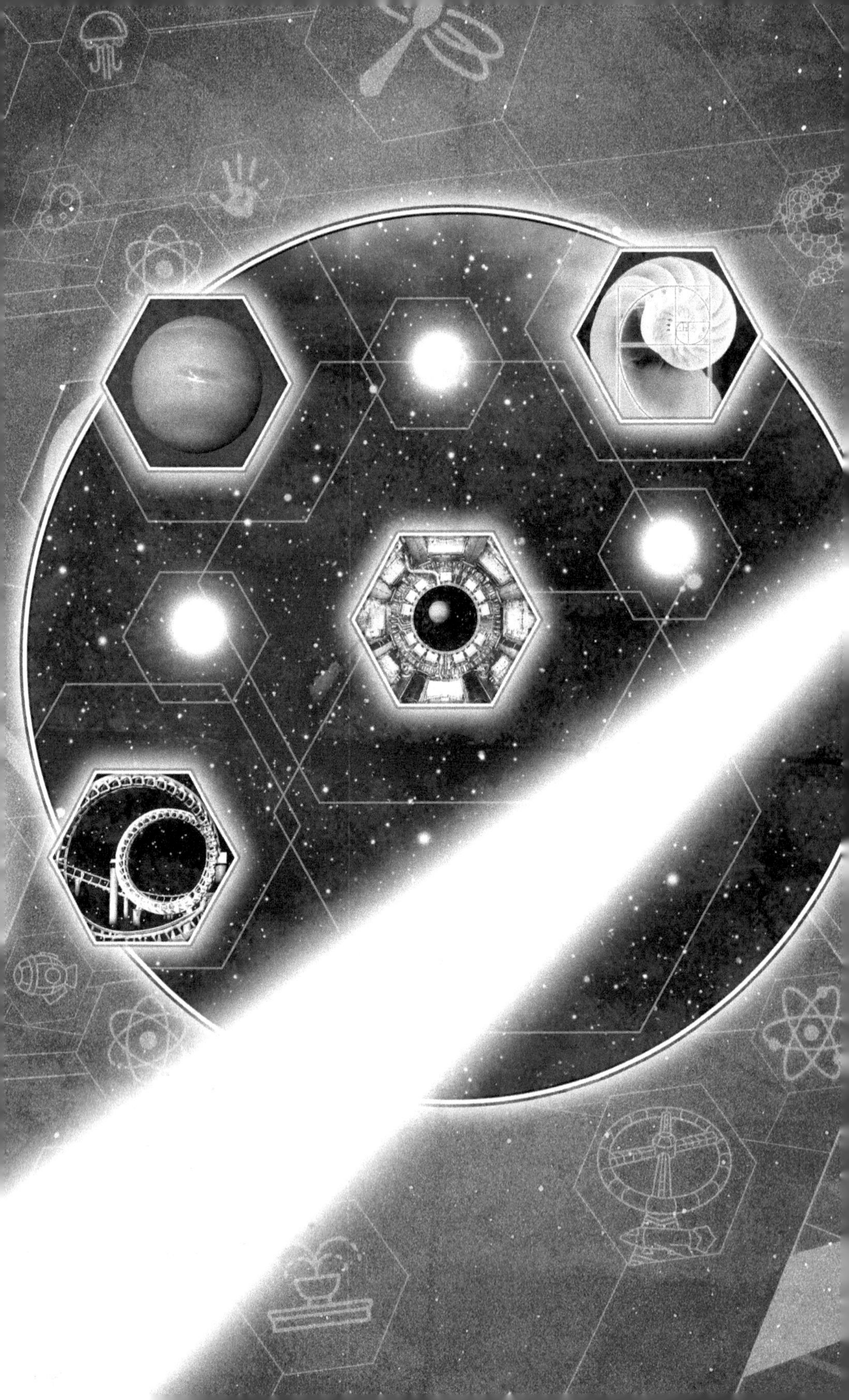

UNCERTAINTY

GEMMA FILES

The ride starts, and you're committed. It goes until it stops. The ride allows no take-backs. It's the most adult thing you can do as a child: throw yourself headlong into the maw of the unpredictable, assuming you'll emerge unchanged.

1

I just want to start out by telling you I work as a physical therapist myself — oh, you got the hospital's reference letter? Okay, good. Yeah, they're good people over there. I've been a contractor on their post-accident physiotherapy programs about eighteen months now. Just to say I know the old joke about doctors making the worst patients. I mean, I'm not a *doctor*, but you get the point. I want to try to cooperate, is what I'm saying.

No, it's not related to work. Not directly, anyway. Well, it involved my work *skills*, but not in a, a professional capacity. See, part of becoming a physical therapist involved also studying yoga, hypnotherapy and guided meditation, which is how I got to where I am today. How I eventually decided to practice my skills on my own mother is a longer, weirder story, but… okay. That's definitely *part* of what I'm here for, I guess.

Basically, it all goes back to the day we found out my grandfather had passed. I didn't know him very well — actually, I didn't know anybody from that side of my family, my mother's side, *very* well, and that was all on my Mom, by her own admission. When I was a kid, she'd tell me they lived too far away for us to visit and didn't make enough money to visit *us*, which sounded legit; most things do, when you're not even eight years old yet. Then I turned eleven, and for the first time ever I managed to get to the mail before Mom did, which is how I found out that hey-ho, Grandad and Gramma Clouthier actually lived just slightly more than twenty miles away from our house in Odessa, Texas, just out past Notrees. So I asked her why we couldn't go visit, and she said: *Because I don't want to, Jael.*

Not like she was mad, or anything, just really calm. It was the calmness that freaked me out a bit, in retrospect.

Did they do something? I asked her, later. She shook her head no. *Did they... not like Dad, maybe?*

Oh no, no. They never even met your dad, honey — well, Gramma did, anyhow. But not Grandad.

Why not?

Just... because.

All right, well. I figured out pretty quick I wasn't going to get any answers that way. Which is why I eventually snuck out to the library a couple of years later and went through every Clouthier in the Notrees phonebook, until one day I got a hold of a nice-sounding lady who seemed both surprised and happy to confirm that yes, she was my Mom's Mom. Grandad was out, she said, but he'd love to talk to me too, if I wanted to call back later.

I did, and he did. We had a long chat, during which I told them pretty much everything about me — not that there was much to tell, at thirteen. I said I wanted to meet them, and Gramma started to say *yes, please,* but then she broke off. There was a pause; I thought I could hear them muttering to each other, the receiver turned away. Then Grandad's voice again, asking carefully: *Does your Mama know about this, Jael, sweetie? That you called us, I mean?*

Um... no sir, not really.

Well, hm. Another, longer, pause. Then, at last: *...maybe best not.* And again it was kind of freaky, because when he said that his voice went so flat it sounded just like Mom's, whenever she talked about him.

I think the idea I got from then on was that this was something a bit too raw to pick at, something Mom would have to tell me about herself, if she ever did. So I put it away in a little box inside, and I — didn't ever *forget* about it, exactly, but it wasn't like I was hurting for relatives on my Dad's side of things, even if I didn't meet any of them until I was about five. That was when Dad — who originally hadn't been anything but a brief summer fling, as far as Mom was concerned — hooked up for good with a girlfriend who Mom liked a lot better than she'd ever liked him, and those two hung around like they'd met in high school or something; his and her extended family became mine as well, to the point where I actually dated one of "Aunt" Sally's nephews for a year before I left for college. Big barbecues, lots of holiday dinners, and here and there I'd still call Gramma and Grandad Clouthier, though always making sure Mom was out of the house or asleep before I did. Except one time, when I said goodbye, looked up and found her standing right there, looking at me silently from the doorway.

How's Mama? she asked, after a long, excruciating minute.

Uh — good, she's good. Treatment went well; they think they got all the melanomas. Probably won't have to do radiation, if she checks out well in a week or two. She nodded, like she'd been expecting it, and the moment was just so *odd* I couldn't stop myself from asking: *You want to know about Grandad, too?*

For a second there I saw something flicker in her eyes and froze, like she might've thought I was making fun of her, or like I'd said something awful. I'd never seen her like that before — almost like she was going to cry, or hit me, or both. But: *No thank you, Jael,* was all she replied, at last. And turned away.

Gramma died five years ago, and I went to the funeral, but Mom didn't. She said she was sick. And when Grandad died, which would be... the start of last year, I think... I told her I was going, so could she come with me? She just shook her head.

You already know I'm not going to do that, baby. So why ask?

Oh my God! Look, what the hell exactly is it you have — had — *against Grandad, Mom?*

Jael, I never had anything *against that man. He just....*

What? He just what?

She stopped, thought. Said, finally: *He wasn't my father.*

What, like — genetically? Gramma had an affair, is that what you're saying?

No, God! No. It's a long story, Jael. It's... I don't think you could... understand it, really.

Seriously?! I'm a full-grown woman, Mom, for Christ's sake; got a degree, a job and everything, and this has gone on long enough, don't you think? So tell me, and let me *figure out if I'm somehow qualified to grasp what the fuck it is you're saying, or not. Tell me, goddamnit.*

So she took a breath, and did.

The point of a ride is that it ends. It creates a liminal space for us to inhabit, but we don't have to live there. It collapses when we get off; it's the same every time, but not really.

Never again.

2

We never really had a lot of money, so going to the places like Disneyland or any of the big Six Flags parks was never a vacation option, whenever I'd ask about it — usually after seeing a commercial on TV, like any kid. But the first thing Mom asked me was if I remembered the summer a travelling amusement park set up in a local mall's parking lot, when I was fifteen, and of course I did. Anybody would.

See, I hadn't really cared much to go for its own sake; I'd seen the park already and all the rides were kid-level at best — tiny Ferris wheel, carousel, cheap-ass haunted maze, like that. But one afternoon a sort-of boyfriend swung by my summer job store and asked if I wanted to hang out with him and his crew there. *We got beer*, he said, which interested me a lot more than his friends' company. So when my shift ended, I left a message on my Mom's phone and rode off with them. And about two hours later, we're all near enough one of the entrances to see my Mom's car, like, *screeching* into the lot, and she bursts out, sees me, sprints over, grabs me and starts shaking me, looking me up and down and going, *Jael, are you okay?! Tell me you're okay!* Like that. So after about a minute of this she drags me to the car. The drive home's long enough for her to calm down, but I'm too freaked out to say anything, and when we pull into our driveway she lets out this huge shuddering sigh and apologizes. But all she ever said when I kept asking why was: *It doesn't matter.*

Until, finally, now. She asks me if I remember OmniPark.

Yeah, you know the place; it closed in — when was it, 2004? No, 2003. When I heard about it as a kid I'd wanted to go, and Aunt Sally was down, but my Dad insisted it was a lot more boring than the hype made it sound. *Not a goddamn roller coaster worth the name in the entire place*, he said, then: *Sorry, Monica,* to my Mom, though I could tell she wasn't really mad. When I looked up the rides online, this year, I could understand why

Dad felt that way; he just wouldn't have found all that stuff interesting. He's not dumb, but he's really... practical. Not exactly an isn't-it-amazing-how-weird-the-universe-is kind of guy.

Then again, I never thought my Mom was, either.

What happened, Mom told me, happened back in 1995, when I was only about a year old. You already know my Dad wasn't in the picture; not that Mom wanted him to be, but it was still hard for her. So when my Grandad offered to take her out for an impromptu vacation day while I stayed with Gramma, both Gramma and Mom thought this was a marvelous idea. "I know how strange this is going to sound to you, Jael," Mom said to me, "but I was really close to my Pa, back then. He really was kind of like my best friend. We both loved science, we'd both wanted to go to EPCOT for years, and so when OmniPark opened up less than an hour's drive away we both promised each other we'd go, when we could. But with the time and the money, we just never somehow managed it — and it was doubly hard to scare up either after you were born, of course. I think Pa must have been saving for a couple of years to pull it together. So this was... this was like a dream come true.

"And it was an amazing day." I remember how her face softened, how she gave this half-smile, and I remember the lump in my throat when I saw her eyes were wet. "We went on all the rides we could — well, *almost* all; we skipped the Time Tunnel, because by then it was the crappy kids' version. But we went through the Story of Man, the Amoeba Escape, the Quantum Catastrophe...that one was a disappointment too, because I'm expecting stuff about real quantum physics, entanglement and the Many-Worlds theory, all of that, and instead we just get a light-show that's really kind of boring. Still. There really never was anyplace quite like that park. Everything I ever read about EPCOT says OmniPark blew them out of the water."

...What's that? Oh. Well, yeah, I think that was part of why they closed down. The place *was* incredibly expensive to run, especially with all the renovations they kept having to do, the ride revisions. When I was researching the place, I remember wondering to myself how they ever broke even, even at the ticket prices they had to charge. But this is all incidental.

The important thing, my Mom told me, was the last ride. The one they'd saved for the end. Nebula Quest.

At the start of every ride, there's always that moment where the bar comes down and locks, where the track engages — the part where you know it's too late to back out. Nothing you do can stop it, now: Hold on or don't, kick out, scream — the ride just keeps going. That's the best, for me, and the worst.

The best, because it's the worst.

3

I've looked up what Nebula Quest was supposed to be about — a bunch of hyperspace jumps through an experimental Stargate or whatever, looking for some nebula that's disappeared; going out further and further and further, past the Andromeda Galaxy and the Virgo Supercluster, so far into the future it'd take a journey through a black hole to get the riders back where they were supposed to be. But that's not how Mom described it to me, because to hear her tell it, she'd forgotten almost everything about the ride aside from the way it'd made her *feel*. No giant OmniVision screen or digital sound effects, no laser light-show, no gyroscopic rotations, no chemical photography tour of the Crab, the Horseshoe, the Hourglass nebulas.... She remembered sitting down in the two-person bubble next to Grandad Clouthier, squeezing his hand as they got locked in; there'd been a woman talking throughout, the Navigator, who started out okay but ended up sounding crazier and crazier the farther they travelled. (*But that's how all the rides were, one way or another,* Mom reminded me, here — *can't have science without mad science, apparently. Not if you want to sell tickets, 'specially at* those *prices.*)

"I remember waiting in line, outside the ride," she said. "The whole place, the Realm of the Stars, was supposed to look like a ring-shaped space station we 'flew' up to in a 'rocket.' Countdown and everything. So we're standing there watching starships arriving, docking, loading and unloading, taking off for other parts of the solar system — incredible stuff. And from inside, just through the portal, we could hear the group right in front of us going through the ride itself, which you wouldn't really think would be possible. It was faint, but... yeah, we could hear them. Screaming.

"It was high and far away, and for some reason it didn't seem like it was coming through the *doors*, so much, as from up above us. Like they were overhead, twisting and turning, hurtling back and forth from one direction to the next: Up and down, east to west, north to south. And every once in a while it was like they turned a corner, suddenly switched from one to the other, faster than you'd think was possible.

"*Sounds scary*, I told your Grandad, and he just smiled and went: *Ooh, very scary, honey!* And we're standing there joking back and forth about how easy it must be to scare those people we hear screaming, you know, charging each other up for the ride, because *we* would never scream like that, not *us*. Because we *love* science, and science fiction, and everything like that... and that was true enough, back then. It'd been true, the whole time we were going through every other part of the Park. By the time we actually sat down in the 'spacepod' ride car and the safety bar clicked in, we'd ramped each other up to the point I half *wanted* it to be real. I *wanted* to go through hyperspace, see the other side of the galaxy. The other side of the universe. Even if it meant I'd never get back, I just wanted to see it. 'Slip the surly bonds of Earth,' like the poem says.

"It didn't turn out that way."

The real function of any ride, as we all know, is to slow down time. To shut up the chattering monkey-mind for as long as we can. Intensity, like gravity, dilates our temporal awareness; ninety seconds feels like three, and like an hour. It makes us forget what those heartbeats in our skull, the ones that are now both jackhammer and achingly slow pendulum, are counting down towards.

Because once you've really grasped that you're going to die, forgetting that fact — even for less than ninety seconds — is the only real experience of immortality any of us can be certain of having.

4

This is the part where what Mom told me stops meshing up with anything you can look up online. I'm not going to ask you to believe it, because I don't think that really matters, at this point. But I think you have to understand how my Mom experienced it, or you're not going to understand why I did what I've done.

What she described wasn't anything like the official Nebula Quest narrative. It was more like — I don't know if you've ever been on one of those centrifuge rides? You know, the kind which spin around so fast that the G-force holds you against the wall, while the floor drops out from under you but you don't fall because the spin's holding you up? I remember Mom saying to me, *All I could think was, "What the fuck did they put a safety bar in for?" We were plastered up so hard against the car's back wall there was nearly two feet of room. We were crushed against one side as well — it felt like luck that Dad was between me and the side wall, 'cause if it'd been the other way around I don't know if I could have kept breathing. I was screaming, of course, bloody murder, all the time; the usual, you know, "Oh my God why did we get on this ride?! Holy Christ let us off! Dad, help, help!" But I could barely even get the words past my lips, because it felt like someone had slapped a huge hand over my face and was smearing everything sideways.*

And I don't know if this was an accident or deliberate, but the lights were only barely working — they'd come on for a few seconds, then black out for what felt like a minute, then back on for another flash. But the weird thing was, what little I could see outside the car, in those flashes? Didn't look anything like the actual ride, as far as the promo photos went. If they looked like anything, it was scenes from the other *rides in the park. That moment when the giant amoeba swallows the car, in* Amoeba Escape; *the isopod swarm in the* Trench Dive; *the sea scorpion leaping out of the water in* Palaeozoa... *Except they all looked wrong, somehow. Worse. Nauseating.*

Though that could just have been the G-force, I guess.

I think the worst part was realizing that Dad was screaming, too. And not the way people normally scream on a ride. Not the way you ever want to hear your father scream. Because if there's shit in the world that can make your father scream like that, then you can pretty much just give up on ever getting a good night's sleep again. At one point I just shrieked out, so hard it hurt, "Christ, I hate you, Dad!" And I meant it. For getting me on this ride, for seeing how much of a coward I was, for showing me how much of a coward he *was. I couldn't make out if he screamed it back, not in words, but I was sure I could hear it anyway. Feel it, on my eardrums. Because I'd dragged him into this, too. Like junkies enabling each other on the chase for that one, sick-making dragon, the perfect rush that'll make you forget everything.*

And then suddenly we were slowing down, and the car stopped spinning, and we slammed back into where we were supposed to be sitting, and I started laughing because of course it was always just a ride, nobody was ever in any danger. And even though Dad was holding my hand so hard it hurt, I was holding on just as tight, and I remembered I loved him and thought how utterly, utterly awful it would have been to go through all that by myself. And I felt terrible for what I'd said but only for a second, because he couldn't possibly have heard me and even if he did he'd know not to mind. And as the lights came on I turned to him, shaking and laughing, and—

—and I realized... it wasn't... wasn't him.

It looked *like him. It was wearing his clothes, his shoes. It had his beard. It had the mole on its cheek my Dad always had. But... the lines on his face were different. Like he hadn't spent nearly as much time in his life smiling. He sat like he was used to slouching; my Dad never slouched. And the look he gave me, as we rolled back into the exit station, wasn't an expression I'd ever seen my Dad wear. It was sour, unsurprised. Mean. Like a man who'd expected to hate the ride the way he'd hated this whole day, and could barely even muster relief that it was over. "There,"* he snapped. *"Done. Last ride. Are you happy now, Monica? Can we go?"*

I just stared at him. He rolled his eyes in disgust. And when the safety bar clicked and rose up, he climbed out without waiting for me. "I'll be in the car," he growled, and stalked off. *I was too stunned even to feel sick.*

He calmed down on the drive home, and apologized. Said he should have remembered how much this all meant to me, even if he'd never cared much for it himself. Asked me if I remembered him getting sick, that time he'd taken me to a traveling park when I was eight — I couldn't even start telling him that we'd never gone to any park together before today. He didn't even drive like my Dad — Dad was a very careful driver, but this guy barely remembered his lane change signals and laughed whenever anyone honked at him for cutting him off. He laughed at me, too, when he saw how freaked out his driving was making me. Not like someone being deliberately cruel, but just... like he didn't get it. Like everything I loved about my Dad was just... gone.

And then we got home, and Mom — your Gramma *— kissed him like she always did, and laughed when he slapped her butt, the way Dad never would have. When he smiled, he looked more like Dad. But even then, I could tell. And I wanted to scream at Mom — why couldn't she* tell? *How could she* not *tell? I mean, she was still her, who she'd always been. But now she was in love with someone else.*

I wasn't ever able to forgive her, for that.

And I never saw my Dad *again.*

People compare amusement park rides to sex all the time; the word "ride" is actually Irish slang for sex. But sometimes I think people miss the critical parallel in that analogy.

Because if the best part of the ride, for most people, is the catharsis of finishing it, the euphoria as you walk away, then the real best part of sex — the whole point of it — isn't the athletics, or even the orgasm. It's the afterglow. Those few minutes of complete relaxation, trust, and safety in someone else's arms. Of total connection, however ephemeral. That's what we go back for, again and again.

Until the first time somebody we ride with doesn't share it.

5

After that was the really awkward part — kind of like you listening to me, right now, thinking: *Well, she obviously believes it, even though there's no fucking way on earth it happened the way she says it did.* The part where you have to keep a real grip on yourself, internally, to stop yourself from just breaking down busting out the c-word — like: C-R-AZY, you ain't got no alibi, you *crazy*, is what I mean. Not... the other c-word.

No, I get it, doctor, seriously. It's okay.

So here I am probing her story, but cautiously, well aware how every question that's supposed to make it make more sense only makes me look more like Scully on *The X-Files*, playing the designated skeptical asshole. Asking things like, *So, was he, like, back to normal next morning?*

No. I told you. He was the same stranger I'd never met before, probably for the rest of his life. I just stopped talking to that guy, after a while.

And nobody else noticed, at all? How could that even work?

That one got me the bitterest smile I've ever seen from my Mom. *Seamlessly,* she answered. *A couple of days later, the guy pointed to all the SF books in his downstairs office, the ones I'd helped my Dad collect, and told me he was tired of hosting* my *books on* his *shelves, that it was time I found a better place for them. Just kind of exasperated. Anything connected to my Dad got explained away as being mine, or changed over without anyone noticing. Like it'd always been that way.*

She said she'd had some vague, faint hope of getting her own Dad back for a little while, if only she could just trick — *this* guy — back to OmniPark. But that melted away pretty quick, given how violently he rejected the whole idea, and besides, she had other stuff to concentrate on; went to school at night, got her own degree and a good job that'd help her not have to rely on the Clouthiers, drifted back into contact with my Dad and Aunt Sally. Made friends. Made a life for herself, and me.

I just stopped saying anything about it, she finished up. *I didn't want to get sent to a hospital, not with you involved. I didn't want to give them any opportunity to take you away from me.*

You think they would have? I couldn't help asking. *I mean, c'mon, Mom, it's not like you were on drugs or beating me up or anything....*

Jael, I don't know. I didn't know *him. I never knew* what *that man might do.*

So that was why she wouldn't go to his funeral, because even after all these years, all she felt about him was *I don't know that guy, he's not MY Dad. I don't know where the hell my Dad went.* Sitting there exactly like always, my smart, strong Mom, and saying this insane fucking thing like she was proud of it; it'd cost her some, obviously, but she'd stuck to it, no matter how much it hurt. Because that was the right thing to do, to honor *her* Dad. And I had to sit there nodding, because what else could I do, in the moment? Thinking: Okay, this is nuts, but she really thinks it's true. Thinking: Oh my God, I can't believe she never told me about this before he died!

Because now it was too late, forever. No possible *way* we could get closure, either of us. Gramma, Grandad... she'd thrown her own parents away, with both hands.

I had to try, though, because this had already ruined enough of her life. Of *both* our lives.

You see that, right?

So say it. I see you want to. *What did you DO, Jael? Why are you here?*

Okay, look....

Should I have gone to someone else? Gotten her to go to someone else? Probably. But you don't know my Mom. That was never gonna work. So—I went another way.

Obviously.

Quivering on the ragged edge of the ride, decision made, and yet. Is there a moment between moments, where things blend? Physics implies so. A moment where you are and aren't committed. A moment where anything — everything — is possible, the cat in the proverbial box, alive and dead simultaneously, so long as you don't look. Where things are still... uncertain.

When does that moment end, exactly? When you see a thing, experience it? Or, and just wait a minute here, could it actually be—

—when you remember it?

6

I studied Nebula Quest, the way it was supposed to be. I learned the script, the Navigator's increasingly terrified/terrifying string of revelations, going out out out out into the black, the empty, the impossible. The plunge through the black hole, back to known space, known time, reality. I scrubbed the boards for anyone who could tell me what the digital sound-effects sounded like, what the laser light-show looked like — *Just give me an approximation, man,* I'd beg (virtually). *OmniPark, Realm of the Stars, right near the end, before they folded for good. I'm trying to help someone recover memories, trying to cure a longstanding case of post-traumatic time-loss. I'm trying to help my* Mom. *You've all got moms out there, right?*

Nerds and geeks, all the way down: They loved it, mainly. You can always find somebody to help, if you only look hard enough. It was harder to get my Mom to agree to cooperate, but...I think she saw it as a way of making peace with me over this, you know? Like she cared more about how I felt than she did about how *she* felt, at this point. Then again, she'd had a whole lot longer to live with it.

There's a guest-room in our house I set up as a little studio about eighteen months back, when I was making extra money and racking up extra practice-time by consulting at home. It has blackout shades, mats, a nice little knock-off Siri clone I can plug my iPad into. We set a date, lay down in the dark together, and I got everything going with a couple of calm-down exercises, some focussing. Eventually, I got her far enough into what seemed like a trance to start the guided meditation. Just set the iPad up in front of her, switched on the tracks I'd gathered and settled back, reading the ride like I was following along on a teleprompter: *And here at the edge of everything, we see the truth of the universe at last, written on pure emptiness — nothing lasts forever. Nothing is static; nothing is constant. Not the planet Earth, not our sun, or our galaxy; not even the universe itself. The only thing that is truly real...*

...is change, itself.

Flux and motion, endless creation, endless decay. Time like a ribbon looped through everything and breathing itself back and forth into being, pulling tight then loosening, over and over again. And all of what we know we can never really know at once just spinning, spinning, spinning away from the one tiny point which blew us out into being from nothingness, chained us to entropy and shot us out further and further, until even the atoms, the particles, the dust that makes us up relax their bonds upon each other and we, what? Keep on going, forever? Break apart? Slowly move back inwards, faster and hotter and hotter and faster, 'til it happens all over again?

I don't know what she saw, lying there, inside her head. Hell, I don't even know what *I* saw, after a while: Not the room, not my Mom, not the iPad's flickering patterns. Just gyroscopic swings through blackness, gravity's awful crush and the sick-making lurch as it let me go, only to snatch me back again. Just a series of holes opening from nothing into nothing, outside, inside, things I couldn't have named if I'd tried. Hating myself for doing this, for trying this, for being butt-stupid arrogant enough to think I could ever heal her wounds; hating *her*, for having those wounds, in the first place. Because *You did this to yourself, Monica Clouthier, you crazy fucking bitch — you see that, right? Don't you? Who the hell else could have done it, if you didn't?*

Just my own voice, my body, my *reality*, all falling away, down the hole. Down the funnel, the twisty straw, towards the event horizon. Beyond it.

On the ride, nothing can ever be truly certain, except that the ride ends. Not if: It will. It does. When, though? That's an entirely different question. Less certain.

Or, maybe — the very opposite *of certain.*

7

I woke up face-down, half on and off the mat, with blood in my mouth. I think I must have fallen straight forward onto the floor, chin-first. The iPad had run out of charge; the room was dark, shades still drawn. It'd been dusk when we started, but now it was later, full night. And my Mom...

I could see her sitting up, the shape of her humped into herself, watching me where I lay but not helping, not even reaching out to touch me. Her arms were crossed, hugging her own chest, like she was trying to hold her guts in. She was shuddering, breath ragged, wet. I could hear that she'd been crying.

"Ugh," I said, and spat, without thinking — a bright copper smell, all in my nose and down my jaw, hot-wet. My head banged like a gong. I tried to lever myself up and almost puked right there, so I froze instead with my fist against the mat, twisting it. When everything got a bit less swimmy, I spat again, and asked, not looking up: "Mom, are you okay? You sound...*ugh*. Oh God."

Thinking: *That was such a bad idea.* Thinking: *Did I loosen some teeth? My gums feel raw.* Thinking: *Oh well, back to the drawing board, I guess—*

And still she didn't answer me, just sat there, vibrating. Taking big, wet gulps of air through a narrowed throat. I heard her nose gurgle, and then I was on my feet at last, feeling backwards for the switch. I turned it on, almost at the same second as she looked up.

"It didn't work, Jael," is all she said, her eyes meeting mine and locking on, like she knew I'd want to help her, to make her feel better. Like we *knew* each other.

(but no)

This woman. Nice enough lady, I guess — nothing wrong with her that I could see, aside from how upset she was. And I felt bad about that, like anybody would, anybody human; she was just all red, you know, like she'd been slapped, like she was going to bruise. Like a bruise she'd had all along was coming up through her skin, her wet, sticky skin with its swollen eyes and its streaming nose, its square, grit mouth, the very picture of terrible, invisible pain. Like I could finally see what she'd tried so hard to hide all these years from...*her* daughter, somewhere. *Her* Jael.

She lost her Dad, and she never got him back, and not one damn person in this world, this *universe*, will ever be able to explain to me how, or why. She lost her Dad, just just like I...

(lost *her*)

My Monica.

My Mom.

All at once, and forever: The moment came where I guess she was her and this other person at the same time, and then...it passed. I woke up. I saw. I saw her, this woman who's living in the same house with me today, hugging me every time I come home, making jokes I'm supposed to know. Cooking me food I've never liked. Talking about things we've never done together.

She's not my Mom. Not *my* Mom. I knew it then and I know it now. I can't *un*-know it.

I wish I could.

And the only thing I'm proud of, even today, is at least I never did what she did—my Mom—back when. At least I never let her, this woman, know I didn't recognize her. Because she needed a daughter, just like I need a Mom. Just like I still need one, so bad I'm not going to drive this poor lady away for the crime of not knowing she's not my Monica, just like she doesn't know I'm not her Jael.

I took a minute. I met her eyes. And I made the decision, right then, not to do what she'd done.

"I'm so sorry, Mom," was all I said.

And I hugged her.

8

So again, ask it, doctor. I know you want to. "Why are you here, Jael?"

Well, to tell it, for one. I needed to do that, in a place and with a person who'd, kind of — have to listen. Have to be polite, *professional*, even in the face of this total chunk of weirdness I'm sicking up in front of them. You don't have to believe me; it'd be nice, but I sure don't expect it. But also...I needed to talk it through, for my own sake, and the only person who'd ever really be able to understand the situation the way I need them to is the one person I *can't* do that with.

Because that's the thing I keep coming back to . Whatever else is different, *this* Monica lost her Dad too, lost *her* version of Grandad Clouthier. Maybe the version she lost was the version my Monica wound up with, except who says it even has to be that neat? For all I know there are a thousand versions of all of us out there, and that goddamned fucking OmniPark ride just shuffled through its riders like a drunk Vegas dealer, scattering cards everywhere. And laughing.

And I couldn't do it to her. I couldn't tell her she'd lost her daughter, too.

So for six months I've been putting together this... this mask of myself. Figuring out who she expects me to be and doing my damnedest to shift into it. She seems a lot more like my Mom than that other Mr. Clouthier was like her Dad, so in one way it's easier than you'd think, but in another it's been...it's been a grind. Winging my way through this 24-7 improv act, taking those gut punches when I catch a momentary odd look, laughing our way out of them, wondering if *this* is going to be the moment she goes, *Oh, shit, who the fuck are you?!*

Or just screams, and doesn't stop until I run away, or she does.

Because when you can't stand to lose something, you'll hold onto the best substitute of it you've got. Right, doc?

...Do you think she's with her Dad, now?

Not that it matters. 'Cause how can we know? How would we ever be sure?

What's the point of asking a question you know nobody'll ever be able to answer?

The ride engages. We've already made our choice.

Nothing...nothing...will ever be this certain again.

How could it be?

Omni Oil, LLC
1419 N. Grandview Avenue, Suites 30-40
Odessa, TX 79762

From the desk of
Dalton Meadowcroft Teague

Tuesday, August 15, 1967

My Dearest Evelyn...

As you know, we are up in Montana this week, sinking oil wells into shale beds. We have struck more times than not, so I suppose we should call ourselves fortunate.

But I write to you today not about oil, but about the other things we brought up from that shaft: fossils, shells, and ancient minerals. Marvels from a time before time began.

I sat at my writing desk in my tent, smoking a bit of the old Virginia, and sipping some of Kentucky's finest, as you know I am wont to do on such occasions. And I said to myself: oil is of finite importance. It will only remain valuable for as long as this society, this culture, requires it as fuel for its machinery.

Meanwhile, I gazed upon the other objects arrayed on that desk. The fossils, the minerals, the tiny shells wrested from the bowels of the earth. And I said to myself, "These things will be priceless for thousands of years to come, no matter what fuel may drive our vehicles in that future."

I realize, now, that what we have been drilling for, all along, is not oil, but information: the most crucial resource we can mine out of this planet. And I sat there at my desk looking at my little collection of shells and minerals and fossil fragments, and I came to a decision.

Evelyn, what we will build will not be an enterprise for the distribution of oil, but for the sharing of information: knowledge torn from the Earth. That is what I will stake my name on. And when my epitaph is engraved upon my headstone, I will be remembered not for the oil I brought up, but for the information I excavated, upon which you and I will build a most marvelous wonderland.

Yours eternally,

--Dalton

Letter from Dalton Teague to his wife Evelyn, containing the first known mention of the OmniPark concept.

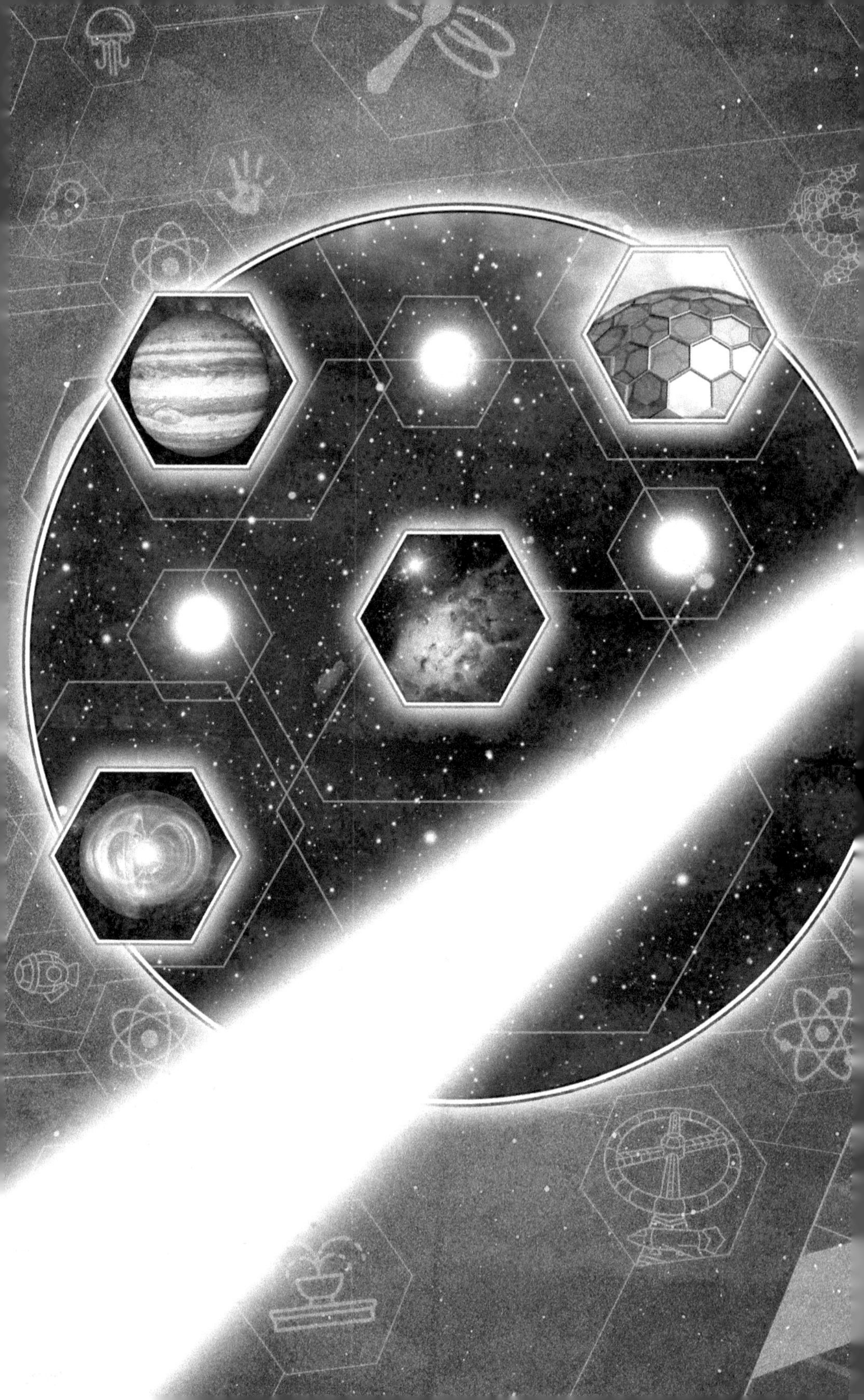

All Those Lost Days

Brian Evenson

1

I only ever visited OmniPark twice. The first time, my parents insisted we go. My father was — in his own words — a "science buff," and my mother was the kind of spouse who felt it her duty to wholeheartedly support whatever her husband suggested. My older brother and I were, I suppose, mildly intrigued by the park, about the things my father and the glossy brochure he had picked up somewhere suggested it contained. We might even have been relatively enthusiastic, right up to the moment we discovered the park was in West Texas, nearly fifteen hours away by car.

Come on, my father said when we groaned, *we'll make a family adventure out of it. It'll be fun!*

That first time was a lot like most of the other vacations my father schemed up for us. It started with a long hot drive from Utah down to Odessa in a station wagon whose air conditioning my dad kept turning off during the most sweltering stretches of road. ("Engines are prone to overheating on days like this," he'd remind us as we gasped for air). Sometimes he'd even turn the heater on and then tell us — "Science in action here, boys!" — how that drew heat off the engine. And no, we couldn't roll down the windows, because that increased drag on the car and give us bad mileage. "If I can stand this," he'd announce from the front seat, casting half-glances back at us as sweat poured down his face, "then you can too."

By the time we reached Odessa, a little past midnight, we were all soaked through and exhausted. We checked in at a little no-name motel on the edge of town; the kind of place people rent more often by the hour than for the night or two. My father had gotten a deal on it, and saw himself as outsmarting the town somehow by not staying closer to the park and paying more. The room's air conditioning was scarcely more functional than our car's had been.

Mercifully, the night cooled off around three in the morning, letting me fall into a dreamless sleep. I only woke when Dad pulled the curtains open and flooded the room with sunlight. He was already dressed and ready to go, Mom too, and couldn't understand what was keeping both me and my brother.

2

What can I say about that first visit that hasn't already been discussed on countless message boards and blogs? We visited all seven of the Realms. We rode all the rides. We ate lunch — not at one of the sit-down restaurants, obviously, but at the cheapest snack stand Dad could locate on the guidemap.

Was it a fun day? Yes. A little strange, not quite like anything I'd experienced before. Sure, fun, yet a little *off* somehow, too. I remember moments of amazement — a few of awe, even — and moments of exhaustion and boredom. A few times I laughed out loud at how hokey an effect seemed, but a moment later I'd become convinced this was all part of a larger plan: I'd been meant to laugh and relax so as to be caught off guard by what followed.

Our parents' constant presence — by which I mean my father's — made it hard to truly lose ourselves in the experience. Half the time my father was expounding on the scientific principles behind a ride and its Realm, while the other half he spent pointing out what he saw as factual or design errors. By that age, we'd learned it was better to let him run on: if we cut him off or told him we already knew what he was telling us, he'd be bluntly offended and would feel the need to give a lecture on respecting your parents. Better by far to nod along and zone out.

By late afternoon my brother had had enough. To be honest, so had I. My brother, though, was older than me, seventeen, which meant he'd been putting up with dad for two years longer. I could tell by the way he was fidgeting and scowling that he was on the verge of saying something that would ruin Dad's mood — which would, in turn, ruin the day for the rest of us.

We were in the Realm of Time, strolling through the garden of the ersatz Victorian mansion, when Dad's veneer of patience began to crack. He had stepped a few paces away to scrutinize a display of statues holding antique timepieces, and was complaining to anyone within earshot that there was no replica of a water clock — that a whole class of ancient timepieces was missing. When no one paid him any attention, his mood began to darken.

It darkened further once we entered the mansion itself and climbed one of the grand staircases leading to the upper rooms. The mansion's library, filled with leatherbound volumes titled with time-related wordplay, struck him as possessed of a levity inappropriate to seriousness scientific endeavor. As he inspected some of the most obviously fictional fossils and "far-future" artifacts I saw his nose wrinkle.

"This whole place is ridiculous," my father announced. "We're skipping the Time Machine ride."

"Why?" my brother asked. I could hear the edge to his voice. "We walked through the rest of this Realm. We should do the ride."

"Why? Because time travel is impossible," said my father.

"Says who?" my brother shot back.

"It's just a ride," I said quickly. "It's probably fun even if it doesn't have much to do with science. Why don't Sam and I go on it quickly and then we'll meet you and Mom downstairs at the Conservatory Parlour." That was the snack shop just below. "You can get ice cream," I added. Dad loved ice cream.

My father hesitated a moment, torn between the thought of enjoying ice cream without having to buy any for his children and his ever-present compulsion to control us. When Mom took his hand, he sighed. Finally he nodded.

"One ride only," he said. "And it's either ice cream or the ride. See you downstairs in twenty minutes."

3

Even after Dad departed, my brother remained in a bad mood. Bad enough that at first I wasn't sure if he'd snap out of it before we had to meet up with Dad again. If he didn't, we'd have a real problem.

We trekked down the tiled hallway from the library to the laboratory, arriving just as a man with thick glasses and wild gray hair took his place at the front of the room and clapped his hands to attract our attention.

The small crowd hushed and listened as he explained how we were about to undertake a great journey — through time rather than space. We would be the first humans besides himself, he claimed, to experience not only the distant future but the full extent of time. He gestured to a wall that had slid silently open to one side of us, revealing a series of wood-paneled vehicles studded with brass knobs and buttons. These, he claimed, were time machines, carefully preset for appropriate destinations. He encouraged us to choose one and step aboard, adding a warning that the voyage was a risky one, and he could not be held responsible for any hazards encountered during our journey.

"Only the truly adventurous need apply," he said. "The meek should feel no shame in leaving this path untrod."

Each vehicle held two people, and so naturally my brother and I clambered together into one and pulled the lap bars down to lock us in place.

4

The ride itself was, more or less, your average carnival attraction. We began by gliding down a tunnel shot through with lights and lasers, the vehicle shaking and spinning, eerie sounds rising chaotically all around us. After a minute or two, we emerged to find ourselves — so the instrument panel claimed — in the year 802,721 AD, beneath a pale-red artificial sky. Clicks and whirrings surrounded us as strange elf-like creatures, meant to be the far-future descendants of humans, swiveled and bent to their tasks in the same endless cycle. They were Eloi — a name I later realized OmniPark had taken from H. G. Wells' *The Time Machine*. They were, obviously, animatronic creations, and functioned far too jerkily and repetitively to be convincing.

"Dad would have hated this," I said.

My brother gave a short barking laugh.

I should have realized that, as with the other rides, this strangely unconvincing moment may have been entirely intentional — a ruse meant to trick us into dropping our guard. Our vehicle suddenly twisted and slipped down into what felt like a dark underground tunnel. The light had dimmed to a deep magmatic glow. The tunnel itself had become uncomfortably humid and warm. The Eloi we had seen above were gone now, replaced by hairy gray-skinned humanoids that a subreddit would later inform me were Morlocks. Where the Eloi had been obviously animatronic, however, the Morlocks moved with startling fluidity. A particularly sharp smell, not unlike chlorine, irritated my nostrils. The Morlocks seemed to be closing in on us, and for some reason I felt genuinely under threat. The control panel of our vehicle flashed a warning and issued commands to manipulate certain levers and knobs. I dutifully focused on doing so, partly so as to avoid having to look at the Morlocks too closely.

Just when they had our vehicle surrounded and escape appeared impossible, the floor opened beneath us and we plunged down into another vortex of light and sound. This one resembled the first vortex in most ways, but something was different here, too: it seemed more real, more like something I should take seriously.

But after the Morlocks, even this plunge through the vortex felt like a respite. I turned, smiling, toward my brother, to share with him the thrill we both must have felt.

But the other side of the vehicle was empty. My brother was gone.

5

My memories of the rest of the ride are vague and tangled. I remember craning my neck and struggling against the bar that held me in the vehicle, howling my brother's name. If I could have wormed free, I would have retraced the ride's path back in search of him. But between the darkness, the flashing lights, and the appearance of a new wave of bizarre creatures, I couldn't figure out how to release the bar.

By the time we passed through the final rooms and found ourselves back in the laboratory, I was near-hysterical. When an attendant finally unlocked the vehicle, I tried to climb out and charge back down the tunnel. A pair of attendants stopped me. I must have made quite a spectacle of myself, but when they made it clear they'd call security if I didn't leave, I finally managed to stammer out a few words about my brother's disappearance.

Once they understood what had happened, the attendants began to take me seriously. Almost too seriously: the way they sprang into action made me feel my fears had not been exaggerated. Those visitors still in the ride were rushed to the unloading dock and hurried out the exit. The ride was shut down, and all guests in line waiting to ride were sent away. While one attendant roped a "Closed for Maintenance" sign across the entrance, the other attendant — a rail-thin man with a pockmarked face — struggled into what looked like a hazard suit. Retrieving a long-handled electric cattle prod from a hook on the wall, he hurried up the tunnel, quickly vanishing from sight.

6

He couldn't have been gone very long, probably no more than ten minutes, though it seemed much longer than that. For the first five minutes or so, all was silence. Not even the remaining attendant spoke.

Suddenly, a series of crackling noises echoed from within the tunnel — the cattle prod, I assumed. Guessing what he might be using it for, what he was driving back, made my imagination run wild.

Then I heard, as if from a great distance, a long, low howl — a sound I could not identify as animal or human.

The remaining attendant placed his hand on my shoulder, and left it resting there in a way I suppose he meant to be reassuring. I realized I had been holding my breath so as to better hear what was happening in the tunnel, and all at once I let it loudly out. The hand on my shoulder tightened, and within the darkness of the tunnel I glimpsed movement.

I saw the hazard-suited attendant, silhouetted by the coal-red lights. He was unaccompanied — or so I thought, until one gloved hand appeared from behind his back, tugging my brother toward the exit. I'd never seen my brother move like this: crouching low and glancing about nervously, gripping that gloved hand. When he emerged into the unloading area, he looked disoriented and exhausted. And that wasn't all that had changed about him. At first I couldn't put my finger on the difference until he came closer, and I saw his chin was covered in a soft growth of beard. Since when had my brother needed to shave? Never, as far as I knew. His face had been smooth this morning, hadn't it?

"Sam," I said. "Where were you? What happened?"

My brother stared back at me, seeming to look straight through me. The attendant released Sam's hand and began to shimmy out of his hazard suit. I reached out and touched my brother's arm. He continued to stare past me.

I shook his arm and called his name, and he blinked.

"It's you," he said, seeming to return to himself a little. Then suddenly he wrapped me in his arms and crushed me against him.

This in itself was strange: our family had never been much for physical displays of affection. I could count on one hand the number of times my brother had hugged me. But apparently his time alone in the tunnel had rattled him. No; it was deeper than that. He was changed, somehow. He smelled different, like stale sweat and grime, with a hint of that sharp scent I'd smelled on the ride.

It wasn't until he released me that I noticed that his clothing was covered in dust, and the right knee of his jeans was torn. *From falling off the vehicle*, my mind offered. He was probably lucky he hadn't gotten more badly injured.

"Why did you climb out?" I asked him.

"They pulled me out," he said.

"'They?'" I asked, but he just shook his head.

And then the attendants were guiding us speedily to the exit, and we found ourselves outside, blinking into the afternoon sun.

7

By the time we reached the Conservatory Parlour, both Mom and Dad had finished their ice cream. Dad made a point of looking angrily at his watch. He opened with a lecture on the importance of keeping track of time, which rapidly flowed into a lecture on the importance of keeping one's promises. How could we lose track of time in a clock-filled exhibit called the Realm of Time? was the general gist. We must've done it on purpose, to spite him.

I opened my mouth to tell my father what had happened, but my brother reached out and touched my arm and stopped me.

"We're sorry," he told our father. "It's my fault. The ride made me sick. It won't happen again."

Dad drew back a little, surprised to find my brother so subservient. He seemed not quite to believe it, and began a new lecture on the importance of telling not only the truth, but the *whole* truth. Under normal circumstances my brother would have fought back, but now he sat quietly, letting Dad's words wash over him, apologizing once more after my father had again had his say.

"Just don't let it happen again," said our father at last, partly bewildered and partly mollified. He gazed around the room and rubbed his hands together. "Well," he said, "What Realm shall we visit next?"

My brother begged off. He still wasn't feeling well, he claimed, and he needed to sit the afternoon out.

"If you think I'm going to run you back to the motel, you've got another thing coming," my father began, raising a finger in warning. But instead of rising to take the bait, my brother said he had no problem waiting back at the Entryway Pavilion.

"But the park doesn't close for another seven hours," my mother said, her voice creased with a hint of worry.

"That's all right," my brother said. "I'll be fine. The time will pass."

When Dad realized my brother was dead-set on sitting out the rest of the day, he launched into a lecture on the value of money — specifically money spent by one's father on a once-in-a-lifetime vacation.

I was probably the only one who noticed that an undercurrent of panic had crept into my brother's refusals.

In the end, our father succumbed. We led my brother back to the Entryway Pavilion, where he found a bench to settle on, and we left him there. At 9 pm when we returned, he was waiting on the exact spot where we'd left him, as if no time had passed at all. He looked up as we approached, momentarily perplexed, as if he didn't recognize us.

The next day, he refused to return to the park. He still wasn't feeling up to it, he claimed. Since my father hadn't yet paid for our second day's entry, he was only too happy to leave him behind in the hotel room. When we returned after an uneventful day at the park, we found him seated on the side of the bed, exactly where he'd been sitting when we departed. Again he glanced up in momentary confusion, seeming unsure where he was, or what he was doing there.

The following day we drove home.

In the sweltering backseat, I tried again to tease out of him what had happened in the tunnel.

"Drop it," he said. When I probed further, he turned to me with a wild look in his eyes, a look that frightened me. Not because I felt threatened by it, but because it was clear how threatened my brother felt — by, what, he wouldn't say.

I dropped it.

8

After that my brother was never the same. It was almost as if he wasn't all there — or rather as if he periodically sunk deeply into his body and had to be recalled to the surface when someone from the outside world tried to interact with him. His responses were slow, and often he blinked around him uncomprehendingly, failing to recognize people and places he had known all his life, recognizing them only after an awkwardly long delay. In those moments, I wondered if my brother had fallen in the tunnel and suffered a brain injury, or if perhaps this was more psychological: post-traumatic stress. At first I tried my best to be patient with him — but the more time passed, the more my patience dwindled. When would I get my real brother back? Who was this stranger who'd taken his place?

"What's wrong with you?" I finally demanded one afternoon when he forgot the way back from the bathroom to his own bedroom. "I know you don't want to talk about what happened in that tunnel, but how bad could it possibly have been? You were only alone for fifteen minutes."

He shot me a piercing look, fully present for the first time in days.

"Fifteen minutes? Is that all it felt like to you?" He considered me with narrowed eyes for a long moment. Then he sat down on my bed and tugged his shirt off.

"Here's what happened," he said. A purplish ragged scar ran from his hip across his chest, terminating in a deep starburst divot taken out of the meat of his shoulder. Not a fresh scar, but an old, faded one.

"That didn't happen in the tunnel," I stammered. "The scar is too healed."

"It did," he said. "I almost didn't survive."

I reached out and touched the scar, half expecting it to be fake, something he'd put on with stage make-up. But it felt real. He let me prod it for a moment and then he pulled away, snatching his shirt from the bed and tugging it back over his head.

Then he sank back into himself and shuffled off to his room, forgetting to close the door behind him.

9

The next year did not go well for my brother. He'd been a good student, but his grades fell precipitously. Teachers began to complain of his unresponsiveness in class; his handing-in of incomplete assignments, or sheets scrawled with gibberish.

The school's guidance counselor scheduled an emergency meeting with Mom and Dad, convinced that my brother might have developed a drug habit—what else would explain his sudden decline? My father tore my brother's room apart looking for drugs, found nothing. My brother just stood by and calmly watched it happen. But if it wasn't drugs, what else could account for this sudden transformation? Mental illness? My father flatly rejected that notion, since to accept it would imply something faulty about his genes, and that premise was obviously untenable. It was easiest for him to decide that my brother had willfully given up and was simply not trying, that it was a failure of character.

My father lectured, cajoled, screamed, but nothing seemed to get through. My brother did manage to limp on to the end of the year, though, and squeak past, just barely, and graduate. The day of his eighteenth birthday, he moved out.

I didn't see him much after that. Sometimes on weekends, my mom managed to coax him over for weekend laundry and a free dinner, but during the week he was unreachable. When I pressed, he mumbled something about working for a local construction company. He made enough for a dilapidated room in a shared apartment on the edge of town, he said, and he'd managed eventually to buy a beater car. My father would often mumble about what a waste it was, him not going to college, him having given up on life, but my brother didn't seem to care.

"Don't be like your brother," my father started saying to me, and before long he had developed that statement into a full lecture.

10

So things went for the next six months, until one night, around two or three in the morning, I jolted awake, startled from sleep by a sound. At first I thought it might be a branch scraping against my window. But no, its rhythm was too deliberate. I was wide awake now, my heart thundering in my chest.

I got up and crept to the window. My brother stood outside, tapping the glass with a pebble. He waved when he saw me, as if it was perfectly ordinary for him to be standing outside my window in the darkness.

I wrestled the window open. "Sam," I whispered. "What are you doing here?"

But he was already clambering through the window and into my room. I stepped back and let him tumble through the window-frame, landing in a heap on the carpet. As soon as he'd regained his footing, he started pacing back and forth, unable to settle.

"What's wrong?" I asked. "Should I wake up Mom?"

He stopped "If I'd wanted Mom or Dad," he said, "I would've knocked on their window. I knocked on yours, didn't I?"

"What do you need me to do?" I asked.

He opened his mouth, and then closed it again, as if he didn't know where to begin.

"Can this maybe wait until morning?" I asked.

He shook his head. "In the light it never seems like as big a deal," he said. "It's only at night that I can grasp the full extent of the problem. It has to be now."

Then he sat down on the bed and began to speak.

11

He had started having dreams, dreams that he was still back there, that he had never left. Could I understand what he meant? How horrible it was? To think that he, or part of him anyway, had never left, was still back there?

"Left where?" I said.

"The Realm of Time! The Time Tunnel!" he said. He had been in there, enjoying the ride, and then they'd dragged him out. Maybe he'd had one arm out of the cart a little, maybe that had been what was wrong, and either his lap bar hadn't been fully locked — or maybe they had a means of unlocking it. That was possible, because even though they weren't smart, they were crafty; he'd found that out from all those months — years, maybe — he'd spent trying to avoid them, trying to stay alive. Because surely I could understand that what had been minutes for me had been much longer for him? And whose idea had it been anyway to build a ride that did something so dangerous — that messed with time?

"I don't know what you're talking about," I said.

He was up and pacing again, seeming not to see me or the room around us.

It was real, he claimed, all real. Or some of it anyway. That first room, no, that was set up to look fake so that you'd just assume the later stuff was fake, another ride. But it was much more than a ride. They had dragged him out and attacked him—I'd seen the scar, hadn't I? They'd done that, and he'd been very lucky to get away, lucky not to have been eaten.

"But who?" I said. "Who are *they*?"

"Why the Morlocks of course!" he snapped. His speech was pressurized now, too rapid. They were real, he claimed, the Time Tunnel wasn't a ride—it was exactly what the inventor had said it was: a tunnel through time. The experience that everyone saw as a simulation was in fact real. At first the Morlocks had been kept at bay by the surprise and wonder of the strange vehicles, but their hunger had eventually driven them to defeat the safeguards and pluck someone out of a vehicle, and he was the one who had been plucked. He had lived there for almost a year, hiding from them, running for his life, surviving by the skin of his teeth. "All those lost days," he said, with great despair. And then they had caught him again, and would have killed him if it hadn't been for a mysterious figure wearing a shiny suit with a weapon that sizzled with power when it touched them and drove them away.

I realized then that something was seriously wrong with my brother. He seemed not even to recognize that the person in the hazard suit who had come for him had been one of the ride attendants.

But, then again, why had the attendant had to take a cattle prod with him down the tunnel? And why had he had to wear a hazard suit?

"And the worst thing," my brother claimed, "is that something went wrong. The shining figure was able to bring me out, yes, but it could only bring part of me out. I was torn in two somehow. Half of me is still in that distant future, still fighting for his life. I need that other half back if I'm ever to be myself again."

He was, he announced, going back into the park, back into the Time Tunnel. He'd go in and try to get the other part of him out. If he succeeded, maybe things would go back to normal and he could again be the person he had been before. If he failed, well, then at least both halves of him would be together, even if they were together in a world that was more like a hell. He wanted someone to know, he said, he had to tell someone, just so at least one person would know what had happened to him if he never came back.

When he was finished, he seemed to sink deeper into himself again. And then he clambered out the window, crossed the lawn, got in his car and drove away.

12

OmniPark security found my brother's car a few weeks later, abandoned on the ground floor of the parking structure. A police investigation unearthed video of him entering the park, then sneaking into the Realm of Time. After that, nothing.

I tried to explain my brother's story to my parents, who responded exactly as expected: Dad furious that I hadn't awakened him when my brother sneaked in; Mom hoping that Sam might have already been found and admitted to a mental facility. Of course, neither of them entertained the slightest possibility that his story held a grain of truth. In the crisp light of that autumn morning, I had difficulty believing it myself.

And that was where we left it. Two years later I headed off to college, and the summer of my sophomore year I found myself taking the long drive down to OmniPark without telling my parents. I would, I told myself, take one more trip through the Time Tunnel, just in case. Just to see if I could find my brother.

But the Time Machine ride was no more. Park Management had stripped out the old ride back in '91, to make room for "Pterry's Time Tunnel" — a ride for children. No Eloi, no Morlocks, and definitely no brother.

I went through anyway, and here and there found evidence of the old ride: the effects that claimed to be pushing the vehicles backward and forward in time were the same, and where the Morlocks had been were still bits and pieces of ruined and rusty machinery that I thought I recognized. Scratched into the side of one of these I thought I saw a crude letter "S," which might, I told myself, have referred to my brother, to Sam.

Or so I thought at the time. To be honest, it was dark and I was traveling quickly enough that I'm no longer sure that I saw anything scrawled on that machine at all.

The first admission ticket stamped on OmniPark's opening day — May 19, 1977 — which Teague kept framed in his office.

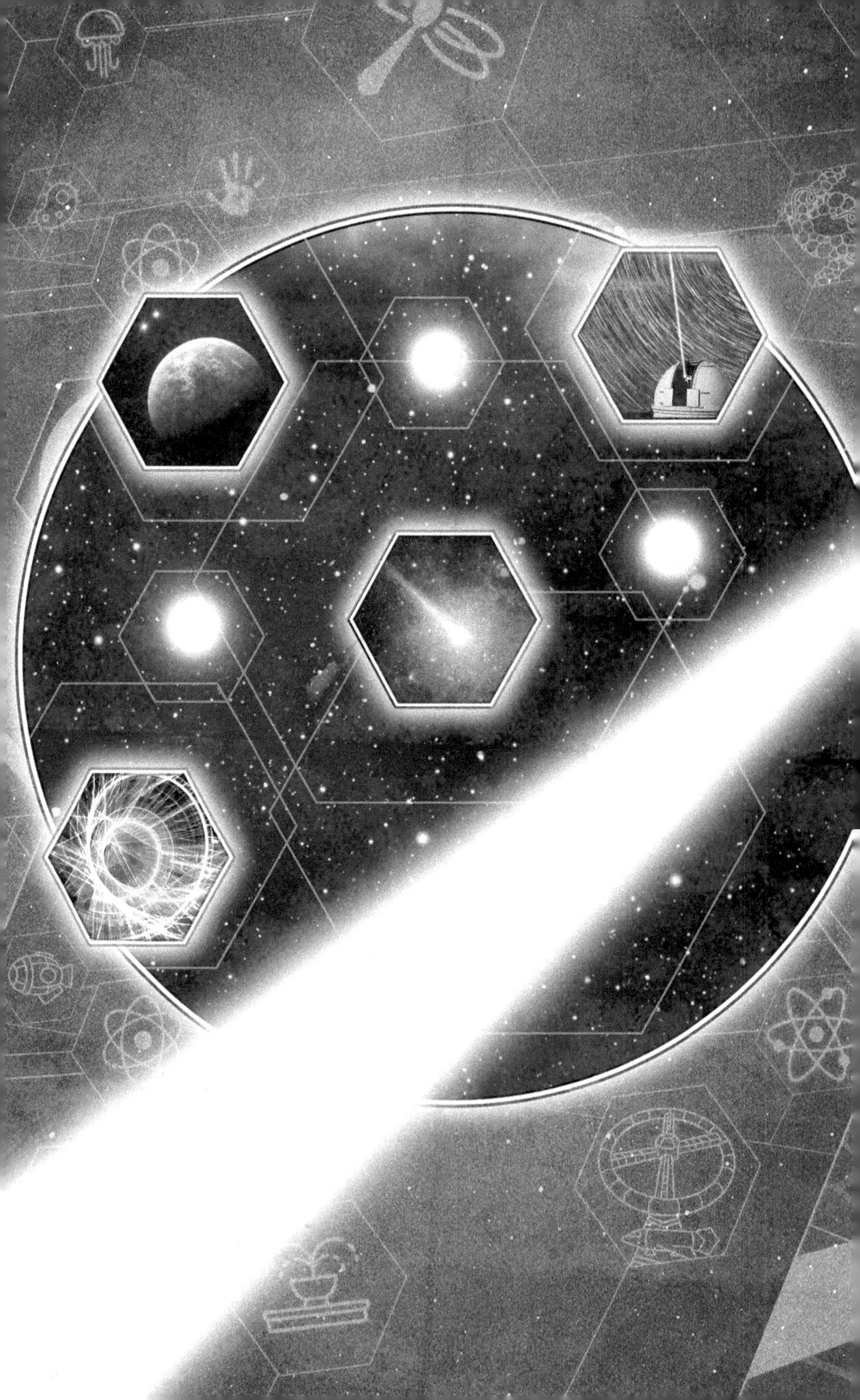

QUANTUM SUMMER

JESSE BULLINGTON & BRENT WINTER

1

When you really got down to it — like, at the quantum scale — everything sucked.

1989 was only half over and already it sucked hard: *President* Bush. The Exxon Valdez. The Mavs not even making the playoffs. Summer in West Texas sucked no matter what year it was. OmniPark especially sucked. What had seemed so magical to Hannah when she was a wide-eyed eight-year old riding the Time Tunnel, or a fourteen-year-old on her first date (with Tim Slidell at the Primeval Zoo), lost its luster after she'd spent a few summers sweating her buns off behind the high-tech curtain. Managers sucked; crying kids sucked; being seen by your carefree classmates in your sweat-stained regulation blue OP jumpsuit and ball cap mega-sucked.

And Hannah? Hannah sucked most of all, the nucleus of suckage that all the other suck orbited around like sweat bees circling a sticky trash can, a veritable subatomic suck particle in the shape of a teenage girl.

The fundamental suckiness of reality had intensified since Julia, Kat, and Evan took off for their epic road trip before starting college in the fall — a trip Hannah could no more afford than tuition at UT like Julia and Evan, not to mention out-of-state like Kat. But bored and lonely as she'd been, when her Alf phone rang on Saturday morning that sucked too, because she knew who was calling her. Call it sucky action at a distance. She'd barely gotten the beige phone out of its fuzzy cradle when she heard Jimmy barking on the other end:

"Hannah! How fast can you be here?"

She considered pretending to be her mom to teach her supervisor a lesson about just assuming she would magically appear whenever he needed her, but there was no point. Even back when she'd had a social life she'd never been able to say no extra dough.

"Morning, Jimmy."

"Can you be here by nine?" Jimmy sounded frantic, but that was his only setting. Hannah squinted at her clock: 8:14.

"You know I live in Midkiff, right?" He didn't answer. He probably didn't know where Midkiff was. Most of humanity didn't. "I live an hour from the park, and I need to shower and—"

"Be here by nine and I'll give you ten bucks cash."

Hannah sat up in bed. "I can make it by 9:30."

"9:15. Ten bucks. Domino's rules — you roll in one minute later, and no bonus."

Hannah hauled ass out of bed, Tasmanian Deviled her way into underwear and a jumpsuit, hit the john, checked herself out in the mirror — *at least put on some mascara*, she imagined her mom saying, *make those baby blues pop* — decided her baby blues would have to do their best unaided, and stopped off in the kitchen to grab coffee and untoasted Pop-Tarts for the road.

"Mornin', Sunshine," Doug said from his customary perch at the dinette, his greasy stubble flecked with crumbs of a suspicious nature. At what point had he decided it was cool to stop wearing pants around her? At least his ratty Iron Maiden t-shirt rode low enough on his lanky hips to obscure most of his tighty-whities. "Figured that call was for you. You gotta grow a pair, kiddo, learn to say no when they try and wrangle you in on your day off. Work'll waste your time just as much as you let it."

Hannah didn't respond to the creep haunting the trailer as she crossed to the cabinet and verified that, yes, he'd indeed eaten the last of the Pop-Tarts she'd bought with her own money, damn it. She slammed the cabinet shut, rinsed out her plastic OmniPark travel cup, spooned in equal parts Folgers and Nesquik, and topped it off with warm tap water. No half-and-half in the fridge, and breakfast was shaping up to be another oily funnel cake at the park. Rad.

"It's a crime they make y'all wear them monkey suits," Doug said. "You'd pull more tips if John Q. Public got a look at them drumsticks."

She almost reminded him that she'd stopped waiting tables at the Park and her mom was now the only waitress in the family, but she'd learned that the first rule of dealing with poltergeists was not to acknowledge their presence — doing so only made them stronger.

"Mornin' baby." Hannah's mom shuffled into the kitchenette, her blue eyes squinting through a cloud of Kool smoke. She coughed wetly and said, "Make you some breakfast?"

"Doug ate all my Pop-Tarts. Again." She kissed her mom on a sour cheek and fled as Doug's scrawny voice skittered after her, promising to buy a whole dang crate of the dang things if she loved them so much, but she really oughta start thinking about how fat her dang bee-hind was swelling up.

The Civic started on the third try, then gobbled up cracked blacktop through barren scrubland as she gambled a ten-dollar bonus against another thirty-dollar speeding ticket. Hannah gripped the steering wheel, leaned forward, and did that thing she sometimes did where she stared at the vanishing point on the horizon and focused intently on outracing time, or compressing space, or whatever it was you had to do to get somewhere faster than was physically possible. It was a doofy little mind game she played with herself, but the doofiness didn't matter. All that mattered was if it worked.

Forty-nine minutes and zero Noids later, the Civic's bald tires screamed to a halt amid the heat mirages already pooling across the employee parking lot. Her Chucks hit the ground running; there was a lot of Park to cover between the backlot and the Realm of the Particle.

Hannah buzzed herself in and flashed her badge at a security guard hunched over an *Archie* comic before hightailing it across the Entryway Pavilion. No time for breakfast anymore, with the weekend crowd around the Omnicolor Fountain slowing her down.

As she skirted the line of guests waiting to be "shrunk down" by the Scalar Portal to enter the subatomic-sized Realm of the Particle, Kenneth spotted her and offered a heat-wilted wave. Like, did he seriously think their shared servitude as Park employees made up for repeatedly snapping her bra strap in Mr. Warburton's class? Serving as a glorified ticket puncher was exactly what his straight-C ass deserved.

But then she'd made honor roll all through high school, and look at her now: Barf Girl.

When the Particle GM had told Hannah he could transfer her out of food service at the Outer Inn and into another sector of the Realm if she put off community college and went full time, she'd jumped at the chance. She was willing to do almost anything to quit waiting tables and tamp down the exponentially increasing fear that she was turning into her mother. But after a few months on "elimination duty," she had to admit she really missed working with undigested food. Who knew that a statistically acceptable minority of guests experienced extreme nausea during the gravity-subverting climax of the Quantum Catastrophe ride? While the Physicist distracted the crowd with his dramatic monologue, it fell to Hannah to unobtrusively deliver branded baggies to anyone who looked like they might go Mount St. Helens.

She buzzed through the employee entrance and walked into a wash of air conditioning so thick and cold it felt like diving into a Slurpee: best part of the Park, right here. Normally she paused to savor the sensation, but her Swatch already read 9:14, so she hoofed it through the maze of white-floored hallways.

The custodial staff worked overnight to rearrange the locations of shops and other features in the Realm's concentric rings — to teach guests about Heisenberg or something — but like everything else at the park, that magic was only superficial, and to go to work every day she had to mash the same sticky button on the same glacially slow staff elevator. 9:15.

9:16.

Hannah stared at the lit down-arrow button and tried to focus on slowing time and compressing space again, but her powers seemed to be failing her.

9:17 when she emerged from the elevator onto Quantum Catastrophe's floor of operations, but Jimmy pressed a sweaty bill into her hand before she could even make her case for fast clocks, slow traffic and sucky elevators. That alone gave her pounding heart pause, even before her pudgy manager said, "We've got a real situation on our hands, Hannah. You up for a promotion?"

She didn't even have to think about it — hell no she wasn't up for a promotion. One look at Jimmy's sweat-beaded forehead, his flushed face, his faded OmniPark tie, and she knew she didn't want to end up like him one day.

A raise, though — that she was up for. She swallowed. "Sure, if the price is right."

She steeled herself for a hard-nosed salary negotiation right there next to the ride machinery, but Jimmy just took off for his office, waving her after him.

"Leon called in," he huffed, out of breath as always. "Said the new ride's making him sick."

Leon played the Physicist during most of Hannah's shifts: that nebbish philosopher-scientist who guided guests on an exploration of the deepest mysteries of the universe as they rode the Quantum Catastrophe. When Hannah first started working at the park, they'd had a different Physicist character, one with a big Einstein wig. His spiel had been all about titanic forces locked in struggle within every atom, their constant dance of attraction and repulsion, irresistible centrifugal force arrested by inescapable gravity, held in a perfect balance that gave rise to the world as we know it. Hannah was fascinated by the idea that the whole physical universe was essentially created on a moment-to-moment basis by an infinite number of tiny wars.

When she and Tim Slidell had gone to the park on their date, Hannah had wanted to ride the Quantum Catastrophe, but Tim said no. *Let's go to the Realm of Man instead,* he'd said with a leer. *I heard if you look in the right cave you can see the Neanderthals doin' it.* That was how Hannah knew she and Tim weren't going to work out.

By the time she'd started working the Quantum Catastrophe herself, the attraction had been updated with a new script and a less wacky host. Now the Physicist talked about how discoveries in quantum physics had proven that everything in the universe — all of time, all of space, everything that has ever existed — is interconnected at the deepest level of reality, which he called "the implicate order." Hannah found that fascinating too, if a bit disturbing. She didn't relish the thought of being interconnected with certain people, like Tim Slidell. Being interconnected with her mom — and her mom's boyfriends and cigarettes and credit-card bills — was problematic enough.

Leon did a decent job of selling the new material, but at first they had him doing it on the old Quantum Catastrophe, which featured a lot of whooshing around and racing forward and shuddering, in line with the struggle-at-the-heart-of-existence theme. It couldn't have been easy, trying to make people feel awed by the timeless presence of eternity when all they could think about was keeping down the Atomic Dog they'd eaten for lunch. Finally the Park updated the ride to match the new theme, and Hannah thought it made for a much stronger combination, but Leon had been acting a little different since the launch. No more palling around in between rides, just staring off into space — Hannah felt bad for not asking him if he was okay.

"What did he say was wrong?" she asked.

"He *wouldn't*," Jimmy said, as if he still couldn't believe it. "He *wouldn't* say. He just said he wasn't coming back."

"Like, ever?"

Jimmy didn't answer, marching them into the office and shutting the door.

"So who's Physicist today?" she asked. "Karl or the new guy?"

"New guy quit and Karl's MIA." Jimmy pressed his palms into his eyes. "Look, Hannah. I know you're a smart girl. I know you like all that stuff." He gestured vaguely in the direction of the ride. "You pay attention to it. And you been paying attention to Leon, haven't you?"

Hannah felt horribly called out, as if he'd just asked her about pillow-humping, but she shrugged and said, "Yeah," with as much nonchalance as she could manage. The truth was she'd hung onto every word of the Physicist's monologue for the first fifteen or twenty times she worked the ride. The long beard Leon wore was obviously fake, and his West Texas accent didn't sound very scientific, but Hannah saw through all that to the monologue itself, a clarion call of truth and beauty and wonder, hailing her from a distant place where such things mattered. Her cynical side wanted to be above it all, to see the lecture as just one part of a sucky ride in a sucky theme park, but according to the Physicist those things only held true on the surface level of reality. If we could find a way to access the implicate order — an idea that the new ride illustrated with trippy special effects — we could transcend our limitations and see reality as it actually is.

Hannah still believed that when you got right down to it, everything did suck at the quantum scale; but maybe if you went even deeper, into the implicate order — the "Realm Beyond the Realms" in Park Speak — then you could escape the suckiness that seemed to infect every other level of existence.

"So you ready to make the jump from understudy?" asked Jimmy. "Think you can play host if I gave you the notes?"

Hannah had to stop herself from visibly sneering. By the end of her second week in the Quantum Catastrophe she had the whole thing memorized and could recite it to herself in its entirety, twice, on the way to work. This was the closest she would get to college for who knew how long, and she intended to absorb every drop of it.

"Sure," she said. "But listen, Jimmy. The money —"

"I'll pay you same as Leon and Karl," he said. "Seven bucks an hour."

That was double her current hourly wage. Her mind went blank. All she could do was nod in what she hoped was a convincing facsimile of self-confidence and business savvy, but Jimmy wasn't even looking at her as he crossed to a tall steel cabinet, opened it, and returned with a white lab coat on a hanger and a pair of chunky black frame glasses.

"Congratulations, doc," he said, handing the items to her. "First ride kicks off in ten minutes. And gimme that damn ball cap."

2

Hannah's first few runs were quantum catastrophes in their own right. She tripped over words in every direction and repeatedly lost her place in the narration. But the guests didn't seem to mind; they were too caught up in the wonders unfolding around them. The ride's marvels gave her the confidence to fully step into her role. Pretty soon she was hitting every beat, even riffing a little when she noticed a geeky kid paying her more attention than his parents.

The day blurred past, too busy to allow her to step back and observe herself the way she usually did a million times a minute. Before she knew it, Hannah was out of the Physicist's command chair at the front of the Quantum Catastrophe and back in the Civic, sore throat belting out an offering of Bon Jovi to the hot night wind. She was the damn Physicist! At seven damn dollars an hour!

She was so excited to tell her mom all about it that she bounded into the trailer and was halfway through the happy news before she realized her mom had been crying into her Kools, the ashtray on the kitchenette counter a bog of wet ash. Hannah's voice trailed off — yet her heart secretly soared. She hated to see her mom so miserable, but Tammy only ever got this down over a break-up. Just when Hannah thought this day couldn't get any better, her mom had finally exorcised the Pop-Tart-stealing poltergeist!

Then the toilet flushed in the back of the trailer, taking Hannah's hopes with it.

"What happened, Mom?" Hannah would've taken her mother's shaking hands, but one held a lit cigarette and the other gripped a sweaty jelly jar filled with Popov and Coke.

"They fired me," her mom croaked, and fell into one of her coughing bouts. She was fully made up for work and still had on her green JD's Cowboy Bar-B-Q t-shirt. Her mascara made an unholy mess of black runnels sliding down her cheeks. Tammy's red-veined blue eyes flicked once at Hannah, guiltily, and down again. "Said I was movin' too slow."

"Real tough titty, alright," said Doug, ambling back down the hall. He'd had the decency to put on jean shorts but had lost his t-shirt in the bargain, as if his sallow flesh could only bear so much fabric at once. "I'll call around tomorrow, get you somethin' better. Just gotta tighten our belts till you're back in the saddle."

Hannah said, "Oh eff you, Doug!" She had never raised her voice at one of her mom's boyfriends, not once, but the residual conviction of the Physicist still flowed through her. "You're the one who needs to get back in the saddle — not that you ever been in it, near as I can tell."

"Y'all know my foot's fucked up!" said Doug. "Bad enough I gotta limp 'round like a cripple without you bustin' my balls 'bout it."

"*Please* quit fightin'." Tammy squeezed her eyes shut, tears oozing around the edges as grey smoke plumed from her nose. "*Please*."

"I'm sorry, baby," said Doug, beating Hannah to the apology. "We'll figure it out. We always do."

"Yeah, *we* do," said Hannah, heading back to her room. She should've known some stupid shit like this would happen. Nothing quantum about these mechanics, just plain old Newtonian suckage: for each break you caught in Midkiff, there was an equal but opposite fuck-up. This was why she hadn't fled with her friends when they all graduated. Kat and Evan and Julia lived in Rankin, the county seat, where the high school was located. Rankin was no utopia, but you could escape its gravity well. Not so with Midkiff. Paradoxically, the smaller town exerted the greater pull, and it wouldn't let her leave.

Dressed as the Physicist, Hannah had told the guests that when subatomic particles became enmeshed in "quantum entanglement," they seemed to communicate with each other faster than light, rendering the very concept of locations obsolete. Yet this thought brought Hannah no comfort. When you entangled with the wrong particle, it didn't matter where you were. Your fates became bound together.

3

"All aboard the Copenhagen Express," Hannah told the guests through her headset microphone as the crew finished checking the safety bars on their individual cars. Hers was at the front of the procession but facing backward, so she could address the whole line of excited faces. As the coaster began to shudder forward, she said, "Thank you for assisting me in this little experiment. Be sure to hold on tight as we enter a world of theoretical mysteries. Pay close attention to everything you observe — at the smallest level of existence lies the potential for infinite change!"

If only. One week on Physicist duty and Hannah had discovered that her life hadn't changed much at all. If anything, the daily grind was even more static than Barf Girl duty — at least with that you had to be vigilant and run around to the different cars. Playing the Physicist offered no such potential for deviation from the routine. Same script, different day.

First she walked the yokels through particles as the building blocks of the universe, their individual cars linked up in a line and trundling along through the holographic stars. Then they entered the wild world of theoretical physics, the magnets that connected each car to the next releasing so they all went slaloming around a padded ring like bumper cars. However, thanks to some ingenuity on the part of the engineers, every car was secretly paired up with another so that whichever direction one of them bounced, so did its twin, while Hannah explained quantum entanglement. Once that segment wrapped up, the floor began to rise and fall beneath the startled guests.

"What are you made of, oh quantum children of the universe?" said Hannah. "Wave or particle, particle or wave — the endless debate of theoretical physics. But what if there are both? What if you particles are actually riding a pilot wave? What if you are surfing the cosmos at the subatomic level?"

At this point jets of water misted the delighted riders, which made no goddamn sense at all — but OmniPark was in West Texas, so every attraction needed to cool folks off at some point. The waves began to subside and the dark of the circular room gave way to a dim blue glow, mirrored walls glittering as a disco ball descended from the ceiling. Just as the final waves evened out and the cars went completely still, the walls began to spin like an autoclave.

As the whirring hum of the motors began to rise, Hannah glanced over to the hidden door in the back and saw Kenneth, who'd been "promoted" to be her Barf Boy, had slipped in with his payload of yacksacks. This was the part that made some people puke, even though their cars had stopped moving. Hannah straightened up in her seat, but her introduction to the implicate order — *Welcome to a place where past, present, and future sit side by side, just like all of you here before me* — died in her raw throat.

Standing hunched over in the center of the floor, amid the motionless particles of the Implicate Arena, was an old woman in a pale green hospital gown. Spangles of light danced along her sticklike legs, spotted arms, wispy white hair, caved-in cheeks. She looked around her fearfully. A nasal cannula perched beneath her nostrils, with tubes running across her cheeks and behind her ears, joined in a clip at her neck.

Hannah glanced at the guests. They all stared expectantly at her; no one seemed to notice the old woman. How the hell had she gotten in here? Hannah glanced at Kenneth, but he was scanning the ride cars, searching for the telltale signs of an impending incident that would require his services. She snapped her fingers at him to attract his attention. He looked at her, and she pointed to the old woman with a dire expression on her face: *Get her out of here.*

Kenneth blinked at where Hannah was pointing, looked back at her, and mouthed *What?* Hannah frowned, snapped, and pointed again, and this time some of the guests turned toward where she pointed. They also stared blankly in the old woman's general vicinity before fixing their attention back on Hannah.

Kenneth sighed, stamped over to the center of the floor and walked right into the old woman, but somehow he didn't bump into her; his body seemed to pass through hers as if she was a hologram. Her mouth gawped and she scuttled sideways to avoid him.

He stood there with his hands raised in a helpless gesture and rotated in a circle, searching for whatever Hannah was pointing at. One of his hands passed through the old woman's abdomen as he turned. She gave another silent cry and swiped at his arm without hitting him. He stopped, looked at Hannah, shrugged, and shook his head. Next to Kenneth, the old woman rapidly strobed in and out of sight as if the lights were flickering just where she was standing. Then she was gone.

Hannah rubbed her eyes. Spending so much time surrounded by spinning mirrors and bizarre visuals was starting to mess with her vision. The old woman must be a random guest reflected out of her ride car and into the middle of the room, with the hospital gown and nasal tubes grafted on by Hannah's subconscious. But after she pulled her shit together enough to give her climactic speech and the guests all filed out of their cars at the ride's end, the old woman wasn't among them. Spooky, but Hannah didn't let herself dwell on it; she just focused on trying to get through the rest of her shift.

Three rides later, the same old woman reappeared at the same point in the attraction, hunched over and terrified, surrounded by oblivious guests in their scattered cars. The woman stared directly at Hannah, jutting out a claw-like finger, shriveled lips moving as if casting an incantation. *Goddamn* spooky. Was this some new feature the engineers were trying out? Everyone suspected that the bastards used the staff and guests as guinea pigs, but if this creepy old woman was a fresh addition to the ride, why didn't anyone else see her?

Hannah scanned the room in the futile hope that Jimmy, or someone else who'd know what to do, would appear. The guests and Kenneth stared at Hannah — she was beginning to worry them. The mirrored walls flashed around and around, containing them all in this moment. A pair of projectors descended from the ceiling on either side of the disco ball, and they threw blurry, phantasmagoric images onto the spinning walls: an Egyptian pyramid sprouted from a desert, transformed into a medieval castle, and then turned into a skyscraper; a woman in a skirted business suit walked out of the skyscraper's main entrance before turning into a perky teenager in a cheerleading outfit, a little girl in water wings splashing around in a pool, a baby emerging slick and wailing into the world.

The display on the walls distracted the guests, but not the old woman. She shuffled straight toward Hannah with menacing purpose. Locked into her ride car and unable to escape, Hannah felt herself begin to freak the hell out. What should she do? She had a ride full of guests expecting her to be in charge of the situation. To them, she was the Physicist — what would a real physicist do right now? A real physicist would probably be curious about the sudden manifestation of apparently inexplicable phenomena. A real physicist would investigate and try to learn more.

But she wasn't a real physicist, and the old woman couldn't be real, either. Whether she was an illusion generated by the ride or a product of Hannah's overactive imagination, she was no more real than the creatures Hannah used to see in her bedroom as a kid, when the pile of clothes on her bedroom floor would take on monstrous features in the moonlight oozing through her window. As the emaciated woman staggered up to Hannah's car, reaching out for her, Hannah did what her mom had advised her to do about the bedroom monsters all those years ago: she closed her eyes tight.

In the blackness behind her lids the words of the Physicist's speech arose, and she delivered the full monologue without a single peek, a prayer to reason, asking it to banish the impossible. When she finally opened them again at the end of the ride, the spinning walls had stilled and the phantom was gone.

Okay. Hannah didn't understand what was happening, but she understood how to deal with it. Same rules as Doug and all the other unwelcome spirits her mom had invited into their lives: pretend they aren't there until reality catches up with you.

She gave the rest of the day's Implicate Arena monologues blind, clamping her eyes shut as soon as she entered the mirrored room and not opening them again until the ride shuddered to its final stop. Would she have to close her eyes for the final speech every time from now on? The guests didn't seem to notice, but what if Jimmy walked in and thought she was tripping or something?

The next day at work, she tried keeping her eyes open in the Implicate Arena on the first ride, and thankfully nothing strange happened. Hannah kept her eyes open during each final monologue until halfway through her shift, when the old woman jumped back in out of nowhere, this time almost right on top of Hannah's car.

Up close, the woman looked exactly like Hannah's Meemaw during her final months, but taller and skinnier. She glared at Hannah with glassy blue eyes set deeply into prominent orbital ridges, the tube on her upper lip flashing in the dim, wavering light as her lips mutely moved and her hand reached out. Hannah glanced over the woman's shoulder at the mirrored walls to confirm what she already knew: this apparition wasn't real.

Sure enough, the old woman wasn't there — but neither was the rest of the Implicate Arena. Instead of guests sitting in ride cars, Hannah saw rows of young people seated at desks, scribbling notes. She didn't see herself presiding over the room as Physicist, either; instead she saw herself seated in the back row, scribbling along with the rest of them.

The overhead projectors dropped down and kicked on, and instead of pyramids rising from the sands the walls showed a time lapse of Hannah transforming from a nervous freshman scrunched down at the back of the lecture hall to a confident senior sitting up straight down front. Then she became the professor standing tall before a new crop of students, hieroglyphic equations dancing across the chalk board behind her.

"Hannah," Kenneth hissed, drawing her back from the daydream that had somehow manifested on the walls. When she blinked the assembled guests back into focus, they disappeared, too — replaced with the old woman. She occupied every car, dozens of her, every one of them clawing at the safety bars that kept them in place. They fought to free themselves, mouths mutely screaming in fear or rage, every pair of milky blue eyes fixed on Hannah, and then one wriggled her skeletal frame free of the car, climbed over the side, crawled across the floor toward —

"*Hannah!*" Jimmy snapped his fingers in her face. The old women vanished — and the guests, too. The empty cars were back in the corral. Jimmy was looming over Hannah, with Kenneth nervously hanging back. "What the hell's going on? You high or something?"

"No way," said Hannah, closing her eyes and willing this nightmare to end. When she reopened them, Jimmy was still grimacing at her. She said, "What happened?"

"Kenny says you zoned out in front of all the guests! Didn't even give the speech!"

"Shit," she said.

"Shit is right. Let's get you out of here. Take the rest of the day off."

"I'm good, I'm good." Hannah felt more alarmed about losing the hours than about the creepy hallucination. "I got a little sick, but I'm better now. I just need to keep my eyes closed during that last part of the ride."

And she was better, so long as she kept her eyes closed when the cars arrived at the Implicate Arena. With each ride, the temptation to peek grew stronger, but she held firm. She couldn't afford to get sick again.

4

When Leon answered the phone, Hannah could tell he was already drunk at eleven-thirty in the morning. She wished she didn't have a well-practiced ear for this shit.

"Hey, Leon, this is Hannah." When Leon didn't say anything, she said, "Hannah Schmidt? From the park? I was your Barf Girl on the Quantum Catastrophe. I got your number from Jimmy."

"Well, you can tell him I haven't changed my mind. I'm not coming back."

"Why not?" She thought she knew, but she needed to hear him say it so she'd know she wasn't cracking up. "Is it because the new ride made you sick?"

"Not sick," he said. "*Sickened*. By that *Christmas Carol* shit. Told 'em Dr. Bohm's Wild Ride belonged in the Realm of the Mind, not the Particle."

What the hell did that mean? Either Leon was really loaded, or he had actually lost his marbles. Hannah's heart pounded, imagining herself ending up like him. That would be almost as bad as winding up like her mom.

"Leon, I'm sorry, I don't understand — "

"Showing you what you would've-could've-should've been," he said over her, "if you didn't settle for eight bucks an hour at OmniPark."

Eight an hour? Jimmy had told her he paid Leon seven! Hannah reminded herself there were more important things at stake here than money — but she would take this up with Jimmy later.

"So you saw things," she said. "I did too. They got me doing it now, playing the Physicist, and I saw... well, it doesn't matter what I saw, because it's not real."

"*Real*." He snorted. "Real as anything else."

"But what does that even mean?"

"You're the Physicist now, you know the script." Leon burped. "Us talking on the phone, you going to work at the park, me taking a piss soon as I hang up — all that shit we think is reality? That's all just the explicate order, unfolding out of a deeper reality underneath it all, even deeper than the quantum level: the implicate, where every goddamn thing that exists — from Odessa, Texas, to the ends of the universe — is connected."

He sounded a little more sober, even if what he was saying wasn't.

"And it's not just everything that exists *now*," he continued. "It's everything that has ever existed or *could* ever exist. So if you ever saw what was in the Realm Beyond the Realms, maybe you'd observe yourself as you *could* be — all the possible yous. I think that's what happened. Fucked me right up. Enlightenment's a bummer."

"But how could the ride make that happen? It doesn't seem to affect the guests or the barf crew."

"They're only in the ride for a few minutes at a time. We're sitting in the driver's seat all goddamn day, repeating the magic words, guiding the way. Terms of the mechanics, I think the engineers put some kind of quantum-level turbocharger under the hood of that ride. You hear things, you know, 'bout all the weird shit they're always pulling in the park, finding ways to make guests think they really jumped through hyperspace or traveled through time."

Hannah didn't know what to say. It all made sense, except for the part where it was impossible.

"Anyway, I gotta go manifest my implicate potential." A can cracked open on the other end of the line. "Give my regards to the ghosts of better tomorrows, but don't look too close — when we gaze at the implicate, it gazes right back."

5

The first time she went back to work after talking to Leon, Hannah found that keeping her eyes closed in the Implicate Arena took even more effort than before, but she had never shied away from hard work. Seeing some phantasmal future — even if it had emerged from the Realm Beyond the Realms — didn't mean shit in the real world. You still had to make it come true. That meant saving every penny she could for community college. She couldn't let herself space out in front of guests anymore, or else she'd lose her job. If that ever happened, Hannah didn't think she'd like the possible future that would come to pass for her.

In between rides she imagined the sequence that might be playing out on the walls of the Implicate Arena when her eyes were closed: tear-streaked conversations with her mom, one last reproachful glance from Doug, a slamming door, a cloud of dust, a sucky roommate in a sucky apartment, debt, poverty, hard work... and then success: good grades, instructors who liked her, classmates who wanted to study with her, advisors who encouraged her, a degree, a scholarship to a bigger school, more studying, more friends, much more hard work, another degree, and then another; travel, conferences, colleagues, students, discoveries, publications, honors, accolades; a career. A life. Her life. It was as if she remembered it all — as if it had already happened to her.

Could she really do it, though? Just abandon Tammy? Maybe her mother was the sinister old woman in the hospital gown, withering away without Hannah to support her. Could Hannah condemn her mom to that fate?

But maybe Tammy could manifest a different reality, too. Maybe without Hannah as a crutch to rely on, another side of her would come to the fore, and she would flourish, and a brighter future would come true.

In her darker moments, Hannah thought maybe the shriveled woman in the hospital gown wasn't her mom at all. Maybe it was Hannah herself, withering away to a dessicated husk at the end of an empty life. She had to avoid that fate at all costs. That was why she kept her eyes closed every single time the ride entered the Implicate Arena. When she got home, she'd tell her mom she was going to apply for community college. Cutting her hours at the park would hobble the family budget worse than Doug's weird foot, but she had to embrace the short-term suck for the long-term radness. Her mom had somehow managed before Hannah started working in high school; she'd do okay without Hannah bringing in all the Wonderbread.

Clambering out of the Civic and walking to the trailer through the muggy night, Hannah felt lighter than she ever had in her life.

Stepping inside the front door felt like having the gravity kick back on at the end of the old Quantum Catastrophe. Tammy sat slumped over in the kitchenette. Without mascara trails to give away her grief, it took Hannah a moment to realize her mom must've been crying for hours.

"Doug's gone. For good this time." A plume of smoke waltzed around the trailer with his ghost. Tammy crushed Hannah's sweaty hand in her bony fingers as she said, "God damn, but I don't know what I'd do without you."

6

"And you're sure?" Jimmy actually seemed concerned, but only the implicate knew if he was worried about Hannah or his own prospects, given how sideways the Realm of the Particle had gone that summer.

"Positive," said Hannah, extending her hand. She felt very adult. The feeling sucked a lot more than she'd expected it to.

"Alright," he said as they shook. "But if you change your mind and wanna step back, I'll understand. No hard feelings."

"Thanks, Jimmy," she said, and put on the Physicist's glasses. She hadn't expected him to listen to her, let alone the higher-ups at OmniPark, but the letter she'd sent advising them to dismantle the Implicate Arena and restore the original Quantum Catastrophe ride had actually worked. Apparently she and Leon weren't the only ones getting sick from it. Jimmy was having a tough time keeping Physicists; Hannah was the only host who had lasted more than a month.

Nevertheless, it would take another month to reengineer the ride, and OmniPark couldn't afford to lose one of its attractions during peak season. After Labor Day they'd put the original Quantum Catastrophe back in, and in the meantime Hannah and the new hosts she was training would just have to shut their eyes during the attraction's grand finale. Jimmy had offered to transfer her back to Barf Girl until they reinstalled the old ride, if it was too much for her — but at her freshly negotiated salary of $8.50 an hour, Hannah felt she could handle anything.

She just had to keep her eyes closed.

Dalton Teague's favorite coffee mug, the very first souvenir created for OmniPark in 1977.

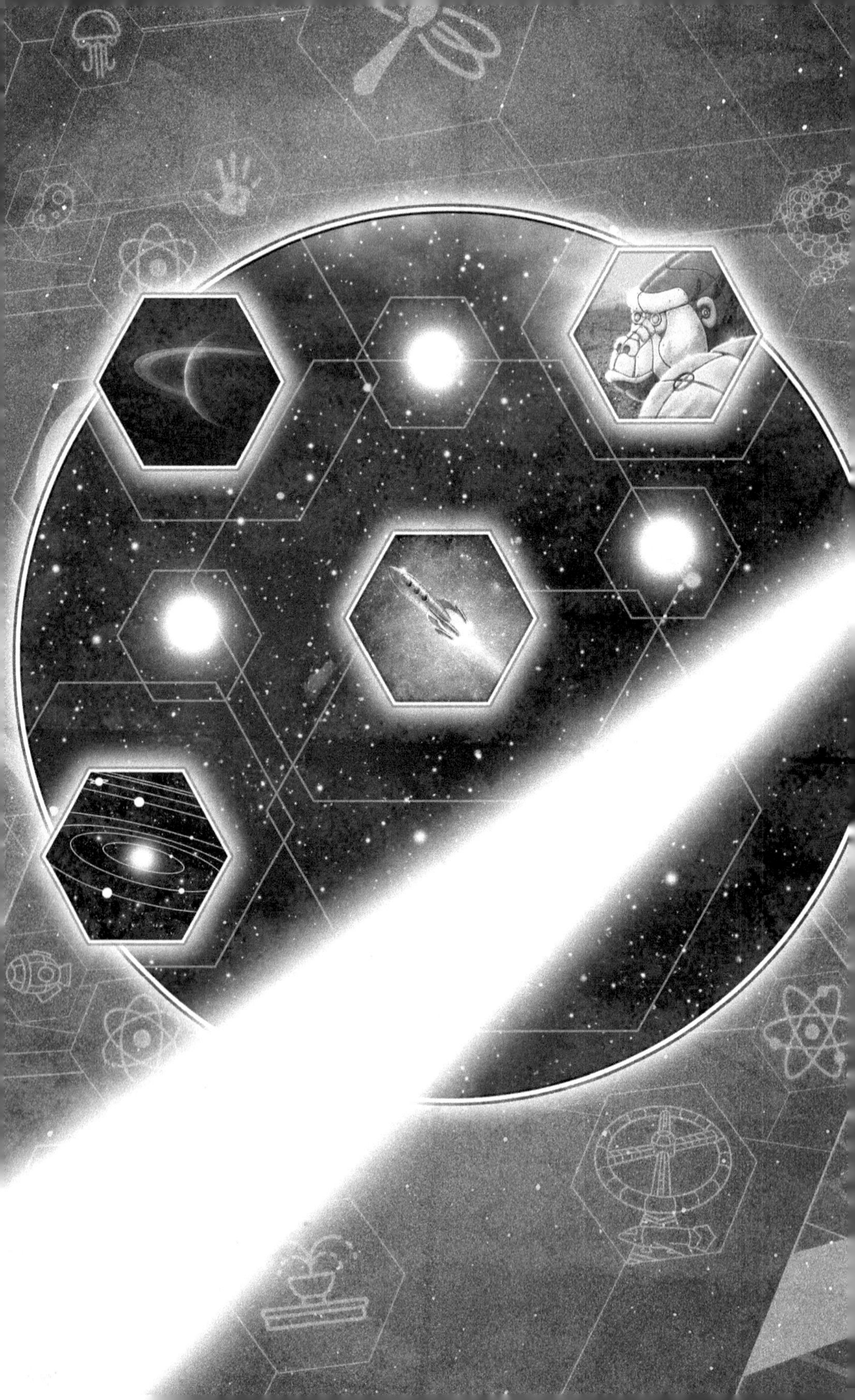

The Robot Apeman Waits for the Nightmare Blood to Stop

Orrin Grey

So, I just talk into this thing? I guess we're making this documentary for fans of the park, right, so I don't have to get too much into what OmniPark was all about — who Dalton Teague was, any of that? What's that? Oh, right, introduce myself. That makes sense…

1

My name is Paul Kirby — no relation to the great Jack — and I was, am, a concept artist. I've worked on a few big movies and a lot of small ones, especially back during the '80s, when I did concepts for stuff like *Seeds of Change* and *Out of Space*. Lately, I've mostly done work for cartoon shows on Netflix. That's all under NDA, so I can't talk about it here… not that it has anything to do with this story.

Anyway, one of my very first gigs was working at OmniPark. Cary Egger, one of the original Technosophers that Teague hired to design the park, hired me to do artwork for his ride concept. Its working title was just "Primal."

That's… will the viewer know what a Technosopher is already? Should I get into that?

2

"Technosopher" was a word that, as far as I know, Dalton Teague made up. To him, it was part engineer, part philosopher and part… I don't even know; wizard, I guess. Technosophers designed the Realms and attractions at OmniPark, but they were a lot more than just hired talent. A few of them — the ones in Teague's private inner circle, I mean — they were… what's the word… practically *revered*. When they spoke, all of us listened.

Teague always told us we were building something truly special at OmniPark. "*Significant*" — that was the word he used. And something about the way he said it made me think he meant more than just the rides. Maybe a lot more. Truth is, I never found out what half the people at that park were working on. There was this whole "eyes-only, need-to-know-basis" thing between different departments. Plus, some of the Technosophers were pretty far out there. Not the easiest folks to make friends with.

That's not to say OmniPark wasn't a friendly place to work. It was nice enough, most of the time — plus the pay was a hell of a lot better than I got doing commissions. That paycheck came with a lot of pressure, though; especially for a design-school dropout like me. This would've been, what, '74, '75? I was still a damn sight wet behind the ears, to say the least. I couldn't have been older than twenty-two. A baby in a button-down shirt.

And I was working for Cary fucking Egger — can I say "fucking" on here? You can edit it out later, right? Yeah, okay.

So, Egger was the Technosopher in charge of my project. He'd been a rocket engineer before he came to work for Teague. A literal rocket scientist — yep, that's what I said, too. Claimed to have worked on the Apollo program, though I never saw any proof one way or the other. But sometimes when he was a few beers deep and high as a kite — which was not all that rarely, let me tell you — he'd make these… *claims*, I guess you'd call 'em, about how "we didn't know the half of it." Whatever that was supposed to mean.

Working for an honest-to-God rocket scientist would've been intimidating enough, but that wasn't the weirdest part. Egger was a Thelemite. He'd known Jack Parsons before he got himself killed in an explosion — "assassinated," Egger said, "by the corporate jaybirds." I don't know what he meant by "jaybirds." He was always using these weird made-up-sounding words.

What? Oh, Thelema... I don't know much about it, to tell you the truth. It's some kind of, like, cult religion that Aleister Crowley came up with. A bunch of people were into it way back when, apparently, but that was before my time. And then it came back as a big counterculture thing in the '50s, I think. Spells, pentagrams, robes and candles. All that witchy shit.

Oh, by the way, Egger wasn't the only rocket scientist on our team. Parsons had some big aerospace cred, too. Word had it he'd done some work with the Department of Defense back in the '60s, during the Bay of Pigs and all that. And he and his wife were even bigger into Thelema than Egger was. In fact, Egger was one of their protégés.

Anyway, Egger had a kid around my age. Long, stringy hair and the palest skin I'd ever seen; almost translucent. Egger called her Theophrastus — the rest of us called her Theo.

Her, yeah. Egger always said she was a hermaphrodite, and that she was one of Cameron's "moon children."

Shit, I'm way off on a tangent now, huh? So... Cameron was Parsons's wife. Marjorie Cameron Parsons, something like that. Later on, she was in some Curtis Harrington films. *Night Tide*, maybe a few others. She was an occultist and an artist and who knows what else. Parsons called her "the elemental woman" and Egger told me he'd summoned her with a ritual he'd done with L. Ron Hubbard — I shit you not.

Anyway, after Parsons died or got assassinated or *whatever* you think happened, Cameron — that's the name she went by — moved out to some ranch in SoCal and started this... group. Sex magic stuff. They were trying to create a new race of "moon children" to serve the god Horus. It always blew my mind how they talked about this shit — like it was all totally normal and made perfect sense. Anyway, I guess Theo was one of the kids that came out of all that.

Where was I? Oh, right, working for Egger. So, Teague hired Egger, who brought along Theo, and Egger hired me and a whole team of other people to work on "Primal," which almost certainly would've gotten renamed if it had ever gone public; which, I suppose this is the part where I say it didn't, though you already know that if you know the park, because it's not in any of the literature, and it certainly wasn't ever on the park map.

We were working in parallel with the folks who designed the "Time Machine" ride — the original one, the *good* one, before they put in that stupid "Pterry Time Tunnel" thing. Our team was tackling the notion of time in ride form, like they were — but from a totally different angle. Egger, from what I heard, got brought on as much because of his Thelemic background as his engineering skills.

"I want every avenue explored," Teague was saying to one of his assistants the one time I actually met him. He'd come down to the shop that morning to inspect some of our character mockups. He had some bean counter at his side — a sour-faced guy in a gray suit who clearly wasn't happy to be there. At first I thought I'd done something to offend the guy, but afterward Egger told me he was Teague's lead accountant — Hapwell, Hapworth, something like that. He was freaking out about how much money the park was wasting on two similar attractions at once, and Teague was pissing him off by ignoring him.

"It's my money," I remember Teague saying that morning. "It will be spent as I see fit." Then he said that stuff about how he wanted every avenue to be explored. He inspected our mockups, asked some really good questions we hadn't even thought to ask, then shook our hands and left. I remember looking into his eyes, thinking, *Holy shit, this is THE Dalton fucking Teague shaking my hand right now*. I was surprised how much he wanted to know about the tiniest details of everyone's work; how he stopped to thank each of us and shake our hands; even the grunts hunched over the drafting tables like yours truly. Yeah. *This guy cares about our work even more than we do* — that was my impression from the grand total of three seconds I interacted with him.

Egger was intense, too; but in a different way. He was a force of nature, that guy. Egger didn't enter a room — he *blew* into it, *sailed* into it. And he never gave anything a pass without completely rearranging it. If you were three-quarters of the way through a sketch, he'd give it one look and send you straight back to square one. But nobody really minded because everything Egger touched, he made better. It was frustrating and inspiring, all at the same time. And when you're that young and that hungry, inspiration is more important than respect.

Back then, I probably would have followed Egger off a cliff. The only thing I didn't like about him was how he treated Theo.

Describe him? I mean, I guess you've seen photos, but they don't do him justice. He had this unbelievably curly, flyaway ginger beard that always reminded me of pubic hair, if I'm being honest. He wore silk bathrobes over his jeans and t-shirts. Almost like he was trying to dress eccentric on purpose, you know? I never knew how much of it was a put-on and how much was really him.

A genius? Wow, that's one hell of a word. I mean, yeah, I think he was. What does "genius" really mean? Somebody who sees the world differently from everyone else, right? Egger did; no doubt about it. He was on a whole other level. I was lucky enough to ride that "Time Machine" before opening day; got to see the "big bang, big crunch" thing at the climax.

I mean, who even comes up with something like that? Egger, that's who. Nobody normal could've thought up those rides. "Genius" was practically a Technosopher job qualification.

But just because somebody's a genius doesn't mean they're stable. Usually the opposite, right? Like, Einstein was a genius, but they say he couldn't tie his own shoes. I never looked that up to see if it's true, but it sure as hell jives with Egger.

So yeah, Egger was a genius; he was also crazy as shit. Most of the inner-circle Technosophers were. I mean, look at it this way: if the rides OmniPark actually built are the most "normal" concepts they came up with, can you even *imagine* what kind of stuff must be locked in the Teague family vault?

Toward the end, I think Egger's craziness started to get the upper hand on him. Maybe that's why "Primal" never opened to the public. And maybe that's a good thing.

3

Oh, don't get me wrong. We *built* "Primal." Shit, my friend Ronnie, who worked on it — died in the Boston Marathon bombing a few years ago, he was in the crowd, poor guy — he hand-painted the sign above the entrance. Big, red claw-slash letters: "Children under 12 should not ride." Hell, I don't think a lot of full-grown *adults* could've handled what we built. It sure as hell wasn't for kids.

I keep calling it a "ride," but Egger never did, because it wasn't a ride in the proper sense at all. You *walked* through it, like a series of museum exhibitions. Which is honestly what it was: a wax museum without the wax, done in latex, silicone and automated motors. Disney would've called it "animatronics," but Egger called it "thaumatropy." You know what a thaumatrope is? It's this little toy from like a hundred years ago. A disk on a string with a picture on either side. Spin the disk, and the two pictures seem to merge. It's the same principle as the movies, just on a much smaller scale. In Egger's mind, that's what we were building — but life-sized, in three dimensions.

"People should be able to spend as much time with each tableau as they need to," Egger used to say. That was the word he used. "Need."

This was back in the planning stages. Attraction concepts were still getting shuffled, stacked and restacked in different Realms, so we weren't sure whether "Primal" was going to go in the Realm of Man — "humanity" would probably have been better, yeah; but this was the '70s — or the Realm of Time.

Oh yeah, the Realm of Life was about evolution, too — but "Primal" was about *human* evolution; specifically the evolution of our emotions, which, according to Egger, were the only parts of us that were real.

"There is the Will," he said. He and Teague both had this way of pronouncing certain words so you knew they were capitalized. "And there is the Spirit — Emotion. Everything else is just chemistry and geology, ghosts and shadows."

According to him, emotions were what set humans apart; not just from animals, but from everything else in the universe, too. It was only through the development of emotions — "a cosmic accident," he called it — that we developed Will. "Animals do not have Will," he said. "They do what they must because they must. They do not choose. Only *we* choose."

So, the idea was to take each guest through the development of every human emotion in order, at least as Egger perceived them. We started in the dark, with Fear. "The oldest and strongest emotion of mankind is fear," was inscribed in red letters above the arched door to the black chamber — a quote from H.P. Lovecraft, who, you have to remember, was not that widely read back then.

That first room. It was my favorite. I always liked designing monsters, and we designed some doozies for that place. So, you came in through the main entrance and passed down this short hallway. Then you walked under those crimson words through a doorway covered with thick black curtains. The room on the other side was pitch dark; deep-in-a-cave dark. It had to be.

Then there was a spark. Most of the rooms were shaped the same way; a circle, with a wide causeway running down the center, blocked off from the rest of the room by heavy bars. The causeway was metal, with a metal grid beneath your feet, so you could see down and to either side. That meant you were surrounded by the visions we'd created.

In that first room, though, there was no way you could know that yet. The spark appeared off to your left, and it grew, slowly, into a fire, which was really just a rotating bulb inside an amber-colored lamp designed to look like it was flickering.

Crouched around the fire were three hominids. One of the things Teague made very clear to us from the start was that we were *not* to design classic movie cavemen. No John Richardson in *One Million Years B.C.* These should be accurate — as much as was possible — depictions of early hominids, our ancestors stuck somewhere between primate and modern humanity.

So these hairy, unclothed things that, nonetheless, had the unmistakable marks of proto-humanity about their faces — at least, if we did our jobs right — were crouched there in the dark, huddled close to that one source of light, just as we expected the guests to do, gathering up against the railing on that side, peering at the tiny fragment of illumination we had provided, so that they weren't expecting it when the monsters came from the other side.

I remember that our first pitches for the monsters were far too tame for Egger. We mocked up your typical cast of Pleistocene predators: saber-toothed cats, huge shaggy bears, even a mammoth. "No," Egger said, when we brought him the sketches. "No, no, no. I don't want a goddamned field guide. I want you to show me *Fear*."

We went back to the drawing board, and brought him sketches of hydras, horned demons, giant octopods. He just shook his head and scoffed. "None of this frightens me," he told us. "Show me Fear."

The things that finally came out of that darkness on the right-hand side of the path would never have passed muster from the bean counters. I know that big mantis shrimp thing in the "Time Machine" was everyone's favorite, even while it also caused kids to climb off the ride crying. But these things we designed would've sent that monster scurrying back into its burrow.

They walked on impossible stick legs, like a Dali painting of an elephant. Their ribboned skin clung to unlikely bones and rags that hung from them; ghost-like, yet all too solid. Their faces were like horse skulls, their eyes pinpricks of light. The limbs that they raised were praying-mantis sickles of hardened bone, lined with tiny mouths and fingers.

They rushed out of the night in a heaving mass, howling like wind through a glacier, swarming over and under and around the walkway toward the fire. For a moment they hovered over the hominids, who raised wide eyes toward the dark.

Then the light went out.

4

So it went, throughout the development of the spectrum of human feeling. Egger had identified what he believed were the eight essential human emotions. Disgust, Exhilaration, Angst, Affection, and so on. I had helped design the monsters for the Fear display, but my baby was one called "Wrath & Regret."

It was *very* simple, compared to the Fear diorama, but I put a lot of work into it. The tableaux was nothing but two hominids, comparatively more advanced than the ones who'd been gathered around the campfire. They were having some kind of a fight: one of them shoved the other then snatched up a rock and bashed his head in.

Anyway, as the rock crushed the hominid's skull, the lights turned to red. We'd coated the backdrop with a special paint so that, when the red light shined on it, the image of the distant valley disappeared, replaced by an expressionist crash of red and black, like a comic book panel.

The injured hominid crumpled to the ground, and his companion stood above him, the rock still gripped in his hand. Then the attacker dropped to his haunches, looking more closely at the wound that he'd inflicted, and — here's the part we were really proud of — the expression on his face shifted as the blood began to pour out onto the ground. Anger to regret, all with one animatronic apeman.

"Nightmare blood," Egger called it. "It has to be the worst thing he has ever seen. Because, for the first time, he knows what it means, and he knows that *he* has caused it. That it will never stop."

The blood pooled on a patch of what looked like just more sand, but was actually a porous synthetic rubber that OmniPark owned the patent on. Kudos to whatever genius cooked that stuff up. It was lightweight, totally stain-resistant, and let the blood slowly sieve through and back into the pump system under the floor, so it would be ready to pour out again when the next group arrived and the scene repeated.

5

Do you need me to say what's happening now? Okay, we are back from lunch and I guess we're going to talk a little bit about me and Theo.

Back then we didn't talk a lot about preferred pronouns and that kind of thing, but you couldn't help but notice the way Egger talked about Theo. He never used pronouns to describe her. Not ever. It was always Theophrastus.

"He says I don't have a sex," Theo told me once, at a time where the double entendre possibilities of that phrase made us both giggle a little. "He says I'm made up of 'equal parts masculine and feminine energy.' But I don't want to be. I just want to be a girl. I want to wear skirts and put on makeup and fall in love with a boy." Here, she lay her hand against my cheek.

"How do you feel when we're together?" I asked her — maybe during that same conversation; maybe another time — and she said that I made her feel, "Like it doesn't matter. Like I can be whatever I want to be, whoever I *am*, and you won't make me change."

I won't say we were in love, but we were in *something*. Both of us were too young to know what the hell we were doing. But we sure found every opportunity to keep doing it.

When Egger was awake and working, he kept Theo at his side every moment. At first I thought she was his assistant, but he hardly ever told her to *do* anything. Mostly she just stood around, watching him work. She wore this weird outfit, sort of like a poncho. I could see her blood pumping through the translucent skin of her neck.

Her long black hair stood out against her skin, and her eyes were so pale they almost didn't have any color at all. It was only when I got closer that I realized they were blue. I lost track of all the time I spent staring into those pale blue eyes, wishing it would never have to end. Course, I had no idea what I was really wishing for. Not then.

Once we'd all been working together for a few weeks, I started catching on to the fact that Theo's constant presence seemed to serve no practical purpose. When I asked Egger about it once, he said it didn't have to make sense to anyone but him. "Her presence helps me to stay in touch," he told me.

"He doesn't treat me like a person," was Theo's response when I bounced that line off her later. "He treats me like… not a *thing*, exactly, but more like a medium. If a person is nothing but Emotion and Will, like he says, then they're like a movie, being shown out of a projector. He treats me like the movie *screen*."

"Then why don't you leave?" I asked her once.

"And go where? Do what? My parents didn't want me. They said that I 'wasn't what they expected.' Now my mom has abandoned the whole Thelema thing. She's a lawyer in Boston; I don't think she'd appreciate a reminder of her past. My dad was in Costa Rica, last I heard. They literally *gave* me to Cary. They signed papers. He's my legal guardian."

"But you're an adult now," I told her. "You can do anything you want."

"Can *you*?" she asked.

Those words are the reason I remember that conversation crystal-clear after all these years. It replays in my head almost every day, even when I don't want it to. *Especially* when I don't want it to. I've had lots of other relationships since Theo. Two ex-wives. I've even got a daughter. She's fourteen. I see her every summer. But that conversation with Theo is the one I always come back to. I didn't understand what she meant back then; not really. But I find it makes more and more sense with every passing year. Can I — can *any* of us — really do what we want?

"Of course I can." I laughed with all the confidence of an artist in his early twenties.

"Really?" she covered a smirk. "You can do *anything* you want?"

"Sure," I said, and kissed her. "And I want to be here."

"Then so do I," she told me. And I believed her.

6

Here's the thing. Back then, I was a kid in love, or lust, or just in the midst of a crush, or something. I was working my first real job as a concept artist. The world was opening up around me like a flower in spring — yeah, it *did* feel that poetic — and yet, at the same time, it was still so claustrophobically small in ways that I didn't even understand. I'd never experienced anything bigger than OmniPark. How could I have guessed what an island our little universe really was?

In that moment with Theo, though, I really believed I was telling her the truth — and that I understood what she was asking. I remember thinking she was… sheltered, I guess. Naïve. She'd never had a normal life, like I had. Never gone to a regular school. Her parents were part of this weird sex magic commune, and she'd been raised by Egger, a brilliant eccentric. I figured she just didn't understand any other life.

But today, I think she understood a lot more than I did, back then. Because the real answer was that of course I *couldn't* do anything I wanted to. No one can. I was a prisoner of everything that had come before that moment. Every prior moment slapping inexorable bonds of cause and effect on the moment that would come next.

Did I *want* to be working on a doomed theme-park attraction? I certainly thought so then, but only because it was better than freelancing. I didn't get to design my own stuff, because all my time and energy went to OmniPark. But of course, she was talking about far more than just that. In spite of what Egger might have thought, I couldn't make things happen by Will alone. Couldn't change my body or who I was. I was stuck being a person. Stuck being Paul Kirby.

I was trapped by circumstance, and by time, like Theo. I was just too arrogant to realize it yet.

"I'm sorry your parents didn't want you," I told her, or something to that effect.

"It already happened," she replied. "It's always happening." At the time, I thought she meant that people rejected her a lot. That made me feel bad for her — but not nearly as bad as I feel now. Now, I think I know better.

"I want you," I told her, trying to make her feel better, showing my ignorance. "I'll always want you."

"You do," she said, giving me a kiss. "And so you always will."

7

Let's talk a little more about the word Egger used to describe what we were building. "Thaumatrope." A disk, like I said, with two pictures, one on each side. Imagine a picture of flowers and a picture of a vase. Spin the disc, and the flowers are inside the vase. Leave it static, though, and you can see the flowers *or* the vase.

So which is real? You can't see both at once except when the disk is spinning. The flowers are always separate from the vase. The vase is always empty. But, at the same time, the flowers are always in the vase.

8

The ride was doomed before it even opened, if I haven't already made that clear. I don't think I realized it at the time. It was just work, and I did it every day, and I didn't think much beyond the next milestone, and the next, and the next after that. But there was no way Teague was ever going to sign off on what we were building. Not as an attraction in a family theme park. It was just another of his experiments — one of many running in parallel the whole time I was there, without me having the first clue about most of them. "Need-to-know," right?

It's easy to say "Primal" didn't make it to opening day because it was "too scary" or "too violent." But I mean, come on. Shattuck's "Wild World of Life" stayed open for a full season, and that bat-shit ride was bloodier than a Manson murder. Nah, the truth is that Egger's idea was too *abstract*. That was the problem. He wanted to build a walk-through of his own understanding of humanity's emotional evolution. That turned out to be *way* too fuzzy a concept to sell, even to Dalton Teague.

When you're doing concept work, your idea's got to be *crisp*. You need an elevator pitch. Your characters should be recognizable by their silhouettes. Theme and conflict have to be clear at a glance. Not because people are stupid or lazy, but because there is a *lot* of information out there. Get too esoteric, and people won't come meet you where you're at. You've no longer got a crowd-pleaser.

Knowing all that, I guess none of us should have been too surprised when Teague — or more likely, his pucker-faced accountant — shut us down. I think we'd finished five of the eight emotions. We weren't building them in order, but in parallel: after Fear, we split up into sub-teams, all racing to complete our designs while keeping Egger satisfied.

I know we'd completed Wrath & Regret, and I know we were done with Affection — the blush-pink tinge of sunset and tangerine silhouetting a slow, tentative embrace that shrunk, gradually, to suggestive darkness. That was where Theo and I had snuck off to be together, when no one was working.

I think Disgust might have been the other one we finished. An animatronic apeman shrinking away from this swampy muck that seemed to be rising up to meet him, maybe? I didn't spend much time in it, though, so don't quote me on that.

The other emotions were in various stages of partial-completion when the shutdown order arrived. "It doesn't matter," Egger said, when they handed him the proverbial pink slip. Management had tried to do it quietly, but Egger never did anything quietly. He flounced. Made sure we all knew how things had gone down. "It's already done!" He shouted over the music at our hastily thrown wrap party, a whiskey bottle in one hand and a spliff in the other. "It'll *always* be done."

That night, he brought bottles of accelerant — paint stripper and poor-man's animatronic lubricant — and poured it all over the inside of the "Fear" scene, soaking the hems of his jeans and robe. I don't really know what happened then, but it started a fire.

He had Theo with him. As always.

9

If this was a movie, I would've been there. Would've rushed into the burning pavilion to get Theo out. But this was real life. After the impromptu wrap party, I went back to the motel up the highway where we were all staying for the duration and sat on the bed, half-drunk and sketching monsters while giant atomic ants menaced a desert town on the TV. I didn't find out what happened until the next morning.

I guess someone on the crew told Teague about Theo and me being together, because I got the call almost as soon as they found her. When I screeched up in front of the hospital, a nurse appeared and ushered me straight to Theo's room. She looked like a mummy, all head-to-toe in bandages. I thought about those old movie mummies with their reincarnated loves, and considered writing Theo a little poem on the theme. Maybe it's best I didn't. It would've been cheap and sentimental anyway — and besides, she never would've gotten to read it. She followed Egger into the dark later that morning.

But for those few minutes, I held the hand the nurse said it was okay to hold, and I told Theo I loved her.

"You did," was the last thing she ever said to me. Her voice was barely a whisper. "So you always will."

10

That's the thing, see. That's what I didn't understand all those years ago. When Theo and I were making love, when I was working on "Primal." Once you make something, it's made. You can't unring that bell.

Oh, you can tear it down, burn the storyboards, destroy the pavilion, scrap the animatronics. I never set foot back inside the remains of the building. I walked down to the site, saw its charred skeleton — the rib-like supports that held up the domes encasing each exhibition, each emotion. And I saw then, maybe for the first time, how much like a human body our ride had been. Each exhibition contained inside an organ, each piece needing the next piece to survive.

But no matter what happens to the physical structure, it still exists, if only as a memory. No, that's not right, not even a memory — because a memory requires a host to remember it. And this is more solid than that. More real.

Time isn't an arrow launched relentlessly forward, after all. That's what Theo kept trying to tell me, if only I'd listened. Matter and energy can never be created or destroyed. Every crystallized moment of time still exists, will always exist, trapped in an endless loop like a gif forgotten on someone's Twitter feed, repeating itself in the dark with no one to observe it. Every moment is infinite, and no moment can ever end. Because it *has* happened. It is *always* happening, over and over again. Big bang, big crunch.

So somewhere out there, our attraction is still waiting for us to finish it. Waiting for a gaggle of excited kids to enter the first chamber. Somewhere, Theo and I are still together in the shadows of the "Affection" pavilion. And somewhere the hominids huddle close to their fire, the monsters are emerging from the dark, that first tentative embrace is underway, and the robot apeman waits for the nightmare blood to stop.

But of course, it never will.

O the curves of my longing through the cosmos,

and in every streak: my being's

flung-outness. Many of them returning

only after a thousand years on the sad ellipse

of their momentum and passing on.

Hastening through the once-existent future,

knowing themselves in the seasons

or airly, as a precisely timed influence

almost starlike in the overwakeful

apparatus for a brief moment trembling.

Venice, mid-July 1912

Dalton Teague's favorite poem, by Austrian poet Rainer Maria Rilke — kept framed in his OmniPark office.

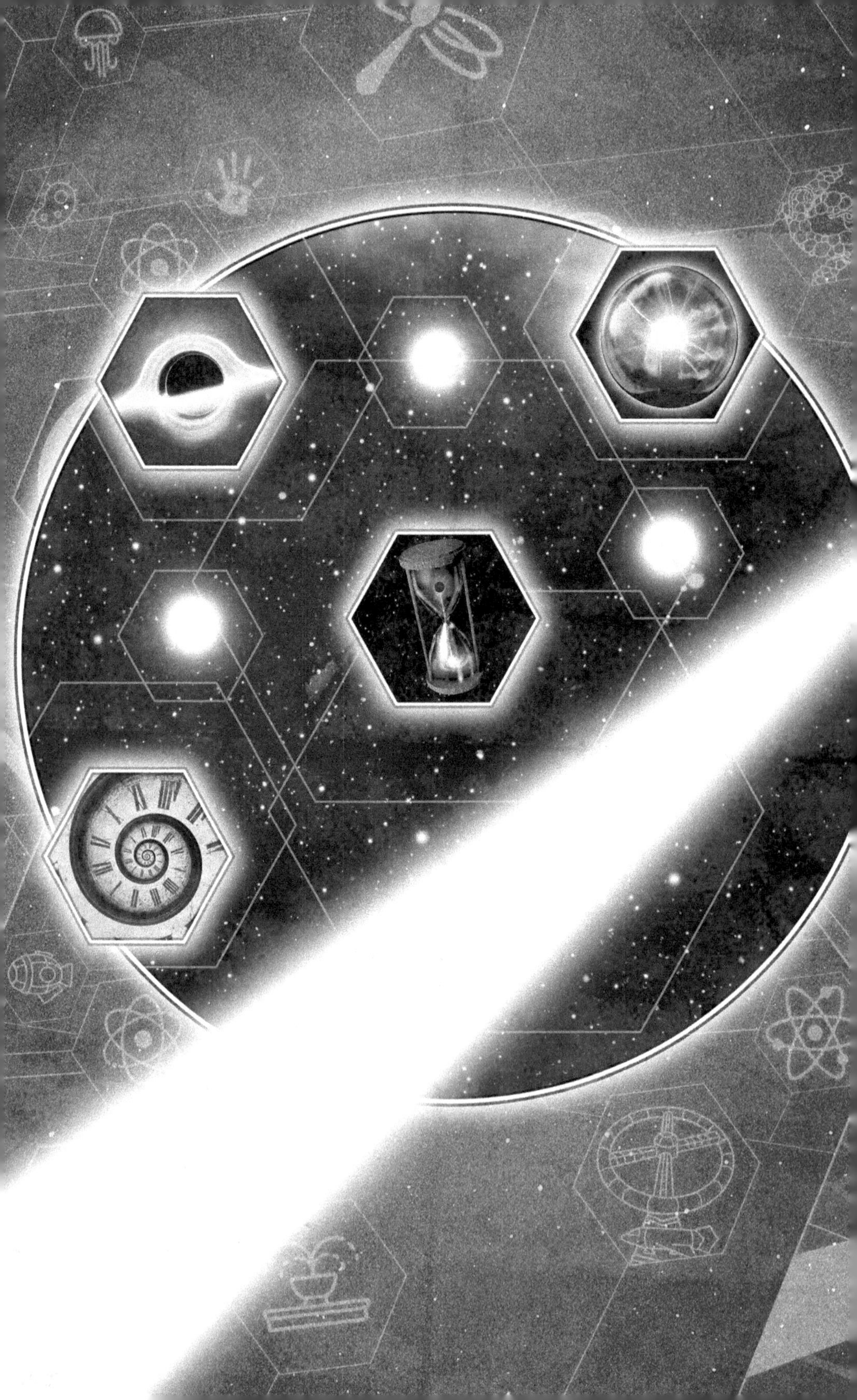

The Secret of Invention

Brad Kelly

1

"What does science mean to you?" Dalton Teague asked him that first day, sweltering in the impossible Texas heat, posed as though quizzing a novitiate on what he meant by 'the Lord.' And when Malcolm stammered through his answer, Dalton held up a hand steady as a plank of wood for all the years he'd worked to manifest his dream. "I don't actually want an answer, young man. I want you here asking the question. Just as we ask it of ourselves each day the sun is so gracious as to rise."

2

Malcolm Fulton had never flown in an airplane, or seen the desert, never even been west of the Mississippi. A well-bred boy from Massachusetts and a straight-A student, he had no vice except the growing conviction that his life must be an adventure: space travel, a journey to the center of the earth, the survival of death. Something. College, almost terminally boring, was only tolerable for the doors it added to his corridor and because it meant that fewer people could tell him "no."

A month before graduation, flipping through an old volume, he found a brochure for OmniPark, a paradoxical tourist attraction amid the creosote waste of west Texas. As a bookmark it made no sense, seemed placed there for him alone. And in the following weeks, he caught himself scrutinizing its pictures obsessively, reading the descriptions, studying the focused and avuncular profile of Dalton Teague, the park's mercurial founder. He fell in a kind of love with the man's self-possessed gaze toward the horizon, as if he saw out there what no one else could. Another character drew Malcolm in: The Inventor, who ministered over the park's Realm of Time in his rust-colored three-piece and the derby hat befitting a Victorian eccentric, the heavy mutton chops and the brass-framed goggles. The park was no rocket trip to distant planets, but the brochure indicated a project steeply illogical and audacious, and Teague's team of Technosophers—a consilience of engineering, storytelling, design, and a sort of technological shamanism—challenged Malcolm's ambitions for himself. At OmniPark, he would find his route toward something real and novel, even if wild and temporary.

Dalton — Dr. Teague, or "Papa" as his inner circle were privileged to call him — hired Malcolm after a single interview. Kismet or karma or brute confidence. And OmniPark quickly became home. An uncanny sense that he'd spent stretches of time here longer than his life. He loved the park's unapologetic and unscientific enthusiasm for science, its attention to detail, and, most of all, its holistic purpose: to enlighten all comers with the deepest knowledge a theme park could aggregate. Each attraction had its charm: The Realm of Life a safari-like adventure through terrain home to creatures long vanished from the earth; the Realm of the Cell a convincing simulacra of the amoeba's violent world; the Realm of Man a wide-eyed march through the struggles our Adams and Eves survived to liberate themselves from the desert, the ice, and the cave.

But the Realm of Time was where Malcolm most wanted to work. Its very existence struck him as though he were a fish finally noticing water. Here, tricks of light and animatronics swept guests on a white-knuckled caper inspired by H.G. Wells himself. Passengers in Victorian contraptions spiraled through a dystopian melodrama, were attacked by mantis shrimp the size of African elephants, endured the Big Bang's kaleidoscope of light and sound. The fidelity to its theme was peerless among all the attractions: the faux-laboratory within the convoluted mansion. The buzzing lights and whirligigs and brass. Even the gimmick was crucial: Time a retro-futuristic substance we once nearly uncovered and have since let slip back into the ether. Soon enough, Malcolm developed his own ideas for this Realm, as though slowly understanding an aspect of Time itself that was real and novel, even if wild and temporary.

But he waited. He did the work asked of him, and that which it seemed others overlooked. He learned rapidly, made friends, became a model young Technosopher, with his eyes always on the Realm of Time and the taciturn Inventor who seemed less a person than an old-timey ghost haunting the park. Time to time, the Inventor seemed to be watching him through those brass goggles. Many mornings they exchanged cursory nods in the Entryway Pavilion, where the man stood waiting as if in hope of encountering Malcolm as he arrived for a day's work. One afternoon, the Inventor simply stood and studied him at his terminal. Fifteen minutes watching Malcolm earnestly type and rifle through the thick file-folders as he sweat. At last Malcolm turned to the Inventor, a fresh render whirring away on his big tube monitor, and the Inventor nodded in response, grave and judgmental even through the goggles.

"Time just going by weren't it?" the Inventor said. "Yeah. That's the way she go'ed." And then he turned and hustled back to his post as if embarrassed.

Weeks passed before Malcolm saw him again. He worked on, increasingly distracted, waiting and then frustrated, disappointed at his waiting. By now he was supposed to be a Mars colonist or an eccentric millionaire. And then, six months into his tenure, Malcolm found a letter in his locker, written in a degraded version of his own hand. He sat down in the break-room to read:

3

Malcolm,

It's the Inventor. That's the name Dalton himself gives me when I finally arrive here. In this timeline, you got here later than I will. Sorry ... than I did. Than I have. It is a very tangled bank. For many of the people who visit OmniPark, I will be, have been, am, the Park's most memorable character. Truest to form. Most reliably who they expect, save my white hair growing grayer by the day and, soon enough, black as on the one in which I was born. But I doubt anyone recognizes how crucial my role is to this place. And not merely the Park's. To the grounds beneath it, to time itself. The air it breathes...

Do you want to know OmniPark's secret? Why this place is so much more than just lights and robots and funnel cakes? You already know, but it is not yet for you. I have held this knowledge for decades now, it seems, and am about to find out. Is this making any sense at all yet?

You see, OmniPark was built over land sacred to the men that came before the old Comanches. A reclusive tribe with no name to modern ears. Speakers, Teague says, of a language more of the Aztecs than the Apaches. Believers in a desert faith more akin to the Yaqui than the Kiowa or Wichita all maps assign to this part of the state. It was here, they believed, that men and women could walk between the Realms. Could peer into the souls of stones and plants. Could dance themselves into the dream world.

  I know I do not strike one as much of a dancer, but I have been older than the man you see now just as you have been younger. By the time I have left this place you'll see nothing but a brittle old fart, but the truth is that fellow is as naive as you will be and are. Such is the most effable facet of the Realm of Time.

  Let me tell you a story, Malcolm. Though you think it is about you, I daresay it strikes me even dearer. Recall your little gang of neighborhood friends? Playing games in front yards and shooting hoops and riding bikes and how you were kind of in love with Eleanor? Some of these kids—Bill and Derek—you have never known less than you know right now. Practically crib-mates; and your mother's friends, too, your father's. You would walk up to any one of their doors and you would knock and you would ask "can Tommy come out and play?" And he would, wouldn't he? I look forward to those days like this morning's coffee.

All of this true. Half of it Malcolm had not even thought of in years. How deep and permanent the gang's friendship had been, and how abruptly it had evaporated. He glanced around the break-room. No one watching, only the cantankerous refrigerator, the rattle of the air conditioner, the clock saying he was five minutes late for work.

  Deeper, come with me. Because there is one day among those who will be the very last time you are all together. You will knock on Eleanor's door and you two will go find Tommy in his driveway skateboarding with Bill. And Derek will come out to find you, Cynthia too. And you will all be in that driveway playing basketball—a game of your own device, remember? Know that you will remember its rules through all the changes you will soon undergo.

  But this last day, I will be just old enough that my amour for Eleanor will hum in my veins and she'll be interested in boys finally—not in that teeny-bopper way, but in actuality; will want to talk and plan and sneak notes. And Bill will be starting to play football and he becomes a rugged kind of man. Derek will move out to Maine to follow his father's work. And then we will be high school kids and the gang we formed nothing but a memory. Like all children: there was a final day in which you came outside to play and none of you knew that this time of your life was over.

  Why tell any of this? Because you have no idea what Time really is. Or perhaps I did not decide but merely followed the tradition of the Inventor before me. The Inventor is not a person. And Time is no arrow. Suffice to say this: Time is a machine. Infinitely complex. And I, me, we… we're the gremlins who run about at night to keep it humming. The Inventor is no mere passenger on this voyage and yet it is more than

I say: A loop. A pattern encoded in all things, which are one thing. I have no analogies that do not sound grandiose, so forgive this: it is an archetype, like a messiah, like a king, like a Shakespeare who redefines the lingua or an Einstein reality or a Dalton Teague who keeps mankind itself leaning toward whatever's next.

4

A stone-age man strode into the breakroom, barefoot, his face daubed with paint, shaking out the fur cape he wore through his shift at the Realm of Man. Malcolm nodded to him, the letter lying on the tabletop like some bit of contraband it was too late to hide. The caveman grunted hello and laughed to himself as he took up the dust-buster hanging there beside the refrigerator. He lay the cape flat and vacuumed at the detritus collected in the fake hair. Malcolm waited, watched him, as the dust-buster screamed, clogged, caught something hard like a penny. After endless minutes, the caveman finished and walked out. Malcolm read on:

5

...but waking up each morning in everyone's yesterday is a bewildering experience. And this may sound like a trap to you, as though the park becomes your prison cell. Nothing could be less true. The park has closed in 2003 and you have worked until the final day. Dalton Teague has no scintilla of greed in him. You will retired as a young man, free to wander the earth, to live in oceanfront villas or hide out in mountain cabins. To travel endlessly as Dalton himself has, seeking some word or image that makes the rest of it all true. And yet, at the same time, you will be an old man living into your youth here. You will split between these two journeys, and others perhaps even grander. And this will happen before you arrive here. And this has happened already.

I want you to consider the true answer to that question Dalton posed. If science is a mere cataloguing of facts, then I have been the poorest of its practitioners. It is, you will find, not an articulation of the system by which this world runs, but a charting of and spacesuit for the nebulous concatenation of reality. Dalton's park, our park, tries to show that. Tries to teach children—and their parents, just as well—that they live in a turbulent sea of harmless chaos. That there is no true end and no true beginning and to pass through the Big Bang or the death of our star is to stand astride the misconception that our time here is limited. You can change the past, if you want, or you can relive it. For you and very few others, this choice is yours.

6

Esoteric doodles comprised the rest of the letter, inscrutable math equations. Malcolm considered whether to hide the thing or throw it away or present it to Dalton. He'd have thought it some joke or derangement if not for the story it told. After a while, he carried the letter with him out into the little alley between the Realms of the Deep and the Stars. The Inventor stood there, recognizable only by the suit he wore, clean-shaven, without hat or goggles. He looked more like an older Malcolm than even Malcolm's father did, or does. His eyes the same color and shape, the same coordinates in his face. And then here came Dalton Teague, deep in thought as always, yet beaming with some unknown joy. Not a drop of sweat on his stiff collar. He stopped beside the Inventor and gazed out across the park as though he could hear a malfunctioning gear somewhere among its rides. A squealing child ran by hollering about dinosaurs, his chuckling father trailing behind.

"It's all true," Teague said with a smile that betrayed a mischievous mood, a knowledge of precisely what would happen. "And we need you, Malcolm, the way everything is now. In other times it will be buried. It will be part of the megalopolis. It will be a mile below the sea."

"Why me?"

"We wanted an astronaut but they were all busy in the first three dimensions."

The Inventor reached out to shake Malcolm's hand and then pulled him in for a hug. "It was all what it is," he said, shaking his head at himself, rambling on until he said something like: "we will be brothered when it happened, everyone. A long time to be…well." He made a motion with his hand like one hastening a slow talker, then stepped back, appearing a bit frustrated with himself, accustomed to hiding it behind his goggles and beard and script. Even in this stammering confusion, though, this inability to speak in one plane of time, the Inventor's voice was clearly Malcolm's own, though scuffed and battered by long experience.

The Secret of Invention

"Are you ready?" Dalton said. "I assure you the adventure far outweighs the cost."

Malcolm glanced at the OmniColor fountain, so brilliant at night but now rather dull by daylight. Both things at once and which was the one to measure it by? He thought of his old friends. The ones the Inventor wrote about. Their routes all laid out ahead before they placed their first footstep. Not for Malcolm Fulton. One lifetime was never enough.

He slowly nodded his head. Dalton and the Inventor led him out across the threshold, from the Entryway Pavilion into the Realm of Time.

They strode down the rails of the Time Tunnel, into the dark corridor before the first real attraction, and Dalton pried a hidden handle from the wall, used this to open a door that Malcolm had never noticed. Teague shone a flashlight down into a stairwell someone had dug into the earth a very long time ago.

"We're there on this side waited," the Inventor said. "It was being completely safe."

Malcolm followed Dalton down the steps and the Inventor closed the door behind them. A sensation of deja vu so potent: Malcolm knew exactly where they were going. Down into the Realm where he would remove his clothing and slip into the black clear waters once again, as he'd done countless times. And in this half-dark now, a vision materialized: his bygone friends laughing in the driveway, his own beard growing thick and white, a vista spreading below him of swooping rock formations and strange trees. And he saw the day the park closed: Dalton locking the front gate with a smile as though it was all of no consequence whatsoever. And then walking with him out into the parking lot and the both of them, this mad dreamer and the Inventor, gazing out across the horizon at something no one else could see.

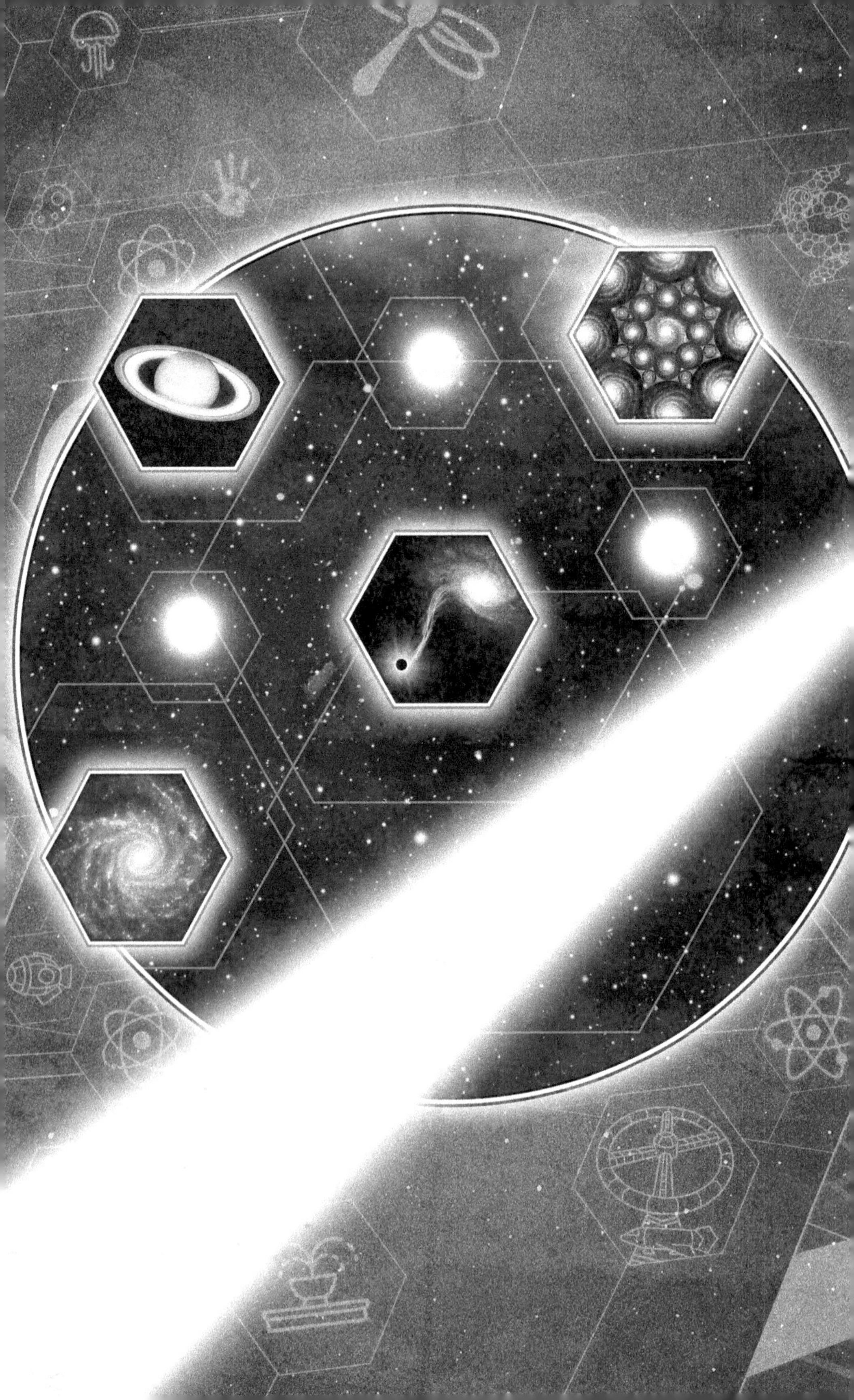

Stellar Nucleosynthesis and the Infinite Power of Love

Alicia Hilton

1

Many people remember August 15, 1969, as the first day of the Woodstock music festival. It was also the day that my father, Naashonon Amor, arrived on Earth and met Dalton Teague, the eccentric Texas oil billionaire. Like many of the hippies at Woodstock, Amor advocated for peace and practiced fluid love. West Texas was a strange place for an extraterrestrial to settle, it's true; but Amor was captivated by Teague's passion for science. Together, they transformed the Teague farm into a commune that attracted some of the most brilliant minds on the planet.

Teague offered to credit Amor with giving him the idea for creating OmniPark, but secrecy was more important to my father than notoriety. When Teague talked to the press about how he'd built a theme park that outshone even Florida's EPCOT Center, he acted as if the scientists that he'd hired were studious intellectuals. The Technosophers were visionaries, sure — but they also loved to party. And while the OmniPark project didn't really kick off until 1974; the first Technosophers joined the commune as early as 1969.

Whereas most of the children who lived on the farm had to guess which Technosopher had impregnated their birth mother, my father's progeny were born with polydactylism, an extra finger on one of their hands. Nathaniel and Nymphas, twins, had bonus pinkies. I was the only sibling born with an extra thumb.

My brother and sister died when they were toddlers. Nathaniel was stung to death by wasps. Nymphas died when a truck plowed into the commune's VW Bus, killing the kids on board, and the Technosopher who was driving them to the local playground.

Naashonon Amor didn't sire any further commune babies after I was born. Mom told me that he'd skipped town the night a meteor struck the commune's barn, causing the roof to cave in. The next full moon, Mom departed from Odessa, carrying me wrapped in a blanket.

Fast-forward seventeen years.

My mother lay in a hospital bed, dying from cancer.

The room was stifling hot, but someone had pulled a blanket up to her chin.

I leaned closer to the bed, trying not to touch the catheter bag that collected my mother's urine. I asked, "Did you say fingers?"

While other people may have heard stranger deathbed confessions than my mother's, that didn't make her request any easier to comprehend.

She nodded. "Closet. Behind the shoes," she rasped.

I glanced at my extra thumb. My stomach churned. "You dug up their graves?" I took a step back from the bed.

"No," she shook her head, eyes welling with tears.

"How did you get the fingers?" Picturing my mom holding a knife, I felt a rush of nausea claw upward from my stomach.

"A doctor, in the hospital," she sobbed. "When they were babies."

My knees began to shake. "I don't believe you," I said. "Why didn't I get surgery?" My extra thumb had always made me feel like a freak.

"I was afraid," she answered.

"Afraid of what?" my voice rose to a shriek.

"I—I thought it protected you."

"Fingers in a jar?" I tried to laugh, but the sound came out as more of a wail.

"Your thumb," she said. Tears rolled down her face.

The sound of a cart, squeaking across the linoleum, made me turn to face the door.

A nurse pushed the cart into the room. She smiled at my mother and asked, "How are we feeling?"

"Diary," my mom repeated under her breath. "Behind the shoes."

I grabbed my purse and ran. *What kind of person keeps severed baby fingers?*

2

Two pinky fingers, dried up and shriveled, shouldn't weigh a lot. Yet the urn felt as if someone had jammed an anvil inside it. Except an anvil wouldn't rattle like a maraca.

I set the urn gently on the ground, and drew a pair of gardening gloves from my jacket pocket. The fabric was stiff, since the gloves were new, but at least I wouldn't get blisters from the jar's hot surface.

The story my mother had written in her diary seemed too outrageous to be believed. I'd always been told I was born in a commune, but how could my father have been an extraterrestrial?

And yet, as soon as I strode into Mom's garage and wiggled the washing machine away from the wall, I found the urn, right where she'd told me it would be.

Don't look inside, Mom had written.

Was it my imagination, or had the jar started to *hum as soon as I'd picked it up*?

I retrieved it from the ground and unscrewed the cap.

The shriveled baby fingers looked like tiny brown sticks — twigs that reeked of rotting flesh.

I shrieked. I couldn't help it. *Good thing the garage door is shut*, I thought.

Once I'd fought my breath back under control, I screwed the cap back on the jar. Instantly, steam began to seep from the seal. I yanked my hand away. God, what a stench.

But my conscience wouldn't let me toss the jar in the trash. How could I deny Mom her final wish?

3

Since it was nearly midnight, I figured I wasn't likely to encounter any witnesses as I dug at the cemetery. All the same I made myself wait a few minutes, listening in the humid darkness, before I swung the gate open.

The grave wasn't hard to find: It was the only plot covered in mushrooms: tiny white fungi that glowed in the dark.

The granite headstone bore a minimalist inscription, too cryptic to betray its secrets to any but our own family: *Naashonon Amor, beloved husband and father.* No birthdate. No death date.

I lay the urn on the wet grass and began to dig.

The moment my shovel cleaved dirt, the mushrooms quivered. Not just the fungi near the shovel blade, but *all* of them. They swayed back and forth, dancing in perfect time to my shovel strokes.

I dug faster, breathing hard with exertion. I felt rivulets of sweat roll down my back, soaking my shirt.

The urn hummed louder, as if a swarm of bees were trapped inside.

After many more sweaty, grunting, panting minutes, my shovel finally struck something hard.

I lowered myself onto my hands and knees and scraped the last of the dirt away with frantic impatience, clawing at the wet earth until my fingernails made contact with the casket's surface.

Raising myself back up, I grabbed the shovel and thrust straight down, cracking the wood.

An odor rose from the coffin, enveloping me like a cloud — sharp and herbal, but not unpleasant. Rosemary?

The fungi made a *popping* sound, and a beam of emerald light lanced up from the coffin, momentarily blinding me.

The urn began rolling under its own power, as if an invisible force was pulling it towards the hole I'd dug.

The ground trembled, shaking so vigorously, that my father's headstone uprooted itself and tumbled to the grass.

The light surged, shifting from green to amber; so bright I could barely see. I stumbled backward, blood thundering in my ears. And another sound, too — almost too high-pitched to hear.

I thrust my palms forward against the searing light, and was surprised to feel something slick and cool beneath my fingertips.

Whoosh.

As suddenly as the light had surged, it abruptly vanished, along with the strange sound.

I blinked, gazing in bewilderment at my surroundings. The hole in the ground was gone, along with the urn and my shovel. Even the headstone that had marked my father's grave had disappeared.

The only remaining physical evidence of the past thirty seconds was a sticky wet residue coating my palms. It looked like water, but it smelled like mushrooms.

4

What would you do if you learned your father was an extraterrestrial?

I talked to my therapist. I said, "My mother kept baby fingers in a jar."

She said, "How does that make you feel?" Her leather chair squeaked as she leaned toward me, wire-rimmed glasses in hand, a well-rehearsed expression of concern knitting her brow.

"It's hard to explain," I told her.

I glanced at my extra thumb. The skin itched, and since last night it had become swollen and red. Not like an ordinary rash. Something was pulsing beneath the surface. I covered the thumb with my other hand.

The therapist seemed not to notice. "In some cultures," she said, leaning back in her chair, "keeping body parts from a loved one is common practice."

"Really?" I glanced up. Amber light gleamed through the window, but it was only headlights. Just an ordinary car.

My therapist nodded. "Queen Victoria wore a locket filled with her husband Albert's hair, after he died. Do you still have the urn?"

I shook my head. "Mom didn't want me to keep it."

I told my therapist a heavily edited version of the events of the past 24 hours. So heavily edited, in fact, that it omitted just about everything except my visit to my mom in the hospital. I didn't tell my therapist that my father was an extraterrestrial, or mention his grave. Or the fact that I'd been feeling an increasingly strong compulsion to drop my economics major and study something bigger; more cosmic.

My thumb was pulsing vigorously by now. Somehow I sensed that if I revealed more, the skin would split.

The therapist gave me a new meditation exercise, along with a tin box full of herbal tea. The tea tasted like mint blended with chamomile, which was nice. But it didn't get rid of my insomnia.

Next morning, I signed into my university's online portal and changed my major: instead of studying economics, I'd become an astronomer. Balancing account books struck me as trite and pointless in comparison to discovering new galaxies.

5

Dalton Teague was a surprisingly easy man to contact — at least for me.

I found OmniPark's main switchboard number in the telephone directory, and a bored yet friendly operator transferred me to Teague's office at the park. I expected the brusque voice of a secretary, but instead it was Teague himself who answered the phone on the very first ring.

"I've been expecting your call, Nania," he said. His voice felt warm, yet distant somehow, as if part of him was somewhere else.

"How — how did you know it was me?" I stammered.

"Your father's grave. I visit it each time the full moon is so generous as to rise."

"But you live in Texas. You travel to Oregon every month?" I pushed my chair back from my desk, and rose to my feet. I paced, though my bedroom didn't leave me much room to do so. I tried to dodge around my bed and ended up stubbing my right toe on the footboard.

"In the Realm of the Stars, distance is fluid." He laughed softly, as if at a joke only he could hear. "I hear you're studying astronomy."

"My mom told you?" I blinked back tears. Not from the sore toe. Five months had passed since my mother's death, yet I still felt her absence like a knife wound every time I woke in the night.

Instead of answering my question, he simply said, "I'm glad you called, Nania. I'll see you very soon."

"You're coming to Portland? Dr. Teague? Are you there?"

But he'd hung up on me.

6

October 23, 1989 was my last day in Portland. It was my eighteenth birthday, and also the day the Space Shuttle Atlantis completed its fifth manned mission and returned to Earth. A new nightclub downtown was throwing a Halloween party, but instead of dressing as a witch or ghoul, I decided to go as myself: an extraterrestrial.

I almost turned back when I saw the length of the line outside the club. My fake ID said I was twenty-one, but the security guard appeared skeptical. He stared at the photo for a long ten seconds, comparing it against my face.

"You look young for twenty-one," he said at last.

"I *am* twenty-one. It's my birthday."

He handed me back the ID. "Happy birthday. Nice antennae."

"Thanks," I said. Extraterrestrials from my father's planet didn't have antennae, but I'd crafted the headband to match my costume because it fit the stereotype.

The guard stopped me again as I tried to sidle past him. "I have to look inside your purse," he said.

Heat rushed to my face. I unlatched my clutch.

He was professional (or disinterested) enough to ignore the box of condoms inside. He was handsome in a rough way, dressed like a biker: black boots, leather pants, and a vest that exposed his tattooed sleeves, both arms covered with weird hieroglyphic symbols.

Finally he nodded for me to shut my purse. "One last thing," he said. "I need to frisk you. Got anything in your pockets that could cut me?"

"I don't have any pockets." The dress I'd sewn was spandex. Pockets would've spoiled my sleek silhouette.

"Raise your arms." His calloused hands skimmed my breasts, then lingered on my butt. "Sorry," he said, though he didn't seem it.

I grinned, surprised at my sudden lack of shyness. "That's okay," I told him. "I'm Nania."

"I'm Jake. See you later?"

"Maybe." I strode past him into the foyer, wearing a grin almost as obvious as my antennae. When I glanced back, he was still watching me, doing a better job of hiding his own smile.

Carried on a rising tide of confidence, I approached the bar, scanning at the drink menu written on a chalkboard above an impressive collection of bottles.

The bartender leaned toward me. "What can I get you?"

"I'll have a Pan-Galactic Gargle Blaster," I said, intending it as a joke.

Imagine my surprise when he smiled, nodded, disappeared behind the bottle rack, and returned moments later with an iridescent green drink in an elongated glass.

My eyes widened as he set my drink on the bartop. I counted out a few bills, adding a generous tip.

This was definitely shaping up to be an unusual evening.

7

It was only after gulping down half of the Gargle Blaster that I realized I'd made a major miscalculation. I hadn't eaten anything since the slice of pizza I'd scarfed down for lunch. Yet I felt fine — light-headed, but not the slightest bit nauseous. So I swallowed the remnants of the cocktail, elbowed up to the bar, and ordered another.

Warm happiness swirled through my veins, impelling me to follow a group of women heading towards the dance floor. A DJ stood high on a platform, spinning synth-pop that made my feet move of their own accord.

The pulse of the bass vibrated through the floor. Reflections from the whirling disco globe drew me inward like a magnet. I pushed past a group of guys clustered around a cocktail table, throwing back shots. I unlatched my purse, pulled out the cross-body strap, and slung it across my chest. When I looked up again, thousands of glowing stars decorated the ceiling.

My platform heels rendered me a little unsteady, but the added height also made it easier to scan the crowd. Most of the dancers wore costumes, some with rubber masks covering their faces. *They must be dripping with sweat*, I thought. The heady scents of floral perfumes and musky aftershave made the air even more stifling — but not stifling enough to drive me away. My mini dress was sleeveless, my legs were bare, and I was riding a wave of newfound confidence and courage.

I approached a guy in a matador costume — but before I could open my mouth to ask him to dance, he turned away to chase after a cheerleader (or at least, a blonde dressed like one).

That guy isn't part of this story, a little voice inside my head whispered. *Tonight's your birthday. Find someone weird and do something crazy.*

I scanned the crowd again, searching for the most attractive guy I could find. It didn't take long to lock onto my target.

He looked like a Freddie Mercury clone — except for his shoulder-length hair, which hung straight and shone pale jade beneath the glimmering lights. His svelte yet muscular body was wrapped in a tight emerald green snakeskin catsuit that seemed almost painted onto his skin. As I drew closer, I noticed he was staring at me, too. I'd never seen eyes quite that color: an intriguing mix of green and pale grey, almost the shade of seawater.

He pushed to the edge of the dance floor, set his cocktail on a table, and shouted, "Do you want to dance?" over the pounding music, making his meaning clear with hand signals in case I wasn't a lip reader.

"Yes!" I shouted back, nodding exaggeratedly.

He took my hand and drew me back into the center; into the lights and music and motion. The texture of his fingers surprised me, until I glanced down at his hand and realized he was wearing snakeskin-patterned gloves to match his costume.

Oh no, I suddenly realized. *I'm actually going to have to dance.*

He began undulating next to me, inching closer already. I tried to match his movements, but mostly just jumped around flailing my arms. He smiled, clearly enjoying my moves.

His fingertips brushed my hair. "Were you born with this color?"

Where was that accent from? I couldn't place it.

I giggled. "No, I don't think anyone is born with green hair. I dyed it."

"You like green?"

"Yes, it's my favorite color."

He smiled. "Your hair is the same shade as your eyes. You're beautiful." Just like that, as if it was the simplest thing in the world.

I felt hot color rush to my cheeks. "Thank you. You're beautiful, too." As soon as the words were out of my mouth, I felt myself blush even more intensely. Good-looking men liked to be called handsome, not beautiful. But it was the truth: he really was beautiful.

His smile widened. "You find me attractive?"

"Yes. Are you a model?"

He chuckled. "I'm an astronomer."

"Really? I'm studying to be an astronomer."

He grinned. "Would you like to see another galaxy?"

"Yes!" My eyes widened. "I mean, of course! That would be amazing."

He placed a hand on my shoulder. "What's your name? I'm Daxton."

"Nania."

"That's a lovely name."

I stepped closer. His aftershave smelled of warm earth and spices I couldn't name. I wanted him to keep touching me, to keep dancing next to me, to stay near me — but instead he took his hand off my shoulder and gestured towards the exit.

"You want to go outside?" he asked.

My heartbeat suddenly quickened. "Yes!" I nodded without hesitation — then reeled in the enthusiasm a little so I wouldn't scare him off. "I mean, sure. Okay. That sounds great!" *Was he going to kiss me?*

As we arrived at the door, I saw that the bouncer had vanished — and the clear night sky had transformed into a deluge, pouring down puddles that were rapidly coalescing into a river. I noticed a coffee shop across the street, but its lights were off.

Daxton said, "My car's in the lot. You want to sit and chat?" He gestured to an olive-green Citroën sedan parked on the corner.

"Yes," I said. Before he could change his mind, I hurried toward the car — but Daxton's long legs gave him the advantage. He'd already unlocked the car when I arrived, and held the door open for me.

"The backseat's more comfortable." He grinned.

I knew he wasn't talking about sitting, but I slid into the backseat anyway. The velvet upholstery felt soft against my bare legs.

He'd just shut the car door when I asked, "Are you from France?"

"No, why?"

"Your car."

"I saw it in a Bond film. Do you like it?"

"Yes. I mean, I do! Are you from England?" I really wanted to know where that accent of his came from.

He chuckled. "No, home is a bit further away." He leaned closer and grasped my right hand.

My extra thumb had stopped itching as soon as I'd quit therapy — but the moment Daxton touched me, it began pulsing again.

He raised my hand to his mouth and kissed it.

"Don't," I said.

"You want me to stop?"

Feeling breathless, I whispered, "My thumb's ugly."

He licked my thumb, sucked on the extra digit, then set my hand in his lap and pulled me closer.

"You want me to kiss your mouth?" he asked.

"Yes." I tipped up my chin and closed my eyes.

His lips awakened mine with gentle kisses.

I opened my mouth and his tongue slipped inside. When I moaned, he began working his way down my neck.

He grasped my purse strap. "Okay if I take this off?"

I slipped off my purse and set it on the backseat. The parking lot was deserted — and it was raining too hard for any prying eyes to glimpse what we were doing. My nervousness vanished as suddenly as it'd appeared. I yanked my dress over my head and threw it on the seat next to my purse.

When I turned back to Daxton, he was wearing what I took for a shocked expression.

Abruptly certain I'd moved too quickly for him, I grabbed my dress and clutched it tight against my chest, covering my lacy teal bra and panties.

"Can I see it again?" he asked.

I sniffed, trying not to cry. "See what?"

"Your tattoo."

I lowered the dress slowly, revealing the map of the solar system tattooed on my right side. The image was rendered in shades of grey, though I'd been planning to add color once I could afford it.

He traced his index finger over the pattern, ever so lightly — then leaned down and kissed Saturn.

I gasped in surprise. Actually it was more of a squeak.

"Is this okay?" he asked.

"Yes."

He moved his head lower.

I said, "Why don't you take off your clothes?"

"Later. Do you want to lie down?" Though his sedan was roomy, the backseat was cramped. I removed my bra and panties, lay back, and waited.

Other guys had fingered me before, but I'd never found experiences as satisfying as touching myself. Daxton seemed to be reading my mind, though, because he was somehow giving me the exact sensations I wanted.

I reached down and grasped a handful of his green hair. "Do you want me to touch you?" I asked, scarcely able to get the words out between gasps.

"Later." He kissed my navel, then worked his way lower until his face was between my legs.

His lips felt incredible enough — but when he began to probe me with his tongue, I felt things I'd never felt before, alone or otherwise.

I'd had orgasms before, but nothing like this. My whole body shook, every muscle clenching in synchrony. Above me I saw a green haze; flashing lights. The last thing I remembered was the sensation of the car lifting off the ground.

8

I woke in a strange room. Everything was green: the huge circular bed, the walls, the ceiling, the shiny piano, the sofas, even the plush shag carpet — all of it done in shades of moss, forest, emerald, lime, pea soup.

What on earth did that bartender slip into my drinks?

I heard a meow, rose onto my elbows, and turned to find the source of the sound. Daxton reclined in a chair next to the bed, a tabby cat cradled in his lap. He was still wearing the green snakeskin suit. At least the cat wasn't green.

Daxton scratched the cat gently between its ears and said, "His name is Maurice. I thought you might like something — or someone — to remind you of home."

Maurice meowed again.

"Where am I?" I yanked off the bedspread, stumbling to my feet in a whirl of dizziness that made me grab the mattress. The jade-colored carpet felt unbelievably soft between my toes.

"My home. At least until we reach Lingonia. Do you like it? I redecorated last night, since green is your favorite color."

None of this was making any sense. How could he have redecorated? Where was Lingonia? This felt too real to be a hallucination. It had to be a dream. I pinched my thigh — and the pinch hurt.

"Would you like breakfast?" He set the cat on the carpet and clapped his hands. A panel in one of the walls opened, and a table slid out. "I have fruit. Or would you care for fish?"

"I'm vegan. Where's Lingonia?"

"Not far." He clapped his hands twice. One of the walls disappeared, replaced by a huge window. In the night sky, I saw distant stars and what looked like Mars, except at least twenty moons orbited the planet. The images were too clear, too real, to be a video.

I screamed.

"I'm sorry. You must be shocked." He clapped his hands and the window closed, replaced by the wall.

"Show me again," I said, once I'd caught my breath.

"Clap your hands twice," he said.

I did, and the window reappeared. Fascinated, I took a few steps closer. The carpet felt soft against my bare feet. One of the moons was rotating. It wasn't my imagination. I turned back to Daxton, and smiled. "I'm hungry. Can we sit on the sofa by the window?"

"Of course." He lifted a pitcher from the table, and filled two glasses with a frothy green beverage.

Suddenly feeling shy, I said, "Where's my dress?"

"You don't need it." He grinned. "The sofa cushions are quite soft."

9

I didn't learn Daxton's other secrets until he invited me to join him in the bathroom. He removed his gloves first. His right hand had two thumbs.

Underneath the snakeskin suit, he looked like a human male, aside from his total hairlessness and conspicuous lack of testicles. Had he been gelded?. No wonder he hadn't wanted to remove his suit back in the car. Tears streamed down my face.

"What's wrong?" he asked.

Sobs shook my body. Tears clouded my vision, making everything blurry.

"Nania, what's the matter?" He stroked my shoulder.

I could barely choke the words out. "You've been castrated."

"No." He shook his head. "I was born this way. Lingonian males don't have testicles."

"Really?"

He nodded. "Lingonian males mate with their tongues."

My jaw dropped. "I'm pregnant?"

"Of course not." He smiled. "Not without your consent."

What he was saying had to be impossible. But when I looked in his eyes, I knew he was telling the truth.

Daxton picked me up and cradled me against his chest. He carried me to the bathtub.

The tub was large enough to be a swimming pool. The water was a perfect 100 degrees — exactly the way I liked it.

A bright yellow fish with pointy teeth darted towards Daxton's leg.

I screeched and gripped Daxton tighter.

He snatched the creature out of the water, popped it into his mouth, and chewed, smiling impishly.

The sound of crunching bones and the coppery scent of flesh made my stomach churn. I swallowed, trying not to retch.

"Let go of me," I said.

He set me down in the water.

Daxton said, "I'm sorry that I'm a carnivore."

"How can this be happening?" I said.

Daxton sighed. "You want to go back?"

I glanced out the window. A spacecraft was approaching, torpedo-shaped, studded with blinking lights, but Daxton didn't seem nervous at all.

"Why did you choose me?" I whispered, my breath mingling with his.

He smiled. "Dr. Teague thought we'd be a good match," he said. "And so did your father."

OMNIPARK

1419 N. Grandview Avenue, Suites 30-40
Odessa, TX 79762

From the desk of
Dalton Meadowscroft Teague

ATTN

Plea

Thi

Fee

If

P

For any further requests, please feel free to **** **** **r press department. Thanks again for your interest in what we are trying to do with OmniPark. I am looking forward to the article.!

Best wishes,

Dalton Meadowscroft Teague

Snapshot of Dalton Teague in front of the OmniColor Fountain on opening night of his park.

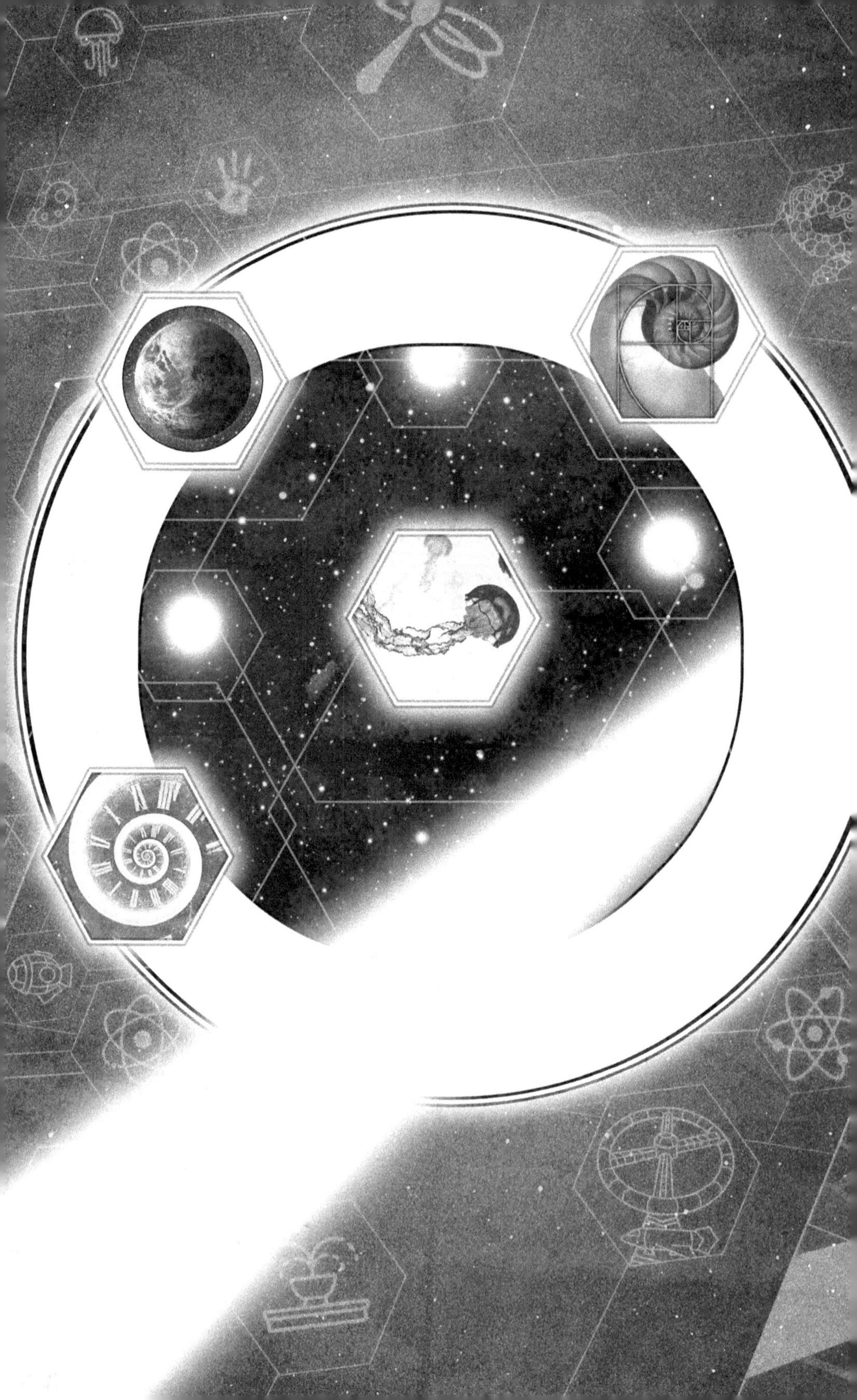

Outside of Everything, There is Nothing

T.M. Morgan

1

I snatched him after a reunion show by Thee Psyckick Temple at South by Southwest. Strolled up to him, lied and told him how big a fan I'd been. Rammed my fist into his nose. He collapsed. I held a chloroform rag over his bleeding proboscis. Into the dark of my van. Gagged. Tied. The joy! God, to have that fucking loser in my grasp.

Drove half the night along Highway 71 and then 87 back to the ruins of OmniPark outside Odessa. The miserable years slipped away as the Entryway Pavilion approached — a pale cathedral towering above the windblown steppe. A quick cut of some chains, then we sped across the weed-spattered parking lot. "The Universe Is Yours to Explore," the sign said.

"Get up," I yelled. The old man startled. He struggled at his constraints, murmured some terrified words through the gag.

"Don't remember me, do you?" I said. "It's been a long time."

2

From the beginning, I knew something was wrong. Falsity oozed from every surface. And the Physicist: with his crazed hair and beard and dark eyes. How cartoonish. When we entered the Realm of the Particle late in the afternoon, my father took the Physicist's hand and shook it vigorously as if the man was an old friend. I glimpsed tears in mom's eyes. Whether from the joy of seeing dad happy or horror at seeing him so crazed, I never knew.

Later, I saw the actor playing the Physicist striding through the Realm of Time's garden as we spoke to the security guards. Without his garb and wigs, he looked like any other fading hippy of the day: lost, confused, meandering from one time-slice to the next. If I had known then, I would have tackled him, pummeled his actor's face with my twelve-year-old fists. But I was still innocent about the singularity I'd just witnessed.

See, my prepubescent brain had run down the calculations, and the output was that for all OmniPark's quasi-intellectual dressings, the place was phony. A con to end all cons. Even as I, mom, and my sister crammed together with the politely nodding guards, spoke over each other about the whereabouts of my missing father, the park held no mystery. Just the opposite, in fact. I'd peeked behind the curtain before I even saw the show. I had wanted real magick, that childhood fantasy where everything fell within the Realm of Possibility. Maybe I wanted it so badly so dad wouldn't look so foolish. Magick. Such a juvenile concept. No one believed my father could just vanish into thin air. Not even me.

Dad had been more manic than usual that week. He'd spent months before our visit tacking up elaborate maps and sketches in his basement workshop; linking them with ropes of red and black string. We all knew better than to raise a fuss. I just hoped this wouldn't turn out like that time we spent two weeks in Savannah investigating haunted cemeteries. Somewhere in the midst of his all-night police interrogation, he'd gotten it into his head that one of us had tattled on him. I'm not sure he ever quite trusted us after that. And who knows — maybe mom told them everything they wanted to hear. It wouldn't have been the first time.

And then OmniPark. From the moment I strolled through the marble arches of the Entryway Pavilion, I nodded my head in appreciation. One couldn't help feeling just a little impressed at the sheer scale and audacity of Dalton Teague's investment. But as we bought our tickets and stepped into the mercifully air-conditioned Pavilion, my main thought was that dad looked apoplectic with dejection. Turns out I'd completely misread his expression: he was awash in pure wonder, astonishment, awe. Looking back — because the hindsight of such things comes so easily — I now know we lost him in that moment. Every step forward from there was inevitable. The attractions, the gravity of the place, had been exerting influence on him for months. On that sweltering Texas morning, OmniPark sucked him down and devoured him.

Funny how I, the kid, knew right away everything was wrong, while he, a grown man with a family, a job, a fully formed identity, plunged headfirst into the park's rabbit hole. I revisited that moment many times in my dreams: his muscles tensed in that nervously expectant posture, polo shirt hung over his plump belly, thinning black hair combed all the way over till it fell into his eyes, whose intensity was only magnified by his coke-bottle glasses.

Forty-two years. That's how long it'd been since dad disappeared in the Realm of the Particle. We moved to Odessa in 1980, hoping that might put us closer to the lawsuit's command center. Lot of good that did. So we bought season passes and launched our own investigation, scrutinizing every inch of the park like wild-eyed detectives — or, on warm summer evenings, organizing a picket line of three outside the park gates, to keep his case warm. The plan slowly got the upper hand on Mom and Regina. Mom's health deteriorated until she died of a stroke in 1995. That drove my sister to the needle, which took her in 2001.

As for me, I lived on for one unquenchable purpose: to expose OmniPark as the deathtrap it was. Dalton Teague's office unsurprisingly declined my repeated requests for an interview. So I went after an easier target: the Physicist — or at least that fucker who played him.

Headshots in mid-80's brochures showed a man losing both his hair and weight. But he kept on playing the Physicist for thirteen years — until 1990, when he co-formed the cult psychedelic band Thee Psyckick Temple, a cacophony that merged squelching noise with psychobabble. His years at the park had clearly gone to his head, convinced him he was some kind of cosmic messenger.

He wasn't the only acid-freak who thought so. As late as 2015, Thee Psyckick Temple still attracted a modest but loyal following on the geezer circuit: sun-weathered hippies who'd protested their way out of three foreign wars, chewing up psilocybin and reliving the glories of youth. The younger set hung around for the liberal psychedelic distribution policy; or maybe because they actually looked up to some of the old lemmings. As for the band themselves, they pranced onstage in impressively limber swagger, decked out like Hendrix in his prime. William, however, did not swagger. He'd been in a wheelchair for a decade at least. Bad hips.

Did I feel bad punching an old guy in a wheelchair? No more than he felt guilty for lying about that day for the past forty-two years. Under ordinary circumstances, I wouldn't have invested the time to track down or rough up a sack of shit like him. But ordinary was long-gone, and it was time for him to own up.

3

I glared into William's dull gray eyes in the haunting quiet of the van, searching for some spark of recognition. "You last saw me in 1990." I lifted him like a sack of straw and shoved him into the wheelchair's worn seat. "That was the last year you played Physicist. Any of this ringing a bell?"

I untied the cord around his head and yanked out the rag. He moaned and spat blood. I persevered as I snatched a bag of tools, tossing it over my shoulder.

"A couple years after dad disappeared, you sat for a deposition with our lawyers. I was just a kid then, but I know you remember me glaring at you across the table. I asked you, 'How much do they pay you to lie?' And you answered with more bullshit. Like you always do."

I duct-taped his extremities to the chair's metal frame. And since he didn't yet feel like answering, I jammed the dirty rag into his stupid maw. The Pavilion's main archway loomed overhead, blocked by rusted gates run through with chains. My trusty bolt cutters made quick work of those, and soon we were wheeling through the Pavilion toward the inner set of doors, which I opened with a hammer. Pale moonlight filtered through the high-set windows like beams from celestial flashlights.

Everything seemed to be going according to plan until I glanced up at the faded banners hung overhead, and the ceiling adorned with intricate scientific drawings of planets, cells, deep-sea fish. But the one that caught my attention bore a sigil of electrons encircling a nucleus that, upon closer inspection, dissolved into a cloud of ghostly particle-waves. It was captioned with Hebraic hieroglyphs, and with one English word in all-caps: *POSSIBILITY*. A rush of icy cold crackled through my bones. Something about this place was *wrong* in a way I couldn't pin down. I rolled us across the Pavilion's cracked tile floor, dodging around the odd bit of detritus that cluttered our path. The interior furniture — mostly church pews — had been long removed, revealing an ornate, multi-pointed star inlaid on the floor. Colorful mosaic tiles formed its interlocking shapes, which wove under and over one another, their surfaces bearing finely chiseled sequences of archaic letters. How many years had this complex geometry lay hidden beneath the feet of countless parents, children, school groups?

I rolled William up before the angular mosaic. "What do you have to say for yourself?" I awaited his response until I remembered I had to extract the saliva-soaked ball of cloth from his mouth. He coughed, spit, wracked his throat, heaved a large clog of red-flecked phlegm.

"What do you want?" he demanded, giving me his best impression of a defiant glare. It was the eyes that betrayed him — those gray eyes dulled by too many ayahuasca ceremonies, but still sharp enough to glimmer with fear, dread, confusion.

"I want to know what happened to my father."

I sniffed, scrunching up my nose at the sharp tang of ammonia and mold, which had whipped up into languid clouds by our intrusion. The spores mindless drifting struck me as malevolent, somehow — a jolt of alertness that warmed my skin like sun rays, raising hot pinpricks along my arms and neck.

"I don't know who you are," he slurred, "and I'm not who you think I am."

I laughed aloud, relishing the echoes upon echoes that reverberated from the vaulted ceiling above. "William Montgomery Sampson." I grabbed him by a tuft of hair, yanked his head back so he had to look me in the eyes. "You played the Physicist here from 1977 until mid-1990. You were here that day in '78 when my father disappeared in the Realm of the Particle. You were here every day I came back to visit after that. And you were there at the deposition, where you lied straight to my face. I know exactly who you are, just as you know who I am. So let's cut the bullshit and talk about what's really on our minds."

He exploded in a frenzied, unsuccessful struggle to free himself. The wheelchair wobbled and tilted up on one wheel. My hands slammed hard on the grips, leaning on the chair with all my weight. I expected him to go limp and plead for mercy, but instead he tensed up like a seizure victim, long white beard flicking like a horse's tail. My eyes fixated on the bald spot at the crown of his head: a liver-spotted tonsure cragged with wrinkles.

Now he was babbling again. The same old bullshit: "I have no idea what you're talking about, please let me go," et cetera. I didn't believe a word of it, obviously. Stuffed the rag back in his mouth, wheeled him around, and rolled him toward a set of locked doors at the far left side of the Pavilion.

"My family gave up in '92," I explained as we rolled past the vine-choked ruin of the OmniColor Fountain. "OmniPark's got a smart team of lawyers, I'll give 'em that. Must be handsomely paid. Bastards strung us along for years, waiting us out, bleeding us dry. I think our own attorneys stopped believing us at some point, if you want to know the truth. Too many 'rational' arguments from your side. Dad ran off to live a new life, they said. Then it was suicide off some lonely stretch of interstate. Then it was a mysterious accident — far away from park grounds, of course. Do they actually train them to do that in law school? Lie, I mean, with a straight face, while they look a grieving wife and kids in the eyes? Must be, surely. Those fuckers lied like they'd trained for it all their lives."

William moaned in pain as we bounced over a pothole in the tiled floor. I paused my soliloquy and gave him a moment to collect himself.

"It was on Quantum Catastrophe, as you know," I continued once he'd quieted down. "That was the ride where Dad let go of my hand. I remember strobe lights, shaking, screams. And I remember you, William, standing in the shadows where you thought I wouldn't see you, watching the whole thing go down. You could've spoken up, you know. Just once, even one time in all these years. But nope. 'Loose lips sink ships' seems to be the word around here. Did Dalton tell you that himself, or was it more of an unspoken understanding?" I shook my head. "Not that it matters now. Forty-two years down this fucking rabbit hole." I hefted my tool bag. "You know, I've got half a mind to take this hammer to you, let you bleed out right here. How's that sound?"

He mumbled frantically behind the gag, which I pried out of his drooling mouth again. "I — you have to understand," he stammered. "Even if I'd spoken up, I would've looked just as crazy as you did."

Well. At least now we were getting somewhere.

"No one would've believed me!" His eyes were wide and more lucid than they'd been all evening. Maybe he was finally coming down off whatever he'd been tripping on at the show. "I would've been fired, and sued down to the shirt off my back for an NDA violation — and that would've been just the start! Do you have any idea what these people can do? No, you don't. You can't imagine what this place really is. The things we made here." He was nearly in tears now — or so I thought, until I realized he was laughing: a long, low, rueful laugh that made me feel he'd gained the upper hand somehow. A quick right hook to his jaw put a stop to that.

I shook my hand and flexed my fingers, thoughts drifting back to The Day. That was what we'd taken to calling it: The Day. The day it happened.

I rarely let my memories dwell on the ride itself, but something about this place brought the scene back with piercing clarity: the ride vehicle gently dipping into a dark tunnel, then sweeping around a curved, glimmering wall to emerge into a wonderland of floating orbs that crackled with electricity. My hand slipped from dad's grip as I gazed in fascination at those dancing spheres of blue lightning. Then I heard mom's voice from the seat behind me: "Dennis?" Confusion and fear already verging on panic. "Honey, where's your father? Dennis? *Dennis!*"

"Where are we going?" William asked, jolting me back to the moonlit present.

I decided on silence. Keep him at full alert, at the peak of attention — ready to answer further queries with scraps of the truth, now that he'd remembered how to tell it. The entrance to the Realm of Life passed on our left, teakwood doors succumbing to termites and rot, laced with tangles of real vegetation overgrowing the wood-carved imitations. William recoiled from the vines, palms outward like the gesture of a religious supplicant.

"Things have changed a lot since the last time we were here," I said, by way of conversation.

"The Realm of the Particle is that way," William gestured toward the Pavilion's far wall. He was really tensing up now. "Isn't that where you want to take me?"

"We're going to the Realm of the Cell first," I said. "Following the pattern."

He straightened up like a puppet on a string. He hadn't been expecting this, hadn't anticipated I'd done my homework.

Oh, but I'd done my due diligence, all right. Twenty-seven thankless years of it, since '93 when mom gave up. I knew all about Dalton Teague's oil fortunes. Learned what little I could about his travels to Morocco and Mongolia and Kurdistan; his obsessions with collecting obscure artifacts and translating dead languages. Back in the mid-90s I'd even paid an underground "documentary filmmaker" for some grainy footage of what purported to be a VIP meeting in the Realm Between the Realms: Dalton's invite-only club that — according to the accompanying booklet — hosted U.S. Presidents, Arab Sheikhs, and members of royal families, along with more cryptic guests who bore resemblances to alleged members of MK-Ultra and the Majestic 12. The footage was too grainy and jittery to make out anything more than human-shaped blobs of color, but it'd made for an entertaining evening.

Then there was the guy from Germany, who'd emailed me out of the blue as our legal case gained notoriety in certain circles. In late '99 he sent me detailed, hand-drawn sketches of the park's layout, indicating sacred-geometrical correspondences that converged on the elaborate sigil mosaicked into the Entryway Pavilion's floor. If one visited each Realm in a particular sequence, he claimed, its true purpose would reveal itself — first through symbol and ritual, then in direct experience.

He might have been a little out there, but he was definitely on to something. The real heart of this place's magick, I'd come to believe, lay in the Realm of the Particle. One might accuse me of bias in that regard, since that was where we'd lost my dad — but the evidence formed a pattern too obvious to be mere coincidence. I was following that pattern now, and William was liking it less with every step.

The night was warm; the moon waltzing behind wispy cirrus clouds. My flashlight beam caught blotches of decay; baroque sculpture devoured by jungle, like the dead gods of some vine shrouded temple. Rodents scurried from my light-beam, making sounds not altogether different from William's periodic yelps. Ghost images darted across my narrow field of vision: shadows that were not shadows, but instead seemed translucent superimpositions.

The only way into the Realm of the Cell was through the Scalar Portal — a simulator that "shrank" guests down to molecular scale. Park lore claimed the Physicist had invented the Portal with the help of his collaborator, the Inventor. In truth, though, it was just another piece of clever engineering, engines and hydraulics long rusted solid.

My hammer made quick work of the chamber's inner and outer doors, and soon we were rolling through a labyrinth of enormous fiberglass cell membranes and protein chains, their once-vibrant colors faded to sickly pinks and yellows. Not much to see here, but the important thing was to keep following the sequence; the geometry. After a few more turns beneath the canopy of an enormous cell nucleus, I abruptly reversed course, crossing back through the central Pavilion to enter the Realm of Time. One snapped lock later, we entered the garden of the Realm's Victorian mansion — once a verdant maze of flowered topiaries, now a wasteland of tangled branches and naked statues, their empty eyes gazing at long-stopped timepieces in a dead facsimile of contemplation.

My eyes were adjusting to the dim light now. The flashlight went back in the bag. A phosphorescent glow, faint, bled from the edges of the failing architecture and plant growth. My eyes playing tricks on me in the dark, perhaps; or maybe some exotic species of fungus. "Do you see that glow?" I asked him. "Of course you do. What is that stuff? Should I be worried?"

William laughed again. "Oh, you should be worried. Hell, *I'm* worried. But you — you haven't got the first clue what you're getting us into. The space between spaces. That's what Dr. Teague wanted to find: the Realm Between the Realms. Not the glitzy one where he entertained his guests, but the *real* one."

I paused, bent down to look him dead in the eyes. Sharp now. Alert. Spilling the beans at last — or some of them, at any rate. "And did he find it?" I asked.

William shook his wispy-haired head. "What happened to your father that day, it...changed Teague, somehow. He shut down the sacred geometry project. Ordered his VIP Realm hollowed out for office space. Fired the more mystical Technosophers. Threatened to fire *me*, too, though I managed to talk him out of it." He shook his head, sighing. "Wish I'd walked out that day. Things only got weirder after that. The satellite launches; those eggs he brought back from God-knows-where. The things we set to breed down in those tanks..."

He shuddered, and might've said more until he caught sight of my shocked expression and clammed right the hell up. No point pressing him now — he wore the look of a man who yearned to snatch his words back out of the air and stuff them someplace they'd never be found.

"Let's stay on topic." I wheeled his chair around again, pivoting back through the Pavilion toward the Realm of the Stars. "I'm here to find out what happened to my father. So how about we make a deal: I pretend you didn't just tell me the last few things you told me, and instead, you tell me some other things I want to know."

"Such as?"

"Such as, do you know how to start it?" I asked.

His brow furrowed. "Start..." Suddenly his eyes widened. "The machine? Are you out of your goddamn mind? Do you have any clue what forces you're playing with—"

I belted him across the face. Call it reflex action. "In case you were thinking of calling me 'kid.' And you still haven't answered my question. Do you know how to get it running?"

"All right, look," he said. "You want the straight dope? I don't know shit about physics, and I sure as hell don't know how to run any machine. I was nobody. I was hired to play a part, and I played it. End of story."

"What part?" I grabbed a fistful of his collar. "What fucking part?"

He sighed miserably. "Isn't it obvious? I'm the scapegoat. I'm the guy who gets paid to be in the wrong place at the wrong time, so I take the fall for Teague's...metacosmic fuckup, or whatever the hell happened on that ride." He spread his hands. "What was it? Your guess is as good as mine. I have no earthly idea where your dad went. Look in my eyes and tell me I'm lying."

I did, and maybe he wasn't. Goddamnit. This complicated things.

"Well," I finally sighed, "if you can't start it back up, then I guess I'll figure it out myself."

A tremor convulsed through William's limbs as he thrashed wildly against his duct-tape restraints. Before I could catch the wheelchair, it rolled downhill toward a concrete chasm where a peaceful river had once flowed. I leaped forward and managed to yank the chair back before he plunged in headfirst and snapped his neck. Among other bones.

"That," I said between gasps for breath, "does not do either of us any good. We both want the same thing: to finish this and get the hell out of here."

My words didn't seem to register. William was shivering, glancing into every shadowy corner as if he expected some lethal threat to leap for his throat at any moment.

I got my breathing under control. Something I'd said had set this off; kicked his fight-or-flight response into high gear. The machine! Despite his repeated denials, he must know how it worked — or at least that it was still functional. My tracing of the park's geometry had got him hot and bothered, but nowhere near as much as my insistence on starting that machine back up. That was the fear within the fear.

"Tell me what it does," I said in a tone that offered no room for disagreement.

"Oh, Christ." He moaned. "Don't you get it yet? It's just a piece of *junk*! Some old '70s computer that automated the ride vehicles. That's all it ever was. Probably hasn't worked in twenty years."

"The more you insist on that, the less I believe it." I leaned back and folded my arms. "So let's take a trip to space, shall we? You know, I think Nebula Quest was the only ride here I ever truly enjoyed. I always liked that bit with the actress — what was she called? The Navigator? Had to be bound and dragged away each time she brought a crew home safe from outside spacetime itself. Now that can't have been an easy job."

To my surprise, he began to cry. This turn of events, combined with the glowing fungi, the phantoms on the walls, and his last few hints about what might still be hanging around this place, was not exactly doing wonders for my mood. "You have no idea," he choked out. "You have no *idea* what we went through for this place."

He was probably right about that. All the same, we rounded the fountain once again, this time heading for the Realm of the Stars.

4

We progressed through the remaining Realms — the Stars and Life — and finally turned our course toward the Realm of the Particle. William offered little more in the way of commentary. He answered my questions in monosyllables, wept softly, and strained against his restraints in an effort to cradle his head in his hands. At last I took pity on him and loosened the duct tape a touch. It wasn't mercy I felt — here, after all, sat the man who'd lied to my face in court; who'd drained our family's meager savings, and who still, even now, held back from giving me the answers I'd come for. But instinct told me he was ready to respond to a gentler touch. Stockholm Syndrome and all that. Build rapport. Keep him talking.

I broke down the door to the Scalar Portal simulator at the Realm of the Particle's entrance, releasing a blast of air so foul it sent me stumbling backwards, gagging and retching. A sludge like dark green mucus coated every surface — including the floor of the Portal room, where glowing bulbs grew so thickly they clogged the wheelchair's spokes, dragging us to a standstill. Good God, what was that stench? It smelled like week-old salmon wrapped in moldy cabbage. I slipped my shirt off and tied it around my face. It helped, a little.

"Do you remember?" I demanded of William as I freed the wheelchair from the weeds and pushed us toward the Scalar Portal's exit. "You stood right there on the platform, ranting about the secrets of the subatomic world. 'Do you feel the quavering?' you asked us, and we did. 'These are the vibrations that underlie all matter and energy in the universe! Prepare to enter the quantum realm!' That was the last thing you said before you opened that door. I'll always remember those words. They're the last words you spoke before I saw you again at the ride, hiding behind your machine while my dad disappeared. Is any of this ringing a bell yet? Hello?"

His head lolled on his chest, tongue dangling from his mouth, a thin trickle of drool slowly soaking his shirt. This was not good. I knelt next to the wheelchair and slapped him. Hard.

"Earth to Physicist!" I shouted. "We're not done here!" No response.

The glow around us increased so subtly that at first I failed to notice it. But gradually, almost imperceptibly, the floor and the walls all seemed alive with illumination of some unfamiliar color. The air pressure dropped even as the temperature and humidity rose. Rivulets of sweat ran down my forehead and neck.

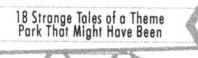

I raced the wheelchair around the curving sidewalks of the Realm of the Particle, dodging between oddly placed buildings whose cracked signs named them "The Outer Inn" and "The Everything in Particular General Store," navigating inward through the concentric rings toward the ride entrance at the Realm's opposite side. Back when the park was up and running, I remembered, these sidewalks had rotated according to some inscrutable clockwork rhythm. Now they lay inert, covered in fungoid slime like every other surface.

Somehow I forced the wheelchair through the fields of viscous growth, balancing William's limp form in his seat, trying to keep breathing through my mouth to avoid the worst of the rotten-garbage smell. We passed through the entrance of "Quantum Catastrophe" — the ride I'd re-ridden countless times since the day I lost my dad. I knew its every corner and curve by heart. Plodding through ankle-deep sludge, shoving William's chair forward with every step, I brought us to the platform where I'd watched him, in-character as the Physicist, manipulate the strange machine's dials and levers at the very moment my father vanished.

Clearing the sludge away with my sleeve revealed a surprisingly rust-free box, about the size of a washing machine. Its sleek mid-century design would've been right at home in a classic episode of *The Twilight Zone* — which was, appropriately enough, exactly where we seemed to find ourselves at this moment.

I gripped two of the levers and wrenched them upward and downward, trying combinations at random, watching for any movement on the gauges and dials arrayed across the machine's surface.

No response from the machine, but a startling one from William: "Please!" he cried, lurching upward in the chair. "I'm begging you, for God's sake, stop!"

I glared at him. "Tell me the sequence."

He threw back his head and moaned. "The sequence for *what*?" he cried. "Do you even understand what this device does?"

I rose to my full height, striding toward him with fists balled at my sides. "I would if you'd fucking *tell* me! That's all I want — just tell me how to undo what you did that day, and we can leave here and never come back." I heaved a deep sigh. "I'm tired of this. Aren't you? Just tell me how it works." I could feel hot rage rising in my chest. "Tell me the goddamn sequence or I swear I will break your face against this thing!"

"No!" he cried, lurching so hard he almost tipped the chair over. "Whatever you do, don't damage it. It has to remain intact."

My eyes narrowed. "Why?"

He gestured toward the machine. "Just push me closer."

"What are you going to do?" I demanded.

"I'm going to show you the damn sequence," he snapped. "Isn't that what you want? Now push me closer."

I nudged the chair into place. He cracked his knuckles — then, without another word, he demonstrated the sequence by motioning with his hands, his wrists still strapped to the chair arms: both the left and right levers had three stop positions where they could move left or right, like a gear shift. That provided for twelve positions. Then he walked me through it a second time while I stood at the console, following his instructions one step at a time: left up, shift, right down, shift, and onward through dozens of combinations, more than I'd imagined any human being could possibly remember—

—and then great engines began to grind.

5

I felt movement not only in this machine, but beneath the floor. Gears, belts, and pistons were waking from long slumber. The smell of burning petroleum rose from cracks beneath my feet, mercifully obscuring the worst of the rancid fungal odor. The glow around us increased until it was nearly blinding, as if something celestial grew.

From behind and beneath the rumbling, new sensations arose: the swell of excited chatter; the buttery sweetness of fresh popcorn. Shadow and swirling color chased each other across my vision. Gliding translucent shapes resolved into clear forms: strolling families, couples, schoolchildren, grandparents.

Despite everything, a smile spread across my face. Here, at last, was the magick. "Now you've done it!" cried the Physicist. "The machine has begun to churn. The nexus is forming. Here we are immortal, and the price is steep: we may dwell in this moment of singularity until the end of this universe, and beyond. That has always been the risk. That's why Teague grew alarmed."

His words hardly registered, because here, in front of me, stood my family: Dad, Mom, Regina — even a little version of me, in brown corduroys and green t-shirt. A moment frozen in time, like a washed-out Polaroid.

William and I remained on the platform. I watched helplessly as my family slipped beyond my reach. For the briefest moment, I imagined Dad glancing up and cocking his head, listening, as if he perceived some faint hint of my presence in a time forever out of step with his.

"Look!" I gasped. "This is when we lined up to board the ride." As I watched my father smile and hug my younger self, my heart seemed to leap from my chest. Tears welled up in my eyes. I'd never wanted anything so badly as I yearned to throw my arms around him, to hold him so tightly he'd never disappear again. "I just have to keep watching," I cried, "and I'll finally see—"

"No." William collapsed back into the chair, his body limp and heavy with exhaustion. "You will not. After everything I've told you, you still don't understand."

I kept my eyes locked on the images of my family, who were nearing the ride entrance area. "What don't I understand?" I demanded.

He heaved a deep sigh. "These images you see are not your father, or your mother, or your younger self. The machine cannot bring back the past; nothing can. All it does is summon ideas, patterns. Things that should stay where they belong."

A thunderous crack split the air as the gears beneath our feet squealed with exertion. The machine's levers shifted back and forth, up and down, in frantic rhythm. Somewhere a circuit tripped, and electricity crackled through the air, blinding me with its sudden brilliance.

A flash. A bang. Complete darkness.

6

The strange glow revealed an empty ride area. The bustling scenes, sounds and smells had vanished, and I found myself sprawled on my backside in a thick layer of reeking fungal sludge. William slumped in the wheelchair to my left.

But not everything had disappeared.

My eyes widened — because there stood dad, dressed just as he had that day: khaki slacks, a blue polo shirt and a white baseball cap. Confusion etched his face. His eyeglasses sat tilted on his nose.

"Dad?"

His eyes widened, too — not with excitement, I realized, but with horror. He raised his hands and gazed at them in revulsion. He ran his fingers over his face, his neck, his chest and stomach. His mouth yawned wide, and he screamed, piercing and raw: a wail neither human nor animal; a howl of denial so absolute it seemed to crack the sky asunder. I covered my ears, but could not escape the despair in his clouded eyes; a hollowness that sucked my life-breath mercilessly into the void between the stars. Even then I stretched out a hand to reach for my father — but as near as he appeared, I understood he was a trillion light-years away.

William had been right all along. This universe of ours is bounded for a reason, and we were never meant to reach beyond its borders. There are distances beyond distance; times beyond time — realms from which nothing and no one should ever return.

"William!" I shouted over the din of my father's shrieking. "I'll send him back! Please — oh God, I'm so sorry."

William only shook his head. After a moment he closed his eyes and began to weep.

The air itself seemed to crack into fractal shards, starting a cascade that tumbled into a howling nothing that disappeared below us. The pit shrieked, a mindless echo of my father's screams, as the sidewalk, the walls, the ceiling and even the sky itself shattered and crumpled, inhaled by the boundless emptiness outside of all things.

When at last the howling ceased, I saw that only the platform, the machine, and the three of us remained in our solid shapes. All else was empty, silent nothingness.

"Son?" My father's hand reached out and finally grasped mine.

Our palms laid flat. A shockwave flushed through me as I remembered that day in 1978, when we'd wandered off on our own, leaving Mom and Regina to their own adventures. As we'd wandered among the Realms, my dad's grip remained firm — not uncomfortable, but tight enough to make sure I wouldn't run off and get lost. "First, the Realm of the Cell," I'd insisted, as we compared the Realm's titanic microbes to the wonder's we'd seen through the microscope he'd bought for my tenth birthday. At one point he leaned down to my height, and said, "Now, son, don't get too excited. There's no such thing as magick, you know."

Wait. This was not my memory. That moment had never happened. Had it?

But now we were off again, hurrying to the Conservatory Parlour in the Realm of Time to enjoy scoops of fresh ice cream — me atop Dad's lap, my hand rubbing the light stubble of his cheek. Such warmth. The sun's glow. And yet when he met my gaze, his eyes were bottomless black pits, and he told me I was sick; that my behavior was hurting him and Mom, and even myself, though I couldn't understand how. By the time we met up with Mom and Regina in the Realm of the Particle, a strange malaise seemed to hover around all of us — a sense of emptiness and cold that I couldn't quite feel, but somehow knew was there, as one knows secret things in dreams.

"Where will you go?" I asked my father, wiping a tear from my cheek. "I need to know where you've been."

Dad smiled, his free hand casually swiping his combover back into place. "Nowhere," he said. "Outside of everything, where there is nothing." He ruffled my hair. "Now come on. Look, it's our turn to board."

7

And there we were, on that afternoon I'd replayed so many times in my memory: climbing into the ride vehicles, letting the lap bar descend and secure us in place, gliding serenely around that glimmering wall of multicolored lights to emerge into a darkened chamber of crackling blue orbs.

The Physicist stood right where he was supposed to be: behind the sleek machine, clad in his white lab coat, manipulating the levers in rhythms too complex to follow. He locked eyes with me as our vehicle neared his station, and held my gaze, his eyes sad and curious all at once. "Play it cool," he stage-whispered behind his hand. "Teague is watching."

My eyes widened — but before I had time to ask any of the dozen questions in my mind, the Physicist delicately released one of the levers and took a step back from the machine. Our car lurched forward into an absolute nothingness that somehow felt as safe and familiar as my own bedroom after I'd turned out the lights. A lone spotlight cast a harsh beam on me from above.

Younger me sat fidgeting nervously beside this thing that bore a vague resemblance to my father. Shards of the dilapidated park hung in the air, reflecting us like a trillion spider eyes.

Then he was gone. And so too was the visual memory. Around me, those shards reflected my father's face along mirrored hallways that spiraled into infinity, his countless mouths wide in unnumbered screams. My breath caught in my throat. I was choking. The thing that looked like my father rose to an impossible scale, dwarfing me like a swaying skyscraper. Its face melted and ran like wax. I hid my eyes, unable to my father like this. But this thing, of course, was not my father. I felt it writhe, turning gelatinous as its joints dissolved. Through its eyes and mouth I glimpsed a void utterly devoid of being: that same howling pit that ached to swallow our universe whole.

My breath returned, and I gulped lungfuls of air, screaming across the crumbling ruins of OmniPark until those screams turned to laughter. I was not of the void; I was here, *now*, in a universe that had been mine to explore all along. I screamed for sheer joy of screaming, for the ecstasy of drawing breath —

— but my screams, I realized, were no more than weak groans, like impotent screams within a nightmare. I was now gazing out at OmniPark from behind those crystalline shards, at a shattered moment stuck in time. Behind me, I felt the cold void, and the slurping things that dwelled there. The things that had taken my father's form.

Through a translucent membrane far below me, I discerned William's shadowy form. I cried out to him until the echoes of my hoarse bleating reverberated within the shards at a deafening volume, drowning out the dregs of my voice with their mocking chorus.

"William!" the infinite numerations of me cried one last time.

But he could not hear me — cannot hear me, and never will. Somewhere, in a time outside of time, his frail figure sits slumped in his wheelchair, plummeting eternally downward from nothing unto nothing.

And somewhere in the ruins of OmniPark, the sleek machine still ticks. The gears still grind, the pistons still pump, the belts still turn. If the world is fortunate, it will keep ticking for a long time to come.

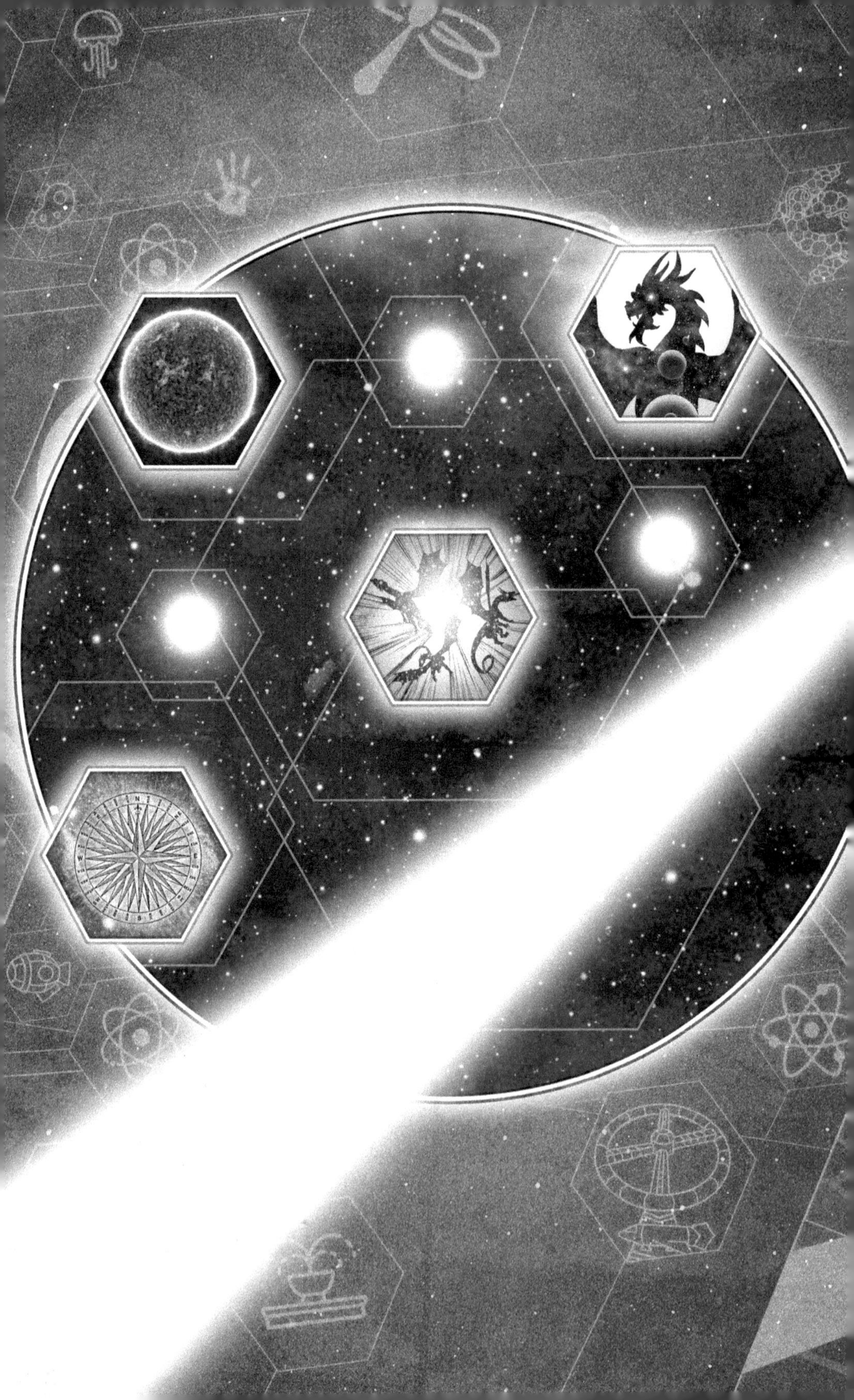

Here There Be Dragons

Katharine Gripp

"Come on, Alix!" Dare's voice echoed around the tiered concrete walls towering above us. The boxy 1970s architecture reflected their shout and tangled the words in eerie reverberations. Faded, psychedelic images covered the walls and floor, shining dizzyingly in my flashlight beam as I picked my way between heaps of broken furniture and derelict piles of trash. The high, narrow windows barely admitted the pale Texas moonlight, and the stale, humid air felt like a musty washcloth pressed against my face.

"Alix!" Dare hollered again, from further inside the abandoned edifice. I played my flashlight around the walls again, trying to figure out why the back of my neck was prickling in goosebumps despite the stifling heat. It was only when I realized no graffiti marked the walls of the abandoned building that I shivered. The park had closed, what — twenty years ago? A place like this should be covered in layers of artwork and tags. This wasn't right. Why was I here again?

"Alix!"

Oh, right. Because love makes you do stupid shit.

I sighed and followed Dare's voice through the dim, cavernous building. The cracked concrete floor with its piles of forgotten rubbish and clusters of long-dead weeds stretched out into the shadows beyond my flashlight's beam like a petrified graveyard. Strange shapes loomed out of the darkness ahead of me: a faded iron submarine, a 1950s-style rocket ship, two plaster mammoth tusks crossed in an arch. What had Dare gotten me into this time?

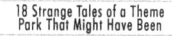

"Isn't this place rad?" Dare's head popped over the crumbling lip of a fountain that sprawled in the middle of this monumental ghost of a pavilion. I could see the faint gleam of their grin in the dusty moonlight.

"It creeps me out," I called back, picking my way toward them around a brown patch of prickly sandbur. "Can we just get this over with?"

"Aw, come on, don't you want to do a little exploring while we're here?" Dare propped their elbows on the fountain rim and waggled their eyebrows suggestively at me. "There are some weird stories about the guy who founded this place. No telling what we might find. Evidence of a secret sex cult? The grisly remains of sacrifices to the theme park gods? The descendants of mutant rats who escaped experimentation and are planning to take over the world?"

I snorted with suppressed laughter. "You watch too many horror movies." I leaned against the concrete lip of the fountain next to them and peered into the shallow bowl. The scariest creatures here were probably the mosquitoes breeding in the puddle of stagnant water at its bottom. "I thought we came here to shoot your video."

"That doesn't mean we can't have a little fun first," Dare murmured, nudging their elbows next to mine and nuzzling their nose into my ear. Despite myself, I felt my heartbeat quicken, my breathing grow shallower, and the air between us crackle with tension. Slowly I raised a hand to the back of their head, feeling the softness of their newly buzzed undercut against my palm as our foreheads pressed together. I pulled their lips to mine, loving the feeling of their skin heating against me, the teasing, the wanting. Before I pulled away, I buried my hand in the shaggy flop of hair at the top of their head, gripping hard enough to make them gasp as we parted. Their eyes sparkled in the moonlight, and I was pleased to note that their breath was as ragged as my own. *This* was why I would follow Dare anywhere.

They grinned as though they could hear my thoughts. "Five minutes?" they pleaded. "I just want to take a quick little look around. See if there's a really awesome place to film."

"Isn't a giant concrete bowl perfect for skateboarding?" I asked. "Why not just do it here?"

They flipped their board over the rim of the empty fountain and jumped down after it, landing next to me. "Well, yeah, but I've done that before. My fans want to see something new and exciting. You know, a time machine, animatronic dinosaurs, an exclusive look into the LSD-fueled playground that used to be OmniPark." I snorted. Our video collabs had so far resulted in mild internet fame, but Dare was always looking for more.

"Fine, five minutes," I said. "But I get veto power if I don't like the spot you choose."

"Thanks, babe!" they gushed, then threw an arm around my neck and kissed me sloppily on the cheek. I ducked out of their hold, fighting off a smile. They hopped on their board and pushed off toward the submarine, weaving around the maze of prickly weeds thrusting up through the concrete.

I followed more slowly, breathing in the silence and stillness that filled the darkness of the empty pavilion in an attempt to calm my nerves, which kept spiking like the needle on a seismograph. I reminded myself I had nothing to be afraid of in this place but asbestos and ghost stories. And possibly rats (although I doubted they were mutants).

Dare has always been the brave one. But one of the things I love about them is how they help me pretend to be braver. They do things like breaking into an abandoned theme park on a moonlit night — and even though I would never dream of doing that on my own, I'll follow them to film their board tricks so that the whole world (or at least their 5,000 YouTube subscribers) can see how awesome they are. When I'm with Dare, the thrill of sharing an adventure with them eclipses my anxiety.

That doesn't mean my anxiety wasn't trying really, really hard to get my attention. As I walked into the old, rusted submarine incongruously rising out of the cracked concrete floor, my pulse thrummed in my ears, and the flashlight in my trembling hand caused the black shadows to jump and quiver.

Dare had entered the door set into the submarine's curved side and propped it open with a dented metal trash can. I stepped across it and caught up with them in the chamber beyond the door, which was designed to look like a small submersible, although I wouldn't have trusted it anywhere near the ocean. Portholes filled with tubes like plastic prison bars were framed by warped brown water stains. The effects of bubbles and light that had once convinced gullible tourists they were descending beneath the water now looked more like broken teeth in a time-worn face. My anxiety bubbled higher as even the faint dregs of moonlight that managed to pierce the gloom of the pavilion behind us succumbed to the smothering darkness of the enclosed space. The sooner I could grab some footage of Dare, the sooner we could get out of this place, and the sooner we'd be snuggled down in their bed, reliving another adventure safely caught on camera.

Dare climbed over the splintered remnants of what looked like theater seats and heaved open another door at the opposite end of the room. Its rusted hinges screamed in protest, a noise that felt like fingernails scraping down the chalkboard of my spine. I followed them quickly through the door into a mercifully larger and brighter room.

"This place is *awesome*!" Dare exclaimed, their voice echoing off the jumbled array of overflowing instruments. Moonlight stole in through jagged arches of broken glass high above us and dripped across the dusty checkerboard floor. No graffiti marred these walls either, and even though the windows above us were broken, no shards of glass glittered on the smooth black-and-white tiled floor.

The sheer volume of it all was overwhelming — it looked like the aftermath of an explosion at a steampunk con. Clocks of all shapes and sizes lay silent behind their cracked and dirty faces, their hands and gears dangling drunkenly down from rotted casings. A table cluttered with nautical instruments had subsided onto a platform whose burgundy carpet had long ago been colonized by mold and mildew. The tarnished metal tubes of a pipe organ sagged against each other at uncomfortable angles. But it was all just set dressing — a couple of the larger pieces of impedimenta had fallen down, revealing nothing but pale, empty patches of drywall behind them. A twisting spiral staircase whose steps had long ago rusted away into copper-colored dust rose upward to nothing.

"It's a little small for skateboarding," I said, looking around the room with a critical videographer's eye. Despite the broken windows, the air felt heavy, old, and tainted, and I still felt the encroaching darkness at my back.

"You're right," Dare replied, kicking their board up and tucking it under their arm. "Let's see what's through here." I grabbed their free hand as they headed into the dark hallway on the far side of the room. They squeezed it tightly and led me onward.

We entered a room filled with maps, faded and peeling off the walls or rolled tightly into tubes, the paper and cardstock yellowed with age, the blues and greens of printed oceans and islands virtually indistinguishable. Old flyers and park maps littered the floor, advertising long-defunct attractions: "See the Great Cetus, Terror of the Deep!" "Grab a bite to eat at the Captain's Table!" "Mariana Trench Dive Schedule (Limit 32 guests per ride)." I played my flashlight over a giant poster hanging above an old cash register whose broken, empty drawer hung open like a hungry mouth. One corner of the large map crumpled and drooped away from the wall, and an ugly brown watermark stained the rest of it. *Here there be dragons*, it read in faded black ink, next to a squiggle that was probably meant to be a sea serpent.

Beyond the map room was a curving hallway containing the wreckage of more steampunk scenery. Empty, cracked glass tanks threw back the refracted beam of my flashlight from their curved sides. Giant metal coils loomed beside them, and panels covered in a multitude of unnecessary gears, levers, and buttons hulked silently on either side of us, crisscrossed by a maze of empty pipes. The metal hallway floor was tilted at odd, unexpected angles beneath our feet, although it seemed sturdy enough as our footsteps rang out on the rusted walkway. The hairs on the back of my neck were standing at alert again, and my breath rasped oddly as I inhaled the stale, musty air.

"I don't think we'll find a good filming location in here," I whispered. There was no logical reason for me to whisper, but something about the darkness pressing in on me made me feel like I needed to. "Let's head back and just film it in the fountain. I'll take some footage of all this weird junk on the way out so people know where you are."

"I just want to see what's through here," Dare cajoled, guiding me toward a closed door at the end of the hallway. I winced at the non-whisper volume of their voice, which sounded as loud as fireworks in this dead place.

We pushed open the heavy double doors together, then stopped and gazed upward, eyes wide with astonishment. We stood in what looked like the middle of a colossal fishbowl, the moonlight glowing through murky green water surrounding its curving walls.

I'd forgotten about the door; it clanged shut behind us, and I whirled and shrieked before I could stop myself, the sound echoing from the Plexiglas walls around us. Dare laughed and squeezed my hand again, then leaned against the metal bar of the door until it squealed open a few inches. "See, in a horror movie, the door would have locked behind us," they said, smiling reassuringly. I sighed — whether in relief or annoyance I wasn't quite sure — willing my heart to return to its normal rhythm. I quickly tugged Dare to me, and buried my head beneath their chin — just for a second, for a small moment of safety and warmth as I regained my composure with their arms wrapped comfortingly around me. Then I let them go, fumbling the lens cover off my camera.

"Let's get this over with then," I whispered, resigned. "It's the perfect spot, right?"

"Totally!" Dare yelped with joy, dropping their board and hopping on it to roll across the empty space, staring gleefully up at the structure around us.

It was an empty, circular room, entirely made of thick plates of Plexiglas — like the fish bowl it had reminded me of, but inside-out: a bubble of air surrounded by water. We stood on a flat, clear platform in the middle of the transparent globe. Once, the clean blue waters of the aquarium must have pressed against its walls, making the OmniPark tourists feel as though they were submerged in the open ocean. But the sun had leached the moisture from the massive tank over the years, and the remaining water swirled thick and green with algae. It sloshed lazily two-thirds of the way up the rounded walls, leaving a thick, scummy residue clouding the glass.

Dare was already boarding back and forth across the floor, rolling up the curved walls of the inside-out aquarium at either end, gaining momentum with each pass. I stayed back near the door and watched them through the lens of my camera, manually adjusting the lighting and focus, searching for the best angle to capture their dark form against the expanse of the moonlit, algae-coated tank. It *was* the perfect filming spot; Dare's image in my viewscreen looked like some alien fish gracefully swimming through the waters of a strange sea. I hunkered down and found an angle where the floor reflected the murky moonlight, and Dare's shadow-image copied their tricks in its transparent mirror. My anxiety eased a little as I focused on the specifics of light, angle, and motion — riding their skateboard was Dare's art; capturing it on camera was mine.

Dare crested higher and higher up the walls, the rumbling of their wheels on the thick panes drumming through the empty chamber. I tried to imagine the soundtrack I'd mix for this video — something hard and driving like the skateboard wheels clattering against the transparent floor? Or dreamy and ominous like the water looming behind the glass? The luminous green sway of the water framed the shot like a frozen tidal wave waiting to crash down on Dare's defiant silhouette floating and flipping across the empty room.

I couldn't get the light quite right; patches of darkness kept creeping in on the edges of the screen. I pulled my eye away from the camera and examined the lens for smudges or scratches. Maybe a gnat had flown into it — it wouldn't be the first time.

But the lens looked clean. I held my camera in my hands and glanced back up at Dare, readjusting the settings to capture them racing across the smooth clear floor, jumping and twisting in the air at every pass. A shadow darkened a corner of the tank behind them, briefly blotting out a patch of the muddy green moonlight.

I blinked, frowning. Had I imagined it? But no: another fragment of darkness snaked along the bottom of the globe before it, too, disappeared.

I shivered, suddenly aware of how damp and dank this room felt in contrast to the warm night outside. Dark patches of mildew sprouted from the floor and the walls, and I suddenly wondered about the integrity of a neglected fifty-year-old glass ball surrounded by literal tons of water. Another shadow, larger, loomed fuzzily in the dark green water behind Dare, then vanished back into the depths before I could discern its shape. The scummy waterline near the top of the room sloshed in waves against the panes.

This tank must once have teemed with all kinds of sea creatures: fish, stingrays, maybe even sharks. If I'd thought about it at all, I'd have assumed they were taken to live in some other aquarium when the theme park closed twenty years ago — but I hadn't thought about it. What if the things that lived in these tanks had been left here to eat each other, to die when the hot sun and the blooming algae rendered their habitat uninhabitable?

And what if some of them had survived?

More shadows darted through the water, behind and below us in our bubble, the closed door behind me our only tether to the rest of the dry, safe world. Dare was oblivious, lost in the joy of speed and precision as they drifted back and forth across the wide, clear bowl. The shadows clustered especially thickly where the wheels of their board scraped the curving walls, the growing patches of darkness smothering the drowned green moonlight. The sloshing waves at the top of the tank grew more tumultuous; the back of my neck felt icy cold, and I could feel the hairs on my arms sticking straight up like porcupine quills.

Maybe it was just my anxiety, or maybe some deep instinct had awakened in me; a long-forgotten dread evolved to keep my tiny mammal ancestors alive in a world of predators. Either way, the feeling was unmistakable. Something was coming.

"Dare…" I whispered, my fear making their name freeze in my throat. The shadows reached higher up the murky green walls. Dare's wheels clattered on the sides of the tank. The water beneath them was black as tar. They hadn't heard me.

"Dare," I tried again, after clearing my throat. Their name felt dry and sticky in my mouth, and still too quiet. My instincts screamed at me to run away, as quickly and quietly as I could, but my concern for Dare rooted me to the spot.

A muffled *thump* sent a vibration through the glass beneath my feet; one of the shadows had crashed against the wall. It slipped along the coating of algae, then slid away, taking some of the vegetation with it and leaving a swirl of torn greenery fluttering in its wake. It only lasted a moment, but that was long enough for me to glimpse something sleek and shiny, with rows of hungry pink suckers embedded in its flesh. As it disappeared back into gloom, I noticed a crack at the point where it had slammed against the glass wall. A spiderweb of thin white lines now spread from a joint between two panes.

Another jarring thump, and another — more sleek ropes of slime and muscle, covered in bulbous suckers, seeking a way to break open our glass room like a clam shell. "Dare!" I screamed, finally finding my voice,

"We have to go *now!*" They heard me this time, startled out of a midair leap, missing their landing and crashing heavily to the smooth floor, their board shooting out from under them and striking the cracked pane. The spiderweb of fractures grew larger, and I thought I could hear trickling water above the sound of the continued assaults on the sphere.

"Alix, what the hell?" they sputtered as I grabbed their wrist and attempted to haul them toward the door. They resisted, trying to pull out of my grasp, and tugged me around when I wouldn't let go. "What's wrong?"

Fear had me in its grip like a tentacle around my throat, and I could barely speak. "Look," I choked, pointing toward the darkest shadow, now surrounded by writhing, ropy arms banging on the walls of the tank. Dare turned, their expression slipping from annoyance to bewilderment to a growing terror that matched mine. For a moment, a nightmare face appeared in the dark water, cold black eyes like oil wells glaring at us above a gnashing, serrated beak... and then it disappeared again behind a roiling cloud of algae.

The waves above us now tossed like the ocean in a hurricane as the creature continued to bash against the sides of the tank. "You win! Let's go!" Dare shouted, stooping to pick up their board and grabbing me by the hand. I felt the floor buckle as we dashed toward the doors, and an ominous thunder filled my ears — the tank had been breached. A wave of foamy, putrid water washed around my ankles. I slipped and almost landed on my kees on the hard floor, but Dare's firm grasp kept me upright.

Please let it open, please let it open, please let it open, I prayed as we splashed and slid toward the door. We threw our weight against it, and it stuck for a heart-stopping moment. I muttered another prayer as we slammed against it, harder, and this time it burst open. Stumbling down the unevenly-floored hallway with its hulking useless machinery, past the map room — a deafening roar, a crack like the world splitting apart, and a tidal wave of dirty green water swept us off our feet. I lost Dare's hand in the rush. I tumbled head-over-heels, trying to breathe, catching glimpses of a writhing tendrils of mottled flesh probing through the hallway after us.

The flood finally dissipated enough to dump me to the floor, where I coughed up all the rancid water I couldn't help but swallow in the tumult. I spluttered and gagged on the black and white checked floor of the room with the high broken windows, amazed that I'd escaped a serious head wound. The moonlight that before had seemed so dull now nearly blinded me as it glittered off the derelict steampunk scenery littered in even more disarray across the room. My camera clattered in front of me on its strap, waterlogged and ruined.

My mind cleared as my lungs fought for oxygen. I was, shockingly, still alive — but where was Dare? I'd lost them in the flood — and then what?

A touch on my back made me yelp in surprise. I jerked around to see Dare, my brave foolhardy love, whole and alive. But their eyes were hollow and haunted, and reflected my own horror back at me. Without a word we ran for the door that opened into the pavilion, slipping on the muck that sloshed across the floor of the tiny submersible entryway.

We clattered over the upended garbage can, kicking it out of the way and letting the submarine door slam behind us. Our wet footprints left a splotchy brown trail as we raced across the dirty floor of the pavilion, the slapping echoes of our feet sending fear lancing up my spine with every splash. The floor seemed miles wide as we passed the fountain at its center. The tall, tiered cliffs of the towering walls loomed above us as we dodged piles of detritus like ship-sinking reefs in a sea of shadows.

At last we emerged into the night, beyond the sagging chain-link fence meant to keep trespassers like us out. We tumbled into the cab of Dare's truck, heedless of our soaking clothes. I felt a stab of fresh panic as Dare fumbled for their keychain—what if they'd lost it in the flood? But the sharp jangle of their keys as they pulled them from a safely zipped pocket flooded me with relief. The rumble of the engine beneath us as the ignition turned was a comforting, familiar growl.

We peeled away in a plume of dust that obscured the ruin of OmniPark in the rearview mirrors. I'd be happy if I never saw it again.

As we reached the highway, the straight, quiet lines of the road stretched in front of us, allowing my heartbeat to slow and calm. We sped westward at 70 miles an hour, my breathing growing more even with every mile we put between us and the thing in that tank. We rolled down the windows, letting the warm night breeze whisk away the foul dampness that clung to our skin and clothes as the wind whipped and tore at our dripping hair. I inhaled deeply, more grateful for every breath than I could've imagined before tonight.

After a few minutes, Dare unstuck their white-knuckled hand from the steering wheel and held it out to me across the center console. I slipped my fingers between theirs — shaking, but reassured by the warmth in their grip. Keeping their eyes on the empty road, they squeezed my hand tightly, then cleared their throat.

"Well, I guess I owe you a new camera," they said. I uttered a strangled sound that could have been a laugh, and felt a tightness in my chest relax, like a clenched fist uncurling.

"Yeah, I guess you do," I managed to shout over the sound of the wind snatching at my hair. It could have been my body that ended up broken and lifeless on that flooded floor instead of just my camera. I sighed and leaned my head on Dare's shoulder, despite the awkward angle of our hands clasped on the console between us. They briefly nuzzled their nose against the top of my head.

"Don't worry," they murmured, and I heard it more through my cheek pressed against the bones of their shoulder than over the sounds of the highway wind in my ears. I sat up and searched their face, hoping to see some reassurance that they really believed there was nothing to worry about, that we'd left the horror of that monstrosity behind us. But they just smiled their mischievous smile, darting a glance at me before turning back to the road ahead.

I knew that look. They were already looking forward to the next adventure, the newest challenge, and daring me to join in.

"Next time," they said, with that smile in their voice, "will be better."

*Original postcard of the OmniPark monorail — kept
framed in Teague's office as part of his collection.*

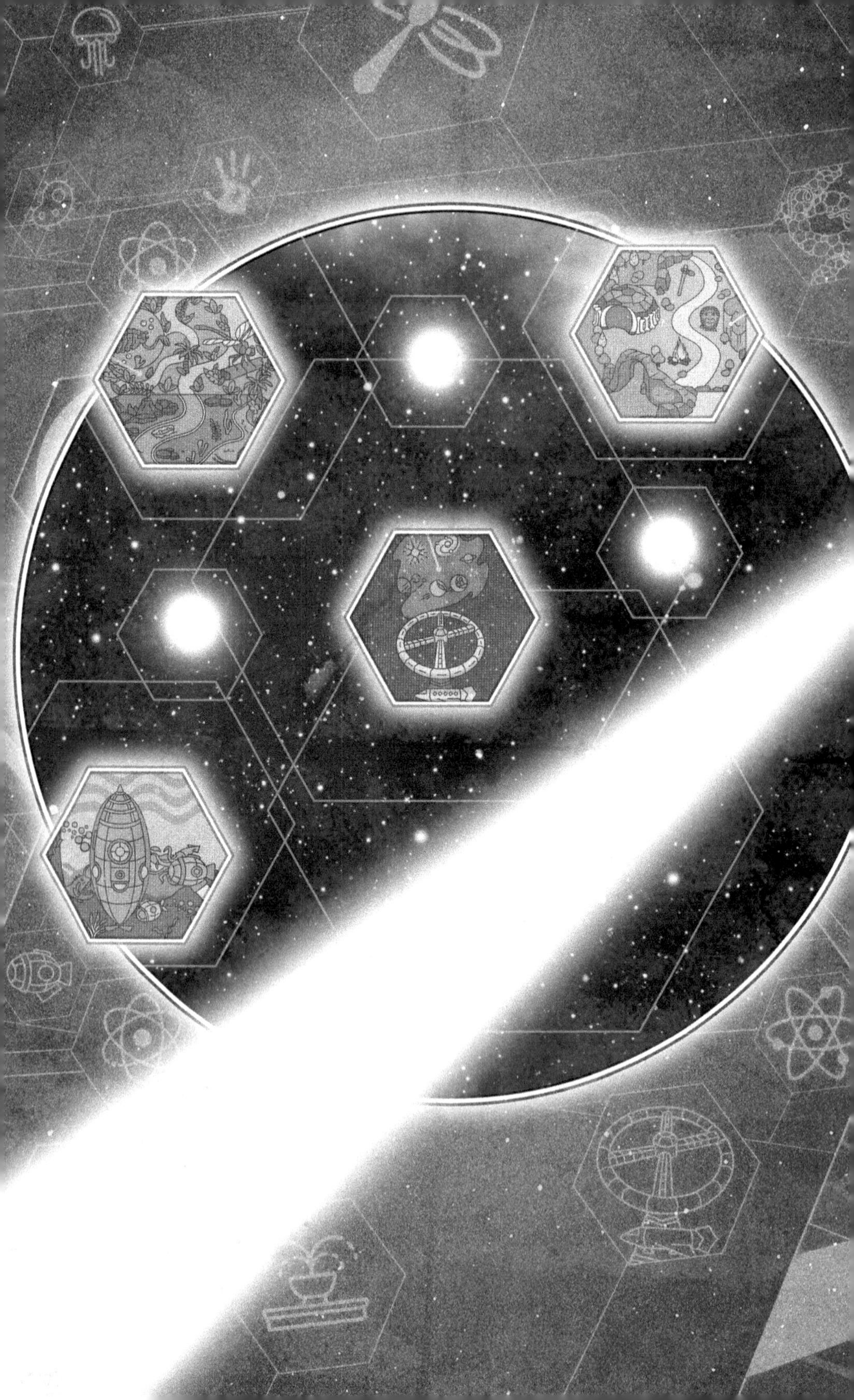

The Ultimate Technosopher's Guide

Anna Maloney

3/14/1997

    Hello! First post! I have to introduce myself! I'm new to GeoCities, but it's the perfect place to journal about OmniPark! I'm Robin Alegria, and welcome to my page. It's all about my favorite place in the world, OmniPark. I'll do a little introduction to the park for people who've never been!

    OmniPark is a theme park in Odessa, Texas — where I live! — founded by oil billionaire Dalton M. Teague (who also has a PhD)! He took seven whole years to explore the world and get ideas for OmniPark, which opened in 1977, when I was five. OmniPark is similar to EPCOT in Florida. It has seven Realms, each themed to a different area of history or science. Both, really. Sometimes one more than the other. There's Life, Cell, Deep (that's about the oceans), Stars, Man, Particle, and Time. The middle of the park has the OmniColor Fountain, but originally it was the Realm Between the Realms, where company parties were held. For a season it was the Wild World of Life ride, which they unfortunately removed because everyone complained about it. I rode that ride a lot during the few weeks it was open, even though it was scary, because I like everything OmniPark makes. The fountain is cool, though.

    I should probably talk a little about me, too. I was born here, in 1972. Now I'm 25. OmniPark opened in 1977, and I've gone to it since then. We got season passes in 1978 onwards and Dad took me on Fridays after school, and sometimes on the weekend. At 7, they started letting me go on my own, and I went almost every day after school. Other kids liked it too, but not as much as me. They thought I was kinda weird for going and knowing so much, but it's the best place on Earth! Why wouldn't I wanna know everything about it?

So yeah. I've been a regular basically since it opened! I still go around once a week. I'm a librarian at the Ector County Library here. It's not six figures, but it's enough to get my special annual pass, which includes parking, discounts on food and merchandise, and late access to the park. OmniPark's open from 8 AM to 9 PM, but with my Platinum Pass, I can stay until 10 PM. Some nights I have that hour all to myself!

So yeah! I'm going to the park in two days, so I'll write about it then. See you soon!

3/16/1997

Hello everyone! I went to OmniPark today! It's around 11 pm right now, because I stayed until 10 even though I have work tomorrow. I'm thinking of asking to change shifts so that instead of having weekends off I have two weekdays off, because there will be less people at the park when I'm there. Surely someone wants weekends off that doesn't have them right now. We close at 6 pm, so I can still go to the park on weekends if I want.

Today I was at the Realm of the Particle. I really like it because it makes you think, and looks cool. It's set up to resemble an atom with electron shells, with concentric circular paths, and the ride in the center. There's a shop in the outermost area, the Outer Shell, and the middle ring, (not the center ring) has the Outer Inn, which is a restaurant. Sometimes the shop and restaurant move, because of the uncertainty principle. In particle physics it's where you never know both the speed and location of a subatomic particle. So, you don't know exactly where things might be. Isn't that neat? The maps of Particle don't specify locations (only areas things might be), whereas all other Realms have specific locations of their restaurant, ride, and themed explorable area.

It's funny, because other things move, too, not just in Particle. OmniPark does renovations, obviously. It's been open twenty years. Announced renovations mean certain areas of certain Realms close until they're done. But there are many other, smaller, unannounced renovations that happen overnight. Things move, plants are replaced, stuff like that. Sometimes stores and restaurants shift. Some of it's simple stuff, but some must take lots of work to do in one night. The only Realm where they don't do that anymore is Time, which got sidelined since they gave it this weird "update" to make it more child friendly. More about that later, today's post is about the Particle!

Not much else to say, actually. The ride, Quantum Catastrophe, is fun. I checked the Everything in Particular General Store, but they haven't added any merchandise I don't have. I have all the merch from every shop. I like documenting everything! That's why I'm a librarian.

I'll probably go back next Saturday, unless I can change my hours, but I'll try to update this page before then. Oh, also, I learnt about guestbooks you can sign to signify you saw my page. There's a link to it on the side! Sign my guestbook!! See you in the next post!

3/17/1997

I didn't expect to update the very next day, but I'm so excited to have this page! Nobody signed my guestbook yet, but maybe everyone's shy. I'll keep this post relatively short, since I'm not visiting the park today.

Probably common questions: Yes, the employees (called Realm Ambassadors) usually know me! They probably think I'm weird for spending so much time there, but they're friendly. Every restaurant knows my regular orders, and usually each Realm's gift shop clerk lets me know when they get new stock I probably don't have. Also, don't read this as bragging, but I know more about OmniPark than them. Ambassadors do immersion training, but they're only trained to know what's necessary. They don't know deep lore or answers to any questions I wouldn't know.

You might be curious why I'm working as a librarian and not for OmniPark — I've tried before, but never got approved. I asked some people hired when I applied and apparently someone recognized my resume photograph as a regular for so long and said something about not wanting to ruin my fantasy? I'm an adult now, and I love the park, but there's stuff I could only learn more about if I worked there. But they've never given me a call back, and you can't exactly find the hiring manager as a park guest, so whatever. The library is a good job.

So yeah! My next post will probably be next time I go! So, see you in my next post! Sign my guestbook!!

3/22/1997

Hello everyone! I went to the park today. It's Saturday, so it was busy! I requested new hours, so starting next month, my days off are Tuesday and Thursdays. Apparently, several people wanted to switch with me to have weekends off! "T" days are usually low numbers, especially in the middle of the day when people are at work or school.

Today I was in Realm of the Stars. Stars is probably the most visually stunning Realm in the park! You get in by getting on a simulation of a rocket that "launches" you to the main part of the Realm, as it's a space station! If any of you are interested in space, this is definitely the Realm for you. It's shaped like a ring, and the walls are all screens that look like windows showing space, full of stars and planets. It's really well done! Don't look too closely and it's easy not to break your immersion. Other "windows" show stuff inside the spaceship, like vegetable gardens and labs.

Paths go to the middle of the station, where the shop, ride, and restaurant are: Orbit One Central, Nebula Quest, and Cosmonaut Café. The best part of this area are the interactive stations where you play with new technology. These update pretty regularly! Tech is always evolving, after all. They get moved around a lot and replaced whenever something is too out of date.

Nebula Quest is about going on a mission to find a nebula the station had photographed but then disappeared, hosted by the Navigator, by taking hyperspace jumps to different places in space. Originally the Navigator was kinda crazy, and kept moving further away from Earth as we looked for the missing nebula, until eventually she got a read on it from really far away. Then she told everyone we weren't just moving in space, but in time, and millions of years had passed so maybe Earth was gone. Fun! She was pretty insane at that point. She took us to places we'd already been, which looked way different as so much time passed. Eventually she decided to try and get us back by going through a black hole, escaping the universe, and running along the curve of spacetime back to our year. Then you ended up back on planet Earth in the proper time and you heard the Navigator dragged away while yelling about seeing time from the outside as you left the ride. A great line she said right before the black hole was, "Either we're obliterated, or we become gods!" It was a good ride, unless you were a physicist, apparently. The ride changed in 1989 because several scientists complained it was scientifically inaccurate.

The update removed all the time elements, so you only jump through space, without leaving the universe. Which totally removes the point of the ride, by the way! (I still like the ride though) They made the Navigator end up unhinged, but at one point she made it clear that the point of the ride is. WAS. That everything is always changing, and that nothing is forever — not even Earth, or galaxies, or the entire universe — except the concept of change itself. Everything was different except us as we went through time, even things that seem like they'll never change like Earth. Dalton Teague has this huge idea that everything is in flux, and I secretly think he built the park to help people to understand that, to get something more out of their visits than just thrills and souvenirs.

Over my time going to OmniPark, I've been slowly getting a better and better idea of his idea for the park, and what Dalton wants it to be. Like Walt Disney and EPCOT, it's meant to be more than just a park. It's easy to say that his "something more" was educating people as he entertained them, which is also true. I mean, the motto of the park is "This universe is yours to explore," and every Realm has inescapable themes of education in them. But there's more to it, an underlying theme of change and evolution. It's a little less obvious in Realms like the Cell and the Deep, but every Realm tries to get the park guests to gain this higher level of understanding of the world beyond just the factual information presented. I mean, every single Realm (except Time now, but every single Realm pre-renovation) is constantly being given minor updates, moving things around, slowly changing over time unofficially.

Next time I go, I'll spend the day in Time. Time is pretty worse for wear after the update, and most people pass on going on its ride if they've already done it unless they have little kids, but you can still catch elements of the old ride, which makes me nostalgic. Plus, I can't really bring myself to hate anything they make, even if I think it's worse than it used to be. Bye for now! Sign my guestbook!

4/1/1997

My heart's still racing. I must believe it was real. Even the attendant didn't see it, but I DID! Nobody ever believes me about stuff like this, but I'm not crazy!

I said I would spend all day in Time next chance I got last post, which was nine days ago. This was my first Tuesday off, and I'd been so busy until today that today was the first chance I got to go since then. There was basically nobody in the park because it's a Tuesday in April when schools are still in session.

This is important. The rides in Time and Stars are the ones majorly renovated, but Time's was way bigger. Originally there was no Pterry the Pterodactyl, and the ride was longer and had a lot more scenes and monsters. But in 1991 the ride was cleaned out and they put in Pterry, removing several parts of the ride, unlike Stars, where Nebula Quest's actual ride was mostly unchanged aside from a few effects and being slightly shortened. In Time, the track was made significantly shorter to remove show scenes. When you ride it, you can still see stuff like old Morlock technology (a species in the original ride) and original track through the red tunnels to the final show scenes where, originally, you were rapidly going back in time and forced into a singularity before the time engine reactivated and brought you back to the present, are still visible.

So the update, Pterry's Time Tunnel, is a kiddie version that is overall a letdown from the original, but apparently OmniPark aren't bowing to criticism like they did with Nebula Quest, and I still ride it sometimes because I can't bring myself to hate something OmniPark made. But it's an inferior ride. People rarely ride it if they haven't been on before, and today was no exception. After stopping in the sitting room when the hour changed to see the clocks all chime and checked the gift shop for any new merch (none) I got on the ride alone. I was one of three guests in the Realm of Time anyway, and the other two were a mother and child too young to be in public school. They were distracted in the sitting room (the child really liked clocks) so I wasn't surprised to be the only one on the ride. What I was surprised about was what the ride was.

I got on the ride vehicle, which still resembles an H.G. Wells time machine because Pterry takes you through time, and then everything darkened, and the ride started into the first scene. But the first scene did not include the start of Pterry's unending dialogue, it started with a man's voice. The familiar voice I hadn't heard in 6 years — the Inventor. I was ecstatic! Had they decided to remove Pterry and bring back the Inventor to some degree? There had been no maintenance on Pterry's Time Tunnel recently, but it didn't really need maintenance to replace voice recordings if the Inventor was only joining as a narrator, or even to replace graphics used in the ride if films just needed to be replaced. That could be done overnight! So, I was super excited! My eyes were bugged out, absorbing as much as possible!

That was not what happened. Because his dialogue continued just as I'd remembered it, and then, after the first time jump scene — where the effects seemed to be the old laser ones instead of the current CGI — my jaw dropped. I was in the distant future of Texas, and the Eloi animatronics were there. No Pterry. And as it continued, the Morlock animatronics were there! They'd been removed in the renovation, but here they were, looking good! That's when I realised the ride was the same as it was pre-revamp. Morlocks, the giant mantis shrimp, the machine malfunction… before I knew it, the track was turning into the section that had been made inaccessible in the Pterry version, through those red tunnels, into the final show scenes. All around me were projections and models showing time going in reverse, taking us through the abandoned scenes, until finally, I was about to go to whatever preceded the Big Bang — and then, like it had always done before Pterry, the time engine reactivated and the ride vehicle completed the circuit and ended at the same room where Pterry's ended, with the Inventor apologizing for us almost being written out of existence.

When I tell you I was white knuckled! The lights dimmed to darkness, and when they brightened, the ride attendant was at my side, asking why I hadn't left the ride vehicle yet. She recognised me as a regular, and was concerned. I must have looked bad, because she immediately helped me out and brought me into the ride's control room to breathe, asking if the vehicle had shocked me or something. I was trying to catch up mentally and said it hadn't… her shirt was Pterry themed, and here, in the control room, I could see the security feeds of different areas of the ride. It was still Pterry's Time Tunnel.

I asked her over and over again if she'd seen the change or if they'd added the Inventor back, but she said no. In fact, she kept implying (as politely as she could) that maybe something was wrong with me. Wrong with ME. But I saw it! She didn't believe me, and walked me to the Realm's employee break room. She had me lie down, gave me aspirin, and went off to get water because she thought I was dehydrated. I was there for some time, staring at the ceiling, thinking about how there was absolutely no way in hell they brought the original ride back in only nine days. Especially if they were only working at night. It took months for the Time Machine to reopen as Pterry's Time Tunnel!

Once she let me, I went back on the ride so many times I lost count. The first time the mother and kid finally got on, and after it was just me again. But it was always Pterry's Time Tunnel. When I got off the last time the ride attendant gave me a sympathetic look and told me I should go home and sleep.

It must sound like I imagined it, but I didn't. It was real. I have to get a better look. I'll update again soon.

4/9/1997

I had work today, but could barely focus. I spent all day doing reshelving work so I could just think — it's mindless once you know the Dewey Decimal system. It's very late. Technically it's already the 10th, but I don't work on Thursdays anymore, so it doesn't matter.

Maybe I shouldn't say this somewhere I put my name, but there's nobody else to tell. I snuck into OmniPark. I went through one of the camera blind spots wearing all black so they couldn't get my features, and I walked so my car wouldn't be on any cameras. I took a circuitous route, so I think I'm safe from them tracking me back home. I knew exactly where to go, and have a good idea where all the cameras face, just from observing the park. Who knew going so often would help with something like this? My hands are still shaking.

I went straight to Time. I know I must have ended up on some cameras, but none of the few employees around saw me or came to investigate. I would have worn their uniform, but again, they never let me work here, so I didn't have one. I went to Pterry's Time Tunnel, got onto the track, and headed into the ride. It's surreal looking at a ride in the dark from a new angle than you've seen your whole life. It was dark, but I wasn't gonna use my flashlight where cameras might see. From being in the control room yesterday, I know there are no cameras in the unused portion of the ride.

I made my way in, and once I was sure I wasn't on film, I turned my flashlight on. It's not a strong flashlight, because then the cameras would be able to pick up light from the abandoned portion of the ride. I hope nobody checks the tapes before they rewrite them. Anyway. I made it, and was in the abandoned show scenes. I don't know what I was expecting, but because nobody can see this part of the ride while on Pterry's, everything was still there. The models, the old projectors, everything. Just off.

Well. Almost everything. With the old ride fresh in my memory, I realised something WAS missing. Something small, easy to miss, especially if all I had to go on were memories from over six years ago. But on the wall, right near some models, a small plaque had disappeared. Straining my mind, I recalled that the small, rectangular metal plate had a line of wiggly symbols that… had something to do with the ride? The only evidence of its removal were the small empty screw holes. No discoloration; it'd probably been removed when the ride was renovated.

But? Why were all the models and old projectors still there? Projectors they could have repurposed or sold, models that could probably be used elsewhere in the ride? Why would they leave everything except… that?

I managed to get home okay. I don't think anyone noticed I snuck in. I don't know if they will, or if they'll even review the tapes if they don't find any evidence of a break-in. I did my best not to leave any. I'll post again soon.

4/10/1997

I was on edge, paranoid someone would single me out and say they knew I snuck in, but nobody did. Thinking over it all night (I got no sleep!) I realised the plaque was. Familiar. I thought maybe I'd seen it somewhere else, other than the Time Machine ride. So, today, I went on Nebula Quest. After my third ride through, I caught it, on the wall, during the transition from when you got on the ride to the OmniVision screen room. An identical plaque to what I remembered. So, I went on The Story of Man, and lo and behold, there it was, on the wall near some models. And on Quantum Catastrophe. And Palaeozoa, and Amoeba Escape, and Mariana Trench Dive — every single ride except Time Machine has one of these tiny plaques, all with the same strange symbols.

Is it Dr. Teague's signature? That'd explain why they're on every ride, but not why they removed it from Time, or why it has weird symbols and not his name. Is its removal from Time a sign he didn't agree with the update? But he's still in charge. Why would he do something he didn't want to do in his own park, and why would the only clue be a plaque removed from a section of the ride the public can't even get into?

Just what are the symbols? Does this have to do with why Time is the only Realm that doesn't get small updates every day? The only Realm that doesn't shift and change like the others? Who disliked Time enough to remove it? How did I ride the original Time Machine ride in 1997? None of the Realm Ambassadors would know anything about that, of course. None of the ones I asked even noticed the plaques. It's not like I can go and ask Dr. Teague what they're for, and if I asked why the one in Time is missing, they'd know I snuck in. What do I do?

4/11/1997

I called out sick today to go back to OmniPark and ride all the rides again, trying to get a better look at the symbols. The ride attendants all seemed worried about me because of how frequently I was re-riding rides, or maybe because I probably look as emotionally weird as I feel. A few checked in on me, and seemed satisfied enough when I lied and said I had a bad day and was trying to cheer myself up. They must know by now how much OmniPark means to me. About halfway through the day I found a bench facing the OmniColor Fountain, and just sat there thinking for a while.

Something… is off. I'm missing something. Something to do with the park always changing. The never-ending march of entropy Dalton Teague wants everyone to learn about and understand when they go to OmniPark. Something with the plaques, with the other Realms shifting even without scheduled maintenance, about why Time was left behind. If only I could talk to Dr. Teague, but I'm not a television reporter or a celebrity. I'm just a librarian. But there are no books with any information about this (I've read every OmniPark book in existence). I thought I knew everything there was to know without being an employee or Dalton Teague himself, but I'm missing something.

Tomorrow night I'm going to go back, see if there's anything else I can catch. Get into the other rides and look closer at the symbols. Copy them down so I can search them up. Get real answers about how things change at night, which Ambassadors do it, and how they do it so quickly with so few people on staff like the night I broke in. I'll get real answers. I know the park well enough not to get caught.

I'll update tomorrow with everything I learn. There's some bigger message Dr. Teague is trying to spread that I didn't pick up on before. Hopefully by my next post, I'll have answers.

4/12/1997

Well. I found. Something. I went through an employee only door while poking around and ended up in an underground tunnel system, really bare bones, connecting all the Realms. Just someplace with offices on site that aren't visible to guests. There aren't cameras there, so I quickly went around looking at doors. They all have name plaques, and one of them said D. TEAGUE. To my surprise, it was unlocked. I couldn't help it and went in. I was closer to Dr.

Teague than I could ever imagine... his office is filled with trinkets seemingly from different countries he's visited, and on his desk, I found it. The missing plaque from Time, on a strange book written in the same symbols. I can't read it, but it was really, really old — ancient, in fact, and for some reason I got the feeling it came from the Middle East... archaic Hebrew!! That's what the writing looked like. I wanted to grab it so badly, but I couldn't. The plaque, however...

Tomorrow I'll come back and put it where it belongs in Time. I have to. In the meantime, I'm going to try and study its symbols. I have work tomorrow, and I'll have time to compare it with our scans of ancient tomes in between my regular responsibilities. See you in my next post!

4/13/1997

I want to preface this by saying I'm NOT crazy! I snuck back in and went straight to Time, screwdriver, plaque, and screws in tow. Still, nobody seemed to notice my late-night entry. But they may notice something now. Anyway. You'll see why I say that.

My hands shook as I put the plaque up and screwed it in, slowly, by hand, but it HAD to be done. The moment all the screws were in, the building itself — the WHOLE BUILDING! — groaned, shifted, and seemed to. Wake up?? I was staring up at the plaque, having fallen over throwing myself back in surprise. My heart was pounding, and I probably would have sat there forever if a voice didn't clear itself behind me. I nearly screamed, but managed not to as I whipped around to see, SOMEHOW, the Inventor. Physically there! The actor who played him was way too old to look like this now! He offered his hand, and I took it, too surprised not to. He was solid as he pulled me to my feet.

As I stared, probably rudely, the Inventor thanked me for putting the plaque back and waking them back up. When I asked what I woke up, the Inventor gestured around to the entire area. The Realm itself was what he meant. But how could that be possible???

I posted yesterday that the plaque's symbols resembled archaic Hebrew. Maybe the plaque worked the way activating a golem worked. The whole Realm, a golem. Each Realm changing because they were alive in some strange way. The Inventor was the projection of the consciousness of the Realm. He nodded, seeming pleased I was putting the pieces together, and led me out of the abandoned area. I was too dazed to protest, remembering the cameras too late — except there were no cameras.

The ride was REAL. The Inventor walked me to the nearest ride vehicle — no longer burdened by a track — and before I could speak, we were off! The Eloi, the Morlocks — I experienced the ride for real! Except the almost dying part at the end. I was astounded! And we got out at each part to inspect the real world! I could touch, feel, run from everything! When we finally got back, I was again white knuckled in the seat, but for a very different reason.

The Inventor offered to take me on an adventure. I… I didn't know what to say. I wanted to say yes, but I also was worried I'd lost my mind, so I told him I had to take a minute to think about it. He understood, and said to come back tomorrow night if I decided to accept his offer. I agreed, and he said he hoped to see me then. I practically ran out of the park.

I spent the next few hours asking myself whether what I'd just experienced could possibly be real. Had Dalton Teague been so consumed by his worship of change that he'd built his whole park out of golems — living creatures that would change with him and keep the park alive? Was such a thing even possible?

I wondered if this could be why Dalton never talked about all the years he'd spent traveling to remote corners of the world. Had he gained some kind of enlightenment, and discovered how to bring real, LIVING change to his park? I don't know. But I do know that it's all real, and I saw it. I know I'm not crazy. So, I've decided to go back tomorrow night, and accept the Inventor's — the Time Golem's offer. What more could I possibly want than even more OmniPark — to become one with the story?

I'll update you when I get back. But for now, see you in my next post, and don't forget to sign my guest book!

[Last Updated: 4/13/1997]

*Original postcard from the Realm of the Stars at OmniPark —
kept framed in Teague's office as part of his collection.*

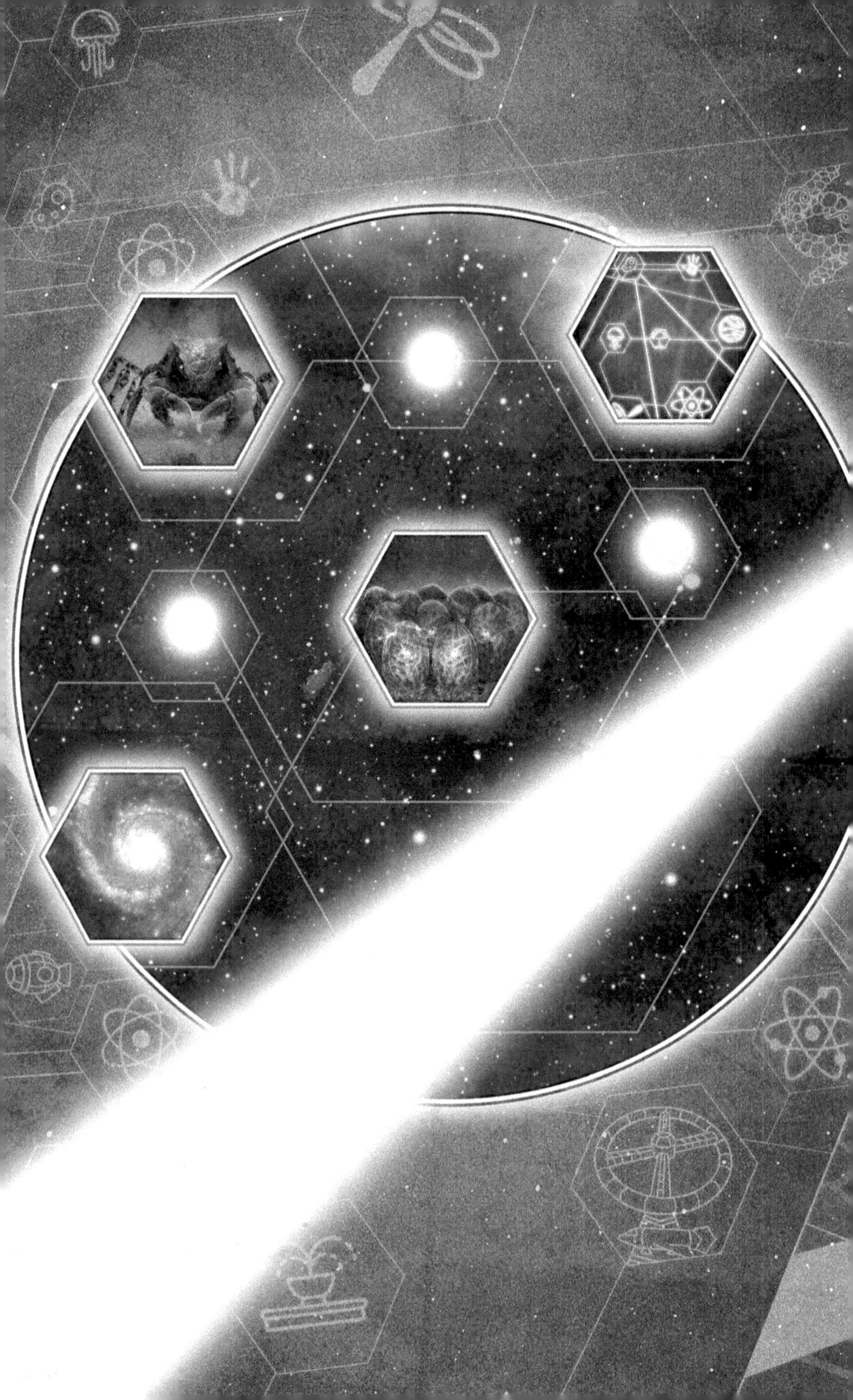

The Bottom-Dweller

Pedro Iniguez

1

It was ten minutes to midnight when Jasper Marvins shuffled inside the Mess Hall, stretching and yawning. He expected the usual ruckus of late-shift Park Ambassadors milling around shooting the shit, complaining of the long haul to come. Instead, the dining room was silent. A handful of employees sat staring at the walls, tapping their fingers on the tables. The puffy bags under their eyes and dead-fish-like slackened jaws spoke of many sleepless nights. He felt their pain.

The Mess Hall wasn't usually open to park employees. This restaurant, located deep in the belly of the *Pequod*, The Realm of the Deep's enormous "submarine," was reserved for guests during open hours. But during the late shift, Jasper and his fellow workers got to dine on crab cakes and cod fillets beneath a cornucopia of lobster buoys, nautical knots and Victorian sailors' portraits. Squinting sidelong through a porthole, Jasper caught a glimpse of animated squid hurtling upward from some deeper hunting ground.

He set his tray beside an old man hunched over a steaming bowl of chowder. His stomach rumbled as he broke off the tail of a crawfish and dangled its bright flesh in front of his mouth. Peculiar blue swirls patterned the meat, like galaxies in miniature. Frowning, Jasper peered closer, the design mesmerizing him with its speckled, spiraling arms. If he didn't know better, he could've almost sworn they were spinning. He shook his head. Couldn't be. Just markings, just camouflage. Some peculiar bioluminescent geometry evolved in the lightless depths.

He dropped the crawfish tail back onto his plate. His hunger had suddenly faded. He rubbed his eyes and took a sip of coffee, hoping it might clear the cobwebs from his mind. He just needed to wake up; that was it. He was seeing things. He was lucky to have the job, graveyard shift or not; and now wasn't the time to risk a psych evaluation by ranting about luminescent sea creatures. This Realm was already plenty weird as it was.

"What's the matter, boy," asked a drawling voice to his left. "You don't like mudbugs?"

"Huh?" Jasper glanced up.

"Mudbugs." The man's face was a wreckage of scars and two-day-old beard. "Crawfish? Bottom feeders? Name's Tyler, by the way." He put out a thick-fingered hand.

"Got it," Jasper said, forcing a smile. "Sorry, not from around here, Tyler. I like 'em alright, just not that hungry, I guess." He dwelled again on the strange spirals marking the crustacean's tail. "Never seen crawfish this fancy," he said prodding the tail with his fork. "Are these local?"

Tyler shrugged. "Fresh, free seafood, that's all I know. One of the many perks of working in the Deep. Eat up, boy! Big day tomorrow. They gonna work you hard tonight."

"Yeah," Jasper said, sliding his dish away. "Summer season starts tomorrow, I know. Looks like quittin' time for you, though."

"Yep." Tyler eased back into his chair. "Earned it, too. Been a hell of a day. Working out some kinks on Mariana Trench Dive. Sometimes the submersible gets caught on the tracks right when the Hive Queen pops out."

Jasper's eyes widened. "You're a Technosopher?"

Tyler shrugged. "Ride engineer. 'Round here, we call it the Mayhem Prevention Department. Fixing stalled rides is the least of it. Can you imagine explaining to Dalton why a busload of first-graders are stuck on a submarine, beggin' to be let off?"

"I wouldn't want to be in that meeting," Jasper agreed.

Tyler huffed. "Me neither. You got kids?"

Jasper shook his head and frowned. "No. Maybe I'm a nihilist, or maybe I'm afraid, but I can't really see myself bringing any into this world, the way things are right now. It would be far too cruel an act. Besides, I couldn't handle that kind of pressure."

"I hear that," Tyler raised his coffee cup in toast.

"What was that thing you said?" Jasper asked. "The Hive Queen?"

"That's what we call her," Tyler sipped his coffee. "Rumor has it she's Teague's fever dream of a sea creature he once encountered in a Mexican cenote. Just a Texas tall tale, though, I reckon. You ask me, she's one of Egger's monsters."

Jasper tilted his head. "Lot of legends around Dalton Teague."

"To say the least," Tyler agreed, chuckling. "Some say he's more than just human — though I'm skeptical of such claims, myself. Hey, what'd they bring you on for, anyway?"

"Me? I'm just a tank cleaner." Jasper suddenly remembered his own coffee. He stirred in cream and sugar as he gave the short version of his story. "I was a diver in the Navy. Did a tour in 'Nam, so I guess that impressed them enough to give me a shot. Tonight's my first shift."

"Hm." Tyler's smile faded and he stirred his chowder. "Big tanks. Lots of fishies. I heard Teague has a lot of pets in there. Personal collection, some say."

"Um," Jasper gulped. "What happened to the last cleaner? Did he get fired?"

Tyler suddenly broke into a fit of coughing, eyes flicking wildly to the right.

Startled, Jasper looked up to see a tall, slender man in a grey three-piece suit and a pale complexion standing beside them, arms folded behind his back.

"Good evening, Mr. Marvins." The man adjusted his thick-lensed glasses, just as he had in Jasper's job interview. *What was his name?* Right: Kurtz; Byron Kurtz, overnight marine-life supervisor. A disturbing smile now stretched across his face. "Would you be so kind as to follow me?" Kurtz extended an arm, making it clear this invitation wasn't optional.

Jasper nodded a goodbye to Tyler, taking a final gulp of coffee before dumping his food in the trash and following Kurtz out of the Mess Hall. His stomach twisted in knots, and he wasn't sure it was from hunger.

2

It was a long, silent walk to the locker room, where Kurtz asked Jasper to change into his wetsuit. By the time Jasper had squirmed into the rubbery contraption, Kurtz was waiting for him at the door, hands folded behind his back. He wore no expression other than a mild smile that didn't reach his eyes.

"Mr. Marvins," he said. "Thank you so much for being a part of our crew here in the Realm of the Deep."

"I should be thanking you, sir." Jasper gulped again, wondering where this was all going.

"Here at OmniPark, we all consider one another family. Some even like to think of Dalton himself as our loving grandfather. At any rate, family looks out for one another — wouldn't you agree?" Kurtz swept a hand toward the hallway, beckoning Jasper onward. All he could do was follow.

They wove through a maze of lamp-lit backrooms and brass-knobbed corridors, finally reaching an antique pull-cord elevator that transported them to a level Jasper hadn't visited yet.

The doors accordioned open, revealing a staging area the size of an aircraft hangar. A series of rafters and catwalks zig-zagged along the ceiling, coalescing into a platform that jutted out over a pool of water stretching the length of a football field. A dozen, clammy-skinned men in wetsuits leaned on the support rails, watching him with the same sleepless look as the employees in the Mess Hall. Each of them carried an aluminum pail in one hand and a spade in the other.

Jasper waved in greeting. The men stood motionless, unsmiling, eyes unblinking.

"Our filters aren't working properly," Kurtz explained. "We've been experiencing a buildup of debris. Food particles, we believe. You're going to need to inspect the filter, which you'll find about thirty feet down, on the left-hand side of the tank. Let's get you into the right gear."

Kurtz waved at the men above. They slowly lowered a winch grasping a bulky atmospheric diving suit. The suit reminded Jasper of Robby the Robot with its mix of concentric spheres, ball and socket joints, and exaggerated bubble helmet. He ran a hand over the gear. A fusion of thick plastic, rubber, and metal components lined the suit like some space-age armor.

Jasper glanced at the men on the rafters again. "Who are they?" he said nodding his head in their direction. "What are the buckets for?"

Kurtz adjusted his glasses, wiping off a smudge with the handkerchief in his pocket. "Those are our cleaners. We use the pails to collect some of the — ah... larger waste, which our filters are unable to dispense of."

Jasper scanned the staging area. A set of flickering fluorescent lights hung from the ceiling, casting a pale glow over the tranquil waters below. He stepped toward the pool, and felt a wave of heat wash over him.

He turned to Jasper. "A little hot for a saltwater tank, isn't it?"

Kurtz placed a hand on Jasper's shoulder and gazed down into the pool, a grin spreading across his tight-skinned face. "We have quite a few tanks in the Realm of the Deep, each housing different species of marine animals. We've compartmentalized different sections in order to simulate their different environments. This tank in particular," he said pointing directly below, "provides a home for a number of… *unique* bottom-dwelling organisms, whose natural habitat is near hydrothermal vents. We keep the temperature just below boiling, though we often have trouble calibrating the thermostat. Which is the reason for the heavy dive suit you'll be donning."

"Bottom-dwelling organisms," Jasper repeated. "Like the Hive Queen?"

"The Hive Queen," Kurtz said, wiping a bead of sweat from his brow, "is only a toy to frighten children. You should know that by now. No, this…" He shook his head. "This is something entirely different, I'm afraid."

Jasper peered down into the pool. His reflection stared back. Glimmering blue spirals unspooled in the blackness of his pupils. He turned away, shivering despite the heat and prepared to submerge.

3

After a crew of engineers fit him into the diving suit, the men in the rafters docked a tether into its spine and submerged him into the murky waters. Immersed in the boiling green brine, he felt like he was cooking alive, even within the protective gear.

As he descended, he noticed a glass barrier on his right-hand side separating his tank from another. Finding his balance in weightlessness, he scanned the adjoining tank, astonished at the variety of aquatic life gliding effortlessly about.

A manta ray barrel rolled gracefully alongside the barrier, its skin glistening under the bright lights. As he dropped farther down, a multitude of bright-colored fish zipped past, then assembled into a large body, and finally banked away as a cohesive unit.

Jasper broke his gaze from the fish and realized the tether had plunged him farther down. He'd been so entranced he'd somehow lost track of time and distance. He shook his head. *Focus.* Here, the waters began to cloud with small particles and the light from above started to fade. He looked up. The distorted outlines of the men on the rafters were barely visible as they peered down on him. His hand probed the top of his bubble helmet for the lamp switch. He found it, flicked it on, and a sharp beam of light cut across the dark water.

The tank's floor was now in view. It had been designed like a rocky, jagged trench and housed barnacles, long, snaking tube worms, and a plethora of zoarcid fish and gastropods. He swung his arms and drifted toward the left side of the tank, where three hoses curved out from the stony floor and fed into a large pump six-feet long. As he checked the fitting for any signs of leakage, he noted the abysmal water quality, caused by food particles, feces, and sediment.

Something glimmered in his peripheral vision just below his feet. About two yards down, nestled in a depression in the rocks, a mound of fleshy, translucent spheres shimmered like stars. Jasper allowed himself to drop down to the bottom of the tank. Once he balanced his feet on the rocks, he focused his light on the spheres. The light penetrated their thin membranes, revealing little squirming embryos inside.

Jasper scanned a network of artificial coral that ran along the leftmost wall of the tank, trying to spot what could have laid the eggs. A small octopus darted past his leg and disappeared into the rocks, smattering a storm of sediment across the water. He gave up his search and traced a fingertip along the thin outer membrane of one of the eggs. The walls had a fleshy, gelatinous consistency, coated with a slimy algae-like residue. He pressed gently against the surface, which bent inward without breaking.

Suddenly, a thousand tiny hooks lashed out at his back, tearing through the tether and the protective metal of the suit, ripping into his skin. The barbs tugged at him, spinning him forcefully around. A spindly leg slashed at his helmet, cracking it. A current of boiling-hot water began to seep through the crack, hissing and steaming in the minuscule space between his face and the lens.

Through the steam, Jasper's lamplight illuminated his attacker. He gazed into a pair of round, obsidian eyes. Like some twisted crustacean, a thick, serrated carapace guarded its head while rows upon rows of legs clawed up and down its belly until its body tapered off into a long, curved tail. The crustacean dwarfed him by about six feet, even now in its semi-curled state.

Jasper screamed into his helmet, the blistering water now rushing into his mouth, scalding his tongue. The beast sank another dozen scythe-like swimmerets into his suit, hooking his belly, pulling him closer. Spindly flagellae shot outward from its underbelly, sending hot pain lancing outward from his groin. His abdominal muscles throbbed and burned as a thousand red-hot needles threaded through his body. He swung his legs upwards, bringing his knees close to his chest. He planted his feet on the creature's belly and tried to push off, but his strength had already faded. His limbs went limp, and he felt himself dragged toward the creature like a helpless doll.

The monstrosity whipped its antennae through his helmet, his temples, digging them deep behind his eyes.

A barrage of images flashed his mind's eye like distorted television channels: spiraling galaxies scattered across the void; colorful planets whirling around alien suns; crustaceans mating with otherworldly lifeforms; a planet resembling earth; a vessel plunging into the depths of a cenote; complete submersion in a dark, frigid lake; the warm, waking waters of a new home; the stern smile of Dalton Teague; eggs hatching; a pack of men scooping her children away; his own, thrashing body impaled on countless rows of legs.

His thoughts centered back on the Mess Hall and the markings embedded on the flesh of his dinner. He heard Tyler's voice echo in his mind: *"Fresh, free seafood… one of the many perks you get working here."* A flood of nausea washed over him as he fought the urge to regurgitate.

Jasper didn't know how, but every image suddenly made sense. History made real through their bond. And the blue swirls: star maps embedded into their being, a genetic language encoding the history of a race of spacefarers seeking to integrate biodiversity into their essence. Every spiral a visited galaxy. Star to star, planet to planet, the seeds of every compatible lifeform were propagated through their eggs.

The antennae withdrew back from his brain and the assault of imagery ceased. Then, the pain returned to his body.

His helmet had now flooded with the boiling, briny water. Through his burning eyes he watched as the creature dispersed a cloudy white mist into the fleshy mound beneath them. Jasper's heart beat like a piston. He wanted to cry. Maybe he already was.

The eggs began to throb, pulsing in time like a clutch of hearts. One by one, they popped, releasing tiny creatures scurrying along the aquarium floor.

The creature opened its mandibles, and Jasper gazed upward one last time, toward a surface he would never see again. Far above him — much too far for him to see or hear — the men on the rafters raised their spades and pails, banging them together in celebration. Kurtz's silhouette stood motionless, his hands at his back. Jasper thought he saw a smile crack across his distorted face.

The creature's mandible pulled Jasper's head gently into its maw.

Your worst fear has come true, it spoke into his mind. *You are to be a father. Thank you, my mate, for the gift of your life.*

Its mandibles snapped, and darkness flooded in.

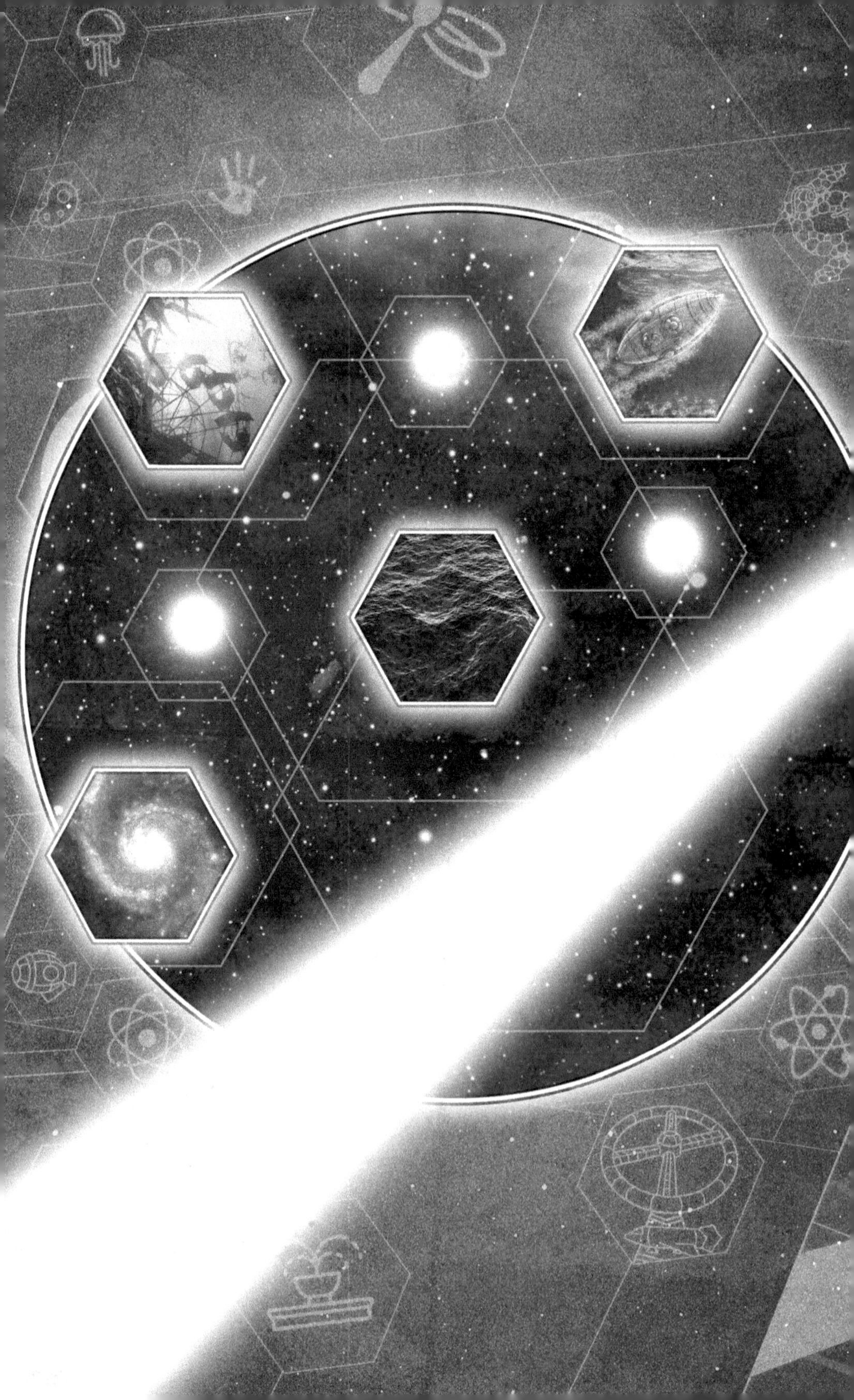

THE FISHERMAN'S LAST CALL

MAXWELL I. GOLD

1

Infinite possibilities of terror, wonder, and fear imbued the black realms of the deep. Unable to truly comprehend the majesty of that darkness within the seas, Eliot Goldberg descended through the wreckage and ruin of the dilapidated theme park one last time, where the Great Gulaplast lay waiting. The old neons greeted him with crackling blinks and tired flickers as his worn leather sneakers pressed over the painted concrete, woeful and beaten by the unforgiving decades.

He never thought he'd see this place again. Not like this, at least. He'd spent his adulthood as a neurotic hypochondriac, a life covered in tissue and Saran wrap, clinging to an irrational fear of water and metal; an almost fanatical juxtaposition to the life he remembered. Eliot's memories of OmniPark weren't like that of so many other kids; though he recalled frolicking under the spectral waters of the great fountain, geometric towers of white and silver cutting against the skies, and seven different worlds as if he were stepping into the past, present, and future all at the same time, mired his young imagination.

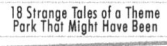

The wildly hot summers spent at the Odessa park consumed his childhood, and his nightmares. Though, Eliot recalled countless nights where coarse words and wry promises were thrown back and forth between his mother and father after he went to his room. Financial squabbles, material concerns, and other basic human needs had consumed every waking moment since his father, Gordon, was laid off from a job at the Odessa National Bank, leaving Eliot's mother to take on more shifts at a diner in town.

Life was all too terrible for the Goldbergs, until the waters once again flowed with color and the fountains bubbled with voices from the deep.

Dalton Teague's corporate ambitions had taken him beyond the board of OmniOil, past the rivers of darkest Africa and through the sweltering Asian jungles back towards a bright glimmering future. Welcome news for some, but the disdain and derision were overwhelming as the metallic beasts and immense steel skeletons loomed high above every single building in the growing Texas town. News came to light that Odessa National Bank, actually purchased by an Ohio company, helped pave the way for Teague's empire of stars, ships, and men. It seemed as if some alien rust monster had planted its hive, attracted every form of life from across the country to this once secluded slice of Americana, now a budding mass of tourism, corporate exploitation and greed.

The Goldbergs didn't seem to notice, though, Gordon was more concerned with the prospect of a job — *any* job. He found part-time work on the park's janitorial staff. The stability of a fucking paycheck was enough for Gordon to give his son a distraction. Teague treated his employees well, very well. Even those at the bottom rungs of his corporate latter. Early access to the Seven Realms, discounted tickets, only the best for OmniEmployees.

"What do you say, Eliot?" His father said one September afternoon, "The park is officially closed for maintenance until tomorrow. How about a VIP tour?"

Ecstatic, Eliot smiled, the warm summer breeze from the lake brushing against his face, "Yeah, dad! That'd be awesome!"

2

Born on the Ohio shores of Lake Erie, Eliot had always loved the water, and all the mysteries lurking within the murky green depths. Though, times had certainly changed for him ever since the family transplanted from the small Ohio town to Odessa. The local library back in New Ashworth taught him the lake's folklore: ancient gods and abyssal creatures, somehow creeping landward from the blackest chasms of the oceans, to seize unsuspecting victims from their unsuspecting lakeside strolls, dragging them to their watery doom with mouth-lined tentacles.

"Can't you hear it, Eliot?" His father asked in a tone of hushed reverence.

Eliot tensed as they strolled along the pier of the man-made lake that divided the neighboring hotel grounds from OmniPark proper. "Hear what?"

"Gulaplast," Gordon said plainly, his janitor's uniform ruffling as air conditioning blew over them.

"Gula-what?" Eliot gazed up, hanging onto every word, every drop, every syllable falling from his father's lips.

"The Fisherman's Last Call," his father said. "At least, that's how the story goes. It's an old folktale. Your grandpa told me when we were living in Ohio. Your mother probably wouldn't want me telling you so," he paused, tilting his head oddly as if scrutinizing watch over the empty pier, the ghostly silhouette of the park towering over them, "let's keep it between us, yeah?"

Secrets held a uniquely esoteric beauty for Eliot; the power of hidden words and dark mentalities wrapped in conscious choice, like some psychedelic drug tasted but once and forbidden forever after. Eliot took a seat on the pier next to his dad, legs dangling above the murky waves, ears twitching and heart racing, wondering what else could be said of the monster under the seas.

"I promise," he said. "Won't tell a soul."

"Gulaplast," Gordon said once more, wiggling his fingers for theatrics. The sun was nestling into the horizon and the first hints of evening cold crept over the water.

"Some say *It* has always been, for as long as the Earth has spun, and perhaps even longer: a beast of unfathomable size and hideous shape. Some say it dwells at the bottom of the Mariana Trench, feeding on our waste and pollution. Waiting."

"Waiting for what?" Eliot gulped.

"To swallow our cities," dad smiled ruefully. "Our skyscrapers, our shopping malls, our suburbs and our homes. Down to the very last Coke bottle."

Gordon snatched the empty bottle from Eliot's grasp, laughing at the boy's startled gasp.

Eliot furrowed his brow.

"So, that's it? A giant trash monster? How did it get here? The Mariana Trench is all the way in the Pacific Ocean. Elliot crossed his arms and frowned. "It's kind of a lame story." But lame or otherwise, the tale sent a chill up Eliot's spine as the wind intensified, whipping the water's surface into whitecaps.

Gordon gazed down, a contemplative look knitting his brow. "Well then, I suppose it's just a story, son. Though Gulaplast's unimaginable size and cunning make it hard to say for sure. A creature like that could easily find its way here, then back to the safety of its watery lair. As the poet philosopher Flavius Gauntius said in his own account of the monster, *For a thousand unparalleled eons, as the ocean brine lapped across the ancient bedrock, a protean creature growing fat, thriving on human waste and refuse had finally stirred awake.*

"Flavius Gauntius," Eliot rolled his eyes. "Yeah right. I've never heard of him."

Gordon only winked and grinned.

Eliot stood there, dumbfounded, listening to his father's tale. Ancient monsters, folk tales, and theme parks? The sun had all but disappeared behind a thin line of trees, followed by a chorus of winds dancing across the green waters as a strange iridescence sparkled under the decaying glow of last daylight.

"You all right, son?" Gordon asked, ruffling his son's bowl cut.

"Sure," Elliot replied. "Just a little cold, that's all."

"It's just a story, Eliot," his dad said, rising from the pier. "There's no Gulaplast. No Fisherman's Last Call. Nothing that's going to devour our home or your Coke bottle," Gordon laughed. "Now, come on. I've got a surprise for you."

The shadow of the skeletal amusement park stood sentinel in the twilight, its jagged smile toothed with long-dead ride pavilions, creaking metal skeletons and bellies of greasy concessions filled Eliot's peripherals as it waited for them.

As they approached one of the employee entrances, Gordon drew an enormously complex set of keys from his pocket.. Being on the janitorial staff, he had access to every nook and cranny of the park, before, during, and after hours.

3

Eliot's hands trembled, limbs like rubber and his brain soft under the pressure of dim nostalgia as he stepped into The Realm of the Deep. Lapping waves from the lake sloshed against the sandy beaches, as if hungering for something, wanting more. The world had certainly grown worn and ragged since the last time he'd walked along this pier. Viruses, reactionary uncertainty, and wild idealisms shook the earth like a cheap antique snow globe riddled with flecks of pale plastic dust. Being away from Odessa for nearly four decades, Eliot had never thought to return here; though he bought the plane ticket only when seeing a news story about the park's closing — the collapse of the final vestige of Dalton Teague's crumbling empire.

Truth be told, Eliot was surprised the park had remained open as long as it had. He'd thought the 1985 "Wild World" tragedy would've shuttered its doors for good. Though, park public relations had neatly swept that story under the rug, just as it had the even less-remembered 1981 disaster in the Realm of the Deep.

Apparently, he was wrong. it was hard to keep a good park down — at least, until the death of its founder.

Everything was just as he remembered it — albeit coated with a thin sheen of dust. The ornate 19th century décor of the library, faux-leather books and Tiffany lamps suspended from the ceiling. Glass and wires crunched beneath his boots as he stepped over discarded jumpsuits, shoes and misplaced tools crusted in verdigris and rust, lost to the annals of time.

"I can't believe it's still here," he sighed out loud.

The Realm's algae-filled water sloshed and slurped against the library's mirrored glass, sending a strange *frisson* up Eliot's spine. "Mariana Trench Dive" — the sign above the ride entrance stood out clear and sharp in his memory. After all, it was the first and last ride his father had taken him on that strange September night when the rest of the park had slumbered. They began in the Pequods's library, then ventured into a massive sea capsule, surrounded on all sides by water that had once teemed with sharks and rays, but now only reeked of algae.

"That was weird," he said, chills running down his spine.

Right, the trash monster. He used to love the water, until his dad told him that silly story, then he began to develop strange and problematic nightmares about things devouring coastlines, slimy filth-ridden tentacles pulling chunks of earth into the blackness of the water followed by the gnashing of great teeth.

"Now, I remember," Eliot looked around at the rusted gold capsule, rows of empty seats leading up to the animatronic figure gazing out through a cracked window with his hands on his hips as if preparing one last great dive: The Fisherman.

"It's been awhile, Dad," Eliot said, taking a seat a few rows back .

"I kind of wish this wasn't how we had to meet again. Or where. Back here, of all places." Eliot cracked his knuckles, twiddling his thumbs, "I wish you'd never brought me to this godforsaken fucking park."

Silence seeped inside the dank room as if he was waiting for a call from the dark. Waiting for the gears of the motionless, inoperable ride to spring to life and answer him. The innards of the sea capsule moaned slightly, half submerged under the lake in a foaming algae soaked. paralysis. Memories long dead, mixed with a crippled nostalgia drifted through the cobwebbed consciousness of his mind as he gazed upon the old Fisherman — who stood statue-still, unchanged, staunch and resolute.

Suddenly a crackling noise thundered through the capsule, wires springing and writhing along the floor in electrified frenzy, as if new life stirred in their copper veins. Ghostly Rossini sopranos, Verdi baritones, and a ghoulish bedlam of strings, tubas, and trumpets warbled through the dusty stereophonic webs, as Eliot's ears bled. It was as if he could taste, smell and hear every memory from forty years ago. Every tinge of rust replaced by gleaming brass; every shelf fresh with cherry-wood lacquer.

A metallic screech sounded from the old Fisherman's joints as the automaton twitched and stretched. As metal bones popped in and out of place, the horrid stench of garbage and rust toxified the atmosphere, spilling into Eliot's lungs, throttling his breath, numbing his sense of smell. A heavy cough erupted from the metal man, followed by silence. Recalling the night with his father, the chills returned, though sometimes things are not as they seem. This wasn't not what he remembered, but then again, he had done everything possible to blot out the trauma.

Eliot gazed at the aged figure, seeking any recognizable detail in its face. The pale latex had peeled away in ribbons, revealing a clockwork of broken gears and seaweed. Two clouded glass eyes stared sightlessly, askew and trembling.

Silence.

The Fisherman coughed again, sparks and trashy embers spilling from his mouth, his voice scratchy like an old phonograph record: *"For a thousand unparalleled eons, as the ocean brine lapped across the ancient bedrock, a protean creature growing fat, thriving on human waste and refuse had finally stirred awake."*

4

"Yup, every nook and cranny," Gordon said, beaming with pride as he pushed open one of the cleverly concealed back doors to the Realm of the Deep.

"Cool," Eliot said.

"Isn't it, though?" Gordon smiled down at his son "This is the Realm of the Deep, where the Fisherman will take us *deep* under the waves to the Mariana Trench," Gordon accentuated his words theatrically.

"The Fisherman?" Eliot trembled as a chill ran through his limbs.

"There are no monsters here, son. It's all just smoke and mirrors. Come here, see for yourself." Taking Eliot's hand, he pulled him closer, Gordon letting him feel the white plastic skin of the shark jutting out of the wall next to the bookcase, "See? All fake."

"Right, fake," Eliot fidgeted once more, still holding the empty coke bottle.

"Son, the bottle?" Gordon said.

The boy clutched the empty Coke. "Do I have to?"

"What are you, scared?" His father stifled a laugh.

"I don't want Gulaplast to get it," Eliot muttered as his dad grinned.

"Okay, suit yourself," Gordon said. "Hang onto the bottle if you want, squirt."

"Now, this was the ride I wanted to show you. It's called the Trench Dive. It actually takes us into the depths of the sea Well, on tracks, but it's pretty damn realistic."

The Realm was adorned with ornate bookshelves, wrought-brass staircases, and antique diving suits gazing through golden portholes as if their phantom pilots were exploring the depths for the first time. It somehow married childhood fantasy with tantalizing hints of mystery and adventure — perhaps even peril on the high seas.

Eliot and his dad took their seats in the second row — almost within reach of the Fisherman, who stood near the center domed window of the capsule dressed in a 19th century merchant commander's robe, the cliché missing leg, and a wide brimmed blue captain's hat as he faced aft, hands at his side, facing away from the invisible crowd.

"What happens now, Dad?" Eliot asked.

"Well, the Fisherman takes us deep under the waves, into the, eh—" Gordon fumbled for a moment, recalling lines from the script. "—Abyssal Zone, where we go on the hunt for elusive sea creatures."

"Then what?" Eliot asked.

"Then we find out what's lurking down there." Gordon smiled. "You never know; we might even encounter..." He reached out and plucked the Coke bottle from Eliot's hand. "A giant trash monster!"

Eliot squealed, dropping the bottle to shatter on the tiled floor.

"Now look at the mess you've made," said Gordon in mock annoyance. "That's going to be my job to clean up, you know."

Eliot pouted, folding his arms and heaving a sigh. "Sorry, dad." Gordon rose up from his seat in exaggerated annoyance, play-acting so outrageously that Eliot couldn't help but laugh. "Well," he said, "the good news is that now Gulaplast can't get it anymore."

"Can't we stay just a little longer?" Eliot asked.

"Yeah, sure," Godron ruffled his son's hair. "Why not?"

Together they sat watching the waters of the lake glimmering along the surface of the glass capsule. Time seemed to fade away into that boundless blueness.

At last, Gordon rose. "All right, time to go grab a broom and clean this up. Wouldn't want the big boss to get suspicious." He tossed Eliot a conspiratorial wink.

Eliot sat along long after his dad had departed, listening to the ticking of gears and the sloshing of lake waters stories above him Curious, the boy's machinations were piqued as he approached the Fisherman.

Twin electric lamps flickered on either side of the Fisherman, casting his face in dancing shadows. Eliot felt drawn to the lights, which seemed to bid him to come closer, to swim within the black shadows of the sea. The old Fisherman's lamp-lit gaze reminded him of something; what was it? A father's gaze. The gaze of a guide and a protector, shining through despite the primal uncertainty in the figure's glass eyes.

How Eliot sensed all this, he could not tell — any more than he knew how he sensed, a moment later, that something had terribly gone wrong.

His father was taking too long. "Dad?" Eliot called out, but the only answer was the echo of his own voice from the ship's polished brass and wood.

Nothing.

The lamps flickered again. Scents of metal rose, along with a heavier undertone: a sharply pungent smell like the stench of rotting trash. The lights flashed in a wild, uneven rhythm, and the stench intensified into a putrid ichor that seemed to coat Eliot's throat and tongue.

"Dad, where are you?" Eliot screamed as the lamps twitched madly. The reek was growing unbearable; Eliot was certain he'd lose his lunch any moment now.

The Fisherman's latex "skin" began to peel from his face. Seaweed and rust spilled from the domed capsule, accompanied by a groaning that Eliot *felt* more than heard; a rumbling that shook the very floor beneath his feet, as if something was eating, gnawing, chewing from the bowels of the lake, hungering for a billion years. Eliot turned and fled from the capsule — but tripped over loose wire he could've sworn wasn't there a moment ago.

He found himself staring up, wide-eyed, into the Fisherman's glaring eyes.

Gears churned behind the automaton's lips, and words guttural and pronounceable mixed with seaweed, rust, and ruin: "Ghulaplast is coming. It is coming now, boy. Run!"

"What?" was the only word Eliot could find to stammer as he stared up into those glass eyes, now suddenly afire with strange wisdom of unimaginable age.

"From the depths," creaked the Fisherman's voice. "From the unimaginable depths, It approaches. Behold — even now, It rises from Its slumber!"

Hot radiations of pain lanced through Eliot's body as electricity crackled through the capsule. Wild cackling chased Eliot back up the staircase, through the exit porthole and back up the Realm's central hallway, past chambers glowing with eerie blue light; tanks crawling with blinking, many-tentacled things that had most definitely not been there before.

Eliot glanced down, noticing for the first time that blood coated his hand, oozing from a deep cut made by one of the broken shards of his Coke bottle. Blackness and greyspace clawed in at the edges of his vision, and soon even that disappeared, leaving only an empty void where memory had once been. He had heard the Fisherman's Last Call.

5

The scars on his hands never healed; not properly.

Eliot never again spoke of his dim memories of that fateful night. The police investigated his father's disappearance for a few days, then gave it up as a lost cause. The drunken lout had threatened to leave town more times than his mother could count, she explained to a pair of bored-looking detectives who closed the case soon after.

Now, back in the capsule again after all these years, his fingers clenched as he stood face-to-face with the old Fisherman. Stepping over shards of broken glass, hands trembling, he clutched the figure's rusted shoulders, breathing in the scent of trash and time.

"I'm home, Dad," he whispered. "Did you miss me?"

*Original postcard of the OmniPark entrance — kept framed
in Teague's office as part of his collection.*

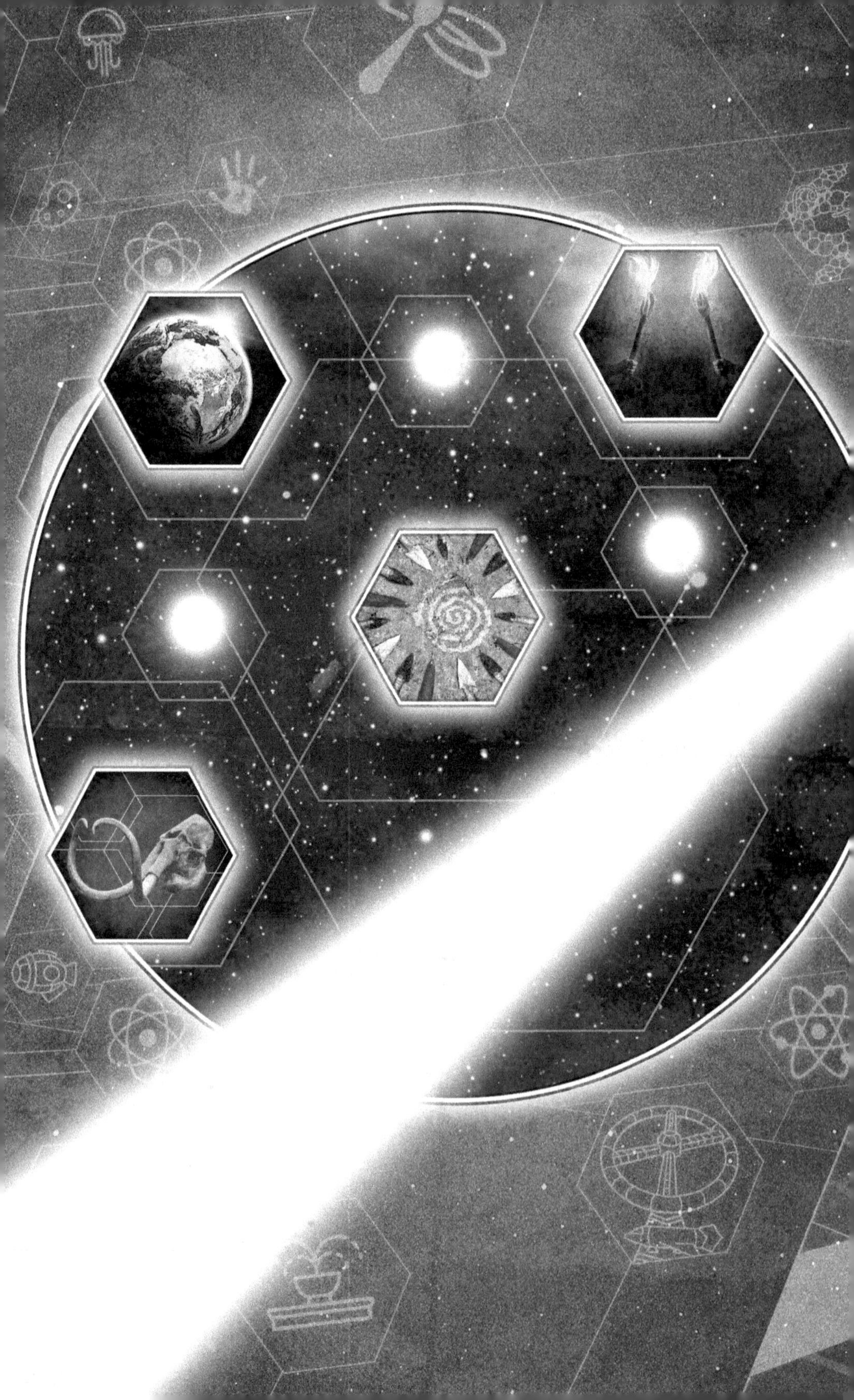

Beyond the Confines of Man

Marshall J. Moore

1

"This is so childish," Roger muttered as he let himself be led towards the Realm of Man. "What are we, twelve years old?"

The attraction entrance was an enormous archway of what Susan assumed must be woolly mammoth tusks, leading into a dimly-lit tunnel. Faint drumbeats thudded from a tinny speaker somewhere inside.

"Come on, big shot," she said. "Lighten up a little. I promise I won't tell anybody you actually had fun here."

She pulled him under the mammoth arch, a strange tingle of excitement running down her spine as the tinny drumbeats grew louder. The tunnel was dark, the ceiling claustrophobically low.

This is what I've been needing, Susan thought to herself. *What this trip was supposed to be. Something new and exciting.*

So far it had been neither of those things.

They emerged out of the low, darkened tunnel into a vaulted chamber shaped like a rough dome, its walls adorned with scrimshawed bones and furry pelts. A small shaft of light lanced down through a smoke-hole overhead, though the storm clouds outside meant that the chamber was nearly as dark as the tunnel from which they'd just emerged.

"'The Great Tent,'" Susan read aloud from a nearby sign. She gazed around excitedly, pointing out the collection of replica Stone Age spears and axes, and the impressively realistic mammoth pelt that stretched across a considerable swathe of the Tent. "Cool, huh?"

Roger didn't answer. Susan turned to see him typing furiously on the keypad of his new flip-phone, hypnotized by the tiny square-inch screen.

"Roger!" Susan said, fighting to keep the irritation out of her voice.

He looked up, annoyed. "What?"

"Could you put that thing down for five seconds?" Susan asked, striving to keep her tone playful. What was the point of all those acting lessons if she couldn't at least put on a happy face for her husband-to-be?

"In a minute," he said, eyes returning to the screen. "It's work."

Of course it was. Roger had barely looked up from his phone this entire trip, except while driving. Susan supposed she should have expected this; he'd complained to her more than once that being an attorney was a twenty-four-seven job, especially if he aimed to make full partner by forty. All the same, this was supposed to be a romantic cross-country road trip from Hollywood to Manhattan, with a Christmas stop in Memphis to visit Roger's parents — a.k.a. her in-laws to be.

With each passing hour, though, it was becoming increasingly clear how low romance ranked on Roger's priority list.

"I'm gonna go get us some coffee," Susan said, forcing a cheerful smile. "You want some?"

"Sure," he said, eyes returning to the phone. "Macchiato if they've got it. With two sugars. Thanks babe."

That was one of the things Susan had liked about Roger when they'd first met. He always had a cup of espresso in hand — never just "coffee," like she drank, but always *espresso*, or something equally European-sounding like cappuccino or latte. And yet, over the past three days on the road, his insistence on finding such drinks in every small town had quickly transformed from charming to annoying.

Forced smile still plastered across her face, Susan marched off in search of some form of caffeine.

2

OmniPark staff were easy to pick out. In this Realm they wore a variety of prehistoric outfits, all of which looked like a lot of thought had been put into them. Both men and women sported fur tunics, leather kilts, body paint, feathers, shell beads, colorful stone amulets and bone jewelry. They looked less like she'd expected cavemen to look, and more like the Indians from the First Thanksgiving. Yet that also felt *right*, somehow.

Incredibly, the Realm of Man had its own coffee stand: The Bean of the Gods. The man who took her order played a passable prehistoric hunter-gatherer: gesturing, grunting and tongue-clicking amicably as he brewed up Roger's espresso. He even wore a rough leather apron — supple and ragged at the edges, as if he'd just tanned the hide this morning.

"Thanks," Susan said as she took the pair of paper cups from the cave-barista. He hooted and chirped in acknowledgement.

"We're new to the park," Susan said, giving him her most winning smile. "Where do we go from here?"

The barista gazed down at her stoically. Susan caught a whiff of his aftershave: something coarse and musky. He grunted and pointed towards the far end of the Great Tent, where another mammoth-bone arch loomed beneath a sign that read, "The Story of Man."

"Thanks, Conan," Susan winked, and set off towards Roger, intent on dragging him into something that'd catch his attention.

3

Five minutes later they found themselves being ushered into a vehicle whose plastic molding did a passable imitation of lashed-together mastodon bones.

"Certainly smells like a woolly mammoth," Roger noted, wrinkling his nose as one of the park's cavewoman attendants checked to make sure the safety bar was fastened across their laps.

The attendant pointed to Roger's phone. Through a combination of pantomime, grunts, and whistles, she indicated that he needed to put it away before the ride could begin.

"Do you have any idea—" he began, but Susan placed a restraining hand on his shoulder, fixing the dour attendant with her most ingratiating smile.

"Let it go, babe," she said out of the corner of her mouth. "You can put the phone down for ten minutes."

Richard opened his mouth to argue, but they lurched forward with unpleasant suddenness as the ride kicked into life. Again Susan heard the distant drumbeats that had first echoed down the entrance tunnel. Hokey as it was, that same thrill of excitement crept down her spine once again.

"Hope this isn't a total waste of time," Roger grumbled beside her. "We're this close to closing the McLaren contract."

Susan gazed down at the glittering diamond ring on her left hand, admiring the way it caught the light. The future would sparkle just as brightly, she reminded herself. They just had to get through this rough patch first. That was all.

4

The ride lurched forward, away from the holding area and into a completely dark room. Susan groped for Roger's hand in the darkness; found it; squeezed. He didn't squeeze back.

Pale blue lights brought the room to sudden life, strobing around the room in a manner that reminded Susan of planetarium light shows. Spectral images of the primordial hunt drifted along the cave walls. Stick figures hurled spears at charging rhinos and fleeing elk. Staccato chanting and complex drum rhythms thundered from speakers in the headrests, accompanied by the shrill hooting of monkeys.

"Welcome to the Story of Man," said a resounding basso voice from speakers in the vehicle's headrests. "Who am I? You may ask. My name is not important, as you'll soon discover for yourselves. For now, you may call me the Anthropologist."

The parade of ghostly figures continued to reenact their hunts across the walls and ceiling of the cave. Examining them more closely, Susan noticed that some were squat, apelike creatures, while others resembled modern humans Most, however, fell between those two extremes: ape and human in equal measure.

"Anthropology," said the narrator, "is the study of humankind."

The revolving images slowed, settling on a handsome young man around Susan's age.

"But how to study such a strange and contradictory creature?" the Anthropologist's voice asked. "As we shall see, the only way to understand mankind is to travel all the way back... to the very beginning."

Beside her, Roger snorted. Susan ignored him, focusing instead on the animated screen as the young man's face began to devolve, growing noticeably less handsome and more like the primitive, apelike creatures that had preceded him in the hunt.

The ride lurched forward again, the Anthropologist resuming his monologue. "To undertake such a monumental journey through time and space, we'll be making use of the Time Tunneler, a device my good friend and colleague the Inventor ...well, invented."

They began to pick up speed. They passed through a tunnel displaying a starfield, which transformed into a river of streaming white lines as their vehicle accelerated.

"They ripped this straight out of *Star Wars!*" Roger protested, so loudly that someone the car behind told him to shush.

"Rest assured," came the Anthropologist's disembodied voice, to Susan's relief, "I have used the Inventor's Time Tunneler on many occasions, and have always returned to our present time healthy and intact. So long as you follow my instructions *to the letter*, I promise that you, too, will return safe and sound."

Susan smiled, charmed despite — or perhaps because of — Roger's annoyance.

"Our first stop," the Anthropologist announced, as a bright light began to grow at the end of the tunnel ahead, "is the Kenyan savanna, circa four million years ago."

They emerged into a brightly lit chamber, baking beneath the light of an artificial sun overhead. As the Anthropologist had promised, it looked exactly like the African savanna she'd seen on late-night Discovery Channel shows. Acres of dry brown grassland and thick, multi-trunked trees spread out into the distance on all sides, though Susan's careful scrutiny revealed the walls of the chamber must have been cleverly painted to give it the illusion of open space. She scolded herself for her momentary slip into skepticism: that was Roger's job. She let the imaginary become real again, settling back into her seat with a smile.

The hooting calls of a howler monkey echoed overhead, accompanied by deeper simian grunts. On either side of the vehicle, small troops of three or four primates plucked and sniffed at nearby branches. The closest of these troops were crouched over a bush, picking through it in search of nuts. Further on, another troop stood around the bloody corpse of a gazelle, brandishing sticks at a pack of big cats that vaguely resembled leopards. The gathered apes hooted and snarled, sending a chill up Susan's spine.

"*Australopithecus*," the Anthropologist announced. "The most ancient of our direct ancestors, barely distinguishable from the less-evolved primates against which they competed for food."

Sure enough, the ride turned a corner to reveal another troop of Australopithecines, this time throwing rocks at a rival group of primates. The only difference between the two groups, as far as Susan could see, was that the Australopithecines stood straight-backed, while their rivals preferred to forage on all fours.

Susan shrieked and shrank back against Roger as one of the nearest *Australopithecus* turned to leer at her, its thin lips peeling back from its broad yellow teeth. Its gaze was human yet inhuman; familiar and other, all at once.

"It's okay!" Roger laughed, pointing. "They're just animatronics, babe. Look."

Peering closer, Susan saw he was right. The apelike creature's movements were stiff, its eyes glassy and dull.

"Jesus," Roger said, still laughing as she leaned away from him. "Remind me never to take you to Disney World. You'd pee yourself on 'It's a Small World.'"

Cheeks burning, Susan turned her attention back to the ride. Though grassy savanna still surrounded them, the lights had dimmed, the domed ceiling above suddenly glimmering with hundreds of tiny stars.

Now the troop of *Australopithecus* huddled together in the grass, arms wrapped around each other. Their hoots and moans sounded pained. Susan found herself leaning back against Roger, imagining how cold that savanna night must have been.

"They are cold," the Anthropologist explained, "because they know fire only as an enemy — not yet as a friend."

"Babe," Roger said, pushing Susan firmly off him. "Ease up, will you? I can't breathe."

"Sorry," Susan muttered as mournful hooting filled the simulated night.

"As you can hear," the Anthropologist continued, "*Australopithecus* has not yet evolved language. They can communicate the simplest of ideas to one another, but each of them is alone in his or her own mind."

They passed into another tunnel, again lit by a simulated starfield jumping to lightspeed. Susan felt a sudden pang of empathy for her ancestors of four million years ago as she and Roger sat in stony silence.

5

The tunnel opened into another chamber, this one an arid-looking canyon of red rocks. Shadows darted along the cliffside above them, too fast and high for Susan to catch more than a fleeting glimpse of humanoid figures.

"We have traveled forward two million years," the Anthropologist informed them, "to Tanzania's Olduvai Gorge, where our ancestors *Homo habilis* have improved upon the hunting methods of their Australopithecine forebears."

The ride turned a corner. Ahead of them Susan saw a herd of animatronic zebras, standing unsuspected as hominid shadows lurked in the rocks behind them. A series of rapid chirps and whistles filled the air.

"As you can hear," the Anthropologist continued, "by imitating the songs of birds, *Homo habilis* has begun to invent something new: language."

The hominid shadows rose from behind their rocks to attack the zebras, spears held high. They looked more human than the *Australopithecines* had, though their heavy brows and thick jaws still resembled those of chimps more than people. The air was full of guttural growls and the panicked braying of zebras.

The vehicles trundled along the bottom of the artificial canyon, approaching a scene of several *Homo habilis* cornering a frightened-looking zebra, their spears levelled at its heart. The ride turned a corner and emerged abruptly from the gorge onto the familiar savanna. The same group of *Homo habilis* now held the remains of the butchered zebra on sharpened sticks, roasting them over a wildfire burning in the grass. As the scents of woodsmoke and roasting meat filled her nostrils, Susan realized with a start that the fire was real.

"Gas flame," Roger said, as though reading her thoughts. "Like the kind that people too cheap to buy lumber use in fireplaces."

Susan bit back the retort that leaped to her tongue: her family had had one of those gas-lit fireplaces, and she'd always loved it as a kid.

"These *Homo habilis* have not yet tamed the fire," the Anthropologist observed, "But they have befriended it."

The ride lurched forward, accelerating suddenly. Susan's heart thudded in time with the rising drumbeat.

"But something is wrong!" the Anthropologist exclaimed, though he sounded more eager than alarmed. "The hunters have become the hunted!"

A guttural chorus rang through the chamber, raising the hairs on the back of Susan's neck. The animatronic *Homo habilis* turned their heads, noticing another group of approaching hominids. These stood straighter, and their eyes gleamed with a cunning, almost human light.

The ride sped past scenes of the *Homo habilis* fleeing desperately from the rival hominids. Those who fell behind were slaughtered with a violence that seemed to belong more in a B-horror film than an educational theme park. Susan closed her eyes as their blood pooled and drained away into the sand.

The vehicle entered a wide-mouthed cave, then lurched to an abrupt stop. The chamber plunged into sudden darkness, though the drumbeats still pounded loudly in Susan's ears. She found herself reaching for Roger's hand again, but he waved her away irritably.

"My dear friends," came the anthropologist's voice in an echoing stage-whisper, "it is imperative that you remain absolutely still and silent. For we are being hunted by *Pithecanthropus erectus*."

A gas vent hissed softly, filling the air with a musky scent that reminded Susan of the primate house at the zoo. Hot air tickled the back of Susan's neck, accompanied by the unmistakable smell of someone — or something — sniffing.

Susan screamed.

She wasn't alone. Other riders yelped in fright as hands emerged in the dark, grasping and pawing at them. Susan felt hot fingers running along her legs, through her hair, down her arms…

"Jesus!" Roger said, and swore so loudly that a child in one of the cars behind them started crying. "What in the hell are they playing at!?"

Susan didn't answer. She'd grabbed hold of one of the hands as it crept along her shoulder, and now she clutched it tightly. It didn't feel animatronic. It felt warm and alive.

The ride began to move again, and the hand slipped from her grip. High-pitched screams echoed through the darkness — not the screams of the riders, but the pre-recorded sounds of the primordial hominids.

"Dear guests," the Anthropologist said, his tone sober. "I am afraid that the *Pithecanthropus erectus* have killed and eaten some of the younger *Homo habilis*. Theirs is a vicious world, and we have no time to mourn the dead — only to be grateful we find ourselves still among the living, as we hurry onward from this nightmare scene…"

Susan leaned her head back, catching her breath. That hand had felt so real…

They emerged onto a wide valley, not unlike those nestled among the Central-California mountains where Susan sometimes took day-trips to clear her head. Low hills ringed the distant rim of the world, across a valley of golden grassland.

"Now we find ourselves in Ethiopia's Great Rift Valley," the Anthropologist said, "Just over one million years later. If we remain quiet and observe carefully, we may catch our first glimpse of anatomically modern *Homo sapiens* — our closest ancestors yet."

A naked man and woman who stood on either side of the tracks, far more lifelike than their more primitive predecessors. Whoever had crafted these animatronics had clearly done so with a great deal of care: a fact made all the more obvious by their anatomically correct nudity. Susan couldn't resist a glance at the male's anatomy — provoking an appreciative smile that he almost seemed to return.

Roger failed to notice any of this, of course. The animatronic woman, however, managed to catch his attention. She was just as splendidly proportioned as her male companion — and Roger paid tribute with a wolfish stare until their vehicle turned a corner and she was lost from view.

"Enjoying the window-shopping, dear?" Susan asked, smacking him on the arm.

"Oh, lighten up," Roger snorted as they passed a scene of animatronic hunters — now armed with primitive bows as well as spears — pursuing an ox across the grasslands.

"No," Susan said, her temper finally getting the better of her. "*You* lighten up! I've been trying to get your attention this whole trip…"

Their argument lasted through several scenes of early human life, and hundreds of thousands of years. As Susan confessed her anxieties about their engagement and moving to New York, the hunters transformed the ox's hide and flesh into primitive tools beneath the watchful eye of a shaman, while women painted scenes of the hunt on the walls. While Roger retorted that she didn't understand the pressures of his job, having never had a real one herself, the human race migrated out of Africa, into the Middle East and Europe, and across all the rest of the continents.

By the time they emerged "less than a hundred thousand years ago," they had lapsed into a silence as frigid as the Ice-Age tundra that surrounded them.

Nearby, human voices chattered and shouted in an unknown tongue. The vehicle rounded a corner, revealing not a hunting party, but a full-tilt battle in progress. A tribe of *Homo sapiens*, clad in tanned leather and body paint loosed a volley of arrows against a band of shorter, thicker-browed Neanderthals — hairy and draped in furs, brandishing stone spears.

"Poor things," Susan murmured. Roger laughed nastily, but she didn't look at him.

Leaving the battle behind, the ride carried them to its aftermath:

not the victory feast of the humans, but a frozen cliffside, where the surviving Neanderthals stood in a circle, mournfully adorning the graves of their fallen warriors with polished stones and bundles of flowers.

Susan blinked back tears — for the fallen Neanderthals, she told herself, and not any other reason.

"Fierce and hardy though they were," the Anthropologist proclaimed with a tone of regret, "the Neanderthals were defeated in the end. For in this age, it is Man's destiny to triumph over all his enemies. How long will Man's reign continue? Only the gods can say."

Susan chanced a glance over her shoulder at Roger. He had pulled out his cell phone, his face illuminated by its small screen. His fingers worked madly as he typed, the ride and his fiancée equally forgotten.

The ride emerged onto a village of crude huts of hide and bone, encircled by a carved fence of mammoth bones. Villagers crouched over cookfires, while others gathered in small groups to weave baskets or chip tools from flint. They spoke to one another in *language* — not grunts or monosyllables, but rich and textured sentences of rhythmic (albeit unintelligible) prose. Unlike their earlier, fiercer ancestors, their eyes shone with kindness and understanding. These were not merely *Homo sapiens*. They were *people*, like her.

Susan felt a strange longing stir in her breast — but before she could put words to it, the ride had hurried them onward to an enormous vaulted cave chamber. It was filled with animatronic hominids representative of all stages of humankind's evolution. *Australopithecus* crouched beside *Homo habilis*, while *Pithecanthropus erectus* hooted softly at the more complex utterances of the Neanderthal. And at the end, standing side by side like Adam and Eve, were *Homo sapiens:* Man and Woman.

"The Story of Man, you see" the Anthropologist said, his voice contemplative, "is not simply the story of *Homo sapiens*. It is the story of all of us."

But his words fell on deaf ears. Susan was busy staring down at the diamond on her left hand, brooding.

"Roger?" she asked softly, as their vehicle pulled into the unloading area, and the Anthropologist cautioned them to remain seated until the lap bar had lifted. No answer.

"Roger," she said again, louder.

He glanced up from his phone. "What?"

"Have you…" she bit her lip. "Have you told your parents?"

"Obviously," he said, rolling his eyes. "They wouldn't like us showing up unannounced—"

"Not that we're coming," Susan amended. "That we're getting married."

Roger opened his mouth, then closed it. Susan saw his Adam's apple working.

The ride ground to a halt, the safety bar lifting automatically. Roger exhaled in relief as he scurried from the car and up onto the loading platform. Susan stayed where she was.

"Roger," she said, gazing up at him from her seat. "Answer the question."

He ran a hand through his sleek blonde hair. "I wanted it to be a surprise."

Susan held his gaze, ignoring the leather-clad ride attendant who'd appeared to check if she needed help exiting the vehicle. She wondered why she'd never noticed how pale and watery Roger's eyes were.

"You forgot," she said softly. She accepted the attendant's hand and stepped out of the car — on the opposite side from Roger, so she was standing in the tunnel leading to The Story of Man. "You forgot to tell them about us."

"I—" Roger began, but was interrupted by a mechanical chime. His hand fell instinctively to the cell phone in his pocket.

"Don't answer that," Susan said.

His fingers worked restlessly, spasming like those of a junkie.

"It's work," he said, his will losing the battle against his fingers as his hands dug into his pocket. "The McLaren deal—"

Susan shook her head. She turned on her heel and strode back up the tunnel, toward the bright lights of the ride entrance. A glance over her shoulder showed Roger standing paralyzed on the platform on the far side of the vehicle, every bit as bewildered as the ride attendant.

His phone chimed again. He fished it out of his pocket and glanced down to read the message.

Susan turned away from her fiance and continued down the tunnel, knowing that when Roger looked up again, Susan would be long-gone.

6

The mastodon-bone ride vehicle stood near the far end of the tunnel, almost as though it were awaiting her like a faithful steed. Susan climbed in, and the vehicle began to move backwards through the ride.

The air grew warmer as Susan rode alone through the Story of Man. The drumbeats, ever-present throughout the exhibit, were growing steadily louder, their rhythm faster. Susan's heartbeat began to match the drumbeats, as if they were awakening something deep inside her; something primal and hungry that she hadn't known was a part of her until now.

The vehicle emerged into the ride's final chamber, where dozens of hominid animatronics stood or crouched in rows, from the apelike Australopithecines to the broad-browed Neanderthals. They looked somehow *realer* than they had before. Maybe it was a trick of the light, but their glassy eyes seemed to follow her as the vehicle carried her further down the tunnel, seeming to accelerate as the drumbeats thundered louder.

The heat had grown almost unbearable now. She shrugged out of her coat, letting it drop to the floor of the vehicle. She peeled off her sneakers, dropping them beside the coat. A faint sheen of sweat stood out on her brow. Her shirt and bra felt strangely cumbersome, so she began to wriggle out of those, too.

She grinned with faint amusement at the thought Roger's reaction to her behavior. But she had left Roger behind, along with any care for what he might think of her. That future was no longer hers.

She unbuttoned her shirt and let it fall behind her, forgotten. She paused before one of the animatronic *Homo habilis* hunters, his face a perfect balance between humanity and the earlier hominids. Susan shimmied out of her skirt and stockings, holding eye contact with the animatronic, as though daring the ancient hominid to take her if he was man enough.

Clad only in her briefs, Susan climbed out of the ride vehicle and strode out of the cave chamber, toward the red-gold light that now shone steadily at its exit. The animatronics watched her depart.

She did not see the *Homo habilis* hunter clamber down from his plinth. He crouched over her discarded skirt, picking up the garment and pawing it in his long-fingered hands, eyes wide with wonder at its texture. He cast a glance at the woman's retreating silhouette, but he did not pursue her.

7

Susan raised an arm to shield her eyes against the radiant light. As her eyes adjusted, an expression of joyful surprise spread across her face. The sight before her was both strange and familiar.

She was standing in the village of the *Homo sapiens*, just inside the fence carved of mammoth bones surrounding the huts. The people were posed just as they had been on her first ride-through — the women and men sewing intricate tunics with bone needles and sinew, the naked children playing about the campfires.

But the village was no longer a diorama; its people no longer animatronics, but beings of flesh and blood, as real and alive as Susan herself. She could hear them singing in rich, powerful voices, rising and falling in an intricate point-and-counterpoint, carrying a rhythm almost too complex to follow. The words were unfamiliar but rich with life and feeling. The village looked out upon an endless golden savanna, lit by a bright sun in a sky of cloudless blue.

Susan beamed with joy as the drumbeats rose to a crescendo. She stepped off the path, feeling the warm savanna sun on her bare limbs, the golden grass tickling her feet.

The villagers glanced up as she approached, though none of them paused in their work. They spoke a word of greeting to her, discernible by tone alone. Susan repeated it to them, and they laughed. Their expressions carried no hint of surprise at her presence; if anything, they seemed to have been expecting her.

A woman near Susan's own age stepped forward. She smiled and pressed something soft into Susan's arms.

Susan unfolded it. It was an animal skin — not a heavy, ugly fur like the coat Roger had given her, but light and breathable, its pattern mottled. It seemed to be a sort of skirt or kilt.

"Thank you," Susan told the woman. Then, in full view of the village, she removed her underwear, standing naked beneath the bright savanna sun. A round of scattered laughter dispelled the last hints of her nervousness. Like Adam and Eve, these people knew no shame in nakedness.

Susan tied the fur skirt around her waist. It fell perfectly into place around her hips, as if tailor-made just for her.

Her new friend held out one more gift: a spear, its carefully grooved flint tip lashed to the sturdy wooden shaft with strips of hide. It was as much a work of art as a tool; to these people there was no difference between the two. Susan wrapped her hands around the shaft, and her heart leaped into her throat. The spear felt like a part of her; as if it had been waiting here for her all along.

She shaded her eyes and gazed out upon the horizon. In the distance she discerned the slow-moving procession of a mammoth herd — startling in its sharpness, as if her eyes had developed a sudden clarity of long-distance vision. A group villagers had already set off in pursuit, loping easily across the golden savanna on tautly muscled legs.

Susan glanced down at the spear in her hand and noticed she was still wearing her gold ring with its glittering diamond. Strange that none of her fellow villagers had noticed this. *Roger*, some distant part of her whispered. She shook her head, as though to clear away from some lingering dream.

She slipped the ring from her finger and let it tumble to the earth. The golden-brown savanna grass swallowed it, though the diamond still glittered where the light caught it.

Spear in hand, Susan followed the hunters toward the mammoth herd, running free beneath the Pleistocene sun. The diamond lay in the dust behind her, forgotten.

Map brochure of the Seven Realms of OmniPark.

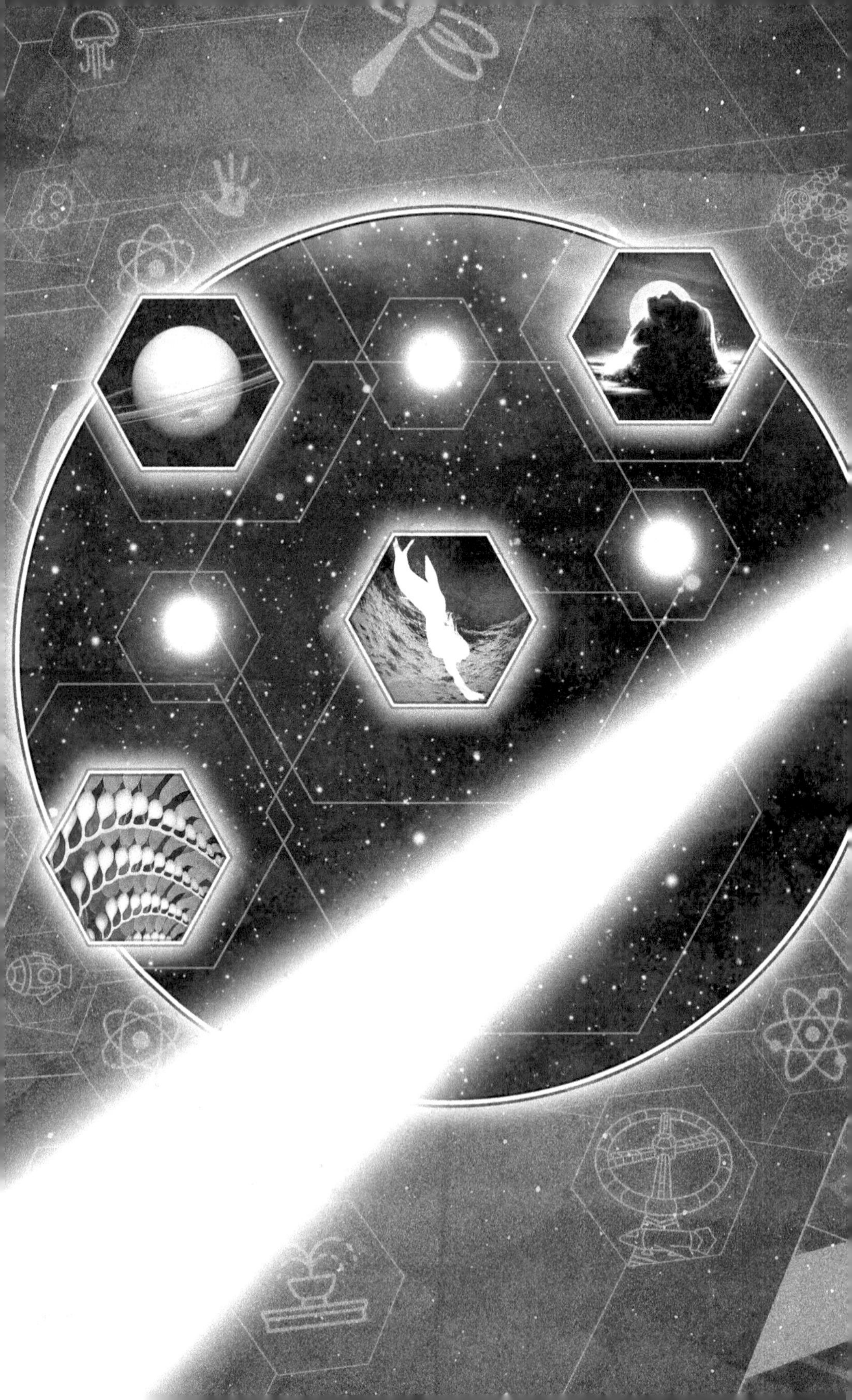

The Selkie Who Loved Buttermilk Biscuits

Susan Murrie Macdonald

1

Neamhnaid woke in strange waters. She recognized none of the fish who swam around her. Worse, she saw neither seal nor selkie of her own clan nearby. She sang out, but none answered.

Neamhnaid blinked. She stared at a human child, a human, Christian child in strange clothes. The child — too young to tell if it were male or female — was not splashing and struggling as humans normally did in the water. In fact, it didn't even look wet.

"Mommy, look! The seal is looking at me!" Jenny Carmichael shouted, pointing at Neamhnaid. "It has yellow eyes."

"Well, if you can look at it, it can look at you," Mrs. Carmichael replied, smiling and calm. "It must be boring for the animals in an aquarium, with nothing to do but stare at the tourists staring back at them."

Neamhnaid saw their mouths move, and heard their voices, but she couldn't understand a word they were saying.

"Look, Mommy!" A little girl exclaimed, pointing excitedly. "There's someone in the water!"

Neamhnaid turned lithely, glancing in the direction the child was pointing. She saw a merbeast unlike any known to her. It was shaped like a human, but the wrong color. She swam closer to investigate, but not too close, lest it be hungry. Too many creatures ate seals.

Neamhnaid swam upward until her head broke the surface. She took a deep breath and peered in all directions. She didn't see her skerry. She didn't see *any* skerries, nor any familiar shoreline.

The shore to her right was odd. No sand, and if it were rock 'twas oddly smooth and monochrome. She pulled herself out of the water onto the concrete platform next to the aquarium pool. She was hungry and shores (even odd ones) meant human food. She had a craving for Christian bread. The shore was rough beneath her fur. She scooted to behind a white plastic barrel and shed her sealskin. The now naked selkie folded her skin neatly behind the barrel. She looked around carefully. Her senses weren't as keen in this form as they were when she was her true self.

2

Xochitl Mendoza, a teenaged cast member in a royal blue Victorian gown, approached the older woman in the white lab coat seated at the breakroom table.

"What are you doing here?" the older woman demanded. "This area is for authorized personnel only."

"Sorry, Dr. Palmer," Xochitl scrutinized the woman's nametag: Tina Palmer, DVM. "This was the closest place out of sight of the customers."

"Guests," Dr. Palmer corrected automatically. OmniPark didn't have customers, only guests. "Who's that over there?" She pointed to the white plastic barrel. "Who's back there? What are you doing?"

Neamhnaid stood, judging it better to come out of her own volition than to be dragged out.

"Lordy, Lordy, Lordy, girl, you are barefoot all the way up," Dr. Palmer marveled. "Are you hurt? Did someone attack you?"

"Andy, close your eyes, or at least turn your head," Xochitl urged.

"Hey, I like the view," Andy confessed. Nonetheless, he politely turned away.

Dr. Palmer stared unabashedly. Neamhnaid looked Xochitl and Andy's age, maybe a little younger. No obvious bruises, no needle tracks on her arm. Her eyes weren't bloodshot, either. They were as yellow as a cat's, but healthy. Her skin was as pale as Wonderbread — and no sunburn, which would have been expected had she been naked long. Short, straight auburn hair, more brownish than red, that didn't quite reach her shoulders. About five-four, and barely over a hundred pounds.

"I'm Dr. Palmer," the vet introduced herself. "These are Andy and," she gaped at Xochitl's nametag and closed her mouth.

"It's pronounced Social. It's Aztec," she said in the weary tones of one who had had to explain it too many times. "What's your name? *Como te llamas?*"

"Neamhnaid"

"N-av-noij," Andy repeated carefully.

"How do you spell that?" Dr. Palmer asked.

"I am not a witch. I do not spell," Neamhnaid replied.

"Were you attacked? Are you all right?" Dr. Palmer asked. A naked teenage girl could hardly have wandered around a park full of tourists with cameras without someone noticing.

"I am not hurt, only hungry," Neamhnaid confessed. "I want Christian bread."

"Hang on a minute. I've got something you can borrow." Dr. Palmer rose from the table. She strode away and stopped at a storage cupboard and came back with a green pile of polyester.

This may be a little big, but it's better than nothing." Dr. Palmer unfolded a green Hawaiian muumuu with an orange floral print.

Xochitl nodded. "That members-only party a few nights ago." She hadn't been invited, not a costumed character's handler, but she'd heard about it; everyone had. The party's theme had been a Hawaiian luau, apparently. Dr. Teague and Miz Evelyn had been there, along with all the Technosophers, OmniPark department heads, and oil millionaires from all over the great state of Texas. Even a few Arab oil sheikhs.

To Andy's disappointment, Xochitl helped Neamhnaid slip into the dress. It was a bit oversized, as Dr. Palmer had predicted, but at least Neamhnaid was no longer barefoot from the toes up.

She was still barefoot, but only on her feet. "Excuse me a moment." She departed again, called Park Security, and returned a minute later with her purse and a pair of Aqua-shoes, black, with neon orange trim.

Xochitl tried not to stare when Neamhnaid put the aqua-shoes on. Her toes were webbed.

The door sighed open and in strode a pepper-haired gentleman in a dark blue uniform. "Hello, I'm Constable Carmichael." He twirled his nightstick and adjusted his domed hat. "I understand you have a minor problem, Dr. Palmer?"

The vet nodded. "These three don't belong backstage. I trust these two to get back where they belong. Someone is probably looking for this young lady. Probably several someones: her family and whoever stripped her naked. Look for drunken college boys whose practical joke went wrong. In the meantime, she's hungry," Dr. Palmer removed a ten dollar bill from her purse and handed it to Carmichael. "Her name is N-av-noij. Escort her to the Captain's Table . They serve Texas buttermilk biscuits with the clam chowder. Are you allergic to shellfish? Can you eat clams?"

"I eat clams."

"Good. Constable Carmichael can get you clams and 'Christian bread.'"

"Thank you."

Once Xochitl had helped Andy rearrange his lobster head, the three young people followed the security guard out of the aquarium area into the main Pequod section of the Realm of the Deep. The four walked down the ship's corridor together. Neamhnaid turned her head at the sound effects of metal creaking. The other three took the minor variations in background noise and lighting changes for granted and ignored them. Park employees dressed like nineteenth-century sailors and Victorian ladies mingled with tourists in shorts and blue jeans.

Xochitl and Andy said goodbye at Barnacle Books.

"Look, kids," the bookstore manager said, "Larry the Lobster is here to read *The Adventures of Molly the Mermaid*." He shoved a plush mermaid toy into Xochitl's hand, and whispered, "Where were you? You're five minutes late."

Xochitl gazed longingly at *Pirates in Petticoats* and *He Sailed With Columbus* on the bookshelves; she had heard all seventeen volumes of the Molly the Mermaid series too many times.

Neamhnaid and Constable Carmichael continued on to the Captain's Table. Practically ignored when it first opened three years ago, it was now considered the best and most popular of OmniPark's sit-down restaurants. An Amerasian woman dressed like Xochitl in a Navy blue Victorian gown, embellished with gold trim and anchor designs and OmnIcons of a stylized jellyfish escorted them to a table. A family of three tourists looked up and waved when they saw them. The daughter of the family, a cute tyke in pink shorts and a pink and white striped shirt, yelled "Grandpa," ran up and hugged the constable.

"Well, hello, Jenny. I was hoping to see you today," Constable Joe Carmichael admitted. He waved at his son and daughter-in-law and shoo'd Jenny back to her parents, then pulled out a chair for Neamhnaid to sit down.

"May I get you a menu, or do you know what you want?" the hostess asked. Many regulars knew the menu as well as the waitresses did.

"Clam chowder and buttermilk biscuits for the young lady, and two chocolate milks, please," Carmichael ordered.

"Right away, sir." She hurried off to turn the order into the kitchen.

"Well, we found my family. Do you see your family, or anyone you know?" Carmichael asked gently.

Neamhnaid turned her head. She did not recognize the human-forms of any of her selkie-clan, nor when she turned to the underwater observation windows did she see any seals, neither her kinfolk nor strangers. "No, Constable."

She smelled clam chowder simmering in the kitchen. In a flash, a waitress in a blue gown and a white apron came scrambling out, balancing a tray upon which sat a white ceramic bowl full of steaming chowder, a plate with two freshly baked buttermilk biscuits, and two glasses of chocolate milk.

"Most restaurants serve oyster crackers with their clam chowder," Carmichael explained, "but here in Texas we serve buttermilk biscuits. Some people dunk 'em into the chowder. Some just eat 'em as a side dish."

Neamhnaid picked up one of the biscuits and bit into it. She smiled widely.

Neamhnaid picked up the spoon and looked at it. It had been years since she had eaten on dry land and longer since she had used human silverware. She dipped the spoon into the bowl. The clam chowder was unusual to her, but good. It was hot.

"Don't burn your tongue. Have a sip of this." Carmichael drank some of his own chocolate milk.

Neamhnaid picked up the glass of brown liquid and took a hesitant, tentative sip. It was cool and sweet. The flavor was unusual to her, but pleasant. She took another bite of biscuit and chewed enthusiastically.

If more Scottish fishermen and farmboys had realized how much the merfolk craved the baked goods they could only get on land, there would have been more baking of oat-bannocks and a lot less stealing of sealskins.

Neamhnaid picked up her second biscuit. She dipped the corner of it into the chowder before taking a bite.

"Good, aren't they?" Carmichael asked.

Neamhnaid nodded. "Very good." She gobbled the rest of the biscuit down, then took another sip of chocolate milk.

The waitress came back to their table. "How is your lunch? May I get you anything else?"

"Good food," Neamhnaid said, swallowing quickly.

"Would you like more buttermilk biscuits?" Carmichael asked.

Neamhnaid nodded. "Yes, please."

"I can handle that," the waitress agreed. "Anything else to drink?"

"No, thank you."

The waitress brought back four biscuits. Neamhnaid ate two and offered the rest to Carmichael, who insisted she eat them.

Neamhnaid finished her clam chowder. She and Carmichael drained their glasses.

"You feel better now with a full tummy?" he asked. She nodded. "Then let's go see if we can't find your family."

She turned her head toward the observation window but saw only cod and halibut drifting by outside.

Carmichael paid for her lunch with Dr. Palmer's money, adding a small tip from his own funds. When Jenny, two tables away, saw her grandfather was getting ready to leave, she dashed away from her own fish and chips and ambushed him with a greasy-fingered hug. "Grandpa, are you going to take me on the Mariana Trench Ride?"

"No, I have to help Nee-av-noug find her family," Carmichael's tongue tripped over the selkie's name.

"Well, maybe they're riding the Trench Dive," Jenny suggested.

Carmichael shrugged. "They might be. Do you want to go on the ride?"

"My family might be diving," Neamhnaid acknowledged the possibility.

"Shall we check out the Mariana Trench?" Carmichael asked.

"Yes!" Jenny leaped, clutching balled fists against her chest.

"All right, Miss French Fries Fingers, you take Nee-av-noug to the ladies' room and wash your hands. I'll go clear this with your folks."

"Grandpa, when it's fish and chips, you don't call 'em Frenchy fries."

"Whatever you call them, your hands need washing," Joe Carmichael insisted.

Jenny led Neamhnaid to the bathroom and showed her how to operate the motion sensor automatic sinks. Neamhnaid was delighted. Jenny took them for granted.

When they returned, Constable Carmichael took the two girls by the hand and down the main hallway of the Realm of the Deep to the Foredeck, where a colored neon sign read "Mariana Trench Dive: An Exploration of the Ocean's Uttermost Chasm."

"Hey, sailor, got room for three more?" Carmichael asked the teenager tending the gate. His felt cap seemed a size too big, and several gold buttons were missing from his navy-blue jacket.

"Aye, aye, Bobby," he replied.

Carmichael nodded. He had known the answer to the question

before he asked. At least twenty guests stood waiting for the submersible ride. The Mariana Trench Dive could handle thirty two people at a time.

Lights flashed as the empty submersible returned to the loading dock. The last group of riders had disembarked just minutes ago in Davy Jones' Locker. Dr. Teague had studied Walt Disney as scrupulously as he had studied Archimedes and Euclid in his youth. All rides let out in giftshops.

"Does anyone need physical assistance into the submersible?" the attendant asked.

A chubby middle-aged woman with salt-and-ginger hair waved her cane. "I might."

"Over here, please, ma'am," the young man called out. "Bobby, can you and your party go first, so you can help her if necessary?"

"Certainly." Carmichael stepped forward. Jenny and Neamhnaid followed him. "Jenny, you get to be first aboard. You go down and find seats for you and Nee-av-noug. I'll be right behind you, helping this lady."

Jenny dashed down a spiral cast-iron staircase. Neamhnaid followed slowly behind her. Then came Constable Carmichael, boots pattering on the tile; and the lady with the cane, inching along one tap at a time. "What can I do to assist you?"

"Just catch me if I fall. Don't worry; my physical therapist has had me practicing stairs." Carmichael started slowly down the stairs, dividing his attention between the girls ahead of him and the lady right behind him.

"Stroke survivor?" Carmichael asked.

She nodded. "Uh-huh."

They reached the bottom of the stairs. She collapsed into the nearest seat.

"Are you all right?" he asked.

"I just need to sit and rest a minute."

"Excuse me, ma'am," another sailor approached them. "Can you move down to the end?" He pointed to the end of the row of seats, where Jenny and Neamhnaid were sitting.

"Not yet, but I will in a minute," she promised.

"Do you want me to stay until you're ready to move on?" Carmichael asked.

"No, I'll be fine if this young whippersnapper can be patient," the lady with the cane assured him. She smiled unevenly, the left side of her lip not curling up with the right side.

"If you're sure you'll be all right, ma'am." Carmichael touched his hat in a mock salute. He tramped down the row of sixteen seats facing portholes to rejoin his granddaughter and Neamhnaid.

Sixteen padded seats on both the port and starboard sides of the submersible faced arrays of oversized portholes lining the walls. The submersible, true to its name, did travel underwater — via keel-mounted wheels locked into a cleverly concealed track. A few feet away from the last seats in each row, a dais lay behind a red velvet curtain.

"Please move down to the last seat in the row and find a seat," the crewman directed. When all the passengers were seated, the red velvet curtain opened, revealing a weathered old man in a dark-blue peacoat and trousers. He tipped the skipper's hat from the mane of white hair that curled about his neck and shoulders.

"I am a fisherman. No, I am *the* Fisherman. I've hunted every creature beneath the waves, from sperm whales to giant squid. I've sailed from the Sargasso Sea to the Caribbean to the Mediterranean and the Black Sea. There's only one corner of the ocean I haven't investigated yet, and that's the Mariana Trench, the deepest chasm of the sea."

"The Mariana Trench, the deepest chasm of the sea," several passengers recited in unison with the audio-animatronic Fisherman.

"I built this submersible so I could hunt the sea-creatures that swim there. We are now diving to what oceanographers call the Epipelagic layer of the Photic zone."

A swarm of bubbles covered the portholes as the submersible ride pretended to dive.

The bubbles faded away. Tiger and hammerhead sharks were visible through the portholes.

"Behold the giant manta rays," the Fisherman announced. "And that huge fish there is the delicious tuna. Didn't know they were that big, did you?"

A few of the passengers revealed it was their first time on the ride by oohing and ahhing.

"Do you hear that? Whalesong. Useful creatures, whales," the Fisherman said, "Oil for lamps, ambergris for perfume, whalebone for ladies' corsets, meat and blubber. They're not fish at all, did you know that? They're mammals.

"They need to surface occasionally to breathe air. The mothers give live birth to their calves instead of laying eggs."

"Permission to dive deeper, Captain?" the ride attendant asked.

"We have now proven this vessel is safe for low level dives in the open ocean. Hold tight. We shall proceed to the Mesopelagic zone." As the Fisherman spoke, bubbles covered the portholes again and the light level decreased.

"Precious little sunlight reaches these fathoms. Our lamps illumine but a tiny bubble in this black void. 'Twill be the most light these creatures have ever beheld in their cold, frantic little lives. Behold the giant oarfish! He grows to the length of four men or more — and that's just the ones who've been caught. Takes but little imagination to conceive how sailors spied these creatures undulating beneath their oars, and brought home legends of sea serpents: dragons beneath the waves. Fascinating though they are, however, they make for poor victuals. Meat's a bit like jelly gone to rot."

He'd scarcely finished his sentence when the portholes revealed a new scene — an animatronic sperm whale battling a giant squid. Like titans from some primordial mythos those great beasts fought and tore. The whale thundered in fury, and waves of color coruscated along the squid's mantle.

"And here," said the Fisherman, "we witness the source of another legend: that of the Kraken.'"

"Release the kraken," a half-dozen passengers quoted in unison.

"The giant squid, believed mythical not so long ago, is all too real. His ancient nemesis the sperm whale, on the other hand, has been hunted from pole to pole by men greedy for his oil. As for myself, I wonder about his brain. It's the largest in all the animal kingdom. What unspoken thoughts and dreams do you suppose pass within that behemoth mind, here in the lightless deep?"

The submersible began to shake.

"We shall leave this fellow now to fight another day. He'll live threescore years and ten, just as men do. If a Kraken doesn't get him first, that is."

Now every seat was jostling fit to burst its moorings.. "Dive!" the Fisherman commanded. "This battle of titans has churned up a whirlpool that sucks us deeper! Down we go, into fathoms unplumbed since God first poured this brine beneath the firmament."

Bubbles churned outside the portholes. The air grew cold. The lights dimmed. In that frigid, dark silence, Neamhnaidh found herself abruptly conscious of each new breath. Goosebumps prickled her arms and neck.

"Here, we enter upon bathypelagic zone," the Fisherman declared. "Or as I call it, the Midnight Fathom. It's so cold down here, the water'd freeze if it weren't for the crushing pressure. Not a pinprick of sunlight reaches this deep. Here, we are in a world altogether separate from the land and sky."

"Those who are curious about the sun and other stars are invited to visit the Realm of the Stars and ride Nebula Quest when we return to shore," the ride attendant interrupted.

"This universe is yours to explore," the other ride attendant said.

"Behold!" cried the Fisherman. "Marvellous creatures seen by few who've lived to tell the tale. The anglerfish! The pelican eel! Beasts dredged from the depths of nightmare, to haunt these cold abyssal plains."

Neamhnaidh gazed wide-eyed out the porthole. She had heard of such creatures, but never seen them. Seals did not dive this deep. She had never been beyond the Mesopelagic zone in her home waters.

A bioluminescent squid swam past the porthole. Considerably smaller than the squid that had battled the sperm whale, this one emitted complex sequences of bioluminescent pulses along skin that danced with mosaics of kaleidoscopic color.

"It's not impossible that those colored pulses may be a form of communication, possibly trying to attract a lady squid, possibly trying to warn other fish that about a large, strange predator in the area. The bioluminescence is the only light this far down."

The submersible thunked against something hard that stopped it in its tracks, setting it rocking gently back and forth in the bubbling water.

"Is everyone safe?" the ride attendant asked. It was rare, but sometimes people did fall out of their seats at this point of the ride.

"All fine," one of the passengers assured him.

Outside the portholes, the light shone. A long something floated outside. It looked like a cross between a giant worm and a jellyfish. "A siphonophore, the biggest I've ever seen," the Fisherman announced. "Five hundred feet if it's an inch."

It was so long neither the head nor the tail was visible from the portholes. Jenny and half the other children aboard were out of their seats, putting their heads up against the window for a better view. They jumped back when tentacles slapped against the side of the submersible.

"The siphonophore is a colonial organism. It's a they, not an it. Therefore, wounding one part one the colony may not kill the entire creature. But if you don't try, you don't know. Firing harpoon — now!" The audio-animatronic figure of the Fisherman slammed his palm against a flat red button.

"Ah, that's got their attention. Dive, dive!"

Bubbles covered the portholes again. The temperature dropped enough that tourists dressed for west Texas weather shivered.

"Welcome to the abyssal zone. The only part of the ocean that's deeper is the hadopelagic zone, in the deepest of ocean trenches."

The view through the portholes revealed nothing but blackness. "I'm turning the boat's lights back on now."

The lights outside the boat came back on. The Fisherman pointed ahead to the bow windows. "Do you see that smoking thing? That's a hydrothermal vent. Those things surrounding the vent are tube worms. I'm sure you recognize the creatures trying to eat them. They're crabs. I'll have the crew try to catch a few. Crabs are good eating when they're fried into crab cakes. Look at that. What's that tower looks like a beehive? There are no bees beneath the ocean."

The submersible steered closer to the towering hivelike structure, "Behold!" the Fisherman cried out. A giant ugly white insect-like thing was at the center of the hive structure. "A previously undiscovered species of isopod. That must be their queen," he declared. "Ready harpoons." He raised his audio-animatronic arm and brought it down on the firing control.

Neamhnaid stared through the porthole as the harpoon missed the isopod queen by inches. Scores of warrior isopods emerged from within the hive. With powerful mantis-like pincers, they attacked the submersible. Neamhnaid watched as they tore plates of steel (or perhaps it was aluminum) from the boat's hull. Nuts and bolts floated past the portholes. Water — very cold water — squirted from the edges of the portholes onto the passengers. More water dripped from the ceiling and bulkheads.

"Bugs, Mr. Rico, zillions of 'em," quoted a passenger in a *Star Trek* t-shirt.

"We will either be obliterated or we will become gods," the passenger next to him said.

"Ascend!" the Fisherman ordered. Bubbles covered the portholes and more water sprayed from the porthole rims. Isopod warriors were just barely visible through the bubbles furiously pursuing the submersible.

"My responsibility is to see my passengers safely home, but I will return, and I pledge I shall find the Isopod Queen, and destroy her, if I have to spend the rest of my life hunting her."

The velvet curtains closed, concealing the figure of the Fisherman.

"Great queen, I pledge to serve you and protect you from this foul hunter," Neamhnaid swore.

"Nee, it's just make-believe. It's all audio-animatronics." Jenny tried to reassure her new friend.

Most of the ride the submersible had traveled so slowly and smoothly on its track that the passengers could not feel it moving. Now as it sped to escape the Isopod warriors, the passengers could definitely feel the motion.

Three minutes later, the submersible docked. A bell rang.

"All ashore that's going ashore," a ride attendant belted out.

"Ladies and gentlemen, thank you for joining us for the Mariana Trench Dive, here aboard the *Pequod*," the other ride attendant said. "Please proceed carefully up the staircase. One at a time, please. Mind your step, the deck is wet."

"Do you need help up the stairs, ma'am?" Joe Carmichael asked the stroke survivor.

"No, thank you. I can make it. I just can't make it quickly," she told him.

As promised, she inched up the cast iron staircase. The only time Carmichael had to help her was when she dropped her cane and he picked it up for her.

The exit line let out into Davy Jones' Locker, the largest giftshop in the Realm of the Deep. Neamhnaid followed Carmichael past rows of t-shirts and shelves of maritime themed souvenirs: seashell jewelry, chess sets with Neptune as king and mermaids as queen, with sea horses as knights, and octopi as bishops.

"Well, Nee-av-noug, have you seen anyone you know yet, either family or the ruffians who tried to hurt you?" Carmichael asked.

"I have seen none I know. But no one tried to hurt me. Everyone has been nothing but kind since I came here."

Carmichael rubbed his cookieduster. Dr. Palmer had said she'd found the girl stark naked backstage. She couldn't have walked through the park without a stitch on.

"Grandpa, can we go to Pterry's Time Tunnel and get some ice cream?" Jenny asked.

"You just had lunch a bit ago. You can't be hungry again already."

"I'm always hungry for ice cream," Jenny confessed.

Several places in OmniPark sold frozen bananas and snow cones, but only the Realm of Time, home of Pterry's Time Tunnel, offered an ice-cream parlor worthy of the title.

"Do you want ice cream, Nee?" Jenny asked.

"What is ice cream?" Neamhnaid replied.

"Grandpa, Nee doesn't know what ice cream is. We *have* to get her some," Jenny insisted.

Carmichael stroked his mustache again. A girl with an unpronounceable name who didn't know what ice cream was at her age? Who'd just shown up at the north end of OmniPark stark naked? It was, to quote the King of Siam, "a puzzlement." He saw a young man sneak something into his pocket, excused himself to the girls, and hurried off to stop the shoplifter.

Jenny looked around the shop and saw her parents browsing by the Jacques Cousteau videotapes. She rushed up and hugged them as though they'd been separated for days, not less than an hour. "Mommy, Daddy."

Neamhnaid smiled. With the example of such a loving family in his own clan, no wonder Constable Carmichael was so insistent on her finding her own family. She doubted her mother was worried yet. She was old enough to swim on her own for a while. But she had been dry a long time. Maybe it was time to fetch her sealskin and return to the water. And perhaps back in the water she could find a way to warn the Isopod Queen of the danger she was in.

"I think I know where my mother might be," Neamhnaid whispered to Jenny. "I have to go." She walked off toward the store door.

Jenny followed after her, clutching at her grandfather's sleeve as if to slow him so she could catch up.

Neamhnaid retraced her steps to the Authorized Personnel Only door that led to the backstage area of the main aquarium. She dashed back to the white plastic storage barrel and found her sealskin still there, unmolested. She slipped the aqua-shoes off her feet and pulled the muumuu off over her head.

Carmichael followed her in. He saw the orange dress come up and over her head. He put a hand over his eyes. "Young lady, what do you think you're doing?"

"Thank you for the buttermilk biscuits." She ducked behind the barrel and slipped back into her sealskin. Then she scooted over the rough concrete floor to the water's edge.

Carmichael swallowed hard against something that suddenly seemed to be stuck in his throat. He gawked as the seal stopped at the water's edge and waved a flipper before entering the water. "Nee-av-noug?" He hummed a few bars of 'The Grey Selkie.'

I am a man upon the land
I am a selkie in the sea
And when I am in my own country
My dwelling is in Sule Skerry.

He swore softly. He'd seen some odd things at OmniPark, but none this odd. Some of his co-workers swore the park was built above leylines. He had no idea how to write this up for his report.

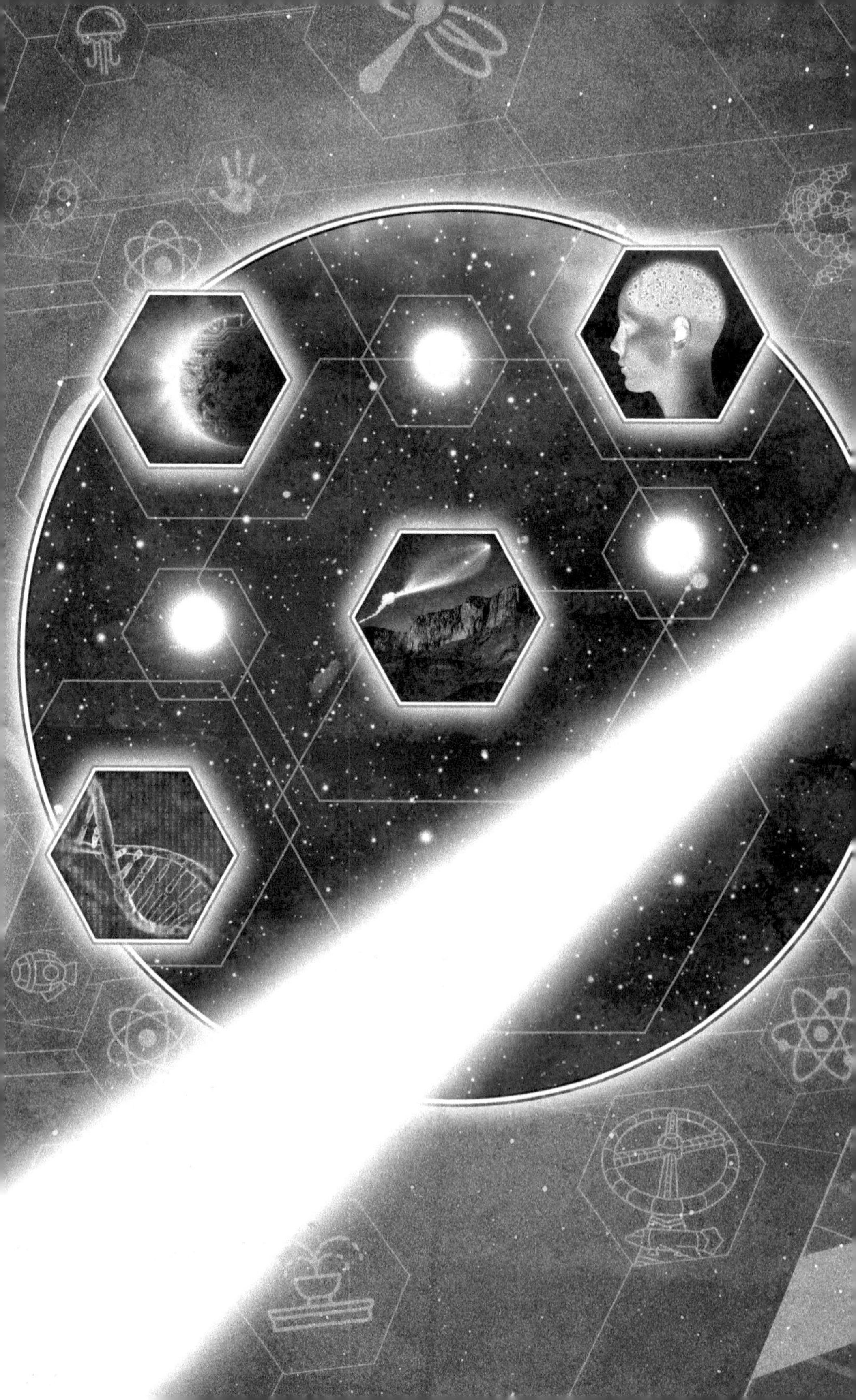

That Which Skulks Among The Stars

Ethan Hedman

1

Aurora drummed her fingers on the steering wheel of her '92 Ford Aerostar as she hummed along to the radio. Her eyes remained sharply focused, never straying from the highway. But her mind was somewhere else; somewhere she drew nearer to with each passing mile.

Over the past several weeks, memories of Aurora's childhood had begun popping into her head. At first they were just fleeting moments, short glimpses backward that brought brief smiles to her face throughout each day. Lately, however, the memories had intensified into vivid daydreams of whole days gone by. And of all those daydreams, none stood out more radiantly than those of OmniPark.

The jewel of West Texas had been the go-to vacation destination for Aurora's family throughout her youth. She had always counted down the days to their visit each summer, and her sudden recollections of all the park's wonders filled her with euphoria as she relived all her past adventures there.

She could still hear the rhythms of archaic chanting thundering out from the Great Tent's Amphitheatre; could feel her fingertips tracing the spines of dozens of leatherbound books in the Inventor's grand library. She recalled the slack-jawed glare of the rowdy Dunkleosteus — a literal fish-eyed gaze that had always made her giggle — and could still taste the hearty crab cakes served with a hearty slather of honey mustard from her meals aboard the *Pequod* submarine.

Each year's OmniPark trips lent fresh wind to Aurora's spirit of adventure. Roaming the Realms made her feel like so much more than just a small-town Texas girl visiting a theme park for the weekend. She became a dreamer among dreams, an explorer venturing between ever-shifting scales, times, and worlds. And as she coasted on her newfound wave of nostalgic bliss, one Realm enraptured her more powerfully than all the others; her favorite place in the world: the Realm of the Stars.

Aurora had fallen in love with the Realm before she'd even stepped inside it; her eyes wide with delight as she clutched the edges of her seat aboard one of its rockets; simulators designed to give an immersive spaceflight experience to the Realm's visitors on their way in. She absorbed every detail of the ringed station as it drew nearer in the viewport, admiring the serene spin which made it seem to dance. The memory of her first ride was so vibrant that Aurora briefly startled as she snapped back to attention at the wheel, glancing up at the first of many OmniPark billboards, heralding that the park was only twenty, ten, and finally just five miles ahead. She set her memories aside, focusing instead on following the roadside proclamations to the correct exit and finding a decent spot in the vast parking structure.

She emerged from the driver's seat, taking a moment to stretch after the long journey. Aurora tingled with anticipation as she left the parking complex. OmniPark was hers to explore again.

2

It was only after she'd passed beneath the towering ceilings of the Entryway Pavilion that Aurora realized how long she'd been away from the park. Her family's last vacation here was in 1990, a whole decade ago, when she was just fourteen. Aurora had hoped to return ever since, but those plans had always been thwarted by school, or work, or some other obligation. Now, as she stood before the OmniColor Fountain at the center of the park, she knew she had achieved something momentous. This trip was a pilgrimage to her past.

She thought about saving her favorite spot for last, but Aurora soon found herself standing squarely before the Realm of the Stars, queued up to board the next entry rocket headed for the station. The simulators had been renovated since her last visit, sporting a sleek, modern take on the aesthetics of retro science fiction. As soon as the rocket took off, the seat rumbling beneath her, Aurora was fourteen all over again. Her eyes sparkled with delight as she took in the stars, thousands of radiant dots scrolling brilliantly in the vault of space, as the rocket broke free of Earth's atmosphere.

Unlike the rockets, the model of the space station itself remained unchanged, much to Aurora's relief. The strains of a Strauss waltz softly wafted through the cabin as Orbit One drew nearer in the viewport. Much to Aurora's relief, the model of the station had remained unchanged throughout OmniPark's many renovations. Its iconic ring rotated just as she remembered it, its gentle spin welcoming her like a greeting from an old friend.

The rocket rumbled smoothly into one of the station's airlock bays, blasting out jets of hissing steam to adjust its angle of approach. The cabin rocked in place before a deep, dull *thud* from below signalled to everyone aboard that the rocket had safely landed.

Aurora waited to unbuckle her seatbelt until the other passengers got up to gather their belongings and exit the simulator. She smiled in recognition as a group of children gasped; the familiar hiss of the rocket's airlock had released a puff of air, causing the young travelers to leap back, giggling in astonishment. As she strolled out of the ride and onto the station, she admired the view along its curved central hallway, beckoning her onward with its countless windows and passageways.

While Aurora wove between squealing children, concerned parents, and an exhausted pair of chaperones struggling to shepherd a junior-high class, she noted the changes made to the station's decor. She grinned as she strode past windows displaying the station's newly remodeled manufacturing zone, delighted by the row of automated arms clicking shuttlecraft components into place.

Like the station itself, the design of these craft had a special place in her heart. The Technosophers assigned to the Realm of the Stars understood the treasure they had in its design; a delicate balance between the aesthetics of classic sci-fi art and the functionality of real-world spacecraft. Their renovations unified that balance with a seamless, artful flair, always staying true to the Realm's past while gazing toward a stylish interpretation of the future.

Ever since her first OmniPark visit, Aurora had dreamed of working here, tweaking the design of this Realm. All she'd ever wanted was to help instill that precious sense of awe and wonder in the next generation of vacationers. Even her choice of vehicle reflected her love for the Realm's designs. The beat up, old Aerostar felt like the closest thing on wheels to a vintage space shuttle, which made Aurora cherish it all the more.

As she reached the station's first major intersection, still weaving through the crowd, she passed into Orbit One Central, the plaza from which all the Realm's activities and attractions branched off. She'd spent hours here in her youth, dabbling with the music machines and art terminals, munching on packaged squares of freeze-dried Neapolitan ice cream from the Cosmonaut Cafe.

But the rest of her beloved station paled in comparison to her favorite spot: the queue for Nebula Quest, the Realm's main attraction, which overlooked the station's largest docking bay. As much as Aurora enjoyed the ride itself, she secretly preferred standing in line, watching starships of all designs and sizes docking, refueling and departing for galaxies unknown. Lost in their comings and goings, she often imagined their crews' adventures on distant worlds; brilliant nebulas looming in their viewscreens as their engines tore across the universe far faster than the speed of light. She always left that hangar promising herself that, someday, she too would find a way to soar among the stars.

Yet on today's long-awaited visit, she felt compelled to pass by the ride's queuing area, continuing along the station's ever-curving hallway. Aurora was perplexed; she wanted nothing more than to see those ships again, to gaze out from the docking bay and dream of galaxies just waiting to be discovered. But her feet kept moving forward, as if under their own power, taking a sharp left at the next intersection. Another abrupt turn came shortly thereafter, and Aurora found herself proceeding down a nondescript corridor of locked doors marked Station Crew Only.

And then, just as suddenly as her feet had changed course, they simply stopped moving. Aurora's brow furrowed in concentration, compelling her legs to carry her back the way she came, back to the comfort of her favorite place on the station. Panic rose in her chest as her limbs ardently refused to submit to her will.

Her gaze scanned the outward wall, a dull, gray surface without the slightest hint of decoration. There were no windows here; no signage to disrupt the endless expanse of riveted plastic.

With a quiet mechanical hiss, a tall panel slid open in the wall, nearly knocking Aurora backwards with surprise. She peered into the opening with curiosity and fear, able to see nothing but darkness within.

"Hello?" she called. "The, uh... the wall's open."

"Please come in," a distant voice responded.

Her feet moved of their own accord again, bringing her forward into the shadows. The panel slid shut behind her, immersing her in darkness.

"This isn't funny," she said, hearing a tremble creep into her voice. "Who are you? Either turn on a light or let me out of here."

The lights clicked on, momentarily blinding her. Aurora raised an arm to shield her eyes, which adjusted to the glare with surprising speed. She glanced upward, seeing all the lights pointed right at her.

"Congratulations, Aurora," the voice said, its gentle tone somehow as familiar as the rest of the station. "You passed the test."

Aurora blinked, squinting, barely able to discern the figure found behind the surge of light.

"Mom?" she whispered, breathless with confusion as her body went limp, collapsing on the fiberglass floor.

3

When she awoke, Aurora found herself sitting on a leather couch, a microfiber blanket having been arranged comfortably over her lap. Her mother sat across from her in an egg-shaped chair, calmly watching Aurora with a gentle grin.

Aurora tried to rise, but found the task impossible, as if she'd been bolted to the couch. "Mom? What is this? What's happening?"

"It's okay, Aurora," her mother said, her voice soothing and soft. "It's all okay now. You found your way home."

"Home?"

"To me. To us. You did wonderfully."

None of this felt wonderful. She didn't know this place, yet it felt as familiar as her own apartment. She didn't even know the woman seated across from her, even as she knew, at the same time, that this woman somehow *was* and most definitely was *not* her mother. She felt the wrongness of it all as a flood of obscured information roiled in her mind, minute details becoming clearer with every passing moment.

"You're not my mom," she found the strength to say, her voice cracking under the words. "Who the hell are you, really?"

The woman smoothed her slacks, scooching forward in her seat. "You recognized me as your mother before. And, in a way, I am. I'm Erika Rowden."

Aurora scowled, a rising frustration burning within her, battling her confusion. "I've never even heard that name."

"I know you haven't; or, at least, you don't think you have. You don't remember me, and that's okay. You're not supposed to at this stage. But please believe me when I tell you that everything's going to be fine."

"Why should I believe you?" Aurora demanded, fruitlessly trying to rise from the couch.

"I just need to ask you some questions. When's the last time you took a shower?"

Aurora blinked. "What?"

"The last time you showered," Erika repeated.

"I... don't know? Why do you care?"

"When did you eat last?"

"What the hell does that matter?"

Erika shrugged. "I'm just curious if you remember eating anything."

"Look," Aurora said. "Whatever this shit is, I'm done. Okay? Finished. Let me out of here, now." Aurora glowered, furious at her motionless legs, agitated with Erika's all-too-patient gaze.

"I understand your frustration," Erika said, leaning closer. "And I promise, you'll be free to do whatever you want as soon as we're done talking. But I need you to think first. Please. Tell me, where did you go to school?"

Aurora furrowed her brow. "If you're *really* my mother, you *know* where I went to school."

"Please, don't deflect the question. You don't even have to answer me out loud. Just *think*, Aurora. Can you remember anything from school? Any school?"

Aurora grunted, glaring down at her paralyzed legs. She felt intangible tendrils probing into her mind, compelling her to recall the schools she'd once attended. But her memories, usually so crisp and vivid, betrayed her. She remembered nothing from school, or of the schools themselves, not even so much as their names. She felt driven to recall her favorite teachers, rival students, class subjects; even something as small as a mascot or a bake sale. But, despite her bitter concentration, there was nothing to recall.

"I don't know," she said at last, swallowing hard as she felt tears welling up in her eyes. "And I don't know why I don't know."

"Yes you do," Erika said, reaching out to grasp Aurora's hand. "You weren't born, Aurora. You were created. Right here, behind the facade of the future, we made you: the culmination of all our highest aspirations. You've already achieved so much; more than we ever dreamed possible. We're prouder of you than you'll ever know. And now you're beginning to remember, just like you're supposed to."

"But my memories," Aurora protested. "All my memories of coming here as a kid..." Her eyes widened. "They're all I remember." She felt a cold twist in her stomach as the truth clicked into place. "Nothing but visiting

OmniPark, year after year... and always coming back here, to the Realm of the Stars."

"That's it," Erika whispered. "You're nearly there. Tell me the rest, Aurora."

"They were never my memories at all," Aurora whispered. "They're *yours*." She gazed into the eyes of the woman seated across from her, the mother she seemed to be meeting for the first time, who she already knew in the deepest part of herself. "You made me," she finally said. "I'm... not human."

Erika nodded, beaming with joy, squeezing Aurora's hand tighter. "You're so much more. I *am* your mother. Your creator. I programmed you to yearn for the stars, just as I always have. To feel awe and wonder at what we may someday find there. And with so many of our shared memories, in a way, you *are* me."

All at once, Aurora's frustrations subsided. She felt a wave of serene contentment wash over her, as inviting as a warm bath. "But... why?"

"Why what?" Erika pressed.

"Why... why everything? Why make me? Why do I exist?"

"Because," Erika said, releasing her grip on Aurora's hand, "we need you. You're more important than you could possibly imagine." She rose to her feet, gazing down on Aurora with the warm affection of a new mother. "I think you'll find you can move again. Care to join me for a stroll?"

4

They walked together in silence through the hallways tucked behind the station's walls, passing through service corridors and storage rooms as they went. At last they reached a small elevator, hidden in a nook behind towering stacks of cardboard boxes. Aurora followed Erika inside, watching her enter a complex code on the elevator's buttons before they rapidly ascended.

A moment later, a soft ping announced they'd reached their destination. The doors retracted smoothly, opening on a small balcony above the queue for Nebula Quest, complete with comfortable seating and a full view of Orbit One's main docking bay. A huge two-way mirror disguised as one of the bay's windows offered a view of the guests waiting in line below without betraying the pair's presence overhead.

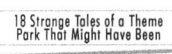

"Clever, isn't it?" Erika asked, nodding toward the window. "The other side displays a computer-generated view of space. All that interstellar traffic we both so love to watch. Dozens of ships, each a world unto itself; all painstakingly designed to evoke the image of a future we aim to attain." She sighed contentedly. "The Technosophers really outdid themselves here in the Stars. It's not the most wondrous thing on park grounds — not by a longshot." Erika smiled furtively, shaking her head. "But it's the greatest marvel our guests are allowed to see."

"It's my favorite place in the world," Aurora said. "But you already know that. And I can't help wondering if I only think that because you do. Or because you want me to."

"You're asking the right questions." Erika said, taking a seat in the nearest chair. "I already told you you're important, Aurora. But you need to understand how complex you are. There are labyrinths of information within you, each designed to be unlocked in your mind as its proper time comes. And as much as you're like me, I also designed you to learn, to make your own choices. Above all, to question everything you're told; everything you experience." Erika gazed out across the winding queue of guests. "You're going to find it difficult to tell the difference between everything that we've given to you, and what you've already given to yourself."

"You can start explaining what's been given to me, then." Aurora paused, taking a deep breath. She realized for the first time that her breathing wasn't functional; it was just an imitation of the real thing. She took the next breath anyway. "You made me here in the Realm of the Stars, I know that, somehow. But I came here on my own, so where was I before driving here?"

"We planted you some distance away. We needed to verify that you could operate alone; make independent, rational decisions. You passed that test with flying colors. You were never ordered to show up at OmniPark, yet you made the choice to come here, all the way to the hidden panel in the wall."

"*Did* I make those choices?" Aurora asked, recalling the uncomfortable intimacy of being drawn to an unknown destination by her own legs and feet. "Where does the programming end? Where do *I* begin?"

Erika nodded, pleased with this line of questioning. "Remember when you woke up in the van this morning?"

"Sure," Aurora said. She'd awoken at a rest stop around the halfway mark of her journey, where she'd pulled over after a twenty-hour driving stretch to catch some sleep. Except now she knew she never started that journey. Her eyes widened. "I've only existed since this morning?"

"You've only been *conscious* since this morning. You've been activated before, many times, to ensure that aspects of your programming were running smoothly. But you won't have any memories of those moments, since you weren't yet wholly *you*. Everything before today has been for just one purpose: to prepare you for this moment."

Aurora lowered herself into a nearby chair. "This sounds like another test."

"Nearly the last one," Erika said. "I know what you're thinking; no, you're not going to be shut down permanently, no matter what you decide about the mission."

"What mission?" Aurora asked, an abrupt sense of excitement rising within her. She wondered if the feeling was genuine or programmed, or if that distinction even meant anything to begin with.

"The short version?" Erika leaned forward. "You're the only being in existence who can do what needs to be done for the future of humanity."

Aurora gazed out across the crowd of clueless tourists. "I think I need the long version."

Erika nodded. "You know who Dalton Teague is, of course."

"Sure. He made all this," Aurora said, tilting her head towards the ride below. "He created OmniPark."

"Yes." Erika reached out, patting Aurora's knee. "If you're willing to think of me as your mother, it's not much of a stretch to think of Dalton as your grandfather. Without him, your creation would have been impossible. He had the vision to understand why you were necessary, not to mention the resources to make you a reality. You're not the only great creation he's grandfathered into existence. This place, this park, means so much more than most people will ever know, and serves more purposes than they could ever guess. A lot of them remain mysteries, even to me." She chuckled. "We Technosophers work on a strict need-to-know basis, let me tell you."

"It's a theme park," Aurora said. "Don't get me wrong; an amazing one, but... what other purposes could it have?"

A coy grin flashed across Erika's face. "Being a theme park *is* its first purpose. OmniPark is an endlessly intriguing playground. It's the reason I chose to study computer science, in fact, after my very first visit to the Stars. Hardly anybody took A.I. programming seriously back then — hardly anyone except for Dalton, that is. He hired me straight out of college and put me in charge of this Realm's automation team."

"I... think I remember all of that, too," Aurora said, furrowing her brow as more memories clicked into place like rediscovered jigsaw pieces. "And I know there's more to it than that."

Erika nodded. "OmniPark also facilitates a great deal of education and research. The Realms grant people new perspectives; ideas they may never have considered in their everyday lives. At the same time, the park gives us the opportunity to observe human group dynamics. It's a complex environment where people feel relaxed and spontaneous, the perfect place to study their behavioral patterns. In essence, OmniPark is a lab they happily pay to visit, year after year. It's not my department, exactly, but we're discovering all sorts of things about how people learn. How desires translate into actions; how fears and aspirations take root in the mind. A lot of that knowledge went into making you *you*."

Aurora's eyes narrowed. "There's more to it than just *that*, too, isn't there?"

"So much more. Some of it's above my pay grade; this place is a wellspring of secrets and revelations, scientific and otherwise. Teague has worked hard to keep most of that research concealed, even from many of his own researchers. The Inventor and the Physicist are more than just actors, you know. They've seen things — wonderful, terrible things." Erika smirked. "There's a bad joke around here: science is never an exact science. Since the beginning, we've wandered into those wonders and terrors in equal measure."

Aurora sat back, rubbing her forehead. "Some joke," she said. "But what does any of this have to do with me?"

"You're my life's work." Erika beamed. "And like all of us here, you're a facet of something greater than yourself. Our dream has always been to soar among the stars. Dalton shares that dream, as he shares many others." She stood up, leaning against the balcony, watching a colossal freighter touch down slowly in the animated window on the far wall of the plaza. "I know you love these ships just as dearly as I do. They've inspired me every day I've worked here, even though they're just shadows of the real thing."

"The real thing?" Aurora repeated, thinking she must've misunderstood.

"Our space program." Erika smirked, watching stars glimmer in the distance.

Aurora raised her eyebrows. "You're saying OmniPark has its own NASA."

"No. I'm saying OmniPark outdid NASA, and everyone else, more than a decade ago. Before you protest, remember: we were able to build *you*, too."

"But, you..." Aurora stammered. "You can't keep something like that hidden. There are satellites. Radar. Someone would have noticed by now."

Erika cocked her head, grinning. "Not yet. We've ventured farther away from our planet than any government agency will be able to for decades to come. And we've done it all under a perfect veil of secrecy."

"Why? I mean, why do any of this?"

Erika returned to the chair next to Aurora's. "Again, this is a bit above my pay grade, but the program's initial emphasis was strictly on exploration and discovery. Before long, Teague shifted its focus to human colonization, hoping to rescue at least some of us from this planet before it turns into a toxic wasteland. But now we're driven by something else entirely."

Aurora nodded. "I assume you're going to tell me what that is."

Erika sighed deeply, bowing her head. "Our losses."

5

Back inside the elevator, Erika entered another complex code, sending them plunging deep beneath the earth. When the doors rolled aside, Aurora thought she was gazing out on an elaborate prototype of some advanced new ride.

"It's no prototype," Erika remarked, seeming to pluck the thought from Aurora's mind. "This is as real as real can be. Welcome to the Aggregation."

They stepped into an enormous bunker, its massive walls stretching outward in a long, smooth curve. Countless lines of spacecraft rumbled and hissed from their illuminated places on the broad concrete expanse. No two ships were quite alike, the lines reflecting versions of development; those nearest to the elevator were the smallest, the lustrous polish of their slender, arched wings glinting off their cockpits beneath the lighting overhead. Farther sat a row of larger craft; bulky, utilitarian haulers which sported cluttered tool arrays on their craggy underbellies. Gallant white behemoths loomed behind all the rest, their ample frames lined with rows of viewports on each side, gigantic sets of potent engines bulging out from their aft ends.

"We've been hard at work developing faster modes of spaceflight," Erika started to explain, "and the engineering team just came up with some brilliant new propulsion techniques for precise thruster maneuverability." As she continued speaking, Aurora felt a trickle of blueprints and equations unlocking in her mind, each accompanying whatever Erika was describing in the moment.

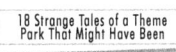

More revelations came swiftly after that; almost too swiftly for Aurora to process. By the time she and Erika arrived at a bulky metal door marked Level 7 Clearance Only, the trickle had become a torrent. She felt as if she'd learned too much at once, or at least that she'd learned it all too quickly. Yet she hadn't learned anything *new* here today. Every tidbit of data had been secreted away inside of her, awaiting the proper code-words to unpack and join the flock of information.

Erika scanned her employee badge against a small panel near the door, causing a tiny, illuminated box to extend from the wall. "Before we enter," she said, placing her thumb in the box, awaiting its affirming beep, "I need you to know that if you make the choice not to take the mission, you aren't going to remember anything you learn inside this room."

"You still haven't told me what the mission is," Aurora said. "How can I make a decision if I don't know what that decision means?"

Erika leaned close to the wall, allowing a tiny lens to scan her retina, before turning back to Aurora with a grin. "Sometimes it's uncanny, just how much you sound like me." She tapped out a code on a large keypad of numbers, letters, and ancient symbols; markings Aurora recognized with vague familiarity from tidbits in her memories of Dalton's hand-scrawled notes. With a press of Erika's hand against a final panel, the door to the room slid open. Inside was nothing but black walls, dim light, a blank screen, and a pair of chairs. "Take a seat," Erika said.

6

Aurora followed the other woman's footsteps, conscious of the door sliding shut faintly behind her. She took a seat in the nearest chair, staring at Erika expectantly. "All right," she said, "I'm listening."

"In just a moment," Erika explained, "I'm going to say a certain word: the final key guarding the most restricted information inside you. Not even I know exactly what that information entails. I designed the key to only decrypt those memories here, behind that vault door. Once you hear the code, you'll know why we need you so badly, and exactly what we've created you to do."

Aurora grounded herself with a deep, simulated breath. "Am I allowed to say no?"

"Of course you are," Erika said. "Dalton was adamant about that. From the moment you woke up today, you've had the power to make and embrace your own choices. You have to decide for yourself whether or not you'll take on the mission. Now," she said, "we've arrived at the moment of truth. Are you ready?"

Aurora nodded, tingling with the same sense of innate excitement she'd felt when she first heard about the mission. "Ready," she said at last.

"Meadowcroft," Erika whispered. And all at once, Aurora *knew*.

She instantly recalled the history of the Aggregation, from that fateful midnight in the park's early days when bulldozers first broke ground on this bunker. She remembered every launch; every whoop and cheer from the control team as each new probe and ship thundered up and out into the great unknown. She remembered the crew's optimism and pride; the friends lost on missions that never returned.

And at last, she knew the reason *why* those missions had never returned: every crewed craft sent beyond the solar system had been crushed to shrapnel in the cold, dark void between the stars.

Only fragments of information ever leaked back; dribbles of data drawn from strong black boxes the crew had managed to retrieve with unmanned probes. Dalton and his inner circle had sat watching the garbled, staticky footage in this very room, their faces pallid with fear in the monitor's flickering light.

She knew what Dalton himself had understood: the truth within the truth, revealed not even to Erika, stored only in the depths of Aurora's encrypted memories. Humanity was far from alone in the universe, but those who had destroyed the explorers' ships were *not* the ultimate enemy. They were little more than wardens; sentries set at the gates of our defenseless solar system, tasked with the quick, merciful termination of all who ventured ignorantly into the black gulfs beyond.

Somewhere in that darkness, far worse things waited. Things that sniffed and slavered in the chasms of spacetime, eagerly awaiting the next interloper to alert them to a nearby garden world. Such places were ripe with soft-bodied creatures to be farmed, harvested, and devoured by the insatiable monstrosities until the heat-death of the universe could bring a bitter and inevitable end to it all.

Aurora was Dalton Teague's response to that great unknown; the defiant fist he'd raised against those ravenous lurkers obscured among the cosmos. In Aurora, curiosity, wonder, and ingenuity had been combined with physical and mental capabilities far beyond those of any human being. She could run full-tilt for miles without pausing for breath and survive indefinitely without food or water; could solve differential equations with tachyon speed while piloting any known spacecraft smoothly through an asteroid field. She could even traverse the great void itself, naked and alone, if the mission were to require it.

She represented a chance; a razor-thin chance, but a real one all the same. Aurora could survive an encounter with these cryptic cosmic wardens; to commune with them, if possible, and return to share her knowledge of that which skulks among the stars.

Cowering in terror had never been an option; Teague's constitution would never have allowed it. He'd understood, from the very first loss, that the only viable response was to observe, investigate, and hope someday to understand.

Aurora's eyes snapped open. "Get me to my fucking ship."

*Snapshot of Teague's desk while assembling his
beloved collection of early OmniPark history.*

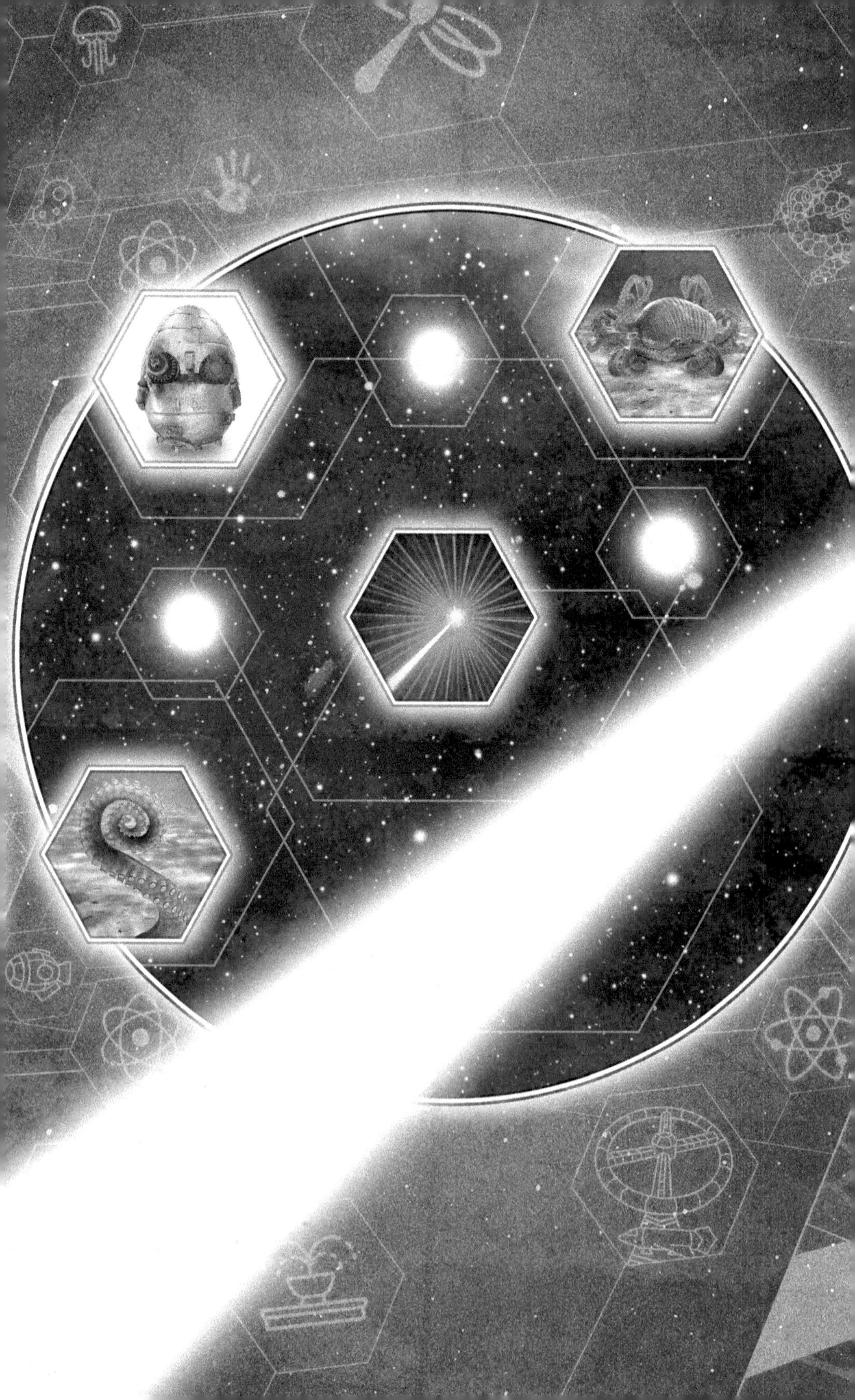

DOWN CAME THE RAINS

JACK BATES

For three consecutive summers in the early 1990s, I was a Realm Ambassador at OmniPark. Then I quit.

I didn't leave my job at the West-Texas theme park because I loathed the week of July 4th, which pretty much stretched from June 30th to July 7th. For those of us who labored in the trenches, the Fourth of July was a week-long battle with overheated, overtired, overstressed tourists. It was grueling — but it wasn't enough to force me to quit.

As a child, I'd fallen under OmniPark's spell-like so many other kids. Passing beneath the arch and hearing the thunderous theme song piped in conjunction with the erupting geysers of the Omnicolor Fountain conjured fantastical possibilities of adventure. I could shrink down to the size of an atom, go back or forward through time. So many paths awaited. It made me feel small to be in someone else's dream turned reality. I walked in a world imagined by a man who envisioned it to be a unique experience on each visit.

In his opening-day speech, OmniPark's founder and chairman said, "This universe is yours to explore." I interpreted those words as a direct instruction; a command. As I grew older, I knew one day I wanted to become a part of OmniPark's world. My plan was to start as a park ambassador, then work my way up to Technosopher — a team member who designed attractions, events, and Realms.

"Remember what happened to the Wizard when Dorothy pulled back the curtain," my father warned.

I told my father Dalton Teague was no illusionist, but a visionary; a genius; and I couldn't wait to work at his side. As soon as I turned eighteen, I applied for a job at OmniPark. I reported to the Library within the Realm of Time for orientation. Zespa Clarke, the woman charged with the placement or removal of park employees, informed us at our interviews Dalton Teague would address us. I arrived an hour before anyone else and secured one of the high back, padded, red leather chairs. After brief remarks from Ms. Clarke, I prepared to meet the man who dreamt the Realms.

The lights dimmed. The bookcases parted. An image flickered on a large screen. After a moment the words, 'A Greeting from Dalton Teague' gave way to an old man it took me a moment to recognize.

I remember thinking, "That's Dalton Teague?" The man on the screen differed from the one we all knew from his weekly TV show, The Realm of OmniColor. The Dalton Teague that appeared before us babbled about continuums. He spoke more to someone behind the camera than he spoke to us.

The first couple of weeks I arrived early hoping to spot Teague taking a pre-opening stroll. In the tranquility before the golden rope was dropped at the entrance to the park, before the eager crowds marched fervently to favorite realms, before Rudolph Xavier's masterful 'Ode to Imagination' trumpeted from hidden speakers, in that space between calm and frenzy, Dalton Teague sometimes walked in the empty park, appearing and then disappearing almost as quickly. My colleagues insisted Teague lived in a secret apartment in one of the realms. Others who saw him complained Teague ignored them.

My own experience was a bit unsettling. During my second year of employment, my duties included street sweeping. I patrolled my assigned area when I noticed a passing of guests quieted. Dalton Teague approached. His presence both frightened and intrigued me.

"Good morning, Mr. Teague."

I stood straighter, smiled wider.

Teague's expression remained constant as he passed through me. A moment later the image disappeared only to reappear behind me.

On my last day at OmniPark, attendance was light for a July afternoon so close to the holiday. Torrential rains plagued us in the wake of Hurricane Arlene in June.

On the day the rains fell the heaviest, my crew chief stationed me outside the Realm of the Deep, a spectacular pavilion with a 60-million-gallon aquazoorium. Numerous hands-on activities awaited visitors exiting the *Pequod* simulator before they made their way into the observation spheres of the aquazoorium.

Guests crammed together to catch a glimpse of Squidbeak, a sixty-foot giant cephalopod. It's milky white mantle cast the impression of a ghostly apparition haunting the water.

I asked several of the veteran employees about Squidbeaks origin. I never heard a plausible explanation of how it made the aquazoorium its home or how it had grown to the gargantuan size. Quietly, rumors circulated amongst OmniPark employees about Squidbeak's appetite suggesting the squid may have eaten its way into giancy. All that's for certain is the park stopped sending in human divers to clean the tank windows after a maintenance man named Horace Ubley swam into the tank to clean it but never resurfaced. A discarded regulator from his air tank was the only indication Ubley showed up to do his job.

After Horace Ubley disappeared, steel grates were placed between the two enormous tanks. Smaller fish could pass through the gaps in the bars but often became chum for Squidbeak. The beast appeared content to stay tucked against the wall until feeding time. People lined up in advance just to glimpse Squidbeak devour the 600 pounds of live fish dumped into the giant squid's semi-private tank. It was like watching a firework erupt within a murky, water-filled bubble. A single, squiggling rocket rising. Then eight arms lined with suction cups and a pair of feeding tentacles all akimbo, curling around fish and pulling them to its razor sharp beak. Finally, exhausted but sated, drifting down and down and down until Squidbeak lay against the wall to digest the meal. The entire activity captured by guests equipped with a variety of still, motion, or video cameras.

Horace Ubley's disappearance wasn't the only odd occurrence to happen at OmniPark, nor was it the last. Nearly twenty years after the park fell dark, strange aberrations continued to plague the land of the Seven Realms.

Still, none were as fantastical as that rainy July afternoon I punched out for the last time.

I stood in a park issued stars and stripes, rain poncho with the hood covering my Realm of the Deep ball cap. Water seeped over the sides of my shoes soaking my socks and chilling my feet. Frustrated and cold, I snuck a smoke while guests rushed into the pavilion to escape the deluge. I could drag my arm inside the poncho and cup a cigarette in my hand beneath the cloak. If I spotted a crew chief approaching, I could drop the butt into the puddle around my feet.

I was taking a puff when I spied an armadillo caught in the rush of water. At least I thought it was an armadillo. It had a shell like an armadillo, and what I thought was a tail like an armadillo. It just didn't move like an armadillo. This particular creature appeared to be squirming its way through the inch or so of water flooding the park. It traced a nonsensical path away from the Omnicolor Fountain — darting left then swooping right until it slithered within thirty feet of me only diverting its trajectory when a sparrow landed on a bench nearby. A tentacle sprang out from the beast and wrapped around the bird. Though it tried to escape, the bird disappeared into the water. Panicked chirping escaped from the tiny bird. The unfortunate sparrow bent and twisted to keep its head out of the water. The octodillo controlled the bird's fate.

A clap of thunder drew my attention to the skies. I had barely turned away from the struggle between the hunter and its prey. Only the bird's beak poked out of the water line.

The improbable man peeked from behind an information kiosk that up until that moment I couldn't recall ever being there. That rainy afternoon I stood outside the Realm of the Deep for a couple of hours. How had I never noticed the information kiosk? It was as if it had appeared out of nowhere. But there it stood, between the grand fountain and me. Peeking around the side was a man in a long raincoat. Rain bounced off the floppy brim of his hat. The metal clasps of his galoshes rattled as he slogged through the puddles. He adjusted welder's goggles over his curious eyes, his hands covered by a pair of soft, leather gauntlets that extended past his wrists. A leather sack drooped off of his right shoulder.

Great, I thought. He's one of those guests.

For some fans, OmniPark became a kind of permanent, space age Renaissance Fair. An opportunity for guests to dress to match the mood or theme of their favorite Realm. They came to OmniPark to escape the daily ennui of routine and enter a fantasy world where they could journey freely in a fantasy world. In the employee lounge we referred to these visitors as Omnigeeks.

The Improbable Man opened two of the lower buttons on his long coat, revealing a pair of plum-colored pants, a white shirt, and a cranberry vest. From the leather sack he produced an elaborate clockwork egg the size of a cantaloupe. All of the intricate, inner cogs and wheels and clapper arms of a pocket watch clicking and whirring inside an egg shaped frame. All of it exposed. No protective case, yet nothing fell out of the frame. The man unscrewed the small end of the egg. He tiptoed through the rising rain as much as a man with buckle galoshes could tiptoe.

I dropped my cigarette. "I wouldn't venture over there."

He pirouetted, tucking the mechanical egg under his arm. "I didn't see you there, Miss Realm Ambassador."

"That's okay. I didn't see you until a second ago."

"That's because I only just arrived."

Why had I opened the door? Clearly, he intended to continue with his fantasy role playing, dragging me into his narrative. Most of the time I could dodge these situations without having to roll my way out with a twenty-sided die. This guest remained persistent.

"Yeah. There's some kind of mutant armadillo over there. It's ensnared a bird."

The sparrow splashed water with its tail.

"The Decapodous Turba are voracious eaters."

"What is that? Some dinosaur fish?"

He spoke as if this were common knowledge. "The Decapodous Turba. From Lolligo Prime. In the Tadpole Galaxy?"

"Uh-huh…"

He persisted. "The Tadpole Galaxy. Four-point-two million light years away. It's practically next door."

My impatience grew. "Was there something you needed, sir?"

He put a finger to his lips.

"Excuse me," I said. "But that's not cool."

"Neither is smoking. On or off the clock. Boom! I got you there, didn't I, Miss Realm Ambassador?" He gestured at my name badge. "Julie M., from Odessa."

"I wasn't smoking."

"You have a burn hole on your poncho."

I wiggled my pinkie finger into the tear in the fabric and that was when the thing with the clockwork egg happened.

The octodillo- to this day I prefer that name to Decapodous Turba—looked directly at us, stretched its tentacles in front of itself, and remained perfectly still.

The sparrow, now free of the octodillo's grasp, fluttered away.

"What is the Deca—"

"Decapodous Turba."

"What is it doing?"

"Disguising itself as a coral plant so we'll lose interest in it and leave."

An aiming device emerged from the back of the clockwork egg. He used the copper crosshairs to direct an azure beam of energy at the octodillo. As the beam retracted, it dragged the octodillo out of the water and into the egg, shrinking the beast to the size of a golf ball. The man screwed the cap back into place. He carried the device with both hands. Several of the exterior cogs and wheels whirred into place. Tiny clapper-arms on tinier springs held in place by even tinier screws clicked off single advancements of ever rotating notched dials. The delicate dynamo hummed. It never ceased to whirr, click, or spin.

"The door," he said.

"What door?"

The man extended his egg holding hands in the direction of a kiosk. "That one."

There was, indeed, a door. I don't know how I overlooked not only a mint green door but the entire green and white, vertically striped kiosk with the carousel topper. The black and gold lettering of 'Information Kiosk' painted on a frosted window pane in the door gave the impression the booth first appeared when OmniPark opened in the '70s. An old time skeleton key stuck out of the lock.

"Would you like me to open it?" I asked.

He seemed to be growing impatient.

"If you wouldn't mind."

I turned the key. "Do you work here?"

"My badge is inside. Hurry, we haven't much time." He slogged through the falling rain and rising waters.

For some reason I thought the interior would be more elaborate. A simple counter top stretched beneath a pull-down metal shade covering a window. Locked in place by a pair of sliding bolts, the shade resembled a blast shield. A pair of white, curved-back, wooden chairs, the kind found in the OmniCone Ice Creamery, faced the window.

The man hurried past me. He balanced the mechanical egg's bigger end on the counter top. Three triangular wings slid out of the egg to help keep it from tipping.

"Here's your key."

He waved it away. "The key is yours. All Realm Ambassadors should carry one."

"What do I need with an old fashion key?"

"Keys are marvelous inventions. They hold memories of the past and unlock doors to the future." He slid the two chairs out from under the counter. "Sit down," he said and occupied the chair on the left.

I slipped the key into my pocket. "I'm not on my break."

"We're way past your shift."

"What does that mean?"

"Please. Sit down."

"Not until you tell me who you are."

He rummaged through a drawer beneath the counter until he

found a lanyard and badge. OmniPark with its universally recognized icon appeared at the top of the badge. Beneath the park's logo was a terrible I.D. photo and a name: Chromaxium Flynn, Technosopher.

The picture on the badge showed a slightly younger, much gawkier version of Flynn. Curly hair, awkward smile. Thick, black framed glasses.

"That's you?"

"Just sit down, would you, please?"

I sat.

He stood.

"Come along." He opened the door. "And bring the egg."

We no longer stood outside the Realm of the Deep. We weren't even facing the Omnicolor Fountain. An infinitely long corridor stretched before us. A constant hum resonated from somewhere further down the hall. Crystals flickered inside glass semi-spheres framed with brass rings.

"Where are we?"

"Miss Realm Ambassador Julie," Flynn said. "Welcome to the Void."

Flynn opened a door I hadn't noticed. It was the kiosk all over again.

"I don't recall any area within the park ever being called the Void, Mr. Flynn. Is it new?"

"The Void is as old as time and as young as tomorrow. The Void exists outside of the Seven Realms. It exists in that space between tic and tock. A gateway between the fabric of reality and the gossamer of fantasy. Between doubt and epiphany. The Void is both here and gone."

Flynn placed the egg on a shelf inside an oval pod. He plugged the square end of a cord into a slot that opened on the screw cap top of the egg. Static filled a monitor screen. Flynn flicked the glass and the octodillo appeared.

In a soft voice, Flynn said, "Hello, beautiful." He pulled on a headset.

The octodillo clicked its beak. A series of dotted triangles, vertical tildys, and concentric circles scrolled across the screen, like closed captioning on a TV. Flynn cracked his knuckles then wiggled his fingers. He typed on a keyboard. A moment later he cracked his neck.

"All right, my little friend," Flynn said. "Let's play twenty-thousand questions. Who are you and why are you here?"

At first all I heard was clicking followed by wet, slurping grunts. After a delay, a disembodied voice responded.

"I request feeding."

Flynn refused to relent. "I'll feed you when you explain who you are and why you're here."

Agitated, the octodillo vehemently hissed and clicked until the artificial voice responded.

"I request feeding."

"How does it do that?" I asked. "All I hear is clicking and slurping."

"Universal Life Form Language Translator. Works on most extraterrestrial species. Never use it on ants. All ants do is sing dirges about eating us from the inside out."

More clicking and slurping. "I request feeding."

Flynn positioned the cursor over a 'Mute' button. He clicked it. "We're not going to get much out of this one."

"So give it some kibble and see what you get. It traveled four point two million miles to get here. It must be starving. I mean, it was going to eat a sparrow."

Flynn thought about it. "Worth a try."

He typed on the keyboard. A sparrow appeared on the monitor. The octodillo caught hold of the bird, chomping off its head. I winced.

"Don't worry," Flynn said. "That's not an actual sparrow. It's been replicated to trick the Decapodous Turba. The containment egg is secretly injecting nourishment through a feeding tube."

Six fake sparrows later, the octodillo revealed its mission.

"Now." Flynn said. "Why are you here?"

"Decapodous Turba Minister of War sent an advance party to Earth to ascertain if the time was right to launch Operation Liberation."

"Who are you liberating?" Flynn asked.

"Supreme Majesty of the Decapodous Turba."

Flynn rubbed his thumb over his fingers. He thought for a moment. "Why do you believe the Supreme Majesty is here?"

"Fifteen Earth years ago, our planet's sun entered into its final cycle of existence. Temperatures rose. We experienced a great drought. In order to safeguard its power, the Decapodous Ministerium placed larvae into capsules and shot them off to find suitable planets to live until a more permanent home could be found for the Decapodous Turba. Of the four hundred million larvae scattered throughout the universe, the closest Supreme Majesty is here. I request feeding."

Flynn flicked a toggle. It muted his microphone.

"Fifteen years ago," I said. "Isn't that when—"

"Dalton Teague built OmniPark, part of which is the Realm of the Deep. The Supreme Majesty has been lurking in the aquazoorium, awaiting the day it could shepherd its people to a new home planet."

"I don't know, Flynn. It feels like the story you're trying to tell is getting too complex."

"Story? What story?"

"This is some kind of immersive experience, right? A park-wide Choose Your Own Adventure?"

"This isn't a game, Realm Ambassador Julie. This is happening."

"Oh? There's more? Feels a little long. The names are confusing."

"This is the start of an invasion. I suspect our little friend here has already relayed his findings to the Decapodous Ministerium. We are under attack."

"Under attack? How?"

"The rain. The Decapodous Turba are terraforming for an easier invasion."

"Do guests pay extra to participate?"

"Listen to me. I need to take this information to the Sanctum. The Directors of the Realms need to be informed. What better place for a carnivorous aquatic species to conquer than a planet composed of seventy percent water? I must alert the Ministerium at once."

"Okay, you do that. What do I do?"

"Wait here. And whatever you do, don't push that button." He pointed at a flashing yellow button.

"Got it. Wait here while you save the world. Oh. And don't touch the yellow button."

"Can you do that?"

I scoffed. "Of course."

Flynn looked uncertain.

"Go," I said.

"I'll return."

Flynn's role playing adventure elevated OmniPark to a more aggressive level. I didn't like the direction the game was heading. I wanted out of the beta test.

I pushed the yellow button.

A yellow laser beam enveloped the octodillo. "I request—"

The yellow energy flared. A million points of incendiary lights focused on a single target. The octodillo vaporized.

I stood in a vacuum quietly drowning in a nervous energy. What had I done? How angry would Flynn be with me? The one thing he insisted I not do I did. Had I terminated all of the Technophers' planning?

The door opened. I didn't know what to make of the expression on Flynn's face. Was he formulating what to say? Was he upset? Angry? Flummoxed? The way the day had been going I feared he'd push a yellow button on me.

"I can explain," I said.

Flynn laughed. "You just saved the planet. That scout was actually an assassin. The Decapodous Ministerium, was attempting a coup — which you, miss Realm Ambassador, have just prevented."

"But I thought Squidbeak was terraforming the planet to make invasion easier."

"Yes, well. It appears old Squidbeak has been secretly informing the Directors of the Realms of this plan since he was caught eating Horace Ubley."

"And now the invasion won't happen because I vaporized the octodillo?"

"Yes. As I said, you have just saved mankind."

"But haven't I condemned the Decapodous Turba to extinction on a dying planet?"

"I wouldn't say extinction. I mean, Lolligo released four hundred million larvae. The Decapodous Minister of Science launched four hundred million larvae to find new homes. Survivors surely exist."

"So I did win."

"We all won."

"So do we all get a trophy? How does that work?"

"Not all victories are rewarded."

"That's lame. There should at least be a coupon for a free scoop of rainbow ice cream at the Omnicone."

Flynn stuck to the script. "Sometimes the only reward is remembering your accomplishments."

"This game is really dark, Flynn."

"It's not a game."

"I mean, that whole thing with eating cloned sparrows was pushing it but ending the game with extinction is just so bleak."

"It's not a game, Realm Ambassador Julie. It is most certainly not a game."

"It has to be, Flynn. It has to be a game. Otherwise, I am guilty of causing millions of deaths of a species just trying to survive. I can't live with that responsibility. So please, tell me this was just a game."

A sadness filled Flynn's eyes. "It was not a game."

"I'd like to go home now. My shift is over."

Flynn capitulated. "I understand."

"How do I get out of the Void?"

"Use your key to open the door."

Flynn pointed across the room at a steel door inside a brass frame.

It wasn't the door he used. I put the key in the tumbler and turned it. The door opened outside the Realm of the Deep.

A great orange sun faded in the evening sky. The storm clouds, like the kiosk with the mint green door, evaporated along with what I remembered of the day.

Thirty years ago I worked my final shift at OmniPark. Ten years after that, OmniPark closed and never reopened. I don't think about any of this until it rains. When thunder rumbles and rain falls, I write down what I remember. I write quickly because as the storm lets up, my memory of that day does the same. It's as if the rain has secrets it rushes to tell me. Later, when I read what I wrote, it feels like someone else's story.

I wonder if, like the Decapodous Turba, Mr. Flynn and his fellow Technosophers foresaw OmniPark's inevitable end approaching. Other times I wonder if the Directors of the Realms had a plan to save OmniPark but failed to implement it. Mostly I wonder about an old, brass, skeleton key tarnished with the same patina coating my memory of where the key came from and why I possess it. I've carried it with me for as long as I can remember, but I have never found a door in which it fit.

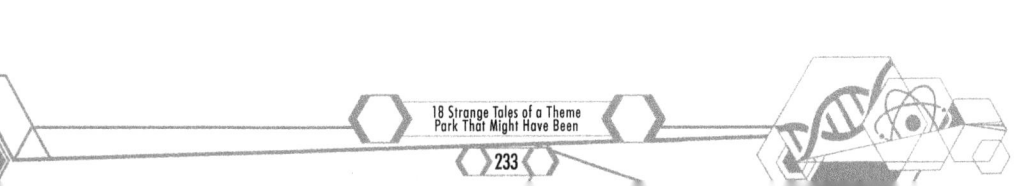

THIS UNIVERSE IS YOURS TO EXPLORE

RYAN CLEMENT

You drive a lonely West Texan highway.

It's been awhile since you remembered your destination. Right now, you need all of your focus just to stay on the road.

It is late. Far too late.

During the afternoon heat, other cars navigated these roads, but now only the coyotes keep you company. Nothing shines but your headlights and the moon.

It is enough.

Billboards pass by. One offers a vaccine-free "Cure for Autism." Another declares "Global Warming is a Hoax!"

One catches your eye. Weathered and rusted, it's barely visible behind the mesquites.

"Visit OmniPark: This Universe is Yours to Explore," it proclaims. "Next Exit."

What do you do?

Keep driving (Go to 41)
Exit (Go to 2)

1

As you run towards the loop's exit, you land in familiar terrain. You push through the Exit turnstile, only to find it reading "Entrance" on the other side. You go through another turnstile, and the same thing happens. And another. And another.

Either the author of this maze made an error or you've become trapped by your own fears. You push on either way.

Go to 1

2

The abandoned parking lot could fit an armada of holiday-makers, but even the tire marks look decades old. The pavement is cracked, pierced by hardy sprouts reaching for the long-set Texas sun. The day's heat still radiates off the black surface as you leave your car.

Signs for OmniPark abound. Most have rusted and fallen over. The stench of lost dreams fills the air. There was a big idea here, once.

You notice a platform. An ancient turnstile blows in dusty winds, creaking quietly, as if to ask you a question.

What do you do?

Return to your car (Go to 41)
Enter (Go to 3)

3

The turnstile creaks as you push it, offering no resistance but locking with a clank once you're through.

Beside the platform, a faint smell of grease reveals a single rail running off in either direction. The rail shakes into crescendo as a bright light glides down the track. Train!

The monorail silently pulls up to the platform. Mechanical doors separate and red handholds swing gently in the empty passenger section inside.

What do you do?

Board the train (Go to 5)
Return to the parking lot (Go to 4)

4

Not feeling the late-night ghost train, you try to leave, but the locked turnstile blocks your path, denying escape.

Go to 5

5

As you board the train, doors seal behind you with robotic precision. Your feet shake as the great machine rumbles to life.

The train looks slick and stylish, a mid-to-late 20th century vision of a future that never was. You grab a hand-hold as it rounds a curve. The scenery outside speeds into a blur through your confused reflection.

Another platform comes into view. You disembark. The monorail evaporates into the night air.

You enter a courtyard of dead trees. As you walk, flashes of green peek out in the dim moonlight. You smell fresh blossoms. Soon, full leaves are visible.

At the courtyard's end, an arch-way guards the entrance to a gleaming-cathedral to technology. Sweeping arches branch off parabolically in impossible directions. You can almost see the sketch marks of some master architect's blueprint. The tower wears murals like a cloak, atoms and planets, cells and animals. Above all, glistening golden spires reach for the heavens themselves.

The place defines grandness.

Epiphanic organ music fills the open chamber as you enter the cathedral. High-set windows filter down the moonlight in golden effervescent rays, revealing an expansive and cavernous inner chamber.

Your footsteps echo on an empty corridor. A figure stands in the centre of the room. Was he there the whole time? He wears a sharp Texan suit, decades out of style. His uncanny figure betrays the illusion. Hologram.

"California has its Disneyland and Florida has its EPCOT Center — so why shouldn't the great state of Texas have her own world-class theme park?" he asks in a drawl. "Welcome stranger! My name is Dalton M. Teague, park founder and chief 'technosopher!'"

The ground sparks and smokes as he speaks. You smell burnt circuitry beneath the tiled floor as the hologram disappears.

The upper echelons of this modern ziggurat seem closed off, but another gateway leads to a flash of colour and dancing water.

Go to 7

6

You find a secret corridor, filled with wires, piping, and concrete. Gone are the magnificent trappings of the Entryway Pavilion or the colours of the fountain. Everything here is utilitarian, practical, pragmatic—structures supporting someone else's dreams.

A floorplan guide, stapled to the wall, gives you some options.

Teague's Office (Go to 38)
The Computer Room (Go to 37)
The Gift Shop (Go to 36)

7

Beneath the sky-scraping spires of the Cathedral of Science, jets of water burst forth in choreographed symmetry, dancing beneath the cloudless sky. Amidst the aquatic ballet, the words "Realm of Realms" are barely discernible.

Paths illuminate before you, each ordained with its own symbolic Omnicon.

Choose one:

The stopwatch (Go to 9)
The planet (Go to 10)
The jellyfish (Go to 11)

The hand (Go to 12)
The particle (Go to 13)
The paramecium (Go to 14)
The dragonfly (Go to 15)
All other exits are *unauthorized*.

8

"Stop! You can't go there!" a voice calls from behind as you push through the "***Authorized* Personnel Only**" door—refusing to play by the rules of this game. You turn and find no one. Was it all in your head?

Go to 6

9

The stopwatch leads to a linear path, where you can't shake the sensation of moving backwards. You walk through a conservatory parlour, filled with marble statues of men, women, and cherubs, all transfixed on one antiquated timepiece or another. A wrought iron gate reads "Realm of Time."

You come upon a mansion both massive and quaint, a warm hug from a bygone era. Steel pipes, ornate clockwork, and cacophonous gadgetry clatter. Burnt coal permeates the air. A figure in a Texan suit watches you from the bedroom window, before disappearing behind a curtain.

As you enter the mansion, gears clink and clank and pipes steam and whistle, but each machine's function remains a mystery.

An ornate staircase winds into upper floors, promising domestic bliss. More stairs descend towards a glowing basement tunnel where a bespectacled mannequin—with wild grey hair and a plush pterodactyl sidekick—holds his hand just above your head.

"To ride the tachyons," his sign reads, "You must be this tall."

Where do you go?

Upstairs (Go to 16)
Downstairs (Go to 17)

10

The planet's path is dark, lit only by small ground beacons, reminiscent of an airport runway. Eventually, an interstellar dashboard is revealed. As you sit down to examine it, robotic arms strap you in as the windshield seals above.

"This is Navigator," an artificial voice announces. "Initiating launch in 3…2…1!"

A figure outside in a Texan suit adjusts his glasses, just before a thunderous explosion behind you thrusts your body flat against the chair. Your cheek muscles contort like cartoon characters under the pressure of multiple Gs. Bright red hexagons flash around you in streaks of light. Everything shakes violently as the sky peels away.

And then… calm. Orbital bliss.

You are weightless, surrounded by a million stars. Across a black canvas, galaxies twirl and tango, planets roll around their stars, and vast nebulae stretch into inconceivable clouds of gas and colour. Behind it all, a constellation reads "Realm of Stars."

Majestic.

A spinning space station, "Orbit One Central," orbits near a stellar nursery, a nebula lit with colours you did not know you could see. The station's outer rings fill with greenhouses, shuttle factories, and habitations. In the centre, a bubbled room shows a cosmonaut with an old Soviet flag.

The onboard Navigator interrupts your thoughts. "Initiating docking sequence."

Go to 20

11

The jellyfish leads you along a damp path, which gets soggier with each step. You traipse through puddles, then lakes, then rolling ocean waves.

Forced to swim in the sloshing darkness, you stumble upon a steel tube sticking out of the sea. Peering inside its hollow interior, you notice a ladder descending into the depths below, with the words "Realm of the Deep" stenciled vertically. As you descend, a figure in a Texan suit closes the lid above, sealing it. Everything rattles as a great mechanical beast awakens.

You climb down to the bridge of a massive atomic age submersible. All around you, steel gauges and chrome dials spin wildly, while a solitary harpoon sits at the ready for the command to fire.

Nausea roils your stomach as the submarine lurches from side to side.

Outside your window, grotesque goblin sharks, bioluminescent jellyfish, jittery isopods, and all manner of primeval sea creatures swim and chase, many with impossibly sharp jagged teeth. Glowing eyes watch from the depth as jittery crustaceans scamper away. A leviathan whale carcass, rots covered in sucker marks.

A skeleton in a fisherman's raincoat occupies the Captain's table with the sign "Eat or be eaten."

Just then, a bright light in the darkness eerily swims towards the bow. As you flash the submarines lights, you realized the light was the lure of a fearsome giant anglerfish swimming into range. Suddenly, it stops. Something has spooked it, something big. You might still catch it.

Let it go (Go to 24)
Harpoon! (Go to 23)

12

As you follow the handprint's path, temperatures drop precipitously. A mild nip turns to biting windchill. You shiver to keep warm. Snow blankets the ground as millions of icy crystals sleet from the sky.

In the distance, a figure in a Texan suit drinks something and walks away.

You follow him, finding yourself in a frozen landscape where woolly mammoths rage against sabre tooth tigers, and colossal ice sheets creep on the horizon.

To your left, a Great Tent stands, hewn from the skins of Pleistocene megafauna. As frostbite nibbles your outer appendages, it may be your only hope.

What do you do?

Enter the tent (Go to 27)
Look elsewhere (Go to 25)

13

The particle's path guides you in circles until you a reach mannequin of a physicist with a long black beard and his hand nearly on the ground. "You must be this short to enter," his sign reads "Remember, you matter."

As you pass through his Scalar Portal archway, you notice the path's width and surrounding plant life growing exponentially. Caught in runaway shrinking, the you glimpse a figure in a Texan suit marking a clipboard, before the world you knew is gone.

You find yourself a particle in a colossal atom. Layer upon layer of sky-like electron shells extend out like a subatomic atmosphere. Translucent neutrinos fly like poltergeists, passing through anything and everything and leaving no trace. Protons crunch down on a central nucleus, pulsing dangerously with positive charge. Electrons race around at dizzying paces, advertising the "Outer Inn."

The air smells electric. The hairs on the back of your neck prickle with trepidation.

What do you do?

Visit the Inn (Go to 30)
Visit the Nucleus (Go to 31)

14

You follow the paramecium's path, fighting through tall grass growing on either side. The grass seems to flicker in a non-existent breeze, always pushing you forward. Once shoulder deep in the grass, you realize they are not plants, but tiny protuberances of a giant cell. Cilia.

A figure in a Texan suit observes you from the shadows as the cilia carry you through a Scalar Portal, shrinking you down to the microscopic level. You close your eyes, ignoring the slimy moisture of the cytoplasm, as your miniaturized body sinks through.

You land roughly on a gelatinous sidewalk of cell membrane, towered over by blue, pink, and green protein structures. Amino acids combine and separate, spelling out "Realm of the Cell." You wipe off the slime.

Strange nano creatures circle above, and beyond a wild red-haired woman looms like a cosmic giant. The light of her microscope may as well be the sun.

"Preparing inoculation." Her voice thunders.

In astronomic movements, the giantess raises the surface on which you sit, turning everything 90 degrees. Lose lysosomes and ribosomes fly past as you cling to a filament. Above, a needle-shaped tower hurtles towards a fleshy surface.

Contact! Skin cells surround everything. You're ejected out of your cell and into the bloodstream.

You float freely along the pulsing current, as red blood cells jumble along like inner tubes on a turbulent river.

An infection blocks the path! Two armies battle over the blood stream. Foreign amoebas wreak havoc on the body's biochemistry, while white blood cells sacrifice their lives defending the body.

Where do you swim?

To the White blood cells (Go to 33)
To the Amoebas (Go to 32)

15

The humidity and mercury rise sharply along the dragonfly's path. Sweat trickles off your brow as fern-like vegetation covers everything. Chlorophyll-filled spores taste bitter in your mouth.

A fast-flowing river stops your progress. A sign with a finger-wagging biologist warns "Beware of insect bites." A Texan-suited figure points binoculars at you before camouflaging beneath the primordial foliage. As you move call out, you lose your balance on the thick wet moss beneath. You fall into the rapids! The current has you now.

Clinging to a log, you cruise through a late Carboniferous ecosystem, filled with alien flora and fanciful fauna. The sounds of chittering insects drive you to madness as you watch for tell-tale signs of movement. Giant centipedes and millipedes wind around the shoreline. An early synapsid comes out of nowhere and snatches one for dinner. A giant scorpion-like eurypterid pokes its head out of the water, only to be gobbled in an instant by a 20-foot amphibian!

In the air above, flying insects spell out "Realm of Life."

As you float downstream, you reach a small patio labelled "Dragonfly Dining Terrace."

What do you do?

Get out (Go to 35)
Continue (Go to 34)

16

The mansion's upper floors overflow with an array of imaginative mechanisms, the "home of the future." Closets on conveyor belts. Cathode ray video phones. Caterpillar-track robots ready to take your drink order. Despite the bravado, none of these contraptions have ever seen a real home. Most have long since been rendered obsolete.

A tinge of sadness pervades the place, a memorial to a lost future.

Before leaving, you notice an old top hat sitting on a coat rack. It makes you seem taller. You may wear it out if you wish.

Go to 9

17

The Time Tunnel vortex spins in chronic fourth-dimensional maelstroms. All pasts, all futures stretch in infinite directions, never-ending spirals of geometric abstraction. You see everything from the extinction of the dinosaurs and to monstrous human descendants chomping on their miniscule kin. The endless wormhole rumbles in its brass-fitted restraints, anxious to break free.

This tunnel could take you from the dawn of creation to the end of time, if you so dared. Its scale alone rattles your soul.

Where do you go?

The Dawn of Creation (Go to 18)
The End of Time (Go to 19)
Return to the fountain (Go to 7) or, if you have explored all of its paths, go to 40

18

The Dawn of Creation crushes you. Every fibre of your being, and all matter, squishes into an impossible subatomic speck. Everything that will ever be comes out of this moment. The entire universe is unfathomably condensed. Even the laws of physics cannot fit.

If you're wearing the top hat, **return to 17**.

Otherwise, you explode, along with the entire universe, in a colossal bang that will ultimately lead to the creation of all matter.

You are the dust before dust, the stars before stars.

THE END

19

The End of Time freezes you in the endless cold of eternal darkness. Everything that ever was or will be has met its destiny. Every movement of every molecule has ground to a halt, reaching perfect energy stasis. No more stars, no more black holes, no future. Nothing but the void. Perfect entropy is the new order, the only order. The universe is dead with none left to mourn. Change itself is no longer constant.

If you're wearing the top hat, **return to 17**.

Otherwise, the great hungry vacuum drains you of every unit of vitality, ripping you apart, particle by particle. You are a frozen husk of matter in colourless, infinite nothingness.

Absolute zero.

THE END

20

Unstrapped from your seat, you gleefully spin in the station's microgravity, twirling to eerie call of synthesizers and theremins. The smooth white walls around you overflow with equipment far too technical to understand.

"Welcome comrade." The cosmonaut beams from the dome, offering vodka with an animatronic arm.

Suddenly, an emergency alarm sounds. "Warning!" The Navigator calls out. "Increased Nebula Activity Detected. Initiating Emergency Evacuation Protocols."

An escape pod opens to your right.

What do you do?

Escape (Go to 21)
Stay (Go to 22)

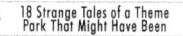

21

You leave the friendly Russian, throwing yourself into the pod. In seconds, it hurtles you through the cosmos as the station implodes in the expanding nebula, iridescent flares ripping through the debris.

After eons crossing time and space, the Texan night sky welcomes your final re-entry, as the pod leaves you in the arms of a kaleidoscopic fountain.

Go to 7 or, if you have explored all of its paths, go to 40

22

You stay for *one* drink with the friendly Russian, knowing it to be your last. You shout "Na Zdorovie" as the station implodes around you.

In deep space without protection, half of you freezes while the other half burns. Your blood expands, cracking your bone marrow. Your eyes and tongue boil.

The nebula pulls you, clutching you inescapably in its gravity. Your atoms merge with the most beautiful display of light and colour you have ever witnessed. The vodka wasn't half-bad either.

It is a magnificent way to die.

THE END

23

You launch the harpoon, bull's-eye! The anglerfish takes it right in its jagged-tooth maw. Impressively strong, the creature drags you and your submarine along for a ride, just as a colossal giant squid, with tentacles as long as a redwood, floats into view. Its blood red purple eye glares at you, before disappearing once more into the abyss.

Realizing your oxygen might be running low, you release the anglerfish and float the submarine back to the surface where multicoloured lights beckon.

Go to 7 or, if you have explored all of its paths, go to 40

24

You let the fish be, but it spooks all the same. Long, fibrous tentacles stem from a creature of unimaginable girth, covering all sides of the submarine in iron-gripped suckers. As the tentacles constrict, seals break and water pours in. You do your best to plug the leaks and restart the engine, but the bridge is swamped. As you breathe your last gasps of air in a dwindling pocket, your final vision is the beak of a colossal giant squid.

You never did like seafood.

THE END

25

Running from the Great Tent, you barely escape with your life. As you flail through the snow, Neanderthal lookouts spy a possible raider. Knapped spear points rain down on you, piercing your leg. As you bleed out over the frozen tundra, they are content to let the blizzard do the rest.

Stumbling through quickly reddening snow, you search for shelter you know you won't find. The memory of warmer places reassures you in your final hours. A cave appears in the distance, but your legs can no longer carry you.

It's unclear whether the cold or the sabre-tooth finally gets you, but the result is largely the same.

THE END

26

You offer the Neanderthals your story and any items you have in trade. They speak in a long-dead language, uncertain of this stranger among them. With no words in common, you mime everything that has happened. The Neanderthals watch bewildered and then do the unthinkable.

They laugh.

The tension released, the elder invites you to join her by the deer, now ready for roasting. The generous Neanderthals share some of their hunt, the freshest venison to ever grace your lips. They regale each other with story after story, using the same human expressions that have withstood the ages. One brings out a flute, and the other a drum. The room erupts in dancing. You clumsily knock over a carving, and the group roars with laughter again. So do you.

As the meal finishes, most turn over to sleep, but the elder leads you through the blizzard outside to a sacred cave, its walls adorned with portraits of wild aurochs and dun horses, beautifully rendered in red, yellow, and black. One wall contains a series of cross-hatched abstract patterns and pictographic symbols. Another sports an unlikely anthropologist, carrying a "Realm of Man" sign.

Finally, you reach a wall where hundreds of hands have been painted in charcoal and ochre. She gestures for you to add yours, and mixes the ingredients. She spits the colours over your hand as you hold it against the wall, leaving your imprint alongside the others. They are nearly identical.

Overwhelmed, you reach out to touch the hand once more only to find yourself reaching into the cool waters of the fountain.

Go to 7 or, if you have explored all of its paths, go to 40

27

Desperate for warmth, you sneak into the tent, where a band of *Homo Neanderthalensis* gather around a fire. The gargantuan stone age construction rests on interwoven mammoth tusks, pelts, and furs—some of which still reek of the kill, as do the Neanderthals.

An elder leads a large-antlered deer towards the fire as the other Neanderthals watch, their thick brows furrowed in anticipation. Using a stone-chipped tool, she slices the deer's jugular in swift motion.

You gasp as the deer strikes the ground, twenty-five pairs of prehistoric eyes turning to you in surprise. Some grab their spears.

Good luck talking your way out of this one.

Tell your story (Go to 26)
Run! (Go to 25)

28

Forgetting yourself, you touch the antimatter particles, obliterating both them and the matter particles of your body in a tremendous explosion of unbridled energy. A chain reaction blazes out like a wave, crashing the matter streams into the antimatter, snapping multiverses out of existence in a spectacular runaway reaction with no one left to observe.

In the world you knew, a mushroom cloud rises over the former OmniPark, undermined and rewritten at its subatomic core.

A quantum catastrophe.

THE END

29

Your strong negative charge attracts you to the positively-charged protons in the nucleus. If you could move like the electrons, zapping across their fields like bolts of lightning, you could maintain your distance, but like a tsunami wave, the force is too strong.

You enter the nucleus, the protons eagerly sapping up your negative energy and turning it positive. As they draw it out, you feel yourself shrinking once more.

The protons seem like planets now, with moon-like quarks stuck together with gluons. The quarks seem strange, yet some are downright charming. They form bonds with each other, forming the words "Realm of the Particle."

At this size, Matter and energy become indistinguishable, particles and waves. Soon you will be little more than a photon.

You see the bleed points into alternate dimensions, exotic realms abundant in anti-matter, verdant universes where dark matter shines bright. You know you must decide quickly, or be lost in this labyrinth, but each decision you consider spawns a myriad of alternate universes branching off like one of those old choose-your-own-path novels.

In the distance, you see path back to the fountain. Particles flow towards it, as they flow everywhere. You could entangle with them, but which do you choose?

The Antimatter Particles (Go to 28)
The Matter Particles (Go to 7
or, if you have explored all of its paths, go to 40)

30

The Inn glows like a ball of energy, tempting you to reach it. Each time you try, it jumps, re-spawning a new at a new location. You try to predict where it will land next, but cannot with any certainty.

Meanwhile, electrons race through your body, increasing its negative charge. As the negative charge builds, you find yourself drawn towards the throbbing Nucleus.

Go to 29

31

In your current state, the positive energy of the Nucleus repels you each time you approach. Perhaps you can reverse your polarity.

Go to 13

32

You seek an alliance with your fellow invaders, but microscopic predators aren't known for diplomacy. The eukaryote's pseudopod morphs around you, enveloping you so tightly you can barely breathe. While its organelles cannot digest you, its membranes will not release you either.

A symbiosis develops where the amoeba consumes your body's excess energy and feeds you enough nutrients to continue your meager survival. In the distant future, your genetic descendants will be the new mitochondria, but this cell remains your prison.

THE END

33

You hope this body's defenders might also be your saviour, forgetting that you're an invader too.

One white blood cell engulfs you, invading every inch of your limbs, searching for an antigen. You struggle in vain, but futilely. Your fate is locked.

THE EN-

But wait!

Stuck in the white blood cell, you course throughout the cardio-vascular system, in and out of the coronary artery. Finally, you find yourself pumped up into a capillary somewhere in the nasal cavity.

The sneeze erupts like a volcano, but it hits you like a hurricane. You are sent screaming out of the nose at 100 mph, cruising once again through the outside air.

A sticky mucous lump breaks your fall. At least there is a fountain nearby you can wash your now normal-sized yourself in.

Go to 7 or, if you have explored all of its paths, go to 40

34

Remembering the earlier warning, you cling to your log as a dragon-sized dragonfly swoops over the terrace. You can sense the disappointment through the myriad lenses of its compound eyes, see its over-sized pincers snap with hunger. The river alone keeps it at bay.

The current pulls you away and over a waterfall into a twisting whirlpool. The swampy green of the Carboniferous gives way to a rainbow, as you emerge geyser-like in a familiar fountain.

Go to 7 or, if you have explored all of its paths, go to 40

35

You seek safe harbour at the Dragonfly Dining Terrace, not realizing the sign was literal. In a single leap, a dragon-sized dragonfly descends upon you, cleaving your torso in its over-sized pincers, picking you apart piece-by-piece until it has had its fill.

Some day, your remains will return to the ecosystem, trapped as part

of the Great Carboniferous Rainforest Collapse, ultimately contributing to the oil deposits that made Teague his billions.

In that sense, you'll always be a part of the park.

THE END

36

The gift shop overflows with stuffed dragonflies, nucleus keychains, and T-shirts reading "I survived the End of Time, and all I got was this lousy top hat." The cash register sits empty.

The entire place is painted like an illusion, with walls and shelves extended long beyond their termini to imaginary vanishing points. Mirrors abound as well, a thousand "you"s extend towards infinity in all directions. You wave, and in a microsecond, they all wave back. "Remember," an animatronic version of Teague calls from the ceiling, "to be a technosopher, all you need is the right **perspective**!"

Through one of the mirrors, a sign reads "Exit to Drop-off Loop"

What do you do?

Exit (Go to 1)
Return to the Corridor (Go to 6)
<upside down: Go…>

37

The computer room is a mess of wires, mainframes, and floppy disks, with a dusty old Commodore 64 awaiting your input.

As you touch a key, the monochrome screen fills with various codes in broken ASCII:

Please recall final characters for passcode

AAATGAACGAAAATCTGTTCGCTTCATTCATTGCCCCCACAATCCTAGGCCTACCCXX/X**Y**
00110011100001010100011011110110101010010010100**O**
UF^4 + 2H^20 − F^4 − H^4 − 0^2 = **U**
(vi^2 * sin(2θ)/g = **R**

You stare at it a few minutes before leaving.

Go to 6
<upside down: …to…>

38

    Teague's office seems more like a laboratory than a managerial post. Cracked beakers, half-completed robots, flimsy devices of unknown purpose abound. At the old wooden desk, books are thrown astray as if a tornado broke through. The few souvenirs of Teague's travels seem scattered and forgotten on the office floor. Before the desk, a scale model of OmniPark depicts its first ideation, disturbed only by the fist-sized crater in the middle. Torn reviews both from Stephen Hawking, accusing the park of being unscientific, and children's crusaders, accusing the park of promoting LSD, cover a dartboard.

    In the wire basket nearby, you spy a fire-tinged letter and save it from the flames. While much of the letter is lost, you can still make out the following words:

    "…orry Dalton, but attendance isn't what it was. We must embrace **change**.

    -Board of Directors"

Go to 6

<upside down: …39>

39

    Having figured out this game, you climb the topmost spire of the Cathedral of Science, each step taking you closer to the Cosmos. On the summit, a hidden observation platform lofts over the seven realms of the park below, laid out before you like a model city in a kid's sandbox—so ahead of its time and yet stuck in the past.

    As you look, the empty park fills with thousands of tiny patrons scurrying over the park like ants trying to rebuild a colony. They run from the dawn of time to end of creation, from the depths of the sea to the heights of the cosmos, from the tiniest particle to the largest galaxy, through the living and the dead. Like children of chaos in search of order. They solve puzzles and ponder their choices. You can even see cars like yours fill up the parking lot. Some also leave. None are all that different from you.

    "Astronauts call it the 'Overview Effect'." A Texan drawl says to your right.

No animatronic or hologram, just a weathered old man barely fitting his Texan suit anymore. And pale, so pale.

Teague offers you a bourbon as you share the view.

"Science is dying in Texas." He offers. "Creationism taught alongside evolution. Flat Earth societies. People burning masks in a pandemic. Moon hoaxes, in the state that steered Apollo! Is nothing sacred?"

Teague catches his breath.

"I created this park to inspire generations to master science. I'm dead two years, and they bury the whole thing. This was my legacy!"

Teague coughs. You give him a minute.

"People often ask me what I was doing all those years I traveled the world. I was gathering data. This world, this universe runs on science and if we… if we…"

Teague clutches his chest in pain, but insists he's okay.

"My fortune came from the same oil now burning the planet. Now I'm just a phantom of a lost dream, and I don't even believe in ghosts."

Teague leans over the edge.

"I too was stuck in my own paradigm, trying each path, following the signs. Charging headfirst into dead-ends, confident I could always just turn back the page. Or skimming to a future at the expense of the present."

He watches you finish your bourbon.

"But you didn't follow the path. Didn't stick to the rules. You took this universe's laws, and broke them, going beyond. You know what we call people like you?"

Your think of words like "cheater" or "deviant," but you've got a better answer: "Technosophers."

Teague smiles, tossing you a shiny silver object. You catch a glistening key engraved with: "This Universe is Yours to Explore."

As Teague fades into the cool night air, you pocket the key and gaze over your new dominion, pouring yourself a fresh bourbon.

You can't help but smile.

THE END!

40

Back in your car, you pull into a roadside motel just outside of Odessa. Your eyes are so weary, that you barely notice yourself requesting a room and receiving the keys.

You lie in bed. Did you wander the park or just your wits? Maybe the morning will make sense of things.

Before you closing your eyes, you spy a bedside binder labelled "local attractions." Inside you find an old dog-eared book, *Tales from OmniPark*.

THE END?

41

You haven't time for curiosity.

Clenching the steering wheel, you slam the gas, revving the accelerator forward down the road. Let OmniPark be someone else's late night gallivant.

The endless highway extends out before you. Soon you forget the sign that barely piqued your interest. It will not be a part of your universe.

THE END

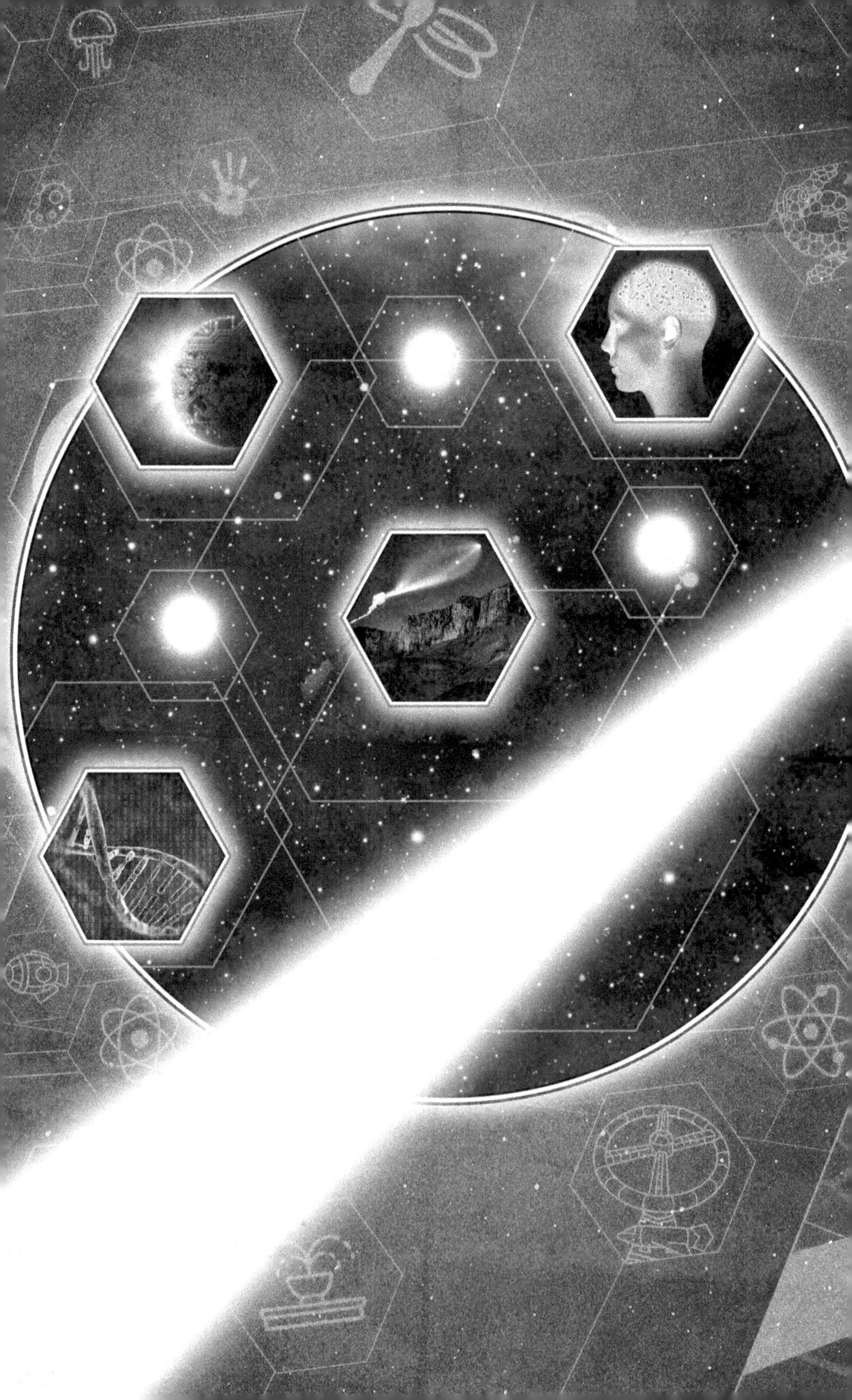

CADENCE: A CODA

TINA MARIE DELUCIA

The heart, despite the body crumbling around it, stubbornly beats on; pumping blood through each vein, from the unmoving toes to the inert brain. Almost oblivious to the destruction around it.

To the fate that awaits it.

When a person becomes a vegetable, every component fails them. The brain no longer sends its buzzing symbols or causes nerves to spark with little pulses. The organs turn sluggish, the intestines erode, the lungs become unable to breathe on their own, and the eyes refuse to see. But the heart. The heart does not fail.

Like any living thing, a theme park needs a heart to thrive. A heart that pumps not blood but electricity and information. Binary code and intricate lines of assembly language endow a single animatronic Neanderthal the power to wave an arm, guide ride vehicles smoothly along their tracks, trigger swells of music and ambient soundscapes from speakers cunningly hidden among flower beds and tree trunks.

The Heart of OmniPark was no muscle, but a climate-controlled room of microprocessor towers. To call it a heart is no mere metaphor, however; for its rhythmic electrical pulses did indeed keep the park alive — kept nerve signals flowing through robotic nerve-endings; directed the circulation of water among topiary gardens and primordial forests; drew up neat arrays of work assignments to be printed for the park's Technosophers each morning. The twenty-six brushed-steel computer cabinets of the OmniPark's Monitoring and Entertainment Control System (MECS) maintained the park through each moment of every day, just as your own beating heart sustains your life from this breath to the one that will follow.

There was a time when it was reliable, perhaps the only thing that could be relied on. It's a thankless job. It's vital, essential, the pressure is astounding. Nestled into the bosom of the Realm Between Realms, it was the center of all things. Though the ground now was occupied by the OmniColor Fountain, it was safe and sound from the pipes. No one paid any mind to it, until something went wrong and suddenly all eyes shifted toward the room of computers. But that did not matter. So long as the park was alive, was entertaining as it ought to be, then it felt something akin to joy.

The Heart had a duty to provide OmniPark everything it needed in order for each Realm to function, for the Fountain to let loose its colorful streams, for joy and awe and wonder to glimmer in the faces of children and parents alike. For the bouncing ono toes, the dragging of parents by the arm into the depths of yet another attraction; another plunge into the unknown. The teasing grins of teenagers, daring one another to step into strange new experiences. The fond winks of parents or grandparents as they too smiled at the park's splendor.

Even when the happy faces grew scarcer, and Realm Ambassadors whispered in worried tones, eyeing exit doors and operational panels. Even then, the Heart beat on, stubborn and oblivious to it's body's slow descent into death and decay. Even after the park's brain perished, leaving the body directionless and confused and in a state between life and death, the Heart continued to pump, and pump, and pump.

Safety, fire prevention, speaker systems, street lights, animatronics, the synching of light and sound with the movement of mouths and arms, doors opening and vehicles movements and smoke pumping and doors closing and merchandising and keeping each Ambassador where they needed to be. All of it relied on waves of impulse flowing from the center.

Each animatronic might have been designed down to the last technically impressive detail, each musical score designed and dreamed up by an expert composer, each track built to withstand not only scores of people but the wear and tear of time. But nothing moved without blood from the Heart, without the pulse from the computers. Without it, all Seven Realms would be no more than useless, phantom limbs without life or connection.

Until one day, something burst.

Power and code failed to reach their destination. Excesses built up. Information pounded against a brick wall that accepted no signals and sent none back. The Heart tried, oh did it try, every failsafe it could call upon, every trick and trap written decades ago in a forgotten dusty manual. It started with one of the Realms, the Realm of Time, and it found itself worrying even more. What would the Realm do without the power it needed?

The Realm of Man followed next, following a pattern as inconsistent as it was unpredictable. "Quarterly," the new data proclaimed. "Seasonally." Cutting off the blood flow and reconnecting it in such a manner did not feel right to the Heart. It did not help the other Realms either. It was as if a valve had suddenly smalled closed, placing strain and tear on the others. The park was not built to work this way — but the nature of the problem continued to elude the Heart.

More technical difficulties. The meticulous lip syncs of the animatronics were suddenly beats off. Effects were falling silent, often causing an attraction to lose the splendor it was so well known for.

It hurt.

MECS remained on red alert on a weekly basis, despite its best efforts. It pumped, pumped, pumped — but the Realms threw it all back. But even as each broken effect was caught, the Heart knew it was running out of fixes. Audio tracks for Cell and Particle were switched off for three full days. In the Realm of Time, Pterry's wings fell off his back, held together only by wires and hydraulic tubes.

Strain upon the core computers weakened the very wires of OmniPark's nervous system. Each flow of impulses to the Realms felt less like the ebb of the ocean and more like straining of a milkshake through a straw.

Someone at the main computer console cried that the place was "fatigued without Teague." Someone else laughed, briefly. Then the room fell into awkward silence.

The Heart ached.

Ride vehicles stopped short, then lurched forward, their power banks howling in pain, buttons flashed in alarm. Cranks moaned with heaving electrical grins as the Heart continued to beat, supplying life to near-lifeless systems. It pushed harder, pumping furiously against failure. Circuits fried. Monitors distorted to the point of illegibility — and still the Heart pumped on.

Even if this was a sham, a mockery of the life it was meant to sustain, it was life nonetheless. It could still bring joy. It could still evoke awe and wonder, even if only in stunted forms. OmniPark was still alive; that was all that mattered. So long as it still had electricity flowing through its circuit boards, the Heart vowed to continue sustaining the life of the park.

It was hot. Fans meant to keep the machines cool were burning out, pushed past their limits. They whirled endlessly, battling a heat that crept in like a living thing. Functions were reduced to the bare minimum necessary to keep the park functioning.

And after that last fluorescence of celebration, the computer center of OmniPark stood silent.

Did It feel something, truly, in the end? The emptiness? Calling upon Time, Man, the Deep, Particles, Cells, Stars and Life itself to hear no call in return? Did a vegetable of a human life truly understand that it was ending as it's heart slowed and slowed giving up its never ending fight? Perhaps.

The tracks were torn from their homes in the floor, lights ripped away from the heavens and hidden crevices, sound speakers dismantled in a flurry of drills and hammers. Murals, once so carefully painted with the utmost creativity and care turned to rubble with swings of sledge hammers. It could feel it, somehow, all of it. As each little bit was torn from it. Each severing of a wire. Each time hydraulics were drained away and discarded. As animatronics were lifted from their show scenes, as set dressings were ripped away and heaped into piles on cold floors.

The computers, so essential in bringing the lifeblood of the park to its various Realms, were soon dismantled. Crowbars, drills, hammers, and wrenches pulled, pulled, pulled at the buttons and bolts on the floor, screens were smashed in and pulled apart wire by wire. The noise was too much to bear. The screaming metal grinding up against each other, the crackle and pop of electricity, the snapping of film and shattering of plexiglass into a heap of metal mess and rusting rot.

The heart is a tenacious organ, and the computer Heart of OmniPark too was tenacious even as all power was siphoned away. Sparks, clinging onto whatever life it could. Whatever life it could once more flow into the park's Realms. The flicker of the Navigator's eyes, so rigid in an ancient endoskeleton. The Physicist's mouth, forever cracked and worn under his beard flapping open to give a defiant declaration. The Anthropologist's myriad of lights upon the final show scene of *The Story of Man* fading out slowly. Screens once so dark and blank once again were filled with static, with garbled lines of data and code, with program feedback.

For one brief corusating moment, the park erupted in color and sound and life. Kaleidoscopes of cell membranes and hyperspace jumps glimmered in brilliant hues of red and purple.

But these were the desperate death rattle of a heart in final throes of purpose. It changed nothing. One final push, one final beat of the park's electric Heart could not bring its worldpark back from the brink of death. One final defiant howl of life in a world gone silent.

Lights filled theaters, walkways and paths were once again alive with song and sound. Ride vehicles glided efficiently upon their tracks. The joy, the spark of life long since close to being extinguished was suddenly a full flame again: a crescendo of entertainment as — for the briefest flash — each Realm remembered its potential.

Then the Heart fell silent, and that was that.

Technicians and dismantlers swore no one turned any machine on. Every mainframe had been unplugged; every circuit dismantled and packed away to safeguard the equipment from looters or over-eager fanatics.

So they smashed harder. Core circuitry, tagged to be preserved as the very Heart of the park, was torn out and tossed away.

OmniPark's universe might have been theirs to explore, but its life had always been the Heart's to give.

Dalton Planned An

8th

Realm.

Guess its **NAME** and win a **PRIZE**...

Visit
https://www.reddit.com/r/OmniPark/
for details on how to enter

Also published by
house Blackwood

The Cradle and the Sword
An ancient Mesopotamian historical opera of sweeping scale and grandeur

The Willows Anthology
100+ original neo-Victorian stories by Brian Evenson, Gemma Files and many others

www.HouseBlackwood.net